W0010113

For my wonderful husband Karl, with all my love. Thank you for believing in me and encouraging me to write.

ACKNOWLEDGEMENTS

A very big thank you to the following people:

My fabulous cousin Jane Bibby, for listening to me and laughing with me, and for putting me right regarding school procedures.

My indefatigable coach and editor Sarah Williams, who coped patiently with my ineptitude for technology, and without whom none of this would have been possible.

My dear friend Duncan Guest, who without knowing it, helped me with police matters.

The photographer, Roger Sweet, whose image of The Crown is on the front cover, courtesy of oxfordshirevillages.co.uk.

Finally, my late Father is a character in the book. Those of you who know me will recognise him immediately. The rest of you can only guess…

ABOUT THE AUTHOR

Antonia Abbott was born in Aylesbury, but lived in Lancashire until she was four years old. Her father was a senior civil servant with entrepreneurial tendencies, buying various businesses, which were then handed over to Antonia and her mother to look after. Antonia clearly inherited these tendencies, as she has turned her hand to many things, including working in a bookie's office (owned by her mother as one of her father's ventures) and running a country pub.

Privately educated in Berkshire, Antonia loathed school and spent as little time there as possible. Subsequently she has spent most of her life in Berkshire and Oxfordshire. Now happily married, Antonia still lives in Oxfordshire with her husband Karl, and tortoiseshell rescue cat, Purdy. When not writing, Antonia runs a successful IFA practice.

Having always loved reading, Antonia had thought about writing for a long time, but had not had the courage to try. After a chance meeting with a professional writing coach, she decided to write her first book at 58, much to the delight of her husband, who had been telling her for years that she ought to write!

Apart from reading, Antonia enjoys eating out and entertaining, although by her own admission, cooking is not one of her favourite pastimes! She has a passion for cars, and enjoys touring Europe in her BMW convertible. Travelling is also high on the list and she can often be found relaxing on a beach whilst tapping away on her iPad. Formula 1 is another interest and in her late teens and early 20s, Antonia spent a lot of time motor racing marshalling, mainly at Silverstone and Thruxton. When the opportunity presents, she also enjoys dancing.

Antonia is also a collector, particularly of Derby porcelain. She has all sorts of pieces – some dating back to Sansome and Hancock, and on the other side of the scales, a considerable collection of the modern paperweights. She will collect absolutely anything, and has to stop herself from buying! Her collection of silver pill boxes is unusual and fun, but at least they don't take up much space!

She and her husband are very fond of frogs, and have a variety of stone ones adorning the garden, plus one or two in the house. Of course one mustn't forget the Derby frog paperweights.

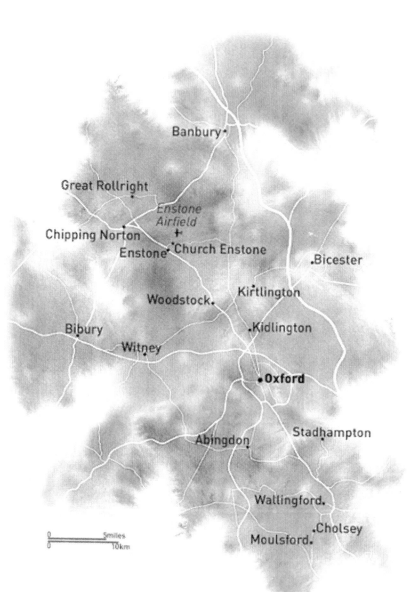

Map of Oxfordshire

CHAPTER 1

At Riverside house, in the pretty Oxfordshire village of Moulsford, party preparations were in full swing for James Rowlands' 21st birthday. Flinging the French doors wide open, James dashed out into the garden to admire the delightful blue and white striped marquee that stood proudly on the wide lawn. The dance floor had been put down and all the tables were dressed in crisp white linen. What's more, although it was only May, the weather had been kind, and the sun shone warm and bright.

The weather perfectly reflected James' mood. He hadn't stopped grinning all day. Not only had his parents given him a brand new Mini Cooper, they were now hosting what he hoped would be a fabulous party, and, what's more, because he had come of age today, he had just inherited £100,000 from his late grandparents.

His mother, Annabelle, was nearly ready. As she put the finishing touches to her make-up she thought back to her own 21st birthday, which had also been her wedding day. That was over 25 years ago now. Her husband Peter had just been promoted to the rank of Flight Lieutenant and they had made a handsome couple. He looked so dashing in his uniform - tall, blond and blue eyed. She remembered how safe she felt as she stood beside him. She paused, mascara brush in hand. How different things might have been. Peter didn't know even now just how much he had transformed her life. Her dark eyes gazed back at her from the mirror thoughtfully and with a hint of past sorrows.

"Enough of that," thought Annabelle to herself, firmly screwing the top back on the mascara. "I must go down and check over the marquee to make sure that everything is exactly as it should be."

Peter was relaxing with the papers. He considered that the party preparations were his wife's domain and he knew that she would have everything organised to perfection. When he heard her familiar light footsteps on the stairs he folded the paper and went to meet her in the hall and together they strolled out through the conservatory and on to the lawn.

As Peter expected, everything did indeed look splendid. The tables with their white cloths, the chairs with their white covers and blue bows, the vases of white roses and the gleaming crockery and cutlery. The caterers had ensured the champagne and beer were chilled and the food was perfectly prepared. All that was needed now were the guests who were due to arrive in approximately half an hour. Peter called over to one of the waitresses and asked her to open a bottle of champagne so that he and

Annabelle could have a quiet drink before the party began. They sipped their champagne and expressed approval. They had bought two dozen cases of it on their last trip to France, from one of the smaller caves that they had discovered on a previous holiday to the famous wine-making region.

"You two look pleased with yourselves," called a voice and they turned to see Annabelle's parents, who were staying with the Rowlands for the birthday weekend.

"Come and try the champagne," shouted back Peter, "and by the way, have you seen the birthday boy recently? He should be here to greet his guests."

"It's all right Dad I'm here," said James as he too walked into the marquee. "I was just keeping an eye out for the band. They've arrived now and are unloading their equipment. I've asked them to park the van as far out of the way as they can."

The Rowlands made a handsome group – Peter in cream slacks and an open necked shirt, with Annabelle beside him, wearing a very fitted emerald green dress and black patent high-heeled sandals. James had chosen chinos and a tee-shirt with the words "birthday boy" printed across the front, which didn't really meet with his father's approval - he would have preferred his son to look a little smarter on such an important occasion, but nevertheless, with his fair hair flopping over his eyes, James Rowlands was a good looking boy. "Shall I take a photo of you all before the party starts?" asked Annabelle's father.

"No thanks," replied Peter, "I'd rather wait for Susie." He glanced at his watch with a frown. "Though that might be a long wait."

Susie was Peter and Annabelle's daughter. She was a couple of years older than James. And she was running late. Again.

*****

Susie hurriedly filled George's Cat Mate dish so that he would survive until her return the following evening, gave him a big kiss and a cuddle, slammed the front door behind her, threw her overnight bag in to the boot of her Mini Cooper convertible, and tumbled into the driver's seat, resentfully starting the engine to begin her journey to Moulsford.

Susie was miffed that James' party was today, as it was one of the rare weekends that she could have spent with her lover Jonathan, as his wife had gone to visit her parents, taking the children with her.

Jonathan worked for the Renault Lotus racing team based on Enstone Aerodrome and Susie had first seen him when he and his wife, Angela, had come to look at Woodstock Academy. Woodstock Academy was an extremely prestigious private girls' school, where Susie was the School Secretary, and where the Browne twins (Jonathan and Angela's daughters) were currently being educated.

Susie had been flattered when Jonathan had called her after he and Angela had visited the school and asked if he could talk to her about the school from her perspective. He had suggested that they get together for a drink after school had finished for the day, and she happily met him in The King's Arms Hotel in Woodstock. It was a Wednesday, which was half-price champagne day, and Susie was stunned when she arrived to find Jonathan with a bottle of champagne and two glasses.

There was no way that Susie could have known Jonathan was a serial womaniser, who had found her attractive and thought she could be a great source of amusement. He was even more pleased with himself when he discovered that Susie lived in Enstone, just minutes from the aerodrome. They had been having a passionate affair ever since that Wednesday.

"Bloody James," muttered Susie, as she turned the ignition key. "Why does it have to be his birthday today?" She knew her father would be annoyed that she was late, but not as annoyed as she felt at having to drag herself away from Jonathan. They had been making love all afternoon and their time together was precious, so she hadn't wanted it to end, and she'd been forced to run around getting ready at the very last minute. She desperately hoped her mother wouldn't be too critical of her appearance – Annabelle was always immaculately turned out and she was a lot to live up to. Even with the addition of the diamond solitaire that had been left to her by Peter's mother, Susie wasn't 100 per cent convinced that her high street dress was quite up to scratch, although she had managed to find matching red shoes. Unusually for Susie, the shoes had heels, which brought her up to a statuesque six feet. That would annoy her brother, as she would look taller than him. This thought made her feel slightly better, as she yanked at the handbrake and shoved the car into gear.

*****

The gravel flew in all directions as Susie drew up at Riverside House. She tucked the Mini round the corner by the garage, so that it would be as out of the way as possible and leave room for the other guests' cars. She was dismayed to see that some people had arrived already. It would not go down well with her parents that Susie had not been part of the welcoming party. She'd got it wrong again.

Sighing, she got out of the car and locked it, thinking it best to leave her overnight bag in the boot until later, and just get herself into the garden and blend in with the party. As she slipped through the side gate, across the patio and on to the perfectly manicured lawn, Susie was a little dismayed to see Peter straight ahead of her. "Hello Daddy," she called out.

"Hello Susie," he replied. "How is it that you always manage to be late?

You've known about this party for months, so there really is no excuse."

"I'm sorry, Daddy," replied Susie. "I'm really not sure why I'm so late, just me being hopeless as usual, I suppose." She tried out what she hoped was a disarming smile, but her father still looked at her with stern disapproval. "Well, I'm here now, and looking forward to a great evening."

"Mmn," was Peter's reply, as he turned to greet some other guests.

Susie quickly made her way to the marquee where she found James talking to a pretty girl and a tall, dark chap. She was introduced to them as Jennifer and David. James went to college with Jennifer and David was her brother. Susie chatted for a few minutes and then moved off to find her mother and her grandparents. Grandma and Grandpa were delighted to see Susie and greeted her with enthusiasm, telling her how lovely she looked in her red dress. A waitress passed and gratefully Susie accepted a glass of champagne. "First today," she smiled as she sipped the perfectly chilled glass of bubbly. "Nice champagne Mummy," said Susie.

"Yes, darling, it is good. Your father and I brought it from France, specially for the party."

At that moment another waitress approached the group, looking extremely flustered. "Excuse me, Mrs Rowlands. Please may I have a word in private?" Annabelle excused herself and walked away with the waitress. "Is there a problem of some kind?" she enquired. "I'm afraid so, Madam, there are two police officers here asking to see you. They're standing just over there."

CHAPTER 2

Annabelle walked over to the two police officers and was immediately shown a warrant card by Detective Inspector Franklin. She confirmed who she was. "What's this all about?" Annabelle enquired, her mind racing. Could it be a speeding offence? No, she would hardly be visited by two detectives for driving too fast! Had either of her children done anything? Whatever could the police want with her? She knew that no-one close to her could be dead, as they were all here at the party.

"It's a complicated issue, Madam, which will take a little while to discuss. I can see we have called at a very inappropriate time." said DI Franklin. "What time tomorrow would be suitable for us come and see you? We are sorry to have intruded, but the matter is somewhat urgent."

"Goodness me," said Annabelle. "Could we leave it until 5.00 pm please? As you can see, we are having a party, and as it's my son's 21st birthday, we also have a family lunch planned for tomorrow."

"Certainly," said the DI. "5.00 pm it is then. May we wish you a very good evening, Madam."

"Urgent?" thought Annabelle. What on earth could have happened that involved her and was sufficiently urgent for two detectives to visit her at home on a Saturday evening?" She had knocked a door mirror off a car last week and not stopped, but then no-one could have seen her. "Oh no, surely not Malcolm?" She thought she had seen someone lurking outside the house the other week and there had also been one or two phone calls where the line had remained silent. "Oh well, I suppose I'll find out soon enough." She squared her shoulders, lifted her chin, and turned back towards her guests.

Returning to the party, Annabelle anxiously looked for Peter who was deep in conversation with a group of young people – clearly James' friends. He beckoned her over. "You're looking rather pale Belle, is everything OK?" he enquired, slipping an arm around Annabelle's waist. She nodded feeling it inappropriate to discuss the matter in front of their guests. Peter looked relieved and proceeded to introduce his wife to the little group.

As soon as she could, Annabelle drew Peter to one side and told him what had happened. "Whatever can it be?" she asked her husband. "The Inspector said it was urgent. I can't imagine what this can all be about."

"Try not to worry, darling," said Peter in what he hoped was a convincing tone. What could the police want with his wife? "Keep smiling, Belle. This is James' night, and we mustn't let anything spoil it for him.

After all, if it were that serious, the police wouldn't care that we were having a party. They could have asked you to go to the station with them."

"I suppose so," said Annabelle, then quickly tried to put a smile on her face as her mother walked over looking quizzical. "You two look deep in conversation, is anything the matter?"

"Oh, you know Mummy, we're just worrying that everything will go off well."

"Oh Annabelle," replied her mother, "I've never known you organise anything that wasn't a great success." Annabelle leant forward and kissed her mother's cheek.

"Thanks, Mummy," she responded, forcing a cheerful note into her voice.

On the other side of the room Susie and James were chatting. "How does it feel to be 21? Have you decided how you're going to spend the money?" she asked. "Are you going to take some girlfriend that you haven't introduced me to on a long and expensive holiday?"

"You know me, Suse," James replied. "There's no-one important in my life. Speaking of which, I see that you've come on your own tonight. Is there no-one special in your life either?" How Susie wished she could confide in her brother, but she knew it was far too risky.

"No, no-one special," she said with a smile. "Has the car arrived yet?" she swiftly changed the subject.

"Yes, it has," replied her brother. "It's in the garage. Would you like to have a look? I didn't go for a convertible, though. They're for girls and hairdressers." Susie laughed and said she could wait until tomorrow, as one Mini Cooper was really much the same as another.

An hour passed pleasantly enough with the waitresses unobtrusively topping up drinks and passing round canapés. Then at 8.15 pm Peter walked over to where the band had set up and borrowed a microphone to announce that dinner was served. Everyone made their way over to the beautifully presented tables, the family all sitting together. Peter and Annabelle were very conscious that they must put up a good front as they wanted the evening to be happy. The food was delicious. The catering company had done the Rowlands proud. Bowls of all kinds of salads had been put on the tables prior to the guests taking their seats, and then they were served from an array of delicious cold meats. This was followed by profiteroles and finally cheese boards were placed in the middles of all the tables. James' health was drunk amidst much gaiety, and then the dancing started.

During all the festivities Annabelle's mind was racing. "Could Malcolm have managed to get into trouble and somehow have implicated her? Could he be expecting her to bail him out?" It was no good, she was going to have to confess to Peter about Malcolm, but when would she get the chance this evening? It definitely had to be before the police returned the next day.

Susie was dancing with a variety of young men, all the time wishing that one of them could be Jonathan. "Still," she thought to herself, "not long now till Monaco." Jonathan was flying her out so that she could see the Grand Prix. Accommodation had been very difficult to find at short notice, but Susie was delighted to know that she would be staying at The Hotel de Paris, and that her room would be overlooking Casino Square so that she would get a good view of the cars as they came into the square. She was flying out on Friday evening, and Jonathan was hoping that he would be able to meet her himself at Nice and then drive her to Monaco. This thought kept Susie going as she danced the night away, smiling as she watched her parents jiving very respectably. She made a mental note to ask them to teach her how to do it, as Susie loved dancing, but did not know how to dance to rock and roll music.

At midnight the band stopped playing. A few guests had drifted away already and the remainder took their leave. "Let's go inside and have a nightcap," Peter said to his wife taking her hand and leading Annabelle back into the house. They slipped into his study, where Peter poured them each a large brandy. "It was a great evening Belle," he said. "As usual you planned it all to perfection."

"Thank you, darling," his wife answered, "but there's something I need to tell you Peter. It may have something to do with the police and why they want to talk to me." Might it indeed? thought Peter. I've got a nasty little secret that could implicate you with the police as well, but I'm not going to tell you what it is, unless I absolutely have to.

Nervously twiddling her glass in her hand, Annabelle began to talk, "I've never told you this Peter, because I suppose I didn't really think it was my secret to confide, but I have a half-brother, Malcolm. My mother gave birth to him when she was very young and he was adopted. I didn't know about him myself for years, not until he managed to trace Mummy, in fact. I think it's a very painful subject for her and I think she only told me once she felt she had to. Anyway, he's a bad lot and always in and out of trouble, and I've given him money in the past to try and help him. Last time I gave him £1,000 and told him that was it but I'm wondering if he's in some kind of trouble with the police and wants me to bail him out? One of my reasons for wondering about Malcolm is that I thought I saw a car hanging around outside our house on the road a few times recently. I hope you aren't cross with me darling?"

"I would rather have known that your brother was coming on to you for money so that I could have stopped it," replied her husband, "but as for being cross with you, of course not." Peter's thoughts circled round and round as he silently pondered what he had done that could cause Annabelle grief. "I think I'd like a cigar before bed. Why don't you go up and I'll join you shortly?"

As soon as Annabelle left the room Peter went to his desk and started searching for the papers which might have prompted this unexpected visit from the police. He'd either been very clever or a proper fool.

Unable to find what he wanted, he shrugged, locked his desk, turned off the lights and climbed the stairs to bed. He was disturbed by the possibility that the police might be after him. But then, what was life without a challenge?

*****

Annabelle was up early next morning, still worrying about the police and why they wanted to see her. After a cup of coffee she went to have a look at the debris left from the party. The caterers had done a sterling job and everything had been removed, down to the last table napkin; all that was needed now was for the marquee company to disassemble the marquee but that wouldn't happen until the following day. They had been so fortunate with the weather, Annabelle thought to herself, as May could be a very cold month indeed. Her mind turned again to the detectives. She could not think of any reason why they could possibly want to speak with her, other than the dreaded Malcolm. She felt the tension building up in her neck and shoulders. That damned man.

Hearing sounds of activity from within Riverside House, Annabelle went back inside to find out what everyone would like for breakfast. It was good to see both her children at the breakfast table as Susie didn't come over as often as Annabelle would have liked. Annabelle felt that her daughter was sometimes secretive and silently wondered why. Anyway, today they were all together and her parents were there as well. They would be leaving after lunch to drive back to Derbyshire and Annabelle was pretty certain Susie would be slipping away too, as soon as she felt it reasonably polite to do so.

Susie was in a world of her own. She had texted Jonathan both before she went to bed last night and first thing this morning and he hadn't replied. She knew that his wife was away so what on earth was he playing at? She had been rather hoping to get away from Moulsford immediately after lunch and meet up with him but this was looking less likely. Mechanically she helped her mother clear away the breakfast dishes. "It's nice to have you here, darling," Annabelle said to her daughter. "I really feel that we don't see enough of you. Perhaps we could meet up at Bicester Village and do some shopping together. How about us doing that this coming weekend?" Susie turned hot and cold both at the same time. That was her Monaco weekend!

"I'm really not sure, Mummy. I'll have to check my diary. I think Grace is planning on coming to stay then."

"Oh that would be nice," replied Annabelle, "I haven't seen Grace in ages. It would be lovely to catch up with her as well." Oh God, worse and worse thought Susie to herself as she smiled weakly at her mother. She really was going to have to come up with a good story to get out of this one!

The family spent the morning quietly. Peter was engrossed in *The Telegraph* and his thoughts about his wife and the police. Trying to gain Brownie points, Susie went to the village shop and bought another selection of newspapers for everyone else. She then went to the garage with James to admire his new car. It was much the same as hers except not convertible and in white with a black roof. "What's going on in your life Suse?" he asked her. "We don't really see much of you these days." Oh, not you as well, Susie thought to herself.

"Well," she said, "I get a long break in the summer. I'm sure we'll see more of each other then. You'll have finished college too. Any plans?"

"I shall try and get on some management trainee scheme," her brother replied. "I know that both Marks and Spencer and BT have good ones."

"Oh go for Marks," laughed Susie, "you might be able to get me a staff discount."

At 12.30 pm (sharp! as Peter was in charge) the family left for the Beetle and Wedge Hotel where they all had a splendid lunch although, certain members of the Rowlands family had rather more to think about than others.

Susie was sitting there scheming as her wretched mother had told her father about Grace's proposed visit and how she was planning on spending the day at Bicester Village with the two of them. Grace was an old friend of Susie's who lived in Manchester. Susie and Grace had known each other since kindergarten and caught up with each other as often as they could. Little did Susie guess that Grace and shopping at Bicester Village were the very last things on her parents' minds.

Annabelle's parents were the first to leave Riverside House after lunch, driving off in their ancient Jaguar. As soon as they had gone, Annabelle told her children about the impending police visit. They were both startled and shocked, having no idea why the police would want to speak with their mother.

Following this revelation, Susie wondered how soon she could decently leave, and then at 4.30 pm announced that she thought she should be going so that her mother could talk to the police in peace. With a relieved smile on her face, Susie jumped into the red Mini and headed out towards Oxford and ultimately home. She still hadn't heard from Jonathan so had decided it was not going to be possible to see him this evening, as no doubt his wife and family would be coming back before too long. Instead, she would have a look through her wardrobe and think about what she was going to take with her to Monaco. She must look her absolute best and most seductive for her beloved man.

*****

Annabelle, Peter and James were sitting discussing the weekend, when the doorbell rang. James excused himself and said he would leave his parents to speak with the police on their own. He whistled loudly and Allsort, his parents' basset hound, came running. "Shall we have a walk by the river?" James asked her rubbing her ears. Taking the frantic tail wagging as a yes, James fetched Allsort's lead and they set off together. Meanwhile, Peter went and opened the front door to find DI Franklin and his Police Sergeant standing there. "Good afternoon gentlemen, do please come in," he said courteously and with an outward air of total calm.

CHAPTER 3

As Susie was dealing with the Sunday evening traffic on her way home to Enstone, Jonathan Browne was letting himself into his house in Kirtlington. He was very pleased with himself, singing "Easy Like Sunday Morning" as he took his overnight bag out of the boot of his Renault Sport. Jonathan loved women and the job he held, as Marketing Manager for the Lotus F1 team, gave him ample opportunity to fuel this passion.

He felt that the weekend had been a great success. His wife, Angela, had taken their seven year old twins to stay with her parents in Cornwall and he had pleaded pressure of work as an excuse not to go. He had spent Friday night and most of Saturday with Susie the secretary. Susie was good company: lively, fun and great in the sack. He wasn't bothered that she'd had other arrangements on Saturday night as, flying back from the Spanish Grand Prix the previous weekend, he'd managed to get the phone number of a rather stunning little air hostess who lived near Windsor and she'd proved more than happy to pick up entertaining him where Susie had left off.

Closing the front door behind him, Jonathan decided to call Angela to see what time she expected to be home. It really wouldn't take long to drive from Kirtlington to Enstone and it would be prudent to see Susie, as he had been ignoring her text messages whilst he was enjoying himself with his trolly dolly. After all, Susie was so convenient and so pleasurable, it would be a shame to upset her.

*****

George greeted Susie with great enthusiasm. He had been on his own overnight and the one thing George really appreciated was human contact and interaction. He rolled on his back and stuck his legs in the air in a gesture of pure supplication. "Hello Georgie Porgie," said Susie, bending down to rub his white tummy. "Have you missed me? I bet you're hungry and would like some delicious dinner." She scooped George's empty Cat Mate dish up from the floor, put the containers in the sink and fetched his normal bowl from the cupboard. George purred happily whilst Susie replenished his water bowl and spooned some Purina into his dish.

Looking at the clock on the kitchen wall, Susie saw that it was a little after 5.30 pm. She was wondering how she would spend the evening when her phone rang, and to Susie's great surprise it was Jonathan. "I've been texting you and you've been ignoring me," Susie cried indignantly.

"I'm sorry sweetheart, I just noticed that I've had my phone on silent and missed all sorts of things," he answered smoothly. "How was the party? Did you meet loads of handsome men and now have lots of new dates?"

"Don't be silly Jonathan, it was a family party and I'd far rather have spent the whole weekend with you. You know that." Mmn, thought Jonathan, Susie did sound a bit miffed. He felt he needed to dangle a carrot. Angela wasn't due home until about 9.00 pm which, even with travelling to Enstone and back, gave him a good two hours. "Why don't you take a bottle of something cold up to bed and I'll join you in half an hour?" he suggested.

Susie didn't need asking twice. She hastily put a bottle of Sauvignon Blanc into the freezer and ran upstairs where she ditched her overnight bag in the spare room before stripping off and heading for the shower. Once under the rushing jet of water Susie washed her hair and body with Molton Brown's Pink Pepper and after a brisk rub with a towel, massaged in the matching body lotion. Quickly she smoothed some mousse through her thick, dark hair then turned her head upside down to blast it with her hairdryer. Satisfied with the results, Susie wrapped herself in her silk kimono and went back downstairs to retrieve the wine before skipping back upstairs and arranging herself on the bed. It wasn't long before she heard Jonathan's footsteps on her path. "The door's unlocked," she called and it was only a moment before the love of her life was climbing the stairs.

*****

As usual, Jonathan had parked his car some way from Rose Cottage, and walked the remainder of the distance. He hadn't noticed the figure standing in the shadows at the entrance to Cox's Lane, but she had spotted him all right and wondered where he was going. She was even more surprised when she saw him go into Rose Cottage. Thinking about what she had seen, she walked slowly away, a puzzled expression on her face.

*****

Susie and Jonathan spent a very pleasurable couple of hours, making love slowly and languorously (privately Jonathan was impressed with his own stamina), drinking wine and chatting. Unsurprisingly, Susie was very excited about Monaco and staying at the Hotel de Paris. She had decided that she would fly out on Friday evening after school, and had told her employers that she had a dental appointment at 10.30 am on the Monday in Chipping Norton, so she would be late in to school that day. She was really hoping that Jonathan would be able to spend at least one night with her. "That could be difficult sweetheart," said her lover. "Monaco is one of the most prestigious events on the Grand Prix calendar so it may be noticed if I go missing, particularly if we win in which case there will be massive celebrations."

"Do you think you could get me into any after race parties?" enquired Susie.

"Sorry, darling, but no. I can't risk someone realising you are with me or wondering who you are. I should be able to pick you up at the airport and we can take it from there, OK?" Susie nodded. She knew she had to accept whatever was on offer. That was the price you had to pay if you had an affair with a married man.

"Anyway, Susie, I must dash now. I'd like to be home to welcome Angela and the twins back. It saves any awkward questions." Again Susie nodded. This time sadly. She would have liked nothing more than to snuggle down with Jonathan and have him there when she woke up in the morning. "Cheer up sweetheart," he said, "I'll be here all night on Wednesday. Angela thinks I'm flying out to Monaco then, when in fact I'm not going until Thursday. Think what you would like to do. Shall I take you out for dinner?"

"Yes please," said Susie. She hated cooking and spent far more time in the nail bar than she did in the kitchen. "Where shall we go?"

"Somewhere remote, where no-one knows us," replied Jonathan. "Why don't you have a look on the internet at work tomorrow and find us somewhere?" he called as he was heading into the shower. He couldn't risk any trace of Susie's perfume clinging to him although fortunately it seemed Angela had a very poor sense of smell.

Ten minutes later, showered and dressed, Jonathan kissed Susie once more and walked down Cox's Lane in the direction of his car. Singing "Easy Like Sunday Morning" once again, he smoothly pulled away and headed for home.

*****

Annoyingly, Angela and the twins were already home when he got back. "Hello Jonathan. Where have you been?" asked his wife.

"Daddy, Daddy," called out the girls, "we've been to the beach and we paddled in the sea." Ignoring Angela, Jonathan held out his arms to his daughters who rushed over for a hug. "Tell me all about your time with Nanny and Grandpa," he said encouragingly, whilst racking his brains to think why he would have been out so late on a Sunday evening when his family were expected home.

"Jonathan, I asked you a question," said Angela a little crossly.

"Sorry darling, what was that?" he enquired, frantically buying time.

Angela repeated herself, "Oh," said Jonathan, "Gerry wanted to borrow some woodworking tools so I dropped them round to him."

"I would have thought as he was the one doing the borrowing he could have come here," Angela retorted, "and what a funny time of night to want to borrow something."

"Oh it could have waited until tomorrow," said her husband, "but we're really busy at the factory getting ready for Monaco. I shall be working some long hours this week so I thought it best to pop the tools round tonight." That was good he thought to himself. By suggesting he was busy at work he might get an opportunity to spend some more time with Susie. "You must be tired with all the driving, Angela my sweet. Can I fix you a drink? And you two should be getting ready for bed," Jonathan said to Emily and Alice. "Upstairs now please and Mummy and I will be up shortly to say goodnight."

Together Angela and Jonathan walked through to the sitting room, where he poured them each a vodka and tonic. "How were your parents?" he asked his wife.

"Disappointed that, as usual, you weren't with me," said Angela.

"I know, Angie, and I'm sorry, but, as I said earlier it's a busy time at the factory. We've got Monaco in a few days and it would be so wonderful if we could be on the podium, or better still, win. I'm busy writing a lot of promotional bumph. It will be much easier for me in the winter. You know that. Why don't we invite your parents up here for Christmas?" That should appease her, he thought to himself.

"That's all well and good," replied Angela, "but who has to do all the cooking and shopping? Not you, is it?" Christ, was the woman never satisfied? he thought to himself.

"Yes, darling, I realise it's more work for you, but we could go out to lunch somewhere in Woodstock – there's lots of choice, and surely to goodness you could do the majority of your shopping on line? I'll see to the booze."

"I suppose it's worth thinking about," said Angela grudgingly. "I expect my parents would enjoy Christmas here, seeing the girls unwrap their presents."

"Good," said Jonathan. "Now why don't you go and read the girls a bedtime story and I'll bring some wine upstairs and then come and say goodnight to them. After all, I think we should have an early night, as I haven't seen you since Thursday." As he said this, Jonathan crossed his fingers behind his back, secretly hoping that Angela would be her usual unwilling self. He really didn't want to finish what had been such an utterly pleasant weekend on a low!

CHAPTER 4

Peter ushered Detective Inspector Franklin and Sergeant Green through to the sitting room, where Annabelle was nervously waiting. She jumped to her feet as they entered and offered the police officers tea. They politely declined.

In as calm a voice as he could muster, Peter invited the officers to sit down. A very flustered Annabelle gestured in the direction of one of the sofas, and the two policemen took a seat, both appraising the room as they did so.

The Rowlands' sitting room was expensively furnished, with a pale green carpet and large cream sofas and armchairs. There were several tables and an elegant sideboard, all of which housed pieces of porcelain and photos in silver frames. Various pieces of art hung on the walls. A couple of Aubusson rugs were placed in the centre of the room. "Mmm," thought DI Franklin, "there's a few bob been spent here, that's for sure."

"I'm sorry that we interrupted your party last evening, Madam, and do hope that it all went well?" enquired the Inspector politely.

"Yes, thank you," replied Annabelle, wishing he would get to the point. "Now how may I help you?"

"Yesterday morning Major and Mrs Williamson's house was broken in to and some valuable antiques were stolen. Unfortunately, Major Williamson interrupted the burglary and was severely beaten by the burglars. He is in a critical but stable condition in hospital. This isn't just a simple case of burglary, but a case of GBH." As the Inspector was talking, Peter breathed a sigh of relief. He was sorry for what had happened of course, but at least he was not implicated in any way. He brought his mind back to what DI Franklin was saying, "So we've come to see you on two issues Madam. As you are the Williamsons' nearest neighbours, we would like you to think very carefully about whether you perhaps saw anything unusual on Saturday between 10.00 am and 11.00 am. Secondly, we would like to show you some photos of the stolen objects. Mrs Williamson mentioned that you have an antiques shop specialising in porcelain, so we would like you to be on the alert, in case anyone tries to sell you any of the Williamsons' pieces."

Annabelle ran an antiques business in the Lamb Arcade in Wallingford. She was renowned for her knowledge of Derby porcelain, having been surrounded by it all her life, as her great grandfather had been a painter at the factory. He had been apprenticed to Albert Gregory, who was best known for his cabinet pieces. She started to look at the photos Sergeant Green produced. "There are certainly some good pieces here," she said, "both Derby and some signed Worcester. Did the thieves get anything else?"

"No, Madam, as I said, Major Williamson disturbed them and they made a hasty getaway. We are waiting for him to be well enough to see if he can give us any descriptions. I say they, but of course it could have been one individual."

As the detective spoke, Annabelle started to wonder about the car she had seen lurking about over the past few days. Should she tell the police or not? She had been wondering whether it was Malcolm but maybe it was the thieves, keeping an eye on the Williamsons' property? Either way, she thought she should say something. "You asked us if we had seen anything peculiar yesterday morning," she ventured cautiously. "Well, I have noticed what I think is the same car parked up on the side of the main road a few times recently." Sergeant Green took out his notebook.

"Could you be more specific please, Mrs Rowlands?" he asked. "Can you give us any actual dates and times?"

"Goodness," replied Annabelle, "let me think. That's difficult to answer. Have you seen it at all Peter?"

"No, darling, I can't say I have," replied her husband. "Do you know what kind of car it was?"

Sergeant Green frowned slightly, "One thing at a time please, sir," he said. "Now Mrs Rowlands, returning to dates and times, can you think of any at all?" Annabelle racked her brains.

"I'm sure it was there on Wednesday afternoon when I came back from seeing my personal trainer," she said.

"What time would that have been, roughly?" asked Sergeant Green.

"About 5.15 pm," said Annabelle.

"Any other specific times that you can think of? How about yesterday morning?"

"Let me see," said Annabelle. "I went to the hairdressers in Wallingford for 11.00 am and was back home a couple of hours later. No, I don't remember seeing it then and that was the only time I went out. As for other times, it really is difficult to know exactly, but I'm sure I saw it the previous weekend at some point. I really am sorry that I can't be more definite."

"How about you, Mr Rowlands? Did you go out yesterday morning?" asked the Police Sergeant. Peter shook his head.

"Now, Madam, please think very carefully. What kind of car was it and what colour?"

"I'm not sure about the make," said Annabelle, "but I am positive that it was black. It was also very dirty every time that I saw it."

"How many times do you think that you saw it?" DI Franklin butted in to the conversation.

"Perhaps half a dozen in the last couple of weeks," said Annabelle, "but it was across the road from our house in that lay-by, so it may have been a while before I realised I was seeing the same car, as a lay-by is a perfectly normal place to park." The detectives nodded.

"One of our main reasons for coming to see you today, Mrs Rowlands, is that you are well known locally as a Derby specialist. Should anyone try to sell you any of these pieces, please say you are interested, but that you will need to make an appointment for the person to come back and see you, as you don't have sufficient cash on hand to pay for them then and there. This will provide you with the opportunity to alert us." DI Franklin handed Annabelle his card. "And please telephone us if you think of anything else. It would be interesting to know whether you see the black car in the lay-by again. We will prepare a statement for you concerning the car and let you know when it is ready for you to sign. Thank you for your help." Rising to his feet, the Inspector indicated to his Sergeant that the interview was over. The police and the Rowlands wished each other a good evening and then Peter escorted the officers to the door.

*****

A little later James and Allsort returned having enjoyed a walk by the river. "What was all that about, Ma?" James asked Annabelle, and she told him briefly about the Williamsons and the porcelain.

"I should have asked the police for copies of the photos," she said to her son. "After all, you will be watching the shop for me when your father and I go to Le Touquet next month. Oh gosh, maybe we shouldn't go now, I don't like the idea of you being here in the house on your own, James."

"I wouldn't worry, darling," said Peter. "It's probably some London gang stealing to order. After all, you're always telling me that Derby porcelain isn't fashionable at the moment."

"Imari isn't popular," said Annabelle, "but a couple of the Williamsons' pieces were rather special. There was a beautiful William Billingsley vase and some impressive Worcester." James listened vaguely, trying to look interested. Although a creative and artistic young man, he was not that enthusiastic about looking after his mother's shop.

"Anyway, I think we could all do with a drink now, don't you?" enquired Peter. "What will you have Belle? There's plenty of champagne left from last night if you would like a glass?"

"Beer for me," said James, heading for the kitchen. "Would you like me to bring you two a bottle of bubbly?"

"Yes please," replied his mother. "I need something to help me relax. I can't stop thinking about the poor Williamsons."

*****

As the police officers drove back to Oxford they passed at least a dozen black cars heading in the opposite direction. They didn't notice that one was particularly dirty.

The car turned into the usual lay-by from where it was possible to see the drive that lead down to Riverside House. It was 6.12 pm precisely. The man at the wheel watched with interest as James and Allsort returned home. After a couple of hours he drove off, and once again his path crossed with that of the detectives on their way to The Old Bakery to inform Mary Williamson that as of an hour ago, she was a widow.

*****

At The Crown in Church Enstone David Timmins was telling Alf, the landlord, about the previous evening's party at Riverside House and what a splendid do it had been. At this point, Alf didn't realise that "one of Jenny's college friends" was in fact Susie Rowlands' brother. Susie popped in to the pub from time to time, and Alf had a soft spot for her, as she reminded him of his own daughter at that age – lively and bubbly and with a good sense of humour. Alf knew David quite well as they lived next door to each other. In fact David had bought the cottage from Alf the previous year, when Alf had got sick of unreliable tenants and decided to put the property on the market. David enjoyed living next door to a pub; particularly this one. Alf was known far and wide for his delicious food and well-kept ale, both of which saved David a lot of time and effort!

"I've got a few quid going spare at the moment, David," Alf said to the young man. "Can you think of a good home for it?" David was an Independent Financial Adviser, who worked for his father in Chipping Norton, and Alf loved having this type of conversation with him.

"You're charging too much for your beer if you've got spare money," joked David.

"Cheeky sod," was Alf's immediate reply. "I'll talk to the bank manager then, if that's how you feel. Perhaps I'm not grand enough to use your services?"

"Oh pull me another pint of your expensive beer and stop moaning," came the reply. As he savoured his pint, David fervently wished that Alf's pub could be full of interesting young ladies, an area in which currently his life was sadly lacking.

*****

About a mile away, Susie Rowlands had bid farewell to Jonathan, and was making a list of all the things she needed to do the following day:

1. Arrange with her neighbour to feed George whilst she was in Monaco.

2. Find a restaurant for Jonathan to take her to on Wednesday evening.

3. Get Euros from the bank at lunchtime.

4. Decide on clothes to take to Monaco.

5. Ring her mother and explain that she was going to stay with Grace next weekend.

Susie felt that the last item on the list would be the most difficult as she was not a natural liar. Pouring herself another glass of wine, she went to bed, to prepare for Monday and the tasks that lay ahead of her.

CHAPTER 5

Woodstock Academy was set in extensive grounds on the edge of the famous Cotswold town. As he dropped Alice and Emily off on Monday morning, Jonathan noticed Susie Rowlands walking in to the main building, accompanied by a little girl. His twins dashed off in the direction of the entrance as most of the younger children thought Miss Rowlands to be rather fun, as she was pretty and giggly and she didn't tell them what to do. He smiled ruefully to himself before heading off to the factory in Enstone. Jonathan was quite happy with the press release he had written and was hoping that, although it would be hectic at work, the lead-up to one of the most prestigious races in the world would be relatively peaceful, for him at least.

Alice and Emily quickly caught up with Susie. "Hello, Miss Rowlands. Did you have a nice weekend?" Emily asked her. Susie always felt a twinge of guilt when she was talking to the twins, in view of the relationship that she had with their father.

"Yes, thank you, I did," she said. "I went home to Moulsford as it was my brother's birthday. What did you girls do?" She quickly turned the focus onto the twins and the other child, whose name was Patricia Symonds. The twins started telling Susie excitedly about their trip to Cornwall to see their grandparents, whilst Patricia stood there silently. Susie felt very sorry for Patsy Symonds. She was a plain, shy child, who found it difficult to mix with the others, who were always poking fun at her and not inviting her to join in their games. "How about you, Patricia? What did you do?"

"Not much, Miss Rowlands," came the reply.

"Well, you had better go to your classroom and I had better go to my office now," said Susie, who had a lot to do, not all of it school business.

Once at her desk, Susie reviewed her list from the previous evening. She decided that she could look on the internet for a suitable restaurant for her and Jonathan for Wednesday evening without anyone being the wiser. She could go to the bank at lunchtime to sort out her Euros but phoning her mother would be trickier, as she didn't want to be overheard.

The morning passed quickly enough and Susie found the time to choose a restaurant and book a table. She decided to drive in to town at lunchtime so that she could visit the bank and then she could phone her mother whilst sitting in the car and not run the risk of being overheard. The conversation with Annabelle went fairly as Susie had predicted it would. Her mother was disappointed that her daughter was going to visit Grace and suggested that perhaps she change it round and that Grace came to visit Susie. Susie had prepared herself for this and explained that Grace had got tickets to a concert and didn't want to miss out on going. She did, however, promise to go shopping with her mother before her parents went to Le Touquet. "Three down and two to go," thought Susie. All she had to do now was think about her packing and make arrangements for George to be fed and watered in her absence.

The afternoon whizzed by and soon Susie was driving home. Before going in to her house she popped next door to see her neighbour, Mrs MacDonald, and asked her if she would look after George, telling the same story about going to visit her friend Grace. Continuity was important when lying, as was a good memory! Mrs MacDonald, who lived alone, was delighted to oblige, as she would enjoy George's company just as much as he would enjoy her feeding him.

Susie went upstairs to sort out her packing. She was hoping that she would get the opportunity to enjoy some of the glamour of Monaco as well as watching the cars going round. Desperately she prayed that Jonathan would be able to spend a reasonable amount of time with her, albeit within the confines of the Hotel de Paris. "Confines," she thought to herself, "it would hardly be a chore to be incarcerated in one of Monaco's finest hotels." Susie had never before been to Monaco and was excited by the whole thing.

Looking in her wardrobe she selected the red dress that she had worn to James' party on Saturday, a little silver backless number that she would never think of wearing in front of her father, and a delicious black galaxy dress that hugged every single curve. She intended to flaunt everything that she had, and this way she would be able to create a different look every evening. She added a denim mini skirt, a pair of white capri pants, an assortment of different coloured tops, a couple of pashminas, a selection of jewellery and, after much deliberation, she managed to pick out just four pairs of shoes and two handbags. All she needed now were her toiletries and her Kindle. Susie gathered everything together and laid it all out in the spare room, ready to pack on Thursday evening, as she would be going directly to the airport from school on Friday. She smiled to herself as she realised she'd forgotten to include any underwear, imagining that Jonathan would probably have been more than happy about that, as she returned to the bedroom to hunt for her sexiest sets. Satisfied that things were under control, she ran downstairs, jumped into her Mini Cooper and drove off to Chipping Norton where she had an appointment at the nail bar. After all, she couldn't be less than perfect when she had Jonathan staying over on Wednesday night, not to mention Monaco.

*****

22

Annabelle was dismayed to see the two police officers getting out of the green Mondeo that had pulled up on the drive at Riverside House. Peter was out playing golf, so she was going to have to deal with them alone. She went to the door and opened it. DI Franklin asked if they might come in and once again Annabelle took them through to the sitting room. "Have you brought the statement for me to sign?" she asked. Sergeant Green confirmed they had, but that they also had some sad news. Annabelle guessed what had happened and nodded gravely as the Sergeant explained that the Major had died on Sunday evening. "This now becomes a very serious matter indeed," said DI Franklin. "This has now become a homicide investigation. Should you be approached by anybody offering you any of the stolen goods, please be careful, and don't alert their suspicions." Annabelle wondered how she was supposed to not alert the suspicions of these people when asking them to come and see her at another time, and desperately hoped that nothing would come of any of this. However, she remembered James saying it would be helpful to have copies of the photos so that he would know what he was looking for when he stood in for her at The Lamb. Sergeant Green said he would arrange for the photos to be supplied.

Annabelle was then asked to check through her statement, and, if happy with it, to sign where indicated. She read it through carefully and then signed.

"We should also add Mrs Rowlands, that if you see the black car parked in the lay by, do not approach the driver, but please do call us," said Sergeant Green. Annabelle confirmed that she would do just that, before showing the two officers to the front door. Just as they were leaving, James drove up in his new car.

Annabelle told James about Major Williamson, but not about the black car, as she was still wondering whether or not it might be Malcolm. "Please God don't let him be a murderer," she thought to herself.

*****

Jonathan's day went well and he finished work earlier than anticipated. Not wishing to go home too early, as he wanted Angela to think he was exceptionally busy, he decided to have a drink at The Crown. It was in the opposite direction to home, but he liked the pub, and often dropped in at lunchtime.

The bar was quiet and Alf greeted Jonathan warmly. "I'll have a pint of Stella, please Alf," said Jonathan.

"Are you ready for Monaco, then?" the landlord asked as he pulled Jonathan's drink.

"Yes, I'm off on Wednesday," came the reply. "I still find certain tracks special, and Monaco's one of them."

"Charlotte's a mad keen Formula 1 fan," said Alf. "She's been to the Grand Prix here but that's as far as she got. I think her dream would have been to see Schumacher win Monaco. Pity he came back, I think. He should have stayed retired whilst he was still at the top." Jonathan shrugged his shoulders.

"Ross Brawn offered him a fortune to come back, so I guess you can't blame him," he replied.

Always on the look-out for attractive women, Jonathan scanned the bar, but was disappointed and decided that chatting to Alf was as good as it was going to get. He knew that Susie came in The Crown occasionally, but he would have seen her car outside if she had been there and quite honestly, he preferred not to be in her company anywhere he was known, as Susie did tend to make it obvious that she was in love with him. He slowly drank his pint, wished Alf a good evening, got in his car and drove off towards Kirtlington and his family.

*****

The nail technician was very talkative and wondered that, as she didn't normally see Susie on a Monday, was she going somewhere special? Susie smiled and throwing caution to the wind, told the girl that she was going to the Monaco Grand Prix with a friend and that she was having a special dinner with her boyfriend on Wednesday. The technician looked impressed and then asked if Susie would like any nail art for these special occasions? Susie declined, thinking what Janet Jennings, the headmistress of Woodstock Academy, would say if she turned up at school tomorrow with decorated nails. Susie always tried to look her most conservative during school hours as Miss Jennings was such a frump.

The nail technician finished her work, leaving Susie with perfect red nails. Susie paid the bill and walked back to her car wondering what she would have for dinner. She had plenty of ready meals in the freezer so she could make a choice when she got home.

CHAPTER 6

"Are you all packed and ready for Monaco?" Angela enquired of her husband at breakfast on Wednesday morning.

"Yes thanks, darling, I am, and I have time to take the girls to school if you would like me to? I'm flying from Birmingham and it won't be a problem as I also have to look in at the factory and collect a spare helmet for Kimi."

"Oh yes, please, Daddy," chorused Alice and Emily. "We shan't see you again until after school on Monday." Their parents smiled at them fondly.

Jonathan was in an extremely good mood this morning. He had managed to extricate himself from staying with the rest of the team and unknown to Susie was planning to share her room in the Hotel de Paris. This had taken a certain amount of engineering as the team did normally all stay together, but nevertheless he had succeeded. He would spring the surprise on Susie over dinner that evening. He knew that she would be thrilled. He smiled to himself. "You look like the cat that's got the cream," Angela observed. "What's making you so happy today?"

"Oh, I'm just thinking what a lucky man I am. Two beautiful daughters and a wife who are all going to miss me as much as I will miss them."

Angela felt a little bemused. Jonathan wasn't normally so happy to be going off to a Grand Prix but after all it was Monaco. No doubt he was thinking about the nightclubs and the Casino. She would have liked to be going with him, but with the twins being so small it just wasn't practicable. She would have to wait until Silverstone, and then maybe take the girls along too.

"What will you do with yourself whilst I'm away, Angela?" Jonathan asked.

"Oh, this and that," came the reply. "Coffee with the girls no doubt. Maybe lunch out. If the weather is as good as it was last weekend, perhaps go for a picnic on Saturday or Sunday. I expect you'd like that, wouldn't you girls?"

"Yes please, Mummy. That would be great. Could we bring a friend too?" asked Alice.

"Wait until nearer the weekend and we'll see what the weather's like," was their mother's reply.

Jonathan got up from the table and collected his suitcase and briefcase. The briefcase was particularly useful as he could fit a fresh shirt and underwear into it. The last thing he wanted was to carry a suitcase into

Susie's house. He kept basic essentials there anyway, such as a toothbrush and a razor. He wondered where they were going to dine that evening, reminding himself to get cash out of a machine first thing. He didn't want Angela checking up on his credit card bill when he wasn't supposed to be in the country!

Alice and Emily put on their blazers and collected their satchels, hugged their mother and made their way outside to where Jonathan's car was parked. He kissed Angela on the cheek, told her that he would miss her and then went and joined his daughters.

Susie also had a smile on her face as she got ready for school. She had put fresh linen on the bed and her best towels in the bathroom in preparation for the evening. She had even bought bread and orange juice from the local shop so that Jonathan could have breakfast in the morning before he left for the airport. She would decide what to wear when she got home from work. Champagne was chilling in the fridge, so everything in Susie's world was organised. She saw Mrs MacDonald looking out of the window, and waved cheerfully to her as she got into the car.

Susie arrived at Woodstock Academy promptly at 8.30 am. She didn't want any hassle this week, as she had to get away dead on the dot on Friday afternoon and she was skiving off on Monday morning. She was quite surprised to see Jonathan dropping off the twins again but didn't acknowledge him. This was neither the time nor the place. Patricia Symonds was waiting for her as usual inside the front door. The child was clearly very unhappy and Susie felt really sorry for her, but powerless to do anything to help her. If ever the opportunity arose Patsy hung around her. The poor child didn't seem to have any friends. Susie wondered whether she should speak to the headmistress about her, or maybe her form teacher.

The school day passed quickly, and it wasn't long before Susie was back in her Mini Cooper heading towards Enstone. She had a knot of excitement in her stomach as she parked her car and as soon as she was inside Rose Cottage she texted Jonathan to let him know that she was home and he could come round as soon as he wished.

Jonathan arrived about half an hour later and Susie threw herself into his arms before dragging him upstairs, along with the champagne. After all, they had three hours before they needed to be at the restaurant. She had booked a table at The Mason's Arms at Swerford, and ordered a taxi so that they could both enjoy a few drinks. After wonderful champagne-fuelled love making, Susie got herself dolled up, and was gratified by Jonathan's smile when she gave him a twirl, making her flirty little dress spin out, perfectly showing off her toned legs.

The silent figure that had watched Jonathan leave Susie's house on the Sunday evening was watching again, and saw them get into the taxi together

*****

Susie and Jonathan were shown to a charming window table at The Mason's Arms. Jonathan ordered another bottle of champagne and once they were sipping it, told Susie the good news that he was planning to share her room at The Hotel de Paris. Susie was over the moon at this and leaned across the table to kiss him. "Oh Jonathan, I do love you so much," she said, a little too loudly for Jonathan's liking.

"Ssh, darling," he said, "you're making people look at us." Champagne and excitement had gone to Susie's head though. She couldn't have cared less if the whole world were watching, and she told Jonathan so. He looked disapproving and asked her to choose what she would like to eat, hoping that the food would help soak up the alcohol and thinking that perhaps the second bottle of champagne had not been such a good choice after all.

Jonathan was not one to have his mood dampened, though and the evening was a pleasant one. The food was good and after three courses and a couple of cups of black coffee, Susie was relatively sober again. Mrs MacDonald heard the taxi pulling up outside Rose Cottage and, looking from behind her curtains, was interested to see that Susie had been out again with the tall man, and that he appeared to be staying the night. Both Susie and Jonathan were oblivious to the fact that they were being observed, thinking only about what was going to happen when they got upstairs.

*****

After yet more languorous love making, the pair arose shortly after 7.00 am, as Susie had to go to school and Jonathan had to drive to the airport to catch his flight to Nice.

They decided it would be best to leave the house separately and that Jonathan should go first so that Susie could lock up. The watchful figure was intrigued to see the same man leaving, with Miss Rowlands waving to him from the front door of her cottage. She peered more closely and saw that Miss Rowlands was wearing a dressing gown, and wondered if she might be ill.

*****

Back in Moulsford the Rowlands family had just finished breakfast. Annabelle was asking James if he would like to help her in the shop, and he was asking how much she would be willing to pay. "Speaking of money, have you done anything with your inheritance, or is it still in the bank?" his father asked.

"No, it's still in the bank, Dad, but don't try changing the subject," replied his son, smiling broadly.

"No, no, seriously James, if you don't know what you want to do with it, you shouldn't leave £100,000 in your bank account," said Peter. "Let's have a proper talk about that. I can't spare the time just now though, as I'm off to Huntercombe for a round of golf."

"Right, Mumsy, let's talk numbers and then I will see if it's worth me considering your offer," said James.

"I didn't realise I had managed to produce such a mercenary child," said Annabelle laughing. "You have just inherited £100,000 from your grandparents. You aren't sure what you are going to do with it and now you want me to pay you for looking after my antiques, when you live at home for nothing. I'll tell you what, you go and open up this morning and I'll come and have lunch with you in the café at 1 o'clock and see what kind of a job you are making of things. There's a couple of boxes of new stock in the garage. Everything is priced up. Let's see how attractive you can make my shop and then we'll talk about money."

That seemed a fair deal to James, so he put the boxes in the boot of his car and drove off to Wallingford. He didn't notice the dirty black car following him.

CHAPTER 7

As James was carefully placing his mother's boxes of antiques inside her shop a Yorkshire terrier bounded up to him, its body wagging. "Oh hello," said James, "Can you smell Allsort?" The dog looked at him quizzically and continued to shake with excitement.

"Don't be a nuisance, Zizi," called a man's voice. James looked up to see a guy with blond hair walking towards him. "Do you work for Annabelle?" the blond guy enquired. "I'm fairly new to the arcade and don't think I've seen you here before."

"She's my mum," replied James, "and as I've just left uni and am starting to think about work she's offered me some part-time here. It gives her more time to do some of the other things that she enjoys and also to look for more stock."

The blond guy held out his hand. "I'm Greg Somerville," he said, "you've already met my assistant, Zizi."

"Pleased to meet you," replied James. "I'm James Rowlands." As they shook hands, James noticed that Greg was wearing what looked like a diamond in one of his ears.

"I have the shop just across the way," said Greg, "so if you need any help, you know where to find me."

"Thanks," said James, "but I have helped my mother in the past, so am probably OK, but thanks for the offer." Privately James wished he looked more like Greg. James was mousey, whereas Greg's hair was blond; Greg's jeans were cut beautifully and he was sporting a pair of well-polished brown loafers. James felt ashamed of his trainers and chain store jeans.

"Well, had better go and have a look round and do some dusting," said the blond Adonis. "Perhaps we can get a coffee or something later?" James nodded in agreement and turned back to his boxes. He ruffled Zizi's fur and she scampered off after her master.

There was a large table in the centre of Annabelle's shop and James carefully moved the items that were already on it to one side, so that he had somewhere to put things as he lifted them out of the boxes. He saw that he had a mixture of porcelain, silver and glass and put his mind to mixing Annabelle's new items with her existing ones to create an attractive display. After all, she would be arriving at lunchtime and James wanted her to like what she saw.

It was a busy morning. The arcade was humming with people - some lookers and some buyers. James was pleased to sell some Mary Gregory glassware and a silver photograph frame. People were in and out, making all sorts of enquiries, and he was delighted to see Greg approaching him with a cup of coffee. "Doesn't look as though you've time to pop up to the café," he said, "so I thought I'd take a chance and bring you a latte." James thanked him and asked Greg how his morning was going, and said that he would enjoy having a look in his shop later on in the day after his mother had arrived. Whilst James and Greg were chatting, the occupant of the black car walked past them unobserved. In fact, no-one in the arcade noticed him on that particular morning. Satisfied with what he had seen, the mystery man returned to his car and made his way back to Moulsford.

Annabelle left the house just after 12.30 pm but by then the black car was nowhere in sight.

*****

Annabelle arrived in Wallingford just before 12.50pm, parked her car and walked along to the Lamb Arcade. She smiled to herself when she saw Greg loitering outside her shop. Upon seeing Annabelle, he too, smiled. "I understand that your son is out to impress you," he said, laughingly.

"Oh yes," replied Annabelle, "and from what I can see from here, he looks as though he's done a good job with the new stock." James had dusted Annabelle's entire stock, and moved things around to mix them with the new items to create an elegant and attractive display. "In view of your sterling efforts I think lunch at The George is called for," said Annabelle. "Would you keep your eye on things for me please Greg? You know my mobile number should someone want to spend a fortune and you feel it necessary to give them a super large discount!"

With that, she took James by the arm and led him round the corner to The George Hotel. They settled themselves at a pleasant corner table and Annabelle asked James about his morning. He told his mother that he had enjoyed re-arranging her shop and that he would be happy to work for her for £50 a day in cash. "I'm sure you would," replied his mother, "but if I'm paying you a proper wage I shall have to charge you for living at home. After all, you're no longer a student." They agreed on a wage of £30 per day, with James continuing to live at home free of charge! Annabelle turned the subject to Greg Somerville and asked James what he thought of him. Her son replied that he thought he was a really nice bloke and that he liked the way Greg dressed and the jewellery that he wore.

"I think I shall have to go shopping in order to match up to him as our shops are so close together," said the young man. Once again, Annabelle smiled to herself. "I would like to have a good look in Greg's shop and perhaps buy him a beer later on," said James. "Can you be around for a while, so that I can do that?"

"Of course," replied his mother.

On returning to the arcade, James went straight across the corridor to Greg's and they were soon deep in conversation again. James suggested that they go for a beer as he knew his mother would look after both shops but Greg said he would prefer to do that later on, after they had closed for the day. James went back to his mother and told her that he was happy to stay for the afternoon if she would like to go home. Saying goodbye to both young men, Annabelle left The Lamb having reminded her son that supper would be at 7.30 pm sharp.

James was delighted to sell a Coalport tea service during the afternoon, as tea sets were not at all fashionable, and came to the conclusion that he was a natural where the antique business was concerned. Whilst sitting there, surrounded by beautiful (and not so beautiful) objects, James' mind turned to the brief conversation that he had had with his father earlier that morning, concerning his inheritance. He was going to spend some money on clothes and a holiday, and the rest he felt he could invest. As he wanted to be independent and not have a lecture from his father on where to invest, James' mind turned to his college friend, Jennifer. He was fairly sure that her brother was a Financial Adviser and as he had met him at his birthday party, James decided to call Jennifer and ask for her brother's number. From their telephone conversation, James was reminded that Jenny's brother was called David and that he worked in Chipping Norton, in their father's practice. James telephoned David and they arranged to meet the following Thursday at the Chipping Norton office.

5.00 pm soon came and he and Greg cashed up. "Where shall we go for a drink?" James asked, deferring to the older man.

"Oh, let's pop round to The George," said Greg. "It'll be quick and easy as your mum reminded you to be home for supper. You don't want to be late." Silently James cursed Annabelle. He was feeling even more gauche and foolish in front of his new friend. He followed Greg and Zizi in to the hotel.

"Back again," said the bar man pleasantly. "A pint of Fosters, is it? It's all right, Greg, don't look so horrified, I'm talking to this chap here. I don't expect you to drink lager. I'll get you the wine list." Once again James was impressed. Greg was well known in the hotel and the bar man also knew what he liked to drink. Greg selected a large glass of Merlot and the pair of them went and sat down.

"I don't know your Mum that well," Greg said to James, "but she's certainly one smart lady. She doesn't look old enough to be your mother. She has a fab style and always looks terrific." James was pleased that his new friend thought his mother to be attractive, but he didn't want to be thought of as a baby.

"She'd be delighted to hear you say that," he replied to Greg, "after all she's going to be 48 next month, so she's no spring chicken."

"Never disclose a lady's age," came the swift reply. At this comment, James once again felt very gauche and hoped that his remark wasn't going to spoil a new friendship.

James enjoyed the time spent with Greg and found out that he lived alone in Cholsey, approximately three miles from Wallingford, and that he had taken his shop in The Lamb the previous month. Prior to that Greg had been selling via the antique fairs and by recommendation, but thought that in a depressed market it could be the ideal opportunity to take a shop, as he felt he needed to be seen repeatedly in the same place, so that potential customers got used to him and started to trust him. He said that he worked in his shop most days and if he wanted a day off, he got one of the other shopkeepers to keep an eye on things for him. All too soon it was time for James to say goodnight to his new friend and to head back home to Moulsford and his supper.

Once again he was impressed as he saw Greg unlock a BMW convertible and lift Zizi on to the back seat. This guy seemed to have it all! However, the one thing Greg hadn't mentioned was a girlfriend which, with his stunning looks, really did surprise James, but then, he didn't have a girlfriend either. He waved to Greg, and set off for Moulsford, pleased with the lovely day he had spent and feeling that his mother would also be happy with what he had sold. He could also impress his father with the news that he had made an appointment to see a Financial Adviser on the day that he had been prompted about his inheritance. All in all a win-win situation on his first working day! Who knew what tomorrow might bring?

CHAPTER 8

Susie felt like a little girl at Christmas as she threw back the curtains on Friday morning. She danced around her bedroom singing "Monaco, Monaco, Monaco," as she got ready for the day. She had checked her packing the night before, and taken the spare keys round to Mrs MacDonald so she could let herself in to feed George. She triple checked her handbag for her passport, tickets and money, then skipped down the stairs to have breakfast. George knew something was happening and was looking sorry for himself. Susie made a big fuss of him and gave him his favourite duck and chicken food pouch. She quickly gulped down her toast and coffee, dumped the dishes in the sink, loaded her car and set off for Woodstock.

There was a pile of papers on Susie's desk when she got to her office; the most important one being a somewhat complex timetable for the second half of the school term. She set to work with vigour as she needed to leave dead on time to drive to the airport at Birmingham. Susie had never been on a plane on her own before and wanted to make sure that she would have her car parked and be at the right check-in desk in plenty of time.

At 2.30 pm she took the new timetable in to Miss Jennings. It had been a ghastly spreadsheet to produce, and she was proud of the results. Sadly though, her employer was not so keen and demanded to have it reproduced in a different format. Susie asked if it would wait till Monday as she was rather busy and needed to get away promptly. At this Miss Jennings raised her eyebrows and reminded Susie of the fact that she would be late on Monday due to her dental appointment and that the timetable was required for the staff meeting at 10.00 am that day. Susie winced as she returned to her desk. Her fingers flew across the keyboard and despite constant interruptions from the telephone Susie triumphed and had produced a new document by 3.30 pm. This time Miss Jennings was happy with the timetable but then told Susie that she must circulate it with a covering memo to all staff members. Susie didn't dare say she had a plane to catch and needed to leave so once again she knuckled down.

Eventually, at 4:43 pm, Susie made it to her Mini and set off towards Birmingham. She was astonished by the amount of traffic on the road. Being Susie, she hadn't given a thought to the fact that it was Friday evening and the rush hour. The traffic crawled agonisingly slowly towards the M40 and as soon as she got onto the motorway Susie put her foot down. Her sigh of satisfaction was replaced by a wail of dismay when a police car came flying up behind her, blue lights flashing, indicating that she needed to pull over. Susie's tummy went tight and her heart sank as she checked first the speedometer and then the time.

Susie was close to tears. It wasn't fair. Why did this have to happen to her? And why today? This was meant to be her special weekend and it seemed that everyone was determined to ruin it for her. She opened her window and waited for the officer to approach. "Good afternoon, Madam. Please step out of the vehicle." Susie fumbled with the door, and swung her legs elegantly out of the car. The officer didn't seem to register her charms. "Are you aware what speed you were travelling at?" he enquired. Susie shook her head sullenly. Of course she knew, but she wasn't about to admit it. "It was 94 mph, madam." The officer did not look remotely impressed. He invited Susie to leave her car, and go and take a look on the police-car dashboard at the record of the speed she'd been travelling at.

"I'm sorry," Susie made a doe-eyed, little-girl face. "I need to catch a flight, you see, and I was late leaving work and really didn't realise I was driving so fast."

"I am now giving you a verbal notice of intended prosecution. Do you have your driving licence please?" the officer replied, completely unmoved by Susie's plight. She leant into the car and rummaged through her handbag until she found her wallet. In the midst of a pile of till receipts was her driving licence which she handed to the police officer, scattering receipts onto the hard shoulder as she did so. After briefly examining her licence, the constable told her to get back into the car and accelerate along the hard shoulder until it was safe to join the flow of traffic. He reminded her that the speed limit was 70 mph. Shaking, Susie did as she was told.

After a great deal of swearing and tears, Susie eventually arrived at Birmingham Airport, found the car park and got herself into the terminal. She scanned the monitor and hurried to the check-in desk. She breathed a sigh of relief when she saw there was no queue, but her jaw dropped when the smug looking girl behind the desk informed her the gate had closed five minutes previously. "But the flight isn't due to leave until 8.00 pm and it's only 7.20 pm," she said.

"That's correct, Madam, but we close 45 minutes before departure, and you have to be at the boarding gate half an hour before departure."

"I could still do that if you would check me in," Susie pleaded.

"I very much doubt it, Madam," came the reply.

"Will you check me in, please?" begged Susie. The girl smiled wearily and picked up the telephone.

*****

As the porter put down his bags, Jonathan still couldn't believe that he had managed to secure a suite in the hotel de Paris overlooking Casino Square. Susie would have the most marvellous view of the race on Sunday, sitting on the balcony. The bill would be phenomenal but it would go straight to the factory in Enstone, so it really wasn't going to cause him any headaches. Life wasn't too bad, all things considered, Jonathan smiled to himself as he started to unpack.

He'd barely had time to finish that thought when his phone started ringing and an extremely distressed Susie started wailing at him. "How in God's name have you missed the plane?" he held the phone away and rolled his eyes as she gabbled her reply, all tears and excuses. He struggled to contain his temper and asked her how she was going to sort this mess out. She explained that she had had to buy a new ticket and the airline couldn't guarantee her a specific flight as flights to Nice were in great demand that weekend, but there definitely wasn't anything else available until tomorrow morning at the earliest. "You'll have to find your own way here, then," Jonathan told her. "If you're arriving tomorrow I shall be in the thick of things and won't be able to come to meet you."

"Please don't be cross with me Jonathan," Susie whined. "I didn't do this on purpose."

"I'm quite sure you didn't," he replied, "but anyone with an ounce of common sense would have taken Friday afternoon off work and not tried to get to the airport in the rush hour. I don't know what you think about sometimes, or even if you do think. This suite is costing a small fortune. What a waste! I really don't want to talk to you now. I'll see you tomorrow – when you get here." With that Jonathan finished the phone call and started to plan how he could best spend the evening.

*****

Susie stared blankly ahead, her eyes welling up with fresh tears. It was all so unfair. She didn't know what to do now and felt totally lost. She couldn't go home. How could she explain to Mrs McDonald? She decided she'd have to get a hotel room here at the airport, which was going to burn a horrid hole into her Monaco money. Feeling extremely sorry for herself, she took a taxi to the Hotel Metropole and checked in. As soon as she got to her room she threw herself onto the bed and burst into floods of tears. Jonathan had never been like that with her before. It wasn't her fault she'd missed her flight. It was all so completely and utterly unfair. After a good cry she re-did her face and ventured downstairs in search of something to eat and drink. As it was a Friday night the hotel was extremely busy. Susie really didn't feel that she could cope with sitting alone in a bar full of people, so she retreated to the sanctuary of her room and ordered from the room service menu. She sat forlornly on the end of her bed eating her burger and chips and drinking her half bottle of Shiraz, watching the flashing lights of the planes as they climbed upwards into the night sky, until, exhausted and heartbroken, she went to bed, alone.

*****

Meanwhile, Jonathan was starting to enjoy himself. He had dined across the square at the Café de Paris and was now heading for The Living Room. He intended to have a few drinks there and see what talent was on offer when, who should he bump in to but the flamboyant figure of Eddie Jordan. The two were old friends and when Eddie knew where Jonathan was going, decided to join him. Naturally the conversation turned to Formula 1, with both men hypothesising as to who would win the race on Sunday. It wasn't the evening that Jonathan had planned, but nevertheless it was a pleasant one and by 1.30 am he was back in his hotel room, alone, for a change. Feeling in need of sex, he sent Susie a text to say how much he was looking forward to seeing her, before drifting into a contented asleep.

CHAPTER 9

James bounced into the kitchen at Riverside House. "I've made arrangements to see a financial adviser, Dad," he chirped brightly. He knew his dad would be pleased to hear this but also that he'd certainly want to put his two-pence worth in.

"That's good to hear," came the reply. "Who is he and what do you know about him? Is he independent?"

"He's called David Timmins. He's the brother of my friend Jenny. They were at my 21st. Tallish chap, dark hair, blue suit." His father shook his head, as the vague description didn't ring any bells. "Anyway, David's based in Chipping Norton. His father owns the company and yes, they're independent. I thought I could go and see Susie on the way back from seeing David. I'm meeting him at his office on Thursday." Peter nodded.

"Mmn," he said, "I'm not telling you what to do, but I think it would be sensible for you to show me any plans that David has for your money before you invest it. I appreciate that you've come of age, but you don't have my experience of investments. Also, do you know anything about this chap, other than that he's your friend's brother?" James sighed inwardly. His father was a control freak and could never let go of anything. Anybody would think he didn't know how important his investment was!

"Well, I'd better get my arse in gear," said James, "Mum's leaving me in charge at the shop today, while she lords it up having lunch with her friends." Peter smiled.

"Enjoy your day," he said. "I'm going to read the paper and then walk up to the Beetle for a pint. See you later."

James whistled happily to himself as he backed his car out of the garage. Fifteen minutes later he was in the Lamb Arcade. Shortly after, Greg showed up, accompanied by Zizi. James' stomach lurched with excitement. The young men greeted each other warmly and then got themselves prepared for what they hoped would be a good day's trading. It was Saturday, so there would be a steady stream of people all day.

"Do you have any plans for this evening?" Greg asked casually, as the last customers left the arcade. James said that he didn't. "Well, do you fancy meeting up for a drink or supper a bit later?" Greg queried. "I need to take Zizi for a walk, but I don't have anything planned apart from that."

"That would be fab," said James with enthusiasm. "What do you suggest we do, or where do you suggest we go?"

"I'll see if I can get a table at The Red Lion," Greg smiled. "Let me have your mobile number and I'll give you a call later."

James drove back to Moulsford feeling on top of the world, wondering what he should wear to go out to dinner with Greg. Greg's clothes were great and James felt very tatty and insignificant in comparison. His mother was in the kitchen, preparing supper and asked how his day had gone. James told her what he'd sold and how much money he'd taken, and she seemed quite pleased with him. He then went on to say that he was going out for dinner with Greg, and wasn't really sure what to wear. Annabelle smiled to herself. She had noticed how well dressed Greg was and liked the idea that her son might begin to show more of an interest in how he looked. "Well, darling, where are you going?" she asked. James explained that Greg was going to try and get a table at The Red Lion and would give him a ring later. "It's only a pub, James, so I don't think you need to worry too much," she said. "What's wrong with your usual jeans or chinos and a polo shirt?"

"Oh, Mum," said her son, "haven't you noticed how good Greg looks? I don't want him to feel embarrassed by me." Annabelle assured her son that he was worrying far too much. After all, he was only going out for a meal with a friend – it wasn't as though he had a hot date with a beautiful girl. Inwardly, James felt it would be far easier to dress for a hot date than for his dinner with Greg.

By 7.30 pm Greg had not phoned, and James was feeling really let down, and not sure whether or not he should call him. They had made a definite arrangement, hadn't they? He was surprised by how hurt he felt by the lack of communication. After all, as his Mother had said, it wasn't as though this was a hot date with a beautiful girl. He wandered in to the kitchen and told his mother that he hadn't heard from Greg and wasn't quite sure what to do. "Don't worry about it," said Annabelle swiftly, "I've made a huge lasagne, so if Greg doesn't come good there's plenty of food to eat here. Just see what happens. Maybe he's got caught up with something. It's hardly the end of the world, is it now?" James decided that the best way to stop worrying would be to switch his phone off. That way he could just put the whole thing out of his mind and do his best to enjoy supper with his parents.

*****

Greg had been most surprised to find his own parents sitting outside his house when he got home. They explained they had been passing by and thought that they would pay him a visit. "You should have rung me," he said, once they were all inside the house. "I can only offer you a drink or tea and cakes. I'm sorry, but I was planning on going out tonight, so I don't have much food in."

"That's all right," said his mother, "We'll take you out for a meal, if you like? We're not in a desperate hurry to get home."

Greg knew that to accept would be the polite and reasonable thing to do, but what about James? He supposed he could have supper with James any time but he didn't see his parents that often. Should he invite James as well? No, that probably wasn't a good idea. "Where shall we go?" he asked his mother. "Do you want to head towards home or would you like to eat in the village? I could try for a table at The Red Lion." His parents agreed that would be fine, so Greg made the call and secured a table for 7.30 pm, deciding that he would call James after he'd had a bit of a catch up with his parents.

The Somerville family spent a pleasant hour chatting about what they had all been doing recently. Greg's parents were particularly interested to know how he was getting on in the arcade, as he hadn't had his shop there for very long. He told them that it was still early days, but that he was reasonably pleased and really enjoyed being his own boss. He also loved being able to take Zizi to work with him and Zizi loved all the attention she got from the customers and other shop owners.

*****

When they got to The Red Lion, they discovered it was very busy and service was a little slower than usual, but that was fine, as they weren't in a hurry. Half way through his main course of succulent fillet steak, Greg remembered James. He glanced at his watch and saw to his horror that it was after 9 o' clock. As soon as it was appropriate, Greg dashed to the Gents, where he sent a hasty text, apologising for the lack of contact, explaining that his parents had arrived unexpectedly, and finished off by saying he hoped to see James in the arcade the following day. That sent, he returned to the table to choose his dessert from an extremely tempting selection. Everyone finished the meal with coffee and Greg and his mother each had a brandy before Greg's parents set off for the drive back to London and Greg sauntered home to his cottage.

Zizi was delighted that her master was home and showed her appreciation by hurling herself at him. Greg laughed and fetched her lead, sending her wild with anticipation of their walk. As he strolled through the village his thoughts turned to James. He noticed that his text had not been answered and wondered whether or not James might be sulking. Time would tell and it certainly wasn't anything he was going to lose sleep over, as he was confident that even if James were sulking, he would be able to win him round. Feeling invigorated by all the walking he had done, Greg took Zizi home and settled down for the remainder of the evening with a bottle of wine and a recording of Il Divo.

*****

A very disappointed James ate supper with his parents. Annabelle's lasagne was delicious, as she was an excellent cook, but James wasn't really in the mood to enjoy it. He decided to take Allsort for a walk so that he could have a bit of peace and quiet, as his father was trying to engage him in yet another discussion about his inheritance and he really didn't want any more of his advice. Before getting the dog's lead, James switched his phone on and found Greg's text, which cheered him up, although he decided not answer it just then. After all, Greg could still have called him as they had arranged, rather than just sending a text. Clipping the lead on to Allsort's collar, the two of them set off. As he went to cross the main road, James encountered a chap coming in the opposite direction. They wished each other a good evening and continued on their way. Neither realised who the other was.

Allsort and James enjoyed their walk, and James felt more relaxed and able to deal with his father when he got back to the house. He was still thinking about Greg's text and asked his mother if she had any plans for the next day. Smiling, she asked him if he would prefer not to do the shop for her, as she would be quite happy to be there herself. It would be the perfect excuse not to cook Sunday lunch and go out for supper with Peter after work. James guessed that she had cottoned on to why he wanted to give the shop a miss and thanked her, saying that he fancied doing some shopping. Again Annabelle smiled. Greg Somerville was certainly having an effect upon her son.

Feeling happier, James fetched a beer from the fridge and went and chatted to his father before heading upstairs for bed. He couldn't understand why Greg had got under his skin so much, but he guessed as he was coming to the end of his student life, it was time to smarten himself up. After all, he would soon be attending interviews, so maybe a suit would be in order as well as some more casual clothes. As he got in to bed, James was debating where he would go for his shopping spree. Maybe Bicester Village, or maybe Reading or Oxford? Wherever he chose, he had the money to spend!

CHAPTER 10

Susie got up stupidly early on Saturday morning, terrified of anything more going wrong. She read Jonathan's text, which immediately made her feel better. It sounded as though he was missing her, which must mean that he had forgiven her. She replied straightaway saying that she was going to the airport in search of a flight, and would keep him updated. Making herself some coffee courtesy of the hospitality tray in her room, Susie decided to skip breakfast and made her way downstairs to check out. Her bill came to a horrifying £153.71 and she glumly handed over her credit card, before jumping in a taxi to the departure building.

The man on duty was most helpful and sympathetic, but said he couldn't guarantee anything currently and suggested that she return at 9.00 am. As it was only five past eight Susie bought a magazine and sat in one of the cafés, sipping a coffee and nervously thumbing through the pages, gazing distractedly at the glossy pictures of perfect looking girls. It took forever for 9 o' clock to come around. When she got back to the desk, the man she had spoken to earlier was no longer there, so she had to go through her story all over again. This time her audience was a very bored looking young woman. After checking her computer screen, the representative told Susie to hurry across to desk no 53, where she could be checked in for the 10.15 am flight. Thanking her, Susie scurried off and checked in.

It took ages to actually get on to the aircraft, but finally she was there, sitting in the window seat in row 7. The chap next to her smiled and said hello as she clambered over his legs to sit down. Susie smiled and said hello back, and then settled herself down with her magazine. The stranger was hell bent on conversation though, so Susie gave in and closed the pages. His name was Paul and he was meeting up with some friends to spend a few days in Nice, staying at the Hotel Beau Rivage. He lived in Derby and worked in Nottingham at the Park Hospital. Out of politeness, Susie asked him what he did there and he told her that he was a nurse. Susie laughed and said that wasn't what she would have guessed he did, so Paul asked her what she would have guessed. Susie told him she thought he looked more like someone who worked in a bank. She then asked him to guess what she did for a living, and Paul said that he thought she was a beauty therapist because she had such lovely nails and was very attractive. Flattered, Susie told him that she was the school secretary at a leading public school and that she was flying out to Monaco to see the Grand Prix. Paul was suitably impressed by this and wondered whether he had the courage to ask Susie if he might see her again. She then went on to say that she was meeting her boyfriend in Monaco and that he worked for the Lotus Racing Team. Paul decided she was out of his league, but they continued to chat pleasantly for the remainder of the flight.

On arrival at Nice, Susie retrieved her bag from the carousel and then made her way to the information desk to find out the best way to get to Monaco. The woman at the desk spoke good English and directed Susie to Nice St Augustin station, telling her she would be able to get a train directly to Monaco. Susie hopped into a cab, keen to get to Monaco as soon as possible, and start making up for lost time. The cab ride only took a few minutes and came to just over 6 euros. Susie fished a 10 euro note out of her purse and told the driver to keep the change. As the taxi pulled away, Susie looked around, only to find she was confronted by a row of unfriendly looking ticket machines and no attendant. The damn machines only took coins. Susie cursed. Why had she let the taxi driver keep the change? She tried in vain to exchange a 20 euro note with a variety of people, but without success. What now? Should she get a taxi to the station in Nice and get a train on from there? Should she get a taxi direct to Monaco, but then would it be able to get near to the Hotel de Paris? What on earth should she do? Was there a bus? If she could find a bus, at least she could explain to the driver where she wanted to go; or could she, as her French was very poor? Susie thought for a moment and decided that all she was doing was wasting time and at this rate there would be no point in her even going to Monaco. She had already lost a night and now it was approaching 1.30 pm local time, so she had lost the best part of Saturday too. Cursing to herself, she set off in search of a taxi. This was supposed to be a beautiful weekend, a real luxury treat, and all she'd had so far was hassle!

Finally Susie found a taxi, and explained to the driver that she needed to go to Monaco, but thought that perhaps the train from the centre of Nice would be the best way. So, the taxi driver took her to Nice Railway Station, as that was really the only part of her garbled conversation that he had understood. Susie was horrified to find the fare was 40 euros. It was proving to be a very expensive Saturday. Still, it would be simple to get to Monaco now. Come hell or high water, she was determined that nothing else was going to stand in her way.

The train was hot and crowded, but Susie felt triumphant. 18 minutes later she arrived at Pont Sainte Devote where she got off the train and started to walk up the hill towards Casino Square. By the time she reached the Hotel de Paris, she felt shattered.

She was soon in the suite and was aware that the chap who had carried her case was hanging about. Suddenly it dawned on Susie. He was expecting a tip! She reluctantly handed over yet more of her rapidly dwindling holiday money to the inanely smiling man, who promptly thanked her and left. Susie took in her impressive surroundings. All she was interested in at this particular moment however, was a drink and a bath, as she felt filthy after all the travelling that she had done. She hunted through the mini bar and grabbed an orange juice, then walked through to the magnificent bathroom and started to run the water in to the huge corner bath. The Hotel de Paris provided very good toiletries, so Susie lobbed in a liberal helping of bath essence and quickly got undressed.

She had not long been in the bath, when, to her great delight, she heard the door opening and Jonathan appeared, looking very pleased indeed to see her. "Why don't you come and join me?" she asked. "There's plenty of room in here for two."

"Indeed there is," he replied, "but I think we might have something more interesting to drink than orange juice." He phoned Room Service and ordered a bottle of the house champagne. As soon as it arrived, Jonathan threw his clothes on to the bed and joined Susie in the bath tub, complete with two glasses of perfectly chilled bubbly.

They kissed slowly and then more fervently, and before Susie realised what was happening, Jonathan was making love to her, right there in the bath. "Mmm, that was fabulous," she sighed after the heat had gone out of their passion. "We must do that again before we leave."

"We should have done it last night," came the reply, "but you were silly enough to miss your plane." Tears sprang to Susie's eyes at the injustice of it all. "Well, you're here now and we're going to have a great time," said her lover. "Let me tell you all about my interview with Jake Humphrey." Jonathan was very pleased with himself as the interview had already gone out live on the BBC and was being aired again the following day during the BBC's race day coverage.

Jonathan was first out of the bath and swiftly replenished their champagne glasses, which he placed on either side of the bed. He then wrapped Susie in a luxurious bath sheet and carried her to the bedroom, where he gently placed her on the bed, propped up amongst the pillows, so that she could enjoy her drink. "When you've finished that, you can unpack and get yourself dolled up," he said, "I've got a taxi booked for 7.00 pm."

"Ooh," said Susie, "Where are we going?"

"We're going to Nice, and that's as much as you need to know for the moment. Now relax and enjoy your drink and if you're a good girl I'll give you a back massage." Susie knew where that would lead, and willingly turned over, letting the towel fall to the floor.

*****

Promptly at 7.00 pm, Susie and Jonathan were in the hotel foyer, waiting for their taxi. The driver was on time, and off they went to Nice.

Jonathan asked to be dropped half way down the Promenade des Anglais so that he and Susie could stroll whilst enjoying the sea air at the same time. Susie was drinking everything in as she walked happily along, holding Jonathan's hand. She had chosen to wear the red dress she had bought for James' party and was looking very beautiful. Jonathan felt good walking beside her.

Eventually Jonathan steered Susie across the road and towards the Negresco. Susie was impressed by the building's elegance, and even more excited when they went inside. Jonathan had booked a table in the Brasserie la Rotonde as he thought Susie would be bowled over by it. He was spot on, as usual. She was mesmerised by the place – the carousel of galloping horses, the big top painted on the ceiling and the automatons that played can-can music every fifteen minutes. They were seated in a cosy side booth that had a fabulous view over the sea.

The cuisine was simple and they both had king prawns followed by salmon served with dainty little vegetables. Susie then chose the lemon tart, whilst Jonathan had a plate of cheese. They washed all this down with a bottle of Sancerre. Susie was in seventh heaven – in an exciting restaurant in Nice, with her lover, what a way to spend the weekend. And, furthermore, she would be watching the Monaco Grand Prix the following day from a balcony at the Hotel de Paris. This really was living! The only sad thing was that she would be unable to share the story of her wonderful weekend with anyone. She wished she were brave enough to trust her secret to a friend, but also had enough sense to realise that it would be far too risky. If no-one knew, no-one could tell tales.

The meal over, the couple walked slowly back along the Promenade des Anglais, where they had a nightcap sitting outside one of the bars. Much to Susie's surprise, Paul from the aeroplane was also sitting at a table with his friends. She waved to him and he waved back. Their drinks finished, Jonathan and Susie hailed a taxi to take them back to Monaco.

Once in their suite, Susie turned to Jonathan and told him that it was one of the best evenings in her entire life and didn't know how to thank him. He suggested that she hurried and got herself in to bed and he would show her how she could do just that. Susie didn't need asking twice. Having expressed her gratitude for a wonderful evening, she snuggled up in Jonathan's arms and fell fast asleep.

CHAPTER 11

Race day dawned, promising lots of sunshine. After waking Susie in order to make love to her, Jonathan called down for breakfast to be delivered to the suite. They sat out on the balcony enjoying coffee, fresh juice and all sorts of pastries. All too soon it was time for Jonathan to don his Lotus livery and set off to the track. Susie asked him what he thought their chances were, as she didn't know a great deal about Formula 1, and Jonathan told her that they were tipped to win. Should that be the case, he reminded her that he would be very involved with an after race party, so she wouldn't see him until very late. Privately, Susie hoped that they didn't win.

After Jonathan had gone Susie spent a couple of hours in the Wellness Centre. Jonathan had very kindly booked her a facial and a back massage. This occupied her nicely until it was time to get in position on the balcony to watch the race. She called down to room service and ordered some smoked salmon sandwiches and a half bottle of wine. Once her lunch had arrived, she settled herself comfortably on the balcony, ready to watch the fun.

One of the Lotus drivers went out on the first lap. Susie smiled to herself as she bit into a sandwich – one down and one to go. She didn't want Jonathan delayed by any race party that evening. In all honesty, she wasn't really that interested in the race and was half watching and flipping through a magazine at the same time, when to her surprise, her phone rang. Expecting it to be Jonathan, she was horrified to see that it was her mother. What on earth could she want? She'd ask something about her weekend with Grace! Shit! What could she say? Susie decided that the best option was to let it ring, see what message was left and then return the call.

*****

In Moulsford, Peter was watching the Monaco Grand Prix, when the camera swung up towards the Hotel de Paris, and who should he see sitting on the balcony with a glass of wine in her hand, but his daughter? "Belle, Belle, come quickly," he shouted. "Susie's on the television in Monaco." His wife came into the room telling him not to be ridiculous and that Susie was staying with Grace. "I'll rewind the bloody thing and show you," said Peter, which he promptly did, and lo and behold, there was Susie, sitting alone on the balcony of the Hotel de Paris. Peter froze the frame so that they could both get a good look, and Annabelle had to agree with him that there could be no mistaking their daughter. "How in Christ's name can she afford to stay there?" raged Peter, "and what's she doing telling us that she's staying with Grace?"

"Calm down darling," said Annabelle, "and let me deal with this. You'll just go off like a bull at a gate. Leave this to me and enjoy the rest of the race." With that she walked out of the room, wondering just what her daughter was playing at and feeling very relieved that James had changed his mind and decided to look after the shop for her that day after all, as Peter was terrible at handling delicate situations and getting to the bottom of this was going to be very delicate indeed, as far as Annabelle could see.

Having made herself a cup of coffee, Annabelle went in to the conservatory to form her plan of attack. She decided that the best thing to do was to ring Susie, ostensibly for a chat to find out how her weekend was going, and take it from there. She dialled Susie's number and was not in the least bit surprised when the phone clicked over to the European dial tone. That confirmed Susie was not in the UK. She wasn't surprised either that Susie didn't answer, and left a short message saying she hoped she was having a lovely weekend, and would she like to come to supper one evening during the week? She specifically did not ask her daughter to return the call, preferring to see how Susie reacted. She finished her coffee and walked back into the snug to tell Peter what she had done and that, furthermore, she didn't want any interference from him.

Peter watched the remainder of the race with similar thoughts going through his mind to the ones that were going through Annabelle's mind. Why had their daughter lied to them? Clearly she was up to no good. He was also very concerned that Susie could not possibly afford to stay in the Hotel de Paris, and as she was sitting overlooking Casino Square, where you got the most fantastic view of the cars, the price had to be astronomical. She must also have been planning this for some time as you couldn't get a room at the Hotel de Paris during the Grand Prix weekend without booking well in advance.

*****

Susie checked her voicemails and listened to her mother's message in dismay, wondering what on earth to do. She was a rubbish liar and her mother would have heard the continental ring on her phone so how on earth was she going to explain that away? Could she say that she and Grace had decided to take a day trip to France? Not really, bearing in mind that Grace lived in Manchester, and anyway, she had told her mother that they were going to a concert the previous evening. That was another fatal mistake. She had no idea what was going on in Manchester and could really trip herself up. Shit, shit and more shit! Perhaps Jonathan would know what to do? Her mother's message had been pleasant and friendly, so perhaps she hadn't noticed the ring tone and all would be well? That was probably the best thing – stick to her story and, if any questions were raised, say her mother must have been imagining the ringtone.

Susie poured herself another glass of wine and went back to watching the race, but with a very uneasy feeling. She was delighted when the other Lotus driver only managed to get 9th place. She thought that gave him some points, so hopefully Jonathan wouldn't be too annoyed that they hadn't won. She started daydreaming about what they might be doing that evening and hoped it wouldn't be too long before Jonathan was back with her.

At around 5.00 pm the door to the suite opened, and in walked her lover with a smile on his face. Susie gave him a forlorn look. "What on earth's the matter?" he asked and Susie explained all about the phone call and the fact that she was supposed to be staying with Grace. "That's simple, " said Jonathan, "your mother hasn't asked you to ring her back, so don't, and when you do get around to it, she'll have forgotten all about the ring tone and if she hasn't, just deny it." Duplicity came easily to Jonathan and didn't trouble him in the slightest, so he really couldn't be bothered with what he considered to be Susie's whinging and whining.

"Let's have a bath and go and hit Nice again. I can't risk being seen with you here, there are far too many people about who know me for me to feel comfortable. I'll run the bath and you get undressed and come and join me." Susie did as she was told, although she was still feeling worried, but knew that she mustn't let her feelings spoil their last evening together, otherwise she might not get another chance to do something similar in the future.

She climbed in to the bath and pretended to show some interest in the race and told Jonathan how much she had enjoyed watching it. He said that the team was not best pleased, but you can't win them all. He then suggested that he got out of the bath first and went and organised the taxi, whilst Susie relaxed for a while, as she was obviously het up from her mother's phone call. This Susie did, turning her mind to the important subject of which dress to wear. Jonathan had told her that they would have a walk around the old town in Nice and find somewhere to eat, so she felt that she shouldn't be too dressed up.

In the end Susie chose her galaxy dress, but made it look more casual with a pashmina and a pair of lower heeled shoes. As usual, Jonathan looked at her admiringly – she looked good from top to toe – beautifully manicured finger nails (he wasn't to know that they weren't her own!), with matching toes, and flamboyant bright red ear rings with a matching necklace. She turned heads all right, did Susie Rowlands, and she was fun to be with, to boot. Kissing her carefully on the cheek, so as not to smudge her make-up, Jonathan escorted Susie downstairs to the waiting taxicab.

The old town was bustling and after a couple of drinks at different bars, they found themselves outside La Luna Rossa in the rue Chauvain, famous for its pasta. The restaurant was hot and crowded, but Susie and Jonathan were fortunate enough to be shown to a table. This was very different from La Rotonde, but equally popular with tourists, and Jonathan was pleased to see that Susie was beginning to relax and enjoy herself. After generous portions of garlic bread, pasta and salad, the two were ready for another night of pleasure.

Back at the Hotel de Paris, Jonathan decided to be brave and took Susie to the American Bar for a drink. They settled down on a large leather sofa and enjoyed listening to the jazz pianist, whilst sipping their last glasses of champagne. "I wish this would never end," sighed Susie. "When will I next see you?"

"Please don't ruin the weekend by worrying about that," replied Jonathan, "you know that I see you as often as I can but you have to understand that I must spend time with my family." Susie felt suitably put down. That was the big problem with a married boyfriend – you never saw him at the weekends. This weekend had been an exception, probably to prepare her for a period of not seeing him. Still, she had two choices and she couldn't imagine her life without Jonathan. Finishing her drink, she suggested that they go to bed, as they both had early starts the following morning. Jonathan signed the bar tab and off they went.

Once Jonathan was slowly undressing her, Susie forgot about all her anxieties as to when she would see him again and decided to enjoy the moment.

CHAPTER 12

James woke up on Sunday morning to the sound of rain drumming against the windows. Getting up and pulling back the curtains, he discovered that it was pouring down. Immediately he decided that he didn't want to traipse around the shops on a day like this, so he would ask his mother if he could change his mind and work in the shop after all.

Dressed and showered he went downstairs to find his parents already eating breakfast. After they had all exchanged pleasantries, James asked Annabelle if she would mind if he worked instead of her as he didn't fancy going shopping in the rain. "Not at all darling," she replied, "that will give me the best of both worlds. Your father is taking me out for dinner tonight, so I don't need to cook and I can spend the day doing as I please. By all means do the shop for me and we can sort out another day for you to have your retail therapy." James thanked her and continued munching on his cornflakes.

As a gesture, James took Allsort for her morning walk before setting off for Wallingford. He was feeling slightly nervous as he wasn't really sure how friendly or otherwise Greg would be. Anyway, he needn't have worried because as soon as he switched on the lights in his mum's shop, Zizi came dashing towards him with her body wagging, closely followed by her master.

"Hi James, sorry about last night," said Greg. "I had a surprise visit from my parents on their way back to London and I totally forgot our arrangement until I was half way through dinner with them. Idiot or what?"

"No problem," replied James, feeling relieved. "I had supper with my parents – my mother is an awesome cook, took Allsort for a walk and then went to bed. Absolutely no harm done."

"Shall we try again tonight?" suggested Greg. James happily nodded his agreement.

Trade was going slowly and time was dragging. James was even considering closing a few minutes early, when a smartly dressed woman in her mid-50s came into the shop and asked James if he were interested in buying a pair of Worcester vases. He replied that he would be interested in having a look, but could say no more than that. He cleared a space for the vases on the counter. His eyes almost popped out of his head as the woman unwrapped a pair of Worcester vases signed by John Stinton. Turning one of them over, he saw the factory year mark for 1918. Alarm bells started to ring, but James couldn't be sure whether these were the ones which had been stolen from Major Williamson.

He managed to smile at the woman, his mind racing. "Unfortunately I can't make a decision on such expensive pieces," he said carefully, "my mother would need to see them and she won't be here today. Is it at all possible that you could call back tomorrow? I'm sure that she would be interested." The stranger smiled back and said that would be fine. They made an appointment for 3.00 pm the following afternoon, and James also had the foresight to ask for her name and phone number. "Thank you so much," he said to her, holding out his hand. "I look forward to seeing you again tomorrow."

After the woman had left the shop James went across the arcade to see Greg. "Are you OK?" his friend asked him. "You look awfully pale."

James sank down on one of Greg's Lloyd Loom chairs and said, "God, I need a drink. Just listen to this Greg." He then told Greg the story of the robbery at Major Williamson's, the fact that the Major had been murdered and that the police had been to see Annabelle about the theft and that he thought he had just been offered two of the stolen vases.

"Calm down," said Greg. "First things first. Go and get the photos and we'll have a look at them and see if you think they were Major Williamson's pieces and then you must ring the police to tell them about tomorrow's appointment. This is really exciting stuff!"

"I'm glad you think so," replied James "I feel a nervous wreck." With that he went and got the folder of photos and took it back to Greg's shop. There was a pair of Worcester vases, but he couldn't see whether or not they were signed by John Stinton. There had been a whole family of Stintons who had worked at the Worcester factory and they had all painted in a similar style. Greg asked James what he thought and he explained that it was impossible to tell. However, his next job was to ring the police, and then ring his mother.

James rang DI Franklin on his mobile and explained what had happened. The Inspector congratulated him on his calmness and said that he and his Sergeant would be at the arcade for 2.00 pm the following day, so that they could work out the best way of handling the situation. Next he rang his mother, only to discover that DI Franklin had beaten him to it.

*****

Annabelle was still reeling from having seen Susie on the TV when the phone rang. She fully expected it to be Susie returning her call and was surprised when she heard the Inspector's voice. She listened to what he had to say and confirmed that she would be at the shop the following day. She then went in search of Peter, who was rummaging through piles of paper strewn across his desk.

"Have you lost something, darling?" she enquired.

"No, no, just having a bit of a clear out." Peter assured her, hastily closing a drawer. "What can I do for you my love?" Annabelle told him about the call from DI Franklin.

"As if I haven't got enough to think about with Susie," she said, "I'll know more about the ins and outs of it all when I've spoken more fully with James. From what the police said, it seems as though he has acted very responsibly in this matter."

"I'm glad that one of them has some sense," grunted her husband. "What's the latest à propos Susie? Have you spoken to her yet?" Annabelle told him that she had left a message, but she wasn't really expecting Susie to return the call.

"Buying time," came the reply. "What the hell can she be up to?" Annabelle shrugged her shoulders and said that they would find out eventually, but that in the meantime Peter must do as he had promised and not interfere.

It wasn't long before James came home, once again telling his parents that he was going out with Greg. "Let's hope so," said his mother smiling. "Your father is taking me to that new Chinese in Wallingford, so you'll have to scout around the fridge if something goes wrong this time. Now, tell me about what happened with the vases."

James recounted his story and then both he and his mother went upstairs to prepare themselves for their evening outings.

*****

Greg had suggested that James come to his house and that they could then walk to the Red Lion if they felt like it or, at the very least go in one car as it was pointless to take two.

James had chosen his clothes very carefully for the occasion. He was wearing cream chinos with a blue open necked shirt and a sweater round his shoulders, and he was painfully aware that his brown slip-on shoes had seen better days. His hair was particularly floppy and annoying the hell out of him and he wondered if part of his shopping trip should take in a hair stylist. Greg's hair was a fab blond colour, making his look a bit mousey by comparison.

Greg and Zizi opened the door together and James stepped inside. He was bowled over by Greg's home. It was a Victorian end of terrace - two up, two down, but boy oh boy, had Greg made it his own. The walls were painted a warm apricot colour and there was an assortment of oriental rugs strewn across the floor. There were two leather sofas and a couple of pouffees; an elaborate chandelier hanging from the centre of the sitting room ceiling and a wild collection of animal print cushions everywhere.

"Wow, this is fantastic," said James, "you have wonderful taste." Greg smiled and thanked him and offered him a drink as they had half an hour to spare before they needed to leave, even if they walked.

Sitting on a sofa, sipping a glass of red wine, James wondered whether he should think about buying a house rather than investing his money. He would have the meeting with David Timmins and see what he had to say. After all, that was what Susie had done with her inheritance and she had a sweet little cottage and Greg's house was to die for. He could definitely learn a thing or two from this chap!

Their drinks finished, the two wandered up the road to the Red Lion – the second time for Greg in two days, as the landlord, Brian Phelps, was quick to point out. "It's your delicious food, Brian, I can't keep away," said Greg, after he had introduced the two men. "Go and sit down, and I'll send Sandra over to take your drinks order," said the landlord. Thanking him, Greg and James made their way across the dining room.

Greg was keen to have a bottle of red wine. James thought he would prefer a beer. As he had already had a glass of wine, he knew that he could only have one more drink and a beer would last longer. Sandra arrived at the table and Greg ordered a bottle of the house red and a pint of Fosters for James. Greg almost knew the menu off by heart and James was happy to go with his recommendations about what to have. Once Sandra had headed off to the kitchen with their food orders, they decided to get to know each other a bit better.

Greg already knew that James lived with his parents in Moulsford, so he asked James what he did with his time when he wasn't working for his mother in the arcade. James explained that he was just finishing a degree in business studies and wanted to get himself on a management trainee programme but that he hadn't quite decided yet and wanted to keep his options open, as he had also just inherited some money, so he could afford to take a bit more time to really think about what he wanted to do with his life.

Greg's ears pricked up at the mention of money. He already liked James, but somebody with money was that bit more attractive still. He then realised that James was asking for information about him, so he engaged his brain and started talking, knowing that he wanted James to feel comfortable around him.

Greg felt a little uneasy talking about himself as he wanted to win James' confidence. He told him that he was 28 and had done an arts degree before opening his shop in the arcade, that he grew up in London and that his parents still lived there. He didn't mention his younger brother, as he didn't feel that would add anything to the conversation. He had bought his house in Cholsey about a year ago, he was enjoying being his own boss but wasn't sure if he could make it as an antiques dealer in the current economic climate. However, he said that it was going well so far – customers seemed to particularly like his jewellery. He finished by saying he was glad to meet a kindred spirit, as he didn't have too many friends in the area.

James was extremely flattered by that remark, as he thought Greg was something else – fab clothes, fab jewellery and with a really magnetic quality. He really would like to be more like him and wondered how, or indeed if, he could ask Greg if he would go shopping with him and help him to smarten up.

The food arrived then, so all thoughts of conversation disappeared as the pair of them tucked in with enthusiasm. As Greg had said earlier, the food at The Red Lion was very good indeed and they certainly made the most of it, finishing off their meal by sharing a splendid cheese board. Greg insisted on paying the bill, saying that meant they could do it again another time at James' expense. James was quite happy with that and felt thoroughly contented as they made their way back to Greg's house.

Once there, Greg invited him in for coffee, which James accepted readily. It wasn't long before the clock hands were heading towards midnight and Greg said that he would have to take Zizi out for her walk. At that point James took the cue to leave, saying that he would see Greg the following day. To James' surprise, Greg gave him a hug before wishing him goodnight.

A very contented James Rowlands got into his car and drove home to Moulsford, thinking that life was certainly on the up.

CHAPTER 13

As the new week began, the Rowlands family all awoke with extremely different thoughts.

Susie was desperately sad that her weekend with Jonathan was soon to be nothing more than a memory, and that all she had to look forward to was the daily grind at Woodstock Academy.

James was feeling really good about the friendship that he and Greg were forming, and was wondering what would happen with the police and the vases that afternoon.

Annabelle's thoughts were divided between her wayward daughter and the mystery of the vases, and Peter was preoccupied by where on earth he'd put those damn papers. After all, he didn't want anything to come back and incriminate Annabelle. He also wondered what the hell his daughter was playing at.

*****

In Monaco, Susie and Jonathan had made love for the last time and Susie was now packing her case before catching the train to the airport. Monaco was back to normal this morning, so she didn't anticipate any snags. As she was booked on the 8.00 am flight, she had to leave the hotel at 5.00 am, without any breakfast. It had been a very short night, filled with passion and already she felt exhausted. Perhaps she would be able to sleep on the plane? She kissed Jonathan lingeringly and managed not to cry, before slipping out of the bedroom on her way to the station.

Jonathan breathed a sigh of relief after Susie had gone, feeling that the weekend had gone well, although still a little miffed that Susie had been a day late. The most important thing, as far as he was concerned, was that they hadn't bumped into anyone he knew. Also, he had had more than his share of fun. Once again he admitted to himself that Susie Rowlands really was something else! He was booked on to the 11.00 am flight, so intended to doze for another couple of hours before packing his case and getting a cab to the airport. Smiling to himself, he turned over and snuggled down to sleep.

*****

Over the breakfast table Annabelle and James discussed their plan of action.

As it was pointless for both of them to go in to the shop first thing, James offered to open up. Annabelle said that she would have an early lunch at home and get to Wallingford in time for James to go and have a bite somewhere before the police arrived. Once James had left, Peter asked Annabelle how she was planning to handle Susie. "I shall let her incriminate herself," replied his wife. "I think I'd like to look her in the eye when I pounce. She can't avoid us forever. Again, Peter, please don't interfere and leave this completely to me. I know what you're like!"

"Yes, yes," replied her husband, "I shall keep out of it – for the moment anyway."

A little later that morning, Annabelle decided to ring the school to speak with her daughter, and was not in the least surprised when she was told that Susie was at the dentist. She left another message.

*****

James and Greg arrived at the arcade at the same time and smiled when they saw each other. As usual Zizi dashed across to greet James, which was something he rather enjoyed. Greg went and got some coffee and the two sat together in Greg's shop, slowly sipping their lattes. "This afternoon should be interesting," Greg remarked.

"Mmm," replied James. He tried to turn the conversation to the previous evening as he wanted to let Greg know how much he had enjoyed himself. He also wondered whether he could ask Greg to go shopping with him, without seeming to be too naïve and gushing. He really needed to find out which day Greg was taking off that week and see if he could fit in with him. He had already asked his mother if he could have Thursday off so that he could go and see David Timmins in Chipping Norton and she had been quite happy about that as she thought he could take the opportunity to look round the antique shops while he was there. James felt flattered that his mother trusted him to buy for her, although he had been told that if anything cost more than £50 he had to text her a photo to get her approval.

Maybe he could ask Greg if he would like to go with him? On second thoughts though, James couldn't really see the shops there offering any clothes that were that upmarket, and he had made a decision that he was going to improve his appearance. Maybe that was why he hadn't been lucky in love, but then Susie always dressed well and she didn't have a boyfriend at the moment. Perhaps he should have a chat with Susie, to see if she had any ideas about how he could smarten himself up.

James came back to earth as he realised that Greg was speaking to him, and telling him that he had customers. James hastily put down the remains of this coffee and crossed the arcade. "Good morning," he said cheerfully. "Do please let me know if I can help in any way at all." The couple smiled at him and explained that they were looking for a gift for a silver wedding, and were thinking of spending in the region of £100. James showed them a variety of photo frames and a couple of silver pin trays, which were all in their price range. He arranged them decoratively on the "wrapping table" and left the pair to make up their minds, saying that he would be just across the way, finishing his coffee.

A few moments later the woman waved to James, indicating that they had chosen something. It was a very decorative square photo frame, priced at £95. James assured them that he thought it was a lovely choice, and that their friends would be pleased with it.

Greg's day had also got off to a good start. His reputation for exquisite men's jewellery was growing, and as James wandered back over to finish his coffee, he passed a very pleased looking young man wearing his newly purchased 18 carat gold chain. Greg looked pretty pleased too and hoped the rest of the day would continue to be as rewarding.

Annabelle arrived just after 12.30, looking wonderful in a pair of jeans, a shirt and her customary high heeled sandals. She had a beautiful diamond collar around her neck, which immediately attracted Greg's attention. "Annabelle, you look fabulous as always," he said, "and your necklace is to die for."

"It is rather good, isn't it?" she replied. "No doubt James has told you all about what is happening this afternoon. I was going to grab a quick bite at home but I thought it would be much nicer to pop down to The George with James. Why don't you join us? Fred will watch both shops, won't you darling?" she said turning to her next-door neighbour, who was almost immediately opposite Greg's shop.

Greg said he would love to join them, so the three went over to The George, where Annabelle ordered a bottle of wine, saying that she and James probably needed Dutch courage!

Lunch finished, they returned to the arcade to await the arrival of the police. At exactly 2 o'clock, DI Franklin and Sergeant Green wandered into the shop, dressed casually, so that they could pose as customers without drawing attention to themselves

Despite the reassuring police presence, Annabelle felt surprisingly nervous as the minutes ticked by until the woman came in with the vases. When she did finally arrive, Annabelle carefully unwrapped the pieces and placed them on the table. "They're certainly beautiful. In fact they're pristine," said Annabelle. "How did you come by them originally?"

"I bought them from an antiques fair in Beaconsfield," replied the woman.

"May I ask why you wish to sell them now?" enquired Annabelle. At that moment DI Franklin stepped forward, and identified himself. The woman immediately paled, and putting her hand to her throat, asked the

Inspector what he wanted. Once the situation had been explained to her, the woman was extremely indignant.

"Are you accusing me of being a thief?" she snapped haughtily. The Inspector assured her that he was doing no such thing, but that he would need her to help with his enquiries. First of all he would need to see proof of purchase, showing where and when she had bought the vases and asked if she were in a position to provide that. The woman responded that she was meticulous with her record keeping and that she had the receipt filed away at home.

At the Inspector's request, Annabelle looked carefully at the vases. They were remarkably like the ones stolen from the Williamsons, but the woman was absolutely definite that she had proof of purchase, so she supposed it could be possible that it was just a coincidence.

DI Franklin was not a great believer in coincidence and so he apologised to the woman for the inconvenience but explained that she would need to find the receipt and to that end his Sergeant would now drive her to her home in Didcot, after dropping him and the vases at the police station. He assured her that the vases would be looked after with the utmost care.

Annabelle re-wrapped the vases and gave them to DI Franklin, who left the shop with his Sergeant and a very angry woman.

"That's one customer I don't imagine we'll be seeing again." Annabelle smiled ruefully as the police car pulled away.

Having decided that she had had enough excitement for one day, Annabelle went home to Moulsford, leaving James to cash up.

Once again, she found Peter in his study. This time he appeared to be going through the cupboards. "Whatever are you looking for?" she enquired. "You never misplace anything!"

"Quite so," he replied, although he still hadn't found what he was searching for and was getting more concerned.

*****

Susie had an uncomplicated return journey to Birmingham, and was soon on her way back to Woodstock, carefully sticking to the speed limit. As she drove, Susie thought about the weekend and what a marvellous time she'd had. She'd felt like a million dollars walking down the Promenade des Anglais on Jonathan's arm. She really did love him and wondered where that left her. She knew in her heart that she was wasting her time with him, but when they were together, it felt so right. Whatever was she going to do?

She reached Woodstock Academy shortly before 11.00 am, as the time difference between the South of France and the UK was in her favour. She parked her car and went to tell Miss Jennings that she had arrived. To Susie's dismay, Miss Jennings told her that her mother had phoned for her, and was waiting to have the call returned. Mechanically, Susie thanked her, and wondered whether she could pretend that Miss Jennings hadn't given her the message and that she hadn't got the message whilst she was in Monaco either. She had let Jonathan convince her that there was nothing to worry about and that she could easily talk her way out of it. Susie knew that her mother was no fool, particularly where she was concerned, and that she was going to have to pull something out of the bag if she had a chance of wriggling out of this one.

Putting her mother to the back of her mind, Susie concentrated on the tasks in hand. Her in-tray was full, so she switched on her computer and started typing. After all, she didn't want the headmistress on her case. It appeared to Susie that her story of a dental appointment had been believed, so now she needed to crack on with her work for the rest of the day.

CHAPTER 14

When she got home to Enstone, Susie went straight round to thank Mrs MacDonald for looking after George. Her neighbour assured her that it was an absolute pleasure, as George was such a lovely cat. "I've put all your post on one of the kitchen worktops, love," Mrs MacDonald called after Susie as she was leaving. Susie thanked her, and taking her suitcase out of the car, rushed in to see George. They were both pleased to see each other, and Susie was cuddling and kissing him when her phone rang. Without thinking, she answered and her heart sank as her mother's voice came down the line.

"I'm glad you're alive, darling, as you seem to be ignoring me," were her mother's opening words.

"Whatever do you mean, Mummy?" asked Susie lamely.

"Well," continued her mother, "I rang you on Sunday afternoon and left a message on your voicemail and then I left another message with Miss Jennings this morning, and still you haven't rung me back. I was beginning to wonder if you'd fallen off the face of the earth." Susie thought rapidly.

"Miss Jennings didn't tell me you'd rung, Mummy. That's very unlike her. I am sorry. As for Sunday, I didn't have any phone messages. Perhaps you dialled the wrong number?"

"Definitely not," replied her mother. "It was your voice on the answer phone. Perhaps there's something wrong with your phone?" she added smoothly.

"Yes, that could be it," mumbled Susie, and swiftly changed the subject. "How are you and Daddy?" she asked.

"We're fine darling, thank you, and wondered whether you would like to come for supper one night this week?"

"That would be lovely, thank you," replied her daughter. "Wednesday would be good for me. Would that be OK with you?"

"Absolutely perfect," said Annabelle, smiling to herself. Purposely she hadn't asked Susie about her weekend. That would keep for another two days. "Shall I make a fish pie, as that's one of your favourites?" Susie said that that would be fab, told her mother how much she was looking forward to seeing her and rang off, congratulating herself, as she felt that she'd got off the hook rather nicely.

*****

Immediately after she had finished speaking to Susie, Annabelle's phone rang again. It was DI Franklin to tell her that the vases which had been taken into her shop were indeed stolen, although they had been purchased in good faith. He was hoping that they might be able to use this information to trace the gang responsible for the break-in at the Williamsons.

However, unbeknown to DI Franklin, an arrest had been made at an antiques fair in Lancashire and all the Williamsons' porcelain had been recovered.

When, in the fullness of time, this became public knowledge, the people of Moulsford breathed a collective sigh of relief.

*****

Jonathan's return to Kirtlington went much more smoothly. He called in at the factory in Enstone and still managed to get home not long after 6.00 pm. Angela was busy in the kitchen and the twins were watching TV. Everyone was pleased to see him. He had bought Angela a large bottle of Gucci Envy at the airport and some Swiss chocolate for the girls. Lots of kissing and hugging took place. Angela produced a bottle of champagne from the fridge, and told him that supper wouldn't be long. Jonathan took a long swig. It was always good to receive a warm welcome. It meant that Angela didn't have a clue about what he'd been up to, but then again, why should she? He allowed his thoughts to stray to Susie for a moment, but then dismissed her from his mind and went into the kitchen to watch his wife cooking.

Jonathan loved Angela's cooking. She was far better in the kitchen than Susie. He breathed a contented sigh as she put the finishing touches to a chicken curry for them and a milder chicken stir-fry for Alice and Emily. He decided to lay the table in order to please his wife. "How was your weekend, Angie?" he asked. "Did you watch the race at all?"

"I saw your interview with Jake Humphrey and thought it was very good, but then I took Alice and Emily out for the day. We went to Stratford and had a picnic by the river. We really need to do more things like that as a family. As it's half-term next week, do you think perhaps we could do something a bit different?"

"What were you thinking of?" enquired her husband. "Don't forget I have to fly out to Canada on Tuesday." Jonathan had been planning to spend some time on Tuesday with Susie as he wasn't flying until early evening, and was loathe to have to give that up. "How about we find a hotel somewhere and go off early on Saturday morning and come back after lunch on Monday?" Angela's face lit up.

"That would be lovely," she said. "Where do you have in mind?"

"I'll have a look on the internet tonight and see what's available." He replied. "You look as though you're about to serve up. I'll go and call the girls."

They enjoyed supper together, and chatted a bit more about the race and Jonathan's interview. Fortunately, Angela didn't ask any awkward questions about Monaco, so he felt very satisfied as he finished the last of the champagne. They told the twins they were going to go away for the weekend. The girls were absolutely thrilled at the thought that Daddy would be coming this time, as they accepted that he often had to be away at weekends. Jonathan asked them where they would like to go, and they chorused "the seaside" in unison. He said that they would have to have a look at the weather forecast as the seaside wouldn't be very nice if it was raining all the time. After the children had gone to bed Jonathan poured himself a brandy and mixed a vodka and tonic for Angela. They sat amicably drinking them and looking at Jonathan's laptop for places to spend the weekend, finally settling on a country hotel in the New Forest, which had a spa and leisure facilities (as both children swam like fish). They agreed that from there they could easily reach the coast if the weather permitted, as Bournemouth was just a short drive away, and if it was dry but not seaside weather, there would be plenty of places to walk. Pleased with themselves, the Brownes retired to bed, where Jonathan set about making love to his wife, but without quite the same level of enthusiasm that he showed to his mistress. Nevertheless, Angela found the experience very pleasant indeed and drifted happily off to sleep. Exhausted by his weekend, Jonathan quickly followed suit.

CHAPTER 15

The gravel scrunched under Susie's tyres as she drove up to Riverside House. She parked her car and then let herself in to her family home. "It's only me, " she called. "Is there anyone there?"

"Hello darling," said Annabelle, coming out of the kitchen. She put her arms round her daughter and the two hugged and kissed. "I've just put the pie in the oven and Daddy should be home in about half an hour. As per usual, he's on the golf course, or more likely the 19th hole by now. What would you like to drink?" Susie asked for an orange juice. Annabelle poured her a glass and carried it, together with her own glass of wine, in to the conservatory.

"Is James not here?" enquired Susie. "I was rather hoping to see him."

"He'll be back shortly," replied her mother. "He's just taken Allsort for a walk." She didn't add that she had asked him not to hurry back, as she had something she wished to discuss with Susie.

Annabelle kept the conversation light-hearted and when her daughter was smiling and relaxed she turned the conversation to the previous weekend. "How was Grace? Did you have a good time together? What did you do?" she asked. Susie took a deep breath and replied that Grace was absolutely fine and that they had hit the shops in Manchester on Saturday afternoon and taken in a show in the evening. They had gone out for lunch together on Sunday, again in Manchester, to a trendy restaurant that she couldn't remember the name of, and then it had been time for her to drive back to Enstone.

"That all sounds very nice," said Annabelle, "it's just such a shame that you aren't telling me the truth."

"Whatever do you mean?" said Susie.

"You know what I mean Susie. Now, would you like to tell me what you were doing in Monaco at the weekend?" Susie almost dropped her orange juice.

"Monaco," she gasped. "I really don't know what you're talking about, Mummy."

"Don't insult my intelligence please Susannah," snapped her mother. "Daddy and I saw you on TV, sitting on a balcony outside the Hotel de Paris. I then phoned you, the call you say that you never had, and the ringtone on your phone was the international one. I would like to know what you're playing at. I'm also intrigued to know how you could possibly afford to stay at the Hotel de Paris over the Grand Prix weekend, when rooms are an extortionate price, so come on, out with it."

"You must have been mistaken. It must have been someone who looked like me," said Susie desperately.

"Nice try, but wrong answer. I really would like the truth now, please," said her mother.

"Well, what if it was me. I'm 23 and entitled to do anything I like," said Susie stubbornly.

"You are entitled to do most things you like, but one of those things is not lying to me," said Annabelle. "I want the truth and I want it now."

"OK" said Susie, "so I went to Monaco to watch the Grand Prix. It's hardly a big deal and the reason I didn't tell you was that I knew you would kick off over how expensive it was."

"Too right," replied her mother. "Knowing you, the way you dress and the lifestyle you enjoy, your credit card is fast approaching its limit, if it isn't there already. Your father and I would have to think twice about staying at the Hotel de Paris during the race weekend and we certainly have more money than you. Whatever were you thinking of?" Susie felt that "sex" was not an appropriate answer as her mother was very cross indeed and anyway that would lead on to other things. She then realised that her mother was still speaking and saying something about not knowing that Susie was even interested in motor racing.

"Oh for heaven's sake," Susie said in the end. "I bought the package off eBay ridiculously cheaply. It was a last minute deal. I didn't tell you and Daddy because I knew you'd go on and on about it – like you are now." She felt really proud of her answer and thought it would be bound to silence her mother.

"I find that extremely hard to believe," said Annabelle. "It couldn't have been that much of a knock down price, as you had already bought it when it was James' party. Anyway, I still don't understand the secrecy and can't accept why you had to lie to me."

"Suit yourself," replied her daughter. "I'm going to get another orange juice. Can I get you another glass of wine?" To Susie's delight, at that point she heard the back door close, and a moment later Allsort was waddling towards her, followed by her brother.

"Hi James, it's great to see you," said Susie.

Annabelle sighed with exasperation. Both she and Susie knew that the conversation wouldn't be continued now that James was home. She walked in to the kitchen to check on her fish pie and dialled Peter from her mobile. "No, darling, I'm not trying to hurry you home," she said, "but I just want to remind you not to mention Monaco in front of James. Susie alleges she bought a deal on eBay. Can you imagine buying the Hotel de Paris on eBay a couple of weeks before the Grand Prix? No, neither can I. I'm determined to get to the bottom of this though. See you soon. Drive carefully."

With that, Annabelle returned to the conservatory, where she found her children deep in conversation. James was telling Susie that he was going to see a financial adviser in Chipping Norton the following afternoon, and suggesting that they should have supper together afterwards. "Fab," said Susie, "let's go to The Crown. Alf does great food. Shall I book us a table?" James said that that was a good idea and that it would be his treat.

It wasn't long before they heard Peter's key in the front door and the family went through to have their supper. As always, Annabelle's fish pie was delicious, and the accompanying vegetables were cooked to perfection. After a glass of wine, Susie felt more relaxed and didn't flinch when her mother reminded her of the shopping trip they had planned to Bicester Village on Saturday. Susie loved shopping and the fact that it was a Bank Holiday weekend wasn't going to put her off. Her mother was usually generous and Susie was optimistic that at the very least they would have a nice lunch together. She was sure that her mother would have forgotten Monaco by then and it also gave her time to think about her story a bit more.

*****

When Susie got home to Rose Cottage, the post was waiting for her on the mat. She put it to one side whilst she fed George and poured herself a glass of wine. She had only had one with her dinner, but saw no reason not to treat herself to another now. She carried the wine and her post through to her sitting room. Susie loved her room. It was at the front of the cottage, and overlooked the lay-by, where she parked her car, and the road, so she could watch people coming and going. Her mother had helped her to choose the furnishings and it was very simply done. She had two small sofas covered in a pink and green material, with a coffee table between them and a book case in one corner. There was an alcove leading to a dining area with a very small square table and four dining chairs and this overlooked her little garden. The room's focal point was the fireplace, which never got used. The hearth was filled with an assortment of candles.

Susie settled herself on one of the sofas, where she was soon joined by George. He climbed onto her lap and circled round a few times, before curling up, purring contentedly. After she had stroked his head for a while, Susie reached for her post and proceeded to open it. There was a card from the nail bar in Chipping Norton, offering her 20 per cent off her next appointment, which she carefully put to one side before turning her attention to an unfriendly looking brown envelope. Susie discovered to her horror that it was an indictment for speeding, and that she was summoned to appear at Stratford Magistrates' Court on Thursday 14 June at 9.30 am. As her brain registered what the paperwork was saying, Susie burst into tears, wondering how she was going to deal with it. She definitely couldn't afford a solicitor, so guessed she would have no alternative but to go to court and plead guilty. Who could she possibly discuss this with? She had never been to court in her life and hadn't a clue what to expect when she got there. Susie decided that Jonathan was her only possibility. She knew she was out of favour with her parents over the Monaco incident and really there was no-one else she could ask as she couldn't see any of her friends having any idea what to do. She looked at her watch and decided that it was too late to text Jonathan and that she would contact him from school the following day. Perhaps he could come round after work? Oh bugger, no he couldn't, because James was taking her out for dinner.

Drying her eyes, Susie decided that more wine was in order. Gently, she pushed George aside and headed for the kitchen. As she knocked back another glass, she let the tears fall as she thought of the unfairness of it all. The stupid summons, her mother prying into her private life, and most of all that she and Jonathan couldn't be together. If only they could tell everyone about their love, none of the other stuff would even have happened. She buried her face in George's thick fur, then polished off the bottle and went to bed, feeling hopelessly sorry for herself.

CHAPTER 16

James set off for Chipping Norton immediately after lunch the following day. He didn't notice the black Golf pulling into its usual spot in the lay-by. He was quite excited as this was the longest drive that he'd taken so far in his new car. James felt very grown up indeed. How many people his age would be driving a brand new Mini Cooper on their way to see a financial adviser? Life was good.

In just under an hour James was pulling in to the car park of The Quiet Woman Antiques Centre a little way outside Chipping Norton. As promised, he was taking the time to look for pieces for his mother's shop. He walked around slowly, finally settling on a pair of small silver salt and pepper shakers, a Derby Posie bread and butter plate and a crystal biscuit barrel. The biscuit barrel wasn't particularly old, but it was good crystal, and the price was right. In total he spent £106. He felt his mother would be pleased by his efforts. He now had time for a quick look around the shops in Chipping Norton itself before his meeting with David Timmins.

James wandered in and out of the various antique shops but didn't spot anything he considered exciting so he made his way over to the offices of Chipping Norton Financial Planners and told the pretty receptionist that he had an appointment with David.

David only kept James waiting for a moment before showing him into a small office overlooking the market square. They exchanged pleasantries before David turned the conversation to James' inheritance. David asked lots of questions, some of which James found hard to answer. He really didn't know what his income and expenditure were. He lived at home free of charge and was just finishing at college. He now had a little job working for his mother. Really his only expenses were his car, the odd night out and a few clothes, although he did admit to David that he wanted to go on a shopping trip as he fancied a new image. David smiled and thought to himself how fortunate James was. That said, James didn't strike him as spoiled in any way and his sister had always said that he was a nice lad. "Jenny could do worse than get involved with James Rowlands," David thought to himself, but then Jenny was happily dating someone, and certainly wouldn't appreciate her brother's opinion on her love life!

He gave James a risk profiler to complete and explained that it would help him to assess the types of funds that would be suitable for him. David also asked more questions about how long James wished to invest for and how much of his money he was prepared to invest. James explained that he didn't really know the answers but that he knew his money was doing nothing sitting in his bank account. He half wondered about buying a flat but David explained to him that that wasn't possible at the moment as he didn't have a proper job. In one way James was quite pleased to hear that, as it was one less decision to make. David suggested that James should keep a portion of his money easily accessible and that they could then look at investing the rest. He then said that the best plan would be to arrange a further meeting where he could present James with some recommendations. James said that he liked the sound of that, and another appointment was made for a fortnight's time.

*****

Susie had arranged to meet James at The Crown at 6.30 pm, but got there a little earlier. She had walked down so that she could enjoy a drink and had over-estimated how long it would take her. Alf was leaning on the bar when she went in and they smiled at each other. "Hello, Susie, love. What's it to be?" Alf asked.

"Hi Alf, I'd like a table for two, please."

"Hot date, is it?" Alf wiggled his eyebrows cheekily.

"Haha, no, definitely not. I'm meeting my brother." Susie laughed.

"Anything to drink while you're waiting?" Alf smiled.

"Ooh yes, I'll have a glass of white, please," she replied. Jonathan had succeeded in weaning her off the dreadful Bacardi Breezers that she had drunk when she first met him, and she was now beginning to learn about wine.

"How about a nice New Zealand Sauvignon Blanc?" enquired Alf, showing her the bottle. Susie agreed with his choice, and asked to open a tab.

She had always liked Alf very much, and wondered whether he might be the sort of person who could help her with her speeding ticket. Sliding onto a bar stool and sipping her glass of wine, Susie told him she'd got a summons. "I've only ever been caught once," replied Alf, "and that was in Moulsford. The week after I was done for doing 40 in a 30, they bloody well put the speed limit up to 40. When the copper stopped me and asked me if I knew what speed I was doing, I was daft enough to say that I didn't. I was only doing 34 and the bastard said I was doing 40. I was hardly in a position to contradict him then, because I would have proved myself to be a liar." Alf's wife, Joan, joined them at this point.

"The funny thing, is Susie, that it was a standing joke around Wallingford that Alf always drove slowly. As one person once said, they went out in the car with Alf and they were overtaken by two bicycles and three pedestrians." Susie laughed at this, and told the couple that her parents lived in Moulsford. Alf went on to say that they used to live in Cholsey and that their daughter had gone to Cranford House School, and asked if Susie had gone there. Susie explained that her father had been in the RAF and that as they had lived all over the place, she had been to boarding school, which she had hated.

"Funny really, that I'm now working as a school secretary, " she said, "but Woodstock's a nice place and I really love living in Enstone. The other huge plus is the fabulous long holidays. I've got all next week off for half term."

"We're having a big barbeque here on Monday, so if you aren't doing anything, come and join us," said Alf. "It's a tenner for the food and you have to pay for your booze. Should be a good do."

Susie looked out of the window and saw James approaching and hastily asked Alf not to mention her speeding ticket, as she didn't want anything getting back to her parents. Alf laughed saying that he understood and gave her a crafty wink as James came into the bar. Susie introduced him to Alf, explaining that James lived in Moulsford and had been to Chipping Norton to see a financial adviser. "Long way to come from Moulsford," remarked Alf, whereupon James explained the connexion between himself and David Timmins.

"This really is an evening for coincidences," said Alf. "First I discover that your family home is in Moulsford when I used to live in Cholsey, and then I learn that you've been seeking financial advice from my next door neighbour. What a small world. Anyway son, what can I get you to drink?" James chose a pint of Stella, knowing that it would have to last all evening, and Susie asked for another glass of wine.

The bar started to fill up and Alf drifted off to talk to other customers, leaving Susie and James with their menus. Susie was explaining to James that the steaks were to die for, when who should walk in, no longer in a business suit, but in a pair of jeans and a polo shirt, but David Timmins. James greeted him and re-introduced him to Susie, explaining that they had met at his birthday party. David ran his eyes appreciatively over Susie. She was wearing a denim mini skirt and a bright pink tee shirt and he thought that she looked stunning. He had a weakness for tall girls, and she was that all right! Even in flat shoes she was as tall as her brother. He suddenly realised that Susie was speaking to him and saying that it must be wonderful to live next door to a pub, particularly one that did such fab food. He agreed with her and explained that was the main purpose for his visit – his supper. James asked David if he was on his own and when David said that he was, suggested that he join them.

Alf came over again, carrying a pint of real ale for David. James explained that David was going to join them and Alf brought another menu. "I shouldn't think you need that, do you?" said Susie with a smile. "I live up the road in Enstone and I know the menu pretty well. I'll bet you know it off by heart." David was interested to learn that Susie lived locally and said he was surprised not to have seen her in the pub before, thinking that he would certainly look out for her in the future.

A waitress came and showed the three to a table in the corner of the restaurant. They continued to chat, whilst waiting for their food to arrive. Susie asked James and David what James was going to do with his money. Her brother promptly told her to mind her own business! Susie laughed, and told David that she had used her inheritance as a deposit on her cottage and wondered whether James was considering doing the same? To shut her up, James told her that he couldn't buy anywhere until he had a proper job. Susie was just about to open her mouth again, when their starters arrived.

David felt it a good idea to change the subject, and asked Susie what she did for a living. That turned the conversation nicely into a discussion about Woodstock, her long school holidays and the area in general. Silence then fell as they enjoyed their starters. Each of the three had their own thoughts. David was thinking what a stunner Susie was, James was wondering whether he could discuss his potential investment with Greg, as he would like a second opinion, and, as for Susie – she was thinking about Jonathan and wishing he were sitting opposite her.

Alf came across after they had finished the meal to check that everything had been all right. As usual, the steaks had been fabulous and they all told him so. His face crinkled into a smile of pride as he said that his steaks were the best for miles around, and asked them if they would like a drink with him. Susie and David jumped at the chance, but poor James had to settle for a cup of coffee as he was driving home.

All too soon James said that he wanted to be getting back, and Susie asked him for a lift. David was disappointed to see her go, but guessed there would be other times. In fact, he went on to suggest that they should do it again in a fortnight's time, after James' second appointment. Susie said that she would have to check her diary and that she would let James know. She wasn't going to commit to anything until she knew if Jonathan was free that night.

*****

James dropped Susie off at Rose Cottage and refused her offer of coffee. As he was driving out of Cox's Lane, he noticed a small figure standing on the side of the road, staring hard at him. He wondered why. He felt that it would only be polite to tell his father a little about his meeting with David, so he headed back to Moulsford, where he found his father in the study, going through the drawers in his desk. To James' surprise, his dad didn't seem particularly interested in anything James had to say. Feeling a little put out, James went off in search of his mother who was curled up watching TV and definitely seemed more interested in his day. James unwrapped his purchases from The Quiet Woman and spread them out on the coffee table. "They're very nice, darling. How much did you pay?" she asked, having examined them all carefully. She seemed pleased when he told her the prices. "We must go out buying together. I think you have a natural eye and I'd like to see you in action. Maybe you should think about antiques rather than a business course. Who am I to advise you though, as I do the antiques for a bit of fun. It's the jam to go with your father's bread and butter."

Peter was still searching through his desk, getting more and more agitated. "Where the hell could those papers be?" He slammed the final drawer shut and went to find his wife and son. There was no more he could do at present.

CHAPTER 17

When he awoke the next morning, Peter made the decision to man up and face his problems head on. What he had done was very foolish. Using insider knowledge he'd bought 3,000 shares in a little known recording company on the nod that it was going to be bought by one of the majors, and had put them in Annabelle's name to protect himself. Almost immediately, he regretted it and decided the best thing would be to get rid of the damn things, as they could come back to bite. Of course, Annabelle knew nothing about any of this.

Taking Annabelle a cup of tea in bed, Peter told her that he was going in to town on the early train as he wanted to go to the office to discuss a couple of things with a colleague. In actual fact, he needed to make a few calls without the danger of Annabelle overhearing what he was saying. He couldn't find any of the papers relating to the deal and in fact he couldn't even remember the bloody recording company's name, so he had a bit of phoning around to do. Annabelle remarked that it seemed to be rather a sudden decision and asked if something urgent had come up. "Kind of," replied her husband. "It's nothing for you to worry about, but there is something I need to sort out, and now seems as good a time as any." Annabelle nodded, and turning her attention to the cup of tea said that she would see him later in the evening. Peter promised to call to let her know what time he would be home.

Not bothering with any breakfast, thinking that he could get something on the train, Peter backed his car out of the garage and headed for Cholsey Station. He didn't notice the black Golf parked on the lay-by, but the driver certainly noticed him.

*****

Annabelle and James had breakfast together and discussed the day ahead. James told his mum that he was still keen to have a day out shopping and he also felt that he needed to do something with his hair and was wondering if she thought Greg would know a decent hairdresser? "I'm sure he would, darling," said his mother. "Perhaps he could also point you in the direction of a few decent boutiques as you seem so set on a make-over. You don't want to see an image consultant by any chance do you?" she enquired laughingly.

"Actually, you know, that might not be a bad idea," replied her son. "Do you know anyone?"

"Yes, there's a girl I met last time I was at the hairdressers. She does a lot of the styling for the salon shows and photo shoots. She's got a good eye," said his mother. "I could find out her details for you if you like?" James said that he would like that very much indeed and she went off to chase it up. James decided that it would be far more grown up to go into the shop looking smarter, rather than asking Greg for help. His mother came back waving a piece of paper with the consultant's name and phone number and he decided to call straightaway.

"She can actually see me at 2.30 this afternoon, Mum," James said to Annabelle, once he'd finished his call. "If I cover the shop this morning, could you do it this afternoon?"

"Certainly," replied his mother, smiling.

James happily headed off to Wallingford and Annabelle went to have a look in the fridge and freezer in order to plan supper for that evening. She thought it likely that Peter would have a good lunch in London, so decided to defrost some trout and worry about what she was going to do with it later. She could nip into Waitrose when she was in Wallingford and pick up some vegetables and other bits - she already had a large delivery coming from them the following morning which should tide them through the Bank Holiday.

*****

James pulled up outside Penny Cook's house on the Wantage Road shortly before 2.30 pm. He wasn't sure what to expect, thinking that it was usually girls who went to image consultants, but what the hell? He wanted to smarten himself up and he wanted some advice. He walked up the path and rang the bell. Penny invited James in and took him through to her studio.

Penny talked about the importance of wearing the right shapes of clothes in the right colours, as these would both make him feel and look better. One of the services she offered her clients was to go shopping with them and she wondered if that might appeal to James? He said that it definitely would and asked for more details. Penny said that they could discuss colours and styles that would suit him now, but that they would need at least half a day to go shopping. She would also need to know what type of clothes he wanted and his budget. James spent about an hour and a half with Penny, which he thoroughly enjoyed, learning about the types of things to wear. He then made an appointment to go shopping with her the following Friday. Penny was surprised that he didn't ask her how much her services would cost, but then she knew that Annabelle dressed well and certainly looked as though she had money. They agreed to meet outside John Lewis in Reading at 10.00 am. In the meantime, Penny suggested that

James should get his hair styled and highlighted as this would definitely enhance his appearance, and recommended he go to Russell at The Cutting Studio in Wallingford.

As soon as he had left Penny, James drove back into Wallingford and walked round to the Cutting Studio, where he made an appointment with Russell for the next Thursday, thinking it important that he should have his new look hair before he went on his shopping trip. He then went home, dying to tell his mother what a fab afternoon he'd had.

*****

In London, Peter had finally managed to dispose of the shares that had been causing him such anxiety. He was seriously miffed to have lost money on them. Still, nothing could come back to haunt him or Annabelle now. It was a pricey lesson to learn, but it could have been much stickier. All in all, he felt he'd got off pretty lightly. He caught the 3.00 pm train from Paddington feeling much calmer. He settled in to his first class carriage with the Financial Times and a large gin and tonic. He then phoned Annabelle to say that he was on his way home. Peter thought she sounded a little tense, but decided that he'd probably just caught her in the middle of serving a customer.

*****

After Peter and James had left Riverside House, Annabelle thought she might as well do some household chores. Her cleaning lady wouldn't be coming in next Monday, as it was a Bank Holiday, and she'd like to have the house spick and span so that she could relax properly over the long weekend. Turning up the radio, Annabelle sang along as she hoovered and polished.

She was making herself a cup of coffee when the doorbell rang. As she wasn't expecting anyone and there was no sign of a car, Annabelle guessed that it would be someone collecting for charity. With a smile on her face, Annabelle opened the door. When she saw who was standing there, her smile froze. "Aren't you going to ask me in?" The nasal whine cut through her like a knife.

CHAPTER 18

Susie woke up still feeling sorry for herself. It was the first day of half term and all she had planned was today's shopping trip with her mother. That could be difficult too, if Mummy started on again about Monaco. She had finally managed to speak to Jonathan about her speeding ticket the previous afternoon and was hurt when he had asked her what the hell she expected him to do about it? She had then asked him if he could come round after work as she would be finishing school early, only to be informed that he was taking his family to the New Forest for a few days, and then flying out to Canada for the Grand Prix. He was coming back from the New Forest on Monday afternoon and leaving for Canada on Tuesday afternoon and no, he wouldn't have time to see her in between. He would be home again the following Tuesday and would have to see what that week brought. So, Susie had a whole week to herself with nothing to do and no chance at all of seeing her man. She decided that she would spend some time phoning the girlfriends that she had neglected recently, to see if they fancied doing something.

She was not due to meet her mother at Bicester Village until 11.00 am, so straight after breakfast Susie started ringing round. Out of the four friends she called, every single one was doing something. None of them invited her to join them and three of them commented that they had not heard from her in ages. That was true and Susie knew it. Since meeting Jonathan she had waited around in case he should be available to see her and she'd not kept in touch with her friends. She realised now that this had been a mistake. A week on her own was going to be bad enough, but how was she going to get through the eight weeks of the summer holidays? She really did need to go away somewhere and if she couldn't convince a girlfriend to go with her, Susie made up her mind there and then that she would go on a singles' holiday. What would Jonathan think about that?

As she was getting into her car, Susie saw one of the school children out with her mother. She said a cheery hello to them and wished them a happy half term. The child thanked her and Susie thought for a moment that she gave her a puzzled look. Shrugging her shoulders and thinking no more about it, she turned the key in the ignition and set off for Bicester Village.

As expected on a Bank Holiday, there was a queue to get in to Bicester Village and then a further queue to find a parking space. Even so, just before 11.00 am Susie was standing by the statue of the polar bear, waiting for her mother to arrive. She had been determined to arrive first, feeling that she needed all the help she could get!

Two minutes later her mother appeared, looking as beautiful as always. They hugged and kissed, and then headed for the shops, arm in arm. Susie thought that her mother looked somewhat preoccupied and braced herself for interrogation over lunch.

A couple of hours passed peacefully enough. Annabelle bought Peter some shirts from Thomas Pink and a gorgeous pair of cream Jimmy Choo sandals and matching bag for herself. Susie looked on enviously. Perhaps she could have a new handbag from Radley? She knew her credit card was fast approaching its limit, but what the hell? It was her birthday in November, but she couldn't really expect her mother to be buying presents for that at the beginning of June!

Looking at her watch, Annabelle suggested it was time for lunch. Mother and daughter wondered where they could go. All the restaurants on site were bound to be full. Should they put their bags in the car and walk in to Bicester? They agreed that was probably the best idea, so they headed off for the town, where they succeeded in getting a table in the Turkish restaurant.

Sitting opposite her, Susie decided that her mother looked a little under the weather, but thought better of saying so. Instead, she asked what she and Daddy were doing for the bank holiday weekend. "We thought about going up to London, but decided against it," said her mother. "The shop is open all weekend so James and I will have to come to some arrangement over that. It should be a good opportunity to sell. Other than that, Daddy and I are going to the Crawford's for lunch on Sunday and, weather permitting, I think they're planning on taking their boat up the river in the afternoon, which should be fun. How about you darling? What are you doing?" Sadly, Susie confessed that she had nothing planned. At this her mother raised her eyebrows and asked if she had spent all her money the previous weekend in Monaco.

"Don't start on that again, Mummy, please," said Susie, pulling a face. "Just be happy for me that I had a good time." Annabelle gave her daughter a very direct look, but decided against saying anything. After what had happened yesterday, she had far more important things to worry about than her daughter's weekend away. She had a difficult decision to make and she would have to make it very soon indeed.

Lunch over, Annabelle paid the bill, and the two strolled back to Bicester Village to resume their shopping. Annabelle was soon carrying lots of bags from expensive shops and Susie still hadn't bought anything. "No doubt you're hard up," said her mother, frowning at her, "after all, Monaco would have been hideously expensive." As Susie was about to make a retort, her mother held up her hand, saying, "Come on, let's go to Monsoon. I know you like their clothes. I'll treat you to a dress." Susie couldn't believe her luck, and was even more delighted when her mother bought her two dresses, saying they both suited her daughter so well that it would be impossible to choose between them. They passed Radley walking back to the cars, as they had both parked on the same car park, and Susie gazed longingly through the window. Her mother laughed and said that as she had had a couple of new handbags, she felt that Susie should have one too. Susie couldn't believe her luck, as she had been expecting her mother to give her a very hard time indeed but then, of course, she didn't know what was going on in her mother's mind after the unexpected visitor the previous day.

Thanking her mother for a lovely day out and her fabulous pressies, Susie kissed her warmly, sent her father and brother her love and the two climbed into their respective cars and set off home.

*****

Annabelle was very preoccupied on the journey back to Moulsford. She had enjoyed shopping with her daughter, but now she needed to think about what on earth she was going to do. Her visitor's nasal tones kept going through her head "You've got until a week today, or else..." What lengths would he be prepared or indeed capable of going to? In her heart of hearts, Annabelle knew that she would have to tell Peter but what, in heaven's name, was she going to tell him? She explored every possibility and couldn't come up with anything. She seemed to arrive at Riverside House very quickly and there was her husband, opening the front door, smiling at her and coming towards the car. "No doubt you have plenty of bags that you need help to carry," he laughed. Annabelle smiled weakly back,

"Yes, I have, thank you darling," she said. "And then, do you know what I would like to do? I'd like us to sit down and enjoy a drink together."

"That sounds good to me," said Peter cheerfully.

CHAPTER 19

Susie returned from shopping with mixed feelings. She was delighted with her new dresses and handbag, and grateful that her mother hadn't asked too many questions about Monaco. On the other hand, she was feeling lonely. The week stretched out ahead of her and the only possibility she had for going out was Alf's barbeque at The Crown on Monday. Hardly the social event of the year! To rub salt in her wounds, Jonathan would be having a wonderful time with his family while she was home alone. Taking a ready meal out of the fridge and putting it in the microwave, Susie decided that things would have to change.

What chance did she have of a holiday this year with Jonathan? Absolutely none at all. What chance did she have of a holiday with anyone for that matter? She needed to do something about it. After supper she would surf the internet for singles' holidays. At least she would be with people in the same boat and it would also give her something to do. Feeling much more positive, Susie spooned George's favourite food into his bowl and got her own meal from the microwave.

As soon as she had finished her lasagne, Susie fished out her iPad and went online. There were plenty of holidays to choose from, so she got going with enthusiasm. After an hour she was feeling far less enthusiastic, as she discovered that "all inclusive from £399" was absolute nonsense and there just wasn't anything reasonable for under £1,000. She had chosen Spain, as it wasn't too far to travel for just a week, but the prices were awful. Susie was terrified that if she chose a holiday for "any age" she might be surrounded by wrinklies, but holidays exclusively for her age group were not only few and far between, they were also very dear. The only available one in August cost £1,129 for a week and was only half board. What should she do? She deserved a holiday, didn't she?

As she searched for a singles' holiday, adverts for dating sites began popping up all over the place. Unable to contain her curiosity any longer, Susie decided to have a look at one or two. She found she couldn't actually have a look at any of the men's details without completing a profile of herself. Should she or shouldn't she? Sod it, she could do exactly what she wanted. She was a grown up, after all. A lot of the sites were free to join, so really, she had nothing to lose had she? She poured herself a big glass of wine to help boost her confidence and quickly started typing, before she could change her mind. She then spent an entertaining couple of hours viewing a variety of profiles, but not being sufficiently brave to contact anybody.

Looking at her watch, Susie saw that it was approaching midnight. She couldn't believe how long she had spent on the internet, without actually achieving anything. Really, the holiday was her first priority. By now, Susie had made her way to the bottom of the wine bottle, and throwing caution to the wind, she got out her credit card and decided to book the holiday in Benalmadena for £1,129. The holiday was in eleven weeks' time, but in order to secure her place, she had to pay in full. Without any hesitation she typed in her credit card number. She now had something to look forward to in August, and she could give Jonathan a taste of his own medicine too. See how he likes being the one who's left behind for a change.

Putting her iPad aside, Susie turned her attention to George. "Well, George," she told him, "I'm going to sunny Spain. How good is that?" The large ginger cat purred contentedly in reply, and settled himself down on Susie's lap for some long overdue stroking.

*****

Annabelle was bracing herself for a very difficult conversation. Whilst Peter had been taking her bags upstairs and sorting out their drinks, she had once again relived the events of the previous morning. His voice had been laced with menace, and where was she going to find £5,000 without letting her husband know what was going on? Would it stop there? Blackmailers were renowned for coming back for more. Why had she been so naïve all those years ago?

Peter came into the snug carrying a tray of drinks and asked her about her day. "What did you find out about Susie and Monaco?" he enquired.

"Nothing," replied his wife. "She was a closed book and basically she told me to mind my own business. I suppose we have to respect the fact that Susie is an adult, and that she is entitled to do as she wishes without telling us. However, I can't forgive her for lying to me about where she was going. And I'm still sure there's a lot more that she's not telling us."

"I agree with you," said Peter, "but we can't force it out of her. I certainly don't believe that cock and bull story about eBay. For Christ's sake, she's never shown any interest in motor racing. Don't look so worried though, Belle, I'm sure everything will unfold in time. Do you think perhaps it has something to do with a man? It seems odd to me that Susie doesn't appear to have a boyfriend. She's a beautiful girl, but then again James doesn't have a girlfriend and he's a good looking lad."

Before Annabelle could answer, the door to the snug opened and James came to join them. "There you are," he said breezily. "How was your shopping trip, and how was Susie? I've had a cracking day at the shop. Just wait till you hear what I've sold."

Mechanically, Annabelle told him about her shopping trip, while Peter went and fetched more drinks.

"Aren't you going to ask me about my day, then?" asked James.

"Of course, darling," replied Annabelle smiling. "What happened that you're so pleased about?" James went on to tell them about the wonderful sales that he had made, including the Spode tea set that had been there for absolutely ages and the two hideous Doulton Lambethware vases. What was more, whilst having a quick look round the other shops, he had come across a pair of pretty silver napkin rings, bought them for £30 and sold them on for £48 the same day.

"Well done, son," said Peter. "I can see you have the makings of a dealer. We'll have you on the London Stock Exchange yet." As he said it, Peter's mind flashed back to the shares he'd unloaded the previous day. He did hope that Annabelle never needed to know about what he had done.

Annabelle was thinking that her moment for confessing to Peter had passed now that James had come home. Smiling at the two of them, she asked her son if he would be joining them for supper. James thanked her, but said that he had been invited to Greg's for a curry. There was definitely a friendship developing there. She walked through to the kitchen to start preparing the evening meal, with her worries still weighing heavily on her mind.

*****

Once the supper dishes were in the dishwasher and James had gone out, Annabelle decided that she would have another go at telling Peter her troubles. She found him with a cigar and a brandy in the conservatory, with the various bits of the Telegraph scattered around him. "Some lovely photos of the Royals," he said handing Annabelle the supplement. "I miss flying them around, you know." He started reminiscing about his days as a member of the Queen's Flight. Annabelle listened patiently, waiting for her opportunity, as she didn't wish to irritate her husband by interrupting him.

She was just about to open her mouth, when the damn phone rang. Peter answered it. "No, no, of course it's not too late," she heard him say. "We'll expect you in ten to fifteen minutes then." Annabelle raised her eyebrows enquiringly as he came off the phone. "It's George and Samantha," he said. "They're going to be passing through Moulsford in about a quarter of an hour and wondered if they could pop in for coffee."

"Right," said Annabelle, getting to her feet. "You go and sort out the coffee machine, whilst I go and make myself look a bit more presentable."

"You look fine, my love," said Peter, also getting to his feet and walking towards the kitchen. Annabelle shot upstairs to change her clothes and freshen up her make-up, thinking that this conversation with Peter was doomed. They were out for lunch tomorrow and this wasn't something that could be rushed. The awful thing though, was that she only had until Friday to sort something out.

Hearing the doorbell, Annabelle hastily sprayed on some Coco Mademoiselle and dashed downstairs to greet her guests.

CHAPTER 20

Sitting beside Peter on one of their luxurious sofas, Annabelle tucked her legs up underneath herself and wrapped her hands around her wine glass, before turning to her husband. They'd had a delicious lunch at the Crawfords and, as the weather had not permitted taking the boat out, were both feeling rather mellow due to the amount of alcohol that had been flowing.

Annabelle took a deep breath. "I did some photographic modelling when I was seventeen, Peter," she said to her husband.

"Did you, sweetheart? You never told me about it," came the reply.

"I didn't tell anyone about it," said Annabelle. "What started out as a bit of fun and some pin money developed into something not so much fun." Peter looked at her quizzically. "Yes," she said, "I was very naïve. I'd managed to get a modelling job locally but didn't tell my parents as I didn't think they'd approve. Then I was introduced to another photographer who asked me if I'd be interested in glamour modelling." Peter raised his eyebrows at this point. "Yes, I know," said Annabelle, "I assumed that glamour modelling meant wearing fur coats and hats and beautiful jewellery, so I couldn't sign the contract fast enough. When I discovered I had signed up to pose naked I was distraught but the photographer said he would sue me for breach of contract if I didn't take my clothes off." Peter laughed at the look on his wife's face.

"It's hardly the end of the world my darling," he said. "I'm sure you were a fabulous glamour model. You still have the most beautiful body."

"It didn't stop there, though," said his wife sadly. "Once he'd taken those first pictures he used them to blackmail me into doing more sessions and the photos really got less and less glamorous, Peter. He told me that if I did as I was told then the photos would just be our secret. In a way, I'd rather he'd just sold them to a magazine. Knowing he was keeping them for himself made me feel disgusting, and meant he still had that power over me. As soon as I turned 18, I moved to London to get away from him, and pushed it all to the back of my mind."

Peter stopped laughing and gave Annabelle his full attention. "Has something happened that's made you want to talk about this now?" He asked, his voice filled with concern. Annabelle nodded.

"While you were in London on Friday he came to the house. He's trying to blackmail me again, but this time he wants money, and if I don't pay, he's going to show the photos to Susie and James. I have until this Friday to find the money. I've got to stop him from showing off the photos. I know he's got them because he brought some of the negatives to show me. I think he must drive the black car that I've seen lurking about, because when I told him that he would have to go as you would be back any second, he told me that you wouldn't, as he'd followed you to Cholsey station and waited whilst you got on the train. He also knew that James had gone to Wallingford to look after the shop for me. He knows an awful lot about us." With this, Annabelle burst into tears.

Peter moved over on the sofa and wrapped his arms around her. "Come on, Belle, dry your eyes. Nothing is ever that bad. We have lots of choices here.

"Do we?" said Annabelle in amazement, blowing her nose hard.

"Of course we have," said Peter. "The most obvious one is to call the bastard's bluff. You tell him he can show the photos to whom the hell he likes and you don't give a damn and he's not getting any money." Annabelle shook her head vehemently at this suggestion. "Alternatively, we can go to the police. What's supposed to happen next?"

"He's going to ring me on Friday morning and tell me where to meet him and I'm to give him £5,000 in cash," said Annabelle.

"Well, that isn't going to happen," said Peter. "Now let's think this through sensibly."

"I really don't want to go to the police," said Annabelle, "Can we not deal with it ourselves?" Peter knew he had to take the lead from Annabelle on this, so he thought for a moment before responding. "Why don't you get him to come here on Friday morning, and then I can be here, too."

"I think he'd be watching the house and want to see you leave and maybe even follow you again to make sure that you had," said Annabelle. "We're going to need to be clever."

"Yes." said Peter gravely, "we certainly are, but he's not going to get away with this. I promise you."

*****

Susie was finding Sunday to be a tough day. She had phoned a couple more friends that she hadn't spoken to for a while, with the same results that she'd had the previous day. They all had plans and she wasn't invited to join any of them, She had mowed her lawn, chatted to Mrs MacDonald over the fence and was now wondering once again how she was going to spend the coming week. She longed to speak to Jonathan but knew that was out of the question as he was away with his family. It hit home to her how wrong she had been to forget about her friends and concentrate on him alone.

She was looking through her emails when she saw that she had one from the dating site which, with the excitement of the holiday, she had completely forgotten about. She eagerly read the message, from a guy called Dave, saying that he had found her profile interesting and did she have a photo? His profile said that he was a 24 year old electrician who liked the cinema and going to the pub and that he lived in Bicester. Dave had a photograph and he looked pleasant enough, so Susie decided she would reply to his message explaining that she was new to the dating site and didn't have a photo and ask him a bit more about himself. "God," she thought to herself, "this is really quite difficult. I don't want to appear too keen and I don't want to appear too nosey either." After all, what on earth did you ask someone you didn't know? Susie thought for a few minutes, then typed a reply and pressed send.

*****

James spent Sunday in the shop. He'd had a great time with Greg the night before. He decided that his new friend was very talented indeed. Not only did he have a fab little house and car, he was also a mean cook. The curry had been delicious and James had felt very relaxed and at home in the little house in Cholsey. He had plucked up the courage to ask Greg if he had a girlfriend, at which point his companion had roared with laughter and said "Hardly." James had been a little puzzled by the reply and was thinking about it as he worked.

Greg, for his part, was also thinking about the previous evening. He found James interesting and attractive, albeit somewhat innocent, and wondered what he should do. Perhaps he needed to be a little more obvious? Clearly the boy liked him, but did it, or could it, go beyond that? "Yes, my love. How can I help you?" he turned to an elderly lady who was peering into one of his jewellery cabinets. She explained that she was looking for a silver bangle for her granddaughter's birthday. Greg turned his attention to the job in hand and found three bangles for the woman to look at. He was delighted when she paid him £130 in cash for a bangle that he had bought for £65.

"That's it, James," he said, walking across the gangway to Annabelle's shop. "Finished for the day. Do you fancy doing something this evening?" James nodded.

"Would you like to come over to Moulsford? You could meet Allsort. We could take her and Zizi for a walk and look in at the Beetle and Wedge. They're fine about having dogs in the bar." Greg said that indeed he did fancy the idea. Now, James inviting him home - that was promising, wasn't it? He returned to his shop and James rang his parents.

His dad answered the phone. "I'm sure that will be fine, James" he said. "Your mother and I had a huge meal with the Crawfords at lunchtime so we're only having a snack this evening. You know what she's like though.

Let me ask her if there is anything that you lads could eat, and then you could invite Greg for supper too." Putting his hand over the mouthpiece, Peter turned to his wife and explained that James had asked if Greg could come over that evening and he was wondering if she would be able to feed them easily?

"If they'll settle for French bread, pâté, cheese and salad, followed by apple pie, they're in luck," Annabelle replied smiling. Peter relayed this information to his son who said that it sounded absolutely wonderful.

James walked across to Greg and said he was welcome to supper if he could survive on bread, pâté and cheese. His friend replied that he could think of nothing better, and drove home thinking about what to wear for his first visit to Riverside House and how best he could impress ex-Wing Commander Peter Rowlands.

In fact, Greg needn't have worried at all. After greeting him and exchanging pleasantries, Peter disappeared off to talk with Annabelle in the Conservatory, whilst he and James ate together in the kitchen with the dogs sitting under the table. After some exploratory sniffing, Allsort had decided that Zizi was probably all right, and lay down with her head on James' foot. She felt that the presence of another dog must mean that they would be going for a good walk later. She was not to be disappointed. Supper finished, leads were clipped on and the four of them set out to walk to the Beetle and Wedge.

CHAPTER 21

Susie awoke on Monday to the prospect of another long and boring day. She guessed that her only source of entertainment was going to be Alf's barbecue and she would have to go to that on her own, but she supposed it was better than sitting at home. Breakfast over, Susie decided she would have a look at her emails and was pleased to see that she had another one from the dating site. Logging on, she discovered that Dave had replied to her message. In answer to her questions, he said that he shared a house in Bicester with a couple of mates and that he drove a van, as he was an electrician. He also asked if she would like to meet up. "Oh God," thought Susie, "He really doesn't sound like the catch of the year. If he's sharing a house, then he's almost certainly renting, and I don't think I can cope with someone with a van." She didn't bother replying, deciding her time would be better spent checking out some more profiles to see if there was anyone that she liked the look of. Before she knew what had happened, two fruitless hours had slipped by.

Susie went to the kitchen, made herself a coffee and raided the biscuit jar. "This won't do," she told George, "I need to make contact with someone before I go down to The Crown. Perhaps the coffee and biscuits will help my brain." Settling herself back down at the dining table, Susie concentrated on the matter in hand. It was amazing how the time disappeared, but by midday she had sent off two messages. One was to a chap called Nick who lived in Oxford and said he was an architect and the other to a Simon who lived in Banbury and said he was a consultant. Doctor? IT? Would she ever find out? They were both nice looking and were both 27. Thinking about it logically, Simon couldn't possibly be a consultant surgeon or physician at the age of 27, so Susie guessed he was involved with IT. Feeling a bit more hopeful about finding a few more fish in the sea, Susie decided to have one last search before calling it a day. She was happily scrolling through the photos of men in her area, when her heart skipped a beat. Smiling out from the screen was a picture of Jonathan! Feeling cold and shaky, Susie read his profile. He admitted to being a married man and said that he was looking for some excitement on the side. He didn't want any commitment and as he travelled with work, he had endless possibilities for meetings. Susie put her head in her hands and burst into tears. She knew that Jonathan was married, but she thought that he loved her. She sat and sobbed her heart out.

After about an hour, Susie decided that she would have to pull herself together. A sad Susie went upstairs, had a soak in the bath and changed into a pair of jeans and a bright red sweater. She carefully applied her make-up so that it was impossible to tell she had been crying, picked up her bag and headed out to the car. It was cold and damp outside, but nowhere near as dreary as she felt.

In less than five minutes Susie was at The Crown. The car park was crammed, with no space even for her Mini, and she was really starting to feel that the world was determined to make her life miserable in every possible way when she saw David Timmins coming out of his cottage. She opened the window to say hello and David suggested that she park in front of his garage. She was quite surprised to find him waiting for her when she got out of the car, so they went into the pub together.

As ever, Alf greeted them warmly. David bought a white wine for Susie and a pint for himself. The pig was roasting outside and a delicious smell was wafting into the bar from the pub garden. Alf told them that it would be ready soon, so David and Susie wandered out and found themselves a table.

David couldn't believe his luck, bumping into Susie again so soon. He told her that he was surprised she was on her own, which made her laugh. He wasn't quite sure he got the joke, but took it as a good sign. She drained her glass in record time and got up to buy both of them another drink.

By this time the garden was filling up, and Alf was happily carving the pig. David and Susie went and filled their plates with slices of the hot meat and all the trimmings. They agreed that it was absolutely delicious.

David studied Susie as she ate. He thought how beautiful she was, but that there was a sadness in her eyes. Noticing her glass was empty again, he asked if she would like another drink and she readily agreed. He'd have to make sure she didn't drive home, but they could cross that bridge later on. He was enjoying himself far too much to worry about it now.

Susie was still seething over Jonathan's online profile. She had intended to flirt with all and sundry in retaliation, but it hadn't crossed her mind that she might actually be attracted to anyone. Maybe it was the wine, but David was looking pretty good right now.

Suddenly it started to rain, so everyone made a dash for the pub, which became extremely crowded. David suggested to Susie that she might like to have coffee back at his cottage, or even another glass of wine? By this time Susie had drunk well over a bottle, but the wine had let her wicked side out, and she thought another glass of wine would be a wonderful idea, so she followed David back to Nag's Head Cottage.

Susie collapsed onto the sofa while David went to fetch a bottle of wine. After she'd downed yet another glass he suggested that a cup of coffee might be a good idea. Susie pouted a bit, but agreed that he was probably right. David went off to the kitchen and Susie hazily wondered how she was going to get home. It was absolutely chucking it down now, so she didn't feel like walking and she certainly wasn't fit to drive. At least she didn't have to go to work tomorrow. That was a definite bonus.

As though sensing her thoughts, David returned with the coffee saying they would have to think about getting her home. He asked if there was anyone she could call to come and fetch her. Sadly, Susie shook her head. "OK then," said David. "I'll call you a taxi. I would have been quite happy to walk you home but it's pissing down and we don't want to get soaked, although the walk would probably do you good!" Indignantly, Susie assured him that she was quite capable of walking herself home, if David would just lend her a waterproof jacket.

He ignored her, and called a taxi.

CHAPTER 22

Thursday was an eventful day for the Rowlands family. James was having his hair re-styled, Susie arranged her first internet date and Peter and Annabelle plotted how they were going to deal with Kevin the photographer.

James was both excited and apprehensive about having something major done to his hair. The Cutting Studio was very upmarket and James felt quite self-conscious sitting among what he considered to be the beautiful people. After a few minutes, Russell came over and ran his fingers through James' hair, asking what he had in mind. James wondered whether he dared add some colour. Russell produced a shade chart and suggested that as James' hair was just long enough, he should put three different colours through it to give it depth. "Gosh," said James, "three?" Russell nodded, and said that he also recommended a deep conditioning treatment followed by a scalp massage, which would leave James both looking and feeling fabulous. "Sod it," thought James. "Why not?" So he agreed to everything that Russell had suggested. He was swathed in a large gown and one of the apprentices brought him a cup of herbal tea to help him relax.

Three hours later, James couldn't believe what he was seeing when he looked in the mirror. His hair shone with subtle lights and was no longer mousey brown, but a rather stunning blond mix that looked very natural. It had also been cut into a proper style, and although he still had hair coming across his face, it wasn't flopping into his eyes. The bill was an impressive £195, but what the hell? He could afford it.

*****

Over in Enstone, Susie was back online. She had arranged to meet Nick for a drink the following evening at the Deddington Arms Hotel. She was still feeling very sore about finding Jonathan on the site, and much as she loved him, she wanted a normal relationship where she could go out and about with someone without him constantly looking over his shoulder, either because he was checking to see if anyone he knew might have spotted them together or because he was checking out another girl. The trouble was that Jonathan was glamorous and exciting, and replacing him was going to be very difficult indeed. Still, she had made a start and as the highlights of her half term week had been the nail bar and Alf's barbecue, a date with a stranger seemed quite promising.

*****

In Moulsford, Peter and Annabelle were working out how they were going to deal with the photographer. He had phoned Annabelle and arranged to come to Riverside House the next morning at 10.30 am to collect the money. James would be out with his personal shopper and Peter would leave the house and slip back unseen. Peter had given Annabelle his dictaphone so that she could get evidence of the blackmail and then they would confront him together and threaten him with going to the police unless he handed over the negatives. Annabelle was worried that he might become violent, but Peter said he wasn't in the least bit worried and that he would knock the bugger's block off, should it become necessary. Annabelle prayed that it wouldn't.

She had just gone through to the kitchen to start preparations for supper when James came home. "Wow, darling, you look absolutely amazing," Annabelle cooed in admiration. "Go and show your father. In fact, I'll come with you. Peter darling," she called, going through to the den, "just look at James' hair. Doesn't he look great?" Peter glanced up from the Telegraph and grunted that James certainly looked different. "Don't take any notice of him," Annabelle told her son, "RAF Officers didn't have exciting haircuts. They weren't called 'The Brylcream Boys' for nothing, you know." They all laughed and Annabelle went back to the kitchen, asking her menfolk what they would like to drink.

A few minutes later, Annabelle returned to the snug with a gin and tonic for Peter, a can of lager for James and a glass of Chablis for herself. As James drank his beer, he thought about Greg and wondered why he was so keen to impress him. No-one had ever had this effect upon him before. Certainly none of the girls he had dated. What did this mean, he wondered? Greg didn't have a girlfriend. Could Greg possibly be gay, and if so, what effect could that have on their friendship? Draining his glass, he thought that perhaps he should talk to Susie about his feelings for Greg. Hopefully they could meet up again next Thursday after he had been to see David Timmins.

*****

When they had finished supper, James took Allsort for her evening walk and decided that he would ring his sister. Susie sounded really pleased to hear from him and told James that her half term week had been very quiet. It was just the opening James needed, so he asked her if she would like to have dinner the following Thursday. That was the day of Susie's court appearance in Stratford so she willingly agreed, thinking she would need something to cheer her up after that. She had already planned on taking a sickie from school that day and possibly the Friday as well, to make it seem more convincing. As they were chatting, Susie decided that she would tell her brother about having to go to court. James listened sympathetically and then asked Susie if she would like him to go with her. They could go up to Stratford together and then she could kill time in Chipping Norton whilst he had his appointment with David Timmins. What did she think? Susie replied that she thought it was a great idea and they arranged that he would pick her up at 9.00 am the following Thursday.

*****

Susie got ready for bed that night feeling better than she had for a while. She had a date the next evening and James was being really supportive. Jonathan would also be back in the UK by the middle of next week, so maybe she would get a chance to see him too? "What do you think about it all, George?" she asked the large ginger cat as she put some treats into his dish. As always, he looked at her adoringly and purred.

CHAPTER 23

James set off bright and early for Reading the following morning. Peter left shortly afterwards. He drove around for a few minutes, until he was sure he wasn't being followed, and then parked up and walked back up to the house through the back garden, so that there was no chance of him being seen.

James and Penny arrived outside John Lewis at the same time. Penny told James that his hair looked fab, and suggested that they go for a cup of coffee whilst they worked out their plan of action. Sitting down at the table, James pulled a piece of paper out of his pocket, explaining to Penny that he had written down a few things that he thought he needed to buy. She scanned the list with a smile and suggested to James that he went for a slightly more grown up look. She also suggested that he concentrated on his footwear, as she didn't consider trainers to look particularly smart.

They finished their coffee and headed off to the shops. Penny suggested that John Lewis would be a good starting point, as they had a variety of different concessions, which should give James some idea of the brands that he liked. The morning whizzed by and Penny helped James make some great purchases. He really couldn't wait to show Greg his new image! Although they had only booked a half day appointment, he asked Penny if he could take her for lunch and then carry on shopping for the rest of the afternoon. He really wanted to make the most of her knowledge while she was there, as he felt it would give him the confidence to go shopping on his own in the future.

Lunch finished, the two of them hit the shops again and James' Mini Cooper was loaded to the roof when he went home. He had spent around £3,000 with Penny's fee, but what the hell – he and Greg were worth it! Penny was delighted too. A new client who had paid her for six hours at £100 per hour. She'd like one of those every week!

*****

Peter and Annabelle sat in the study with a pot of coffee, waiting for their visitor.

Just after 10.30 am the doorbell rang. Peter gave Annabelle a reassuring hug before she went to answer the door. Kevin the photographer looked her up and down with a leering grin on his smarmy face. Annabelle shuddered. "Got my money, have you babe?" he said in his ghastly nasal tone.

"Yes." Annabelle nodded. "But I would really like to have the negatives." Kevin snorted with laughter.

"I'll bet you would. But are you going to make it worth my while, I wonder?"

"I'll do anything you ask, if it means that you keep my children out of it," Annabelle pleaded.

"Yeah, well no offence darlin', but all I'm interested in is your cash and I don't reckon you've got the kind of money that these pictures are worth. I mean, we'd be talking about tens of thousands at the very least."

"Just name your price, I'll find the money somehow." Annabelle knew she nearly had him now.

"All right then, fifty grand for the negatives and another twenty for the prints. And that's a bargain."

"So, if I pay you seventy thousand pounds, you'll give me all the photos and the negatives, and leave me and my family alone?" Annabelle asked.

"Sounds fair to me." Kevin sneered.

"Sounds like blackmail to me," Peter remarked, coming through to the hall from his study.

"I don't know what you're talking about." The photographer bluffed, but it was clear that he was shaken by Peter's unexpected appearance.

Annabelle slid the dictaphone out of her pocket and waved it under Kevin's pointy nose.

"Would you like me to play it back then, to jog your memory. Or shall I just take it straight to the police?"

The photographer went pale. Annabelle smiled sweetly. Peter's voice was like thunder as he spoke.

"Right, now that we are all clear about where we stand, I suggest that you get off our property before I have you arrested for trespassing, as well as attempted blackmail. If you haven't returned all of my wife's photos and negatives within twenty four hours we will be contacting the police, be in no doubt about that and I'm sure that they will be extremely interested in everything that we have to tell them, just as I'm sure that my wife isn't your only victim."

"Yeah, I'll get your stinking photos. Have a good look and see what kind of a slag you married. Or maybe you already know. She never took much convincing, did you darlin?" Kevin spat.

"Don't push your luck." Peter growled. "You've got twenty four hours. Now, get off my property before I change my mind and call the police right now." Muttering all kinds of obscenities, Kevin hurried over to the dirty black car that was parked in the middle of the drive and skidded away.

"Oh darling, you were wonderful," said Annabelle. Peter wrapped her in his arms.

"What a ghastly little man," he said. "That's the worst of it over and done with. And you were wonderful too. In fact, we make a pretty wonderful team." Annabelle buried her head in her husband's chest. She could feel the weight beginning to lift. She prayed that Kevin would return the photos. It almost seemed too good to be true, that she might finally be able to put all of this behind her.

*****

Annabelle couldn't believe how much James was carrying when he came home that evening. She eyed up the bags. "Are you going to let me have a peek inside?"

"Certainly not!" James replied, sounding embarrassed. "You'll have to wait until I choose to wear something."

"Are you doing the shop for me tomorrow?" she asked. "I bet I'll see you wearing something new then." James blushed and headed for the stairs.

"Would you like a beer?" Annabelle called after him.

"You really are the best, Mother," James called back happily.

"Don't I know it!" replied Annabelle, laughing. "By the way, how much did you spend?" James pretended not to hear as he bounded up the stairs, two at a time.

*****

Having sorted out drinks for them all, Annabelle went to find Peter and tell him about James' shopping trip. "And, " she said to him, "I don't want any sarcastic comments. You grunted and pulled a face about his hair yesterday, and I don't want to see you do that again."

"For God's sake, woman, can't you see he's had it coloured?" asked an exasperated Peter. "Only women and nancy boys do that." Annabelle winced.

At that moment, James came in to the room and, taking his beer, took a long and grateful swig. "You look as though you needed that," said Peter. "Was shopping hard work? Your mother always seems to enjoy it." Annabelle glared at her husband. Peter took a deep breath. "Right, both of you go and put on your glad rags and I'll book a table at the Beetle. How about it?"

"Lovely idea darling," said Annabelle, heading for the stairs.

*****

While the rest of her family were preparing for dinner at the Beetle and Wedge, Susie was preparing for her date with Nick. She hadn't been on a blind date before and wondered what on earth she should wear? After trying on a couple of different outfits, she settled on a pair of white skinny jeans, a black cashmere sweater, and a pair of black wedge heeled sandals. From her vast collection of jewellery she selected a large silver pendant on a long chain, a pair of silver hoop earrings and a couple of pretty silver rings. "That'll do," she said to herself.

"Wish me luck, George," she said as she went downstairs. "I'm going to meet a strange man. Well, at least I hope he's not strange. I'm going to meet a man I don't know. Be a good boy while I'm out."

She arrived at the Deddington Arms just after 7 o'clock, to find Nick waiting in the car park for her. He indicated a space where he thought she should park. This irritated Susie straight away, but she obediently shuffled her car backwards and forwards until he appeared satisfied. They then went into the bar together.

Nick got the drinks. Susie decided that discretion was definitely the better part of valour and chose an orange juice. She watched him at the bar and wasn't impressed by what she saw, as he was fiddling about in his purse to find the correct money to pay for the drinks. Eventually he came back, carrying what looked like a half of shandy and her orange juice.

Susie thanked him politely and said that it was nice to meet him and that he was the first person she had met from the dating site, as she had only just joined. He replied that he had met quite a few ladies, but none of them had really been to his liking. Under her breath Susie muttered that she wasn't surprised. For Christ's sake, real men didn't drink halves of anything. She had imagined that Nick would be sophisticated, but sadly that wasn't the case and as he droned on and on about himself Susie wondered where the ladies' loo was and whether she could climb out through the window.

She looked at her watch. It was only 7.45 pm. She couldn't go yet and furthermore her glass was empty and there didn't seem to be any sign of Nick buying her another drink. "Sod this," she said to herself. She turned to her date, saying, "I need another drink. Can I get you anything?" Nick asked for half a shandy. Susie made her way to the bar where she ordered Nick's drink plus a small glass of wine for herself.

The date was hard work, and all she wanted to do was go home. Nick was nice looking, but that's all there was to him. Having stared at her empty wine glass for about 15 minutes, Susie turned to Nick and said she had better be going home. He was clearly unimpressed by this and asked her why she was leaving so soon. Susie garbled an excuse about not having eaten, as she'd had to work late. Nick replied that he thought he had made it clear they were just meeting for a drink. Susie agreed that he had made it perfectly clear, which was why she was leaving now. With that she got up and made her way to the car before Nick had time to say anything else to her. She shot out of the car park and headed back home to Rose Cottage and George, who was far better company than her date had been.

The first thing she did when she got home was to pour herself a very large glass of wine and have another look on the internet. There had to be a man out there for her, other than bloody Jonathan.

CHAPTER 24

Susie spent a lot of time online over the weekend, but didn't really achieve a great deal. She chatted with a few men but not wishing to repeat Friday's disaster, she didn't make any arrangements to see anyone.

After her pancake-flat half term, she was almost glad to go back to school. She was just settling into her work when she received a text. "Will be in UK today – earlier than planned. Do you fancy a guest tonight?" Did she fancy a guest? Did the Pope wear a silly hat? Quickly she replied "Have missed you and can't wait to see you. What time do you think you'll get here?" All thoughts about Jonathan's online profile were immediately erased from Susie's mind as she thought about the evening ahead.

The rest of the morning flew by and at lunchtime Susie went into Woodstock to buy food and booze for the evening. She got some bits and bobs from the deli, and a bottle of decent champagne. Eating was going to take a back seat tonight as far as Susie was concerned.

On her way back into school, Susie was waylaid by some of the girls. She asked one or two of them what they had done over the half term break and the Browne twins told her all about their trip to the New Forest and the lovely hotel they had stayed in, with a big swimming pool. Emily said they had only stayed for two nights at the hotel as their Daddy had to go to Canada for the Grand Prix, but that he was coming home tomorrow and that they were really excited to see what he would bring back for them. Susie couldn't help thinking that they weren't the only ones who were excited to see what Jonathan had for them, only she wouldn't have to wait until tomorrow for her treat.

Susie couldn't wait for school to finish that afternoon so that she could get home and get the champagne in the fridge. She cursed when she saw Mrs MacDonald in her front garden. She was a lovely neighbour, but unbelievably nosey and she always wanted to chat.

"Hello dear," said Mrs M, as Susie went to get her shopping out of the boot, "what sort of a day have you had, then?"

"Hell," thought Susie shoving the champagne as far down in the bag as she could as she didn't want her neighbour to see it and ask any questions. Straightening up, she smiled at Mrs MacDonald, said she'd had a busy day and made some comment about the weather, before apologising that she couldn't stand and chat, but she had some things she needed to get in the freezer as quickly as possible. Mrs MacDonald said that she quite understood and that you couldn't have food going to waste, so Susie quickly scuttled indoors.

Once inside and with the door safely closed behind her, Susie unpacked her shopping and put the champagne in the fridge. She felt the cottage would look better with a few flowers and seeing that Mrs MacDonald was busy talking with another neighbour, she scooted out in to the back garden where she managed to find a few roses which she plonked in a vase. Sadly, she did not possess her mother's artistic flair, or her cooking abilities either. She didn't really know what she'd inherited from her mother in fact. Annabelle was so perfect and petite, so organised and unflustered. Her life seemed utterly charmed. Susie felt useless by comparison.

She went upstairs and ran herself a bath, pouring in a generous helping of bath foam. Whilst the bath was running, she chose her clothes for the evening – a denim mini skirt and a low backed white tee shirt, a pair of silver beaded flip flops, some chunky jewellery and a spray of Calvin Klein's Obsession.

Before stepping into the bath she texted Jonathan and told him that the front door would be open, so that all he had to do was come in. She didn't want him lingering on the door step where prying eyes could see him any longer than was necessary.

*****

Jonathan parked his car in his usual place, took his briefcase out of the boot and walked round to Susie's cottage. It was a pleasant evening and he cheerfully smiled at the little girl swinging on the gate at the top of the lane. The girl smiled back and said "hello". He was somewhat disconcerted to see Susie's neighbour in her front garden, busy weeding her flower border. They wished each other a good evening. Should he walk in to the cottage or should he knock? If he walked in, perhaps the woman would think he was related to Susie and not pay any attention to him? Anyway, for goodness sake, she didn't know who he was and that he was married.

Susie ran into his arms as soon as she saw him. They kissed passionately. "I've missed you so much," she gasped.

"Well, I'm here now until tomorrow morning," he replied. "Let me have a shower while you pour me a drink and then we'll have to think about making up for lost time." Susie opened the fridge door and reached in for the champagne. She waited five minutes, poured two glasses, and carried them upstairs to join her lover. He was still in the shower, so she waited patiently, draped across the bed.

*****

Despite the fact that Jonathan was knackered, the two of them spent a very pleasant evening. Jonathan smiled when he saw Susie's best efforts for supper. Angela was an accomplished cook and extremely well organised; Susie was haphazard at best, but her sexiness made up for everything.

She tried to talk to him again about her speeding ticket and the fact that she had to go to court on Thursday. Jonathan made an effort to listen sympathetically, but really he wasn't interested. It was her own silly fault after all. He also felt that sometimes Susie didn't quite get the plot. Their relationship was based purely on having fun. He didn't want to be bored with any of the mundane details in her life, he had enough of those to deal with at home and at work. Draining his glass, Jonathan suggested that they have an early night.

*****

As his body clock was still on Canadian time, Jonathan woke early the next morning. Susie was sleeping peacefully and, as he didn't want to disturb her, Jonathan showered and dressed quietly and went outside into the back garden, where he sat with a cup of coffee. He didn't realise that he was being watched with interest by a very puzzled little person.

Coffee finished, Jonathan went back inside and poured two glasses of orange juice which he carried upstairs. Susie was awake now and amazed that he had got up and dressed and hadn't made love to her. When she pointed this out to him, Jonathan assured her that would soon be put right. He started to unbutton his shirt.

*****

He wasn't in a particular hurry to get to work, so he lingered over breakfast as long as possible and left the cottage after Susie. He walked her to her car, and throwing caution to the wind, kissed her again and told her that he would see her soon. His words were heard with interest.

Going back inside, Jonathan decided it was time to text Angela and let her know that he was at the airport and that he would see them all that evening. He then switched off his phone so that she couldn't try to call him and discover that he was in the UK after all.

After yet another cup of coffee, Jonathan drove to his office.

CHAPTER 25

Susie drove into work feeling very happy. She had just spent a wonderful evening and night with Jonathan. Surely the thing on the dating website was old and he wasn't using it? Most probably he'd forgotten that it was there. He must love her, because they always had such a fantastic time together. It was going to be a short week too, although for the wrong reason. Susie had decided to skive off work sick on the Thursday for her court appearance, as she was only allowed to take time off during term time for dire emergencies and she had already used the excuse of the dentist for her trip to Monaco. Having already decided that it would look more convincing if she were off sick for two days, that was Friday taken care of, giving her four days away from school. Perhaps she would be able to see Jonathan again on Friday ,if he was at the factory, and there was no reason to suppose that he wouldn't be. She had left him back at Rose Cottage as he hadn't been in a hurry to go to work, wanting to spend as much time with her as possible, (she thought), and the first thing he had thought of when he had been able to get away from Canada earlier than he expected was to come and see her, and he'd brought her a bottle of perfume, so life was indeed good.

*****

Isobel Stanley was taking the third year juniors for their first History lesson since the half term Jubilee break. She really enjoyed this class as it contained some bright pupils who were eager to learn. Her lesson plan for today was to talk about the Queen's Jubilee and what they had all done to celebrate. She started off by telling the class what she and her husband had done. They had gone away for the weekend and gone to Derby Day at Epsom. Mrs Stanley went on to describe the outfit that she had worn, and said that she and her husband had had a glass of champagne to toast Her Majesty, and to make the day even better, her husband had picked the Derby winner and won some money. She didn't tell the children how much, as she didn't want to feel that she could be encouraging them to gamble!

The class was mesmerised with Mrs Stanley's story and asked her all sorts of questions. What was the horse's name that had won the Derby? Had she and Mr Stanley stayed in a hotel? Where was it? Was the food nice? What else had they done that weekend? Isobel answered all their questions and then told them it was time for them to tell her about their weekends and half term week as well.

Had any of them been to the Derby? No. Had any of them been to stay in a hotel? A few hands went up and Mrs Stanley asked the children who had put up their hands to come and stand at the front of the class, so that they could tell the others about their experiences. Five little girls came forward - the Browne twins, Sophie Smith, Molly Fisher and Victoria Newton. Patsy Palmer felt more left out than ever. Those Browne twins were always doing something nice - unlike her. Mrs Stanley asked if any of them had been up to London to watch the river pageant, and Victoria said that she had. She was then asked to tell the class about the hotel where she stayed and what she had done on the day when the pageant took place. Victoria explained that she and her parents had stayed at The Ritz and that the hotel was very beautiful and had big chandeliers. On the day that the Queen sailed down the river, they had watched her from one of the bridges, but she couldn't remember which one. It had been raining, so they had had to wear raincoats and Daddy had sat her on his shoulders so that she could see better. It had been cold and she had been glad to go to McDonald's afterwards for a burger. There then followed a discussion about the river pageant on the Thames.

Sophie and her family had been to the seaside at Bournemouth for the whole week and stayed at The Royal Bath Hotel, which overlooked the sea. She told the class that she could see the sea from her bedroom window. She had shared a room with her older sister, but it had a door straight through to her parents' bedroom, which they hadn't been allowed to close. It had been a lovely holiday.

The Browne twins went next and took it in turns to speak. Emily explained that they had stayed in a hotel in the New Forest and had visited Bournemouth and seen the sea too. Alice said that they hadn't been there for the whole week, as Daddy had had to fly out to Canada for work and that he was coming home today and that they hoped he'd be there when they got in from school.

"Why was he at Miss Rowlands' house this morning, and why did he kiss her and say that he'd see her soon? He's not in Canada, he's in England now," came Patsy Palmer's voice from the back of the class. Emily and Alice looked horrified and as though they were about to cry.

"You're wrong. He wasn't there. He wasn't. He's on a plane," said Emily.

"That's right," said Alice, rushing between the desks and grabbing Patsy by the hair, "He's on a plane coming home. You're making up a story 'cos you have a silly, boring life, with no friends and you're jealous of me and Emily. So there." With that she yanked Patsy's pony tail hard, making the other girl yelp.

Isobel Stanley tried to disentangle the two children who were now slapping and punching each other. Finally she managed to pull them apart.

110

"That is no way for young ladies to behave," she said. "Alice, apologise to Patricia at once."

"Shan't. She's a liar," said Alice stubbornly.

"I won't accept that kind of behaviour Alice," said Mrs Stanley. "Now go and stand outside Miss Jennings' office. I shall be there shortly."

"I'll go with her," said her sister.

"No you won't," replied her teacher, "you'll go back to your seat. Sophie, Molly and Victoria, could you also go and sit down please. Now, Patricia, I'm sure you made a mistake in thinking you saw Mr Browne at Miss Rowlands' house this morning. It was most probably someone who looked rather like him."

"I didn't make a mistake," replied Patsy sulkily. "He was there last night too. And I saw him drinking a cup of coffee in the garden this morning. He's often there. He parks his car round the corner where he thinks no-one will see it, but I do." Emily started to cry.

"Why would my Daddy be staying with Miss Rowlands, Mrs Stanley? We only live in Kirtlington. It isn't far away. He could come home to us."

Isobel did her best to comfort the little girl. "Now, we don't know that it was your Daddy," she said, doing her best to smile and pretend that all was well, "Patricia must have made a mistake. Particularly if Daddy is in Canada at the moment." Patsy persisted that she hadn't made a mistake and Emily continued to cry. The bell went for the end of class and Isobel stayed with the children until the next teacher arrived. Fortunately she had a free period next, so she decided to take Emily to the Staff Room, where she found someone to look after her, whilst she went to deal with Alice.

She found the child where she had told her to be – outside the headmistress's office. "She's a liar," Alice shouted, as soon as she saw her teacher. At that moment Miss Jennings came out of her office, wanting to know why Alice was shouting. Mrs Stanley took Alice into Miss Jennings' office and told the Headmistress about what had happened in her class. Miss Jennings could see that both pupil and teacher were distressed. She also tried to comfort Alice by telling her that Patricia Palmer had probably made a mistake and that there was nothing to worry about. She went on to say that regardless of what Patricia had said, Alice had behaved very badly by pulling her hair and starting a fight, and that she would have to tell her parents about it. For the moment, however, Mrs Stanley would take Alice back to class, where she would apologise to Patricia. Did she understand? Alice nodded mutely. "As you have a free period, Mrs Stanley, I would like a word with you please, as soon as you have taken Alice back."

*****

Having installed Alice safely back in the classroom and having explained to Miss Edwards, the Maths teacher, what had happened, Isobel Stanley returned to the Headmistress's office. Miss Jennings was looking extremely agitated. "We shall have to see Susie Rowlands and hear her side of the story," said Miss Jennings. "I really can't believe that she can be involved in any way with a parent; she must realise how inappropriate that would be. Would you be kind enough to ask her to join us, Mrs Stanley?"

A few minutes later Isobel Stanley returned with Susie Rowlands, who had a puzzled expression on her face. "You wanted to see me, Miss Jennings?" "Yes I do, Susie. Please sit down." The Headmistress indicated a chair and Susie sat down, surprised to see that Mrs Stanley hadn't left the room.

Miss Jennings told Susie that Mrs Stanley had had a very unfortunate incident in her class during the previous period which involved the Browne twins and Patricia Palmer. Patricia had said certain things that Alice and Emily had not agreed with and now Mrs Stanley would explain to Susie what had happened. Susie was surprised and wondered how what had happened in a lesson could possibly affect her. She found out very quickly!

"Hell," she thought, "how can I get out of this one? First Mummy and Monaco and now this."

Susie realised that Mrs Jennings was speaking to her. "I know that both you and Patricia live in Enstone, so I know that she could have been outside your property at various times and observed the comings and goings there. I also know that Mr and Mrs Browne gave a party for the girls' birthday recently and that Patricia went to that party, so I'm quite certain that she would recognise Mr Browne. I am going to have to tell the Brownes about this unfortunate incident as Alice started a fight with Patricia, which is behaviour that is totally unacceptable to Woodstock Academy. We have a nice class of girl here. You must also realise that it would be totally unacceptable for a member of staff to have any kind of inappropriate relationship with a parent. Could you give me your side of the story please?"

Susie decided to try and play for time. She smiled at Miss Jennings and said, " Surely what I do in my own time is up to me, Miss Jennings?"

"I'll take it to be true then," came the reply.

"What do you mean?" asked Susie, somewhat crossly.

"You haven't denied it, Miss Rowlands, so I will assume it to be true."

"And what, may I ask, do you assume to be true, Miss Jennings?" Miss Jennings wrinkled her face in distaste, "Fornicating with a married man, who is a parent of pupils at Woodstock Academy."

"I suppose it would be acceptable if it was Chipping Norton Comp?" snapped Susie. "My God, what a po-faced snob you are." At this insult, Miss Jennings' face turned an unattractive shade of puce.

"Perhaps you'd care to retract that comment, Miss Rowlands," she said. Susie mimicked her,

"Perhaps you'd care to stop being a po-faced snob, Miss Jennings."

Miss Jennings might have turned puce, but Mrs Stanley had blanched and wondered how she could possibly intervene. She could see this interview having disastrous consequences. It did appear to her that Susie and Mr Browne probably were having an affair and even if they weren't, there were going to be some unpleasant questions asked in the Browne household, as even if Miss Jennings didn't contact the Brownes about Alice's behaviour, when they got home, the children would certainly be telling their parents what Patricia had had to say. She opened her mouth to try and calm the situation "May I?"

"You may not do anything but leave the room, thank you Mrs Stanley," said Miss Jennings, "you have become supernumerary." Silently Isobel Stanley left the room.

"I demand to know, Miss Rowlands, whether or not you and Mr Browne have been having a sordid little affair," said Miss Jennings. At this Susie saw bright, scarlet red, and didn't even think before she opened her mouth,

"No, Miss Jennings, we haven't been having a sordid little affair, and for the record what I do in my own time has nothing to do with you at all. However, for your information, you nosey old cow, Jonathan and I have been having a full blown, mad passionate love affair, with unabandoned sex at every opportunity. Does that satisfy you, you po-faced, prim little woman? You've probably never had decent sex. No, on second thoughts, you've probably never had sex at all, shrivelled up old prune that you are. Woodstock Academy this, Woodstock Academy that. Bloody Woodstock Academy's the only life that you have."

"Have you quite finished, Miss Rowlands?" asked Miss Jennings coldly, "because I am going to have to issue you with a formal warning for inappropriate behaviour." Susie cut across her,

"Do you know what you can do with your formal warning? You can shove it up your arse. I've had enough of this place and I'm leaving now. Go find yourself another dogsbody. I'm out of here." With that Susie got to her feet and went out, slamming the door behind her.

CHAPTER 26

Susie felt sick. What the hell had she done? Put herself out of a job, for starters. As soon as she got home, she must text Jonathan and ask him to phone her urgently so that she could let him know what had happened.

She dashed up the front path, and flinging herself on to the sofa quickly texted Jonathan.

"Serious problem. Please call. Xxx."

Fifteen minutes went by and her phone remained silent. Time for another text.

"I really need to speak to you urgently. Please call me. Xxx."

Twenty minutes later she received a reply: "Can't. I'm busy. It'll have to wait."

"Shit, Shit, shit," Susie said to George. "It's 20 past 4. The bloody children will be home soon, telling their mother everything. What am I going to do?" The cat looked up at her adoringly.

*****

Susie's messages had irritated Jonathan. He had only left her that morning, after making her the first person he saw on his return from Canada. What could be that urgent? What sort of a serious problem could she possibly have that he could help with? He was adamant that he wasn't going to dance to her tune by ringing her up immediately. She could wait until the following day.

Arriving back in Kirtlington and opening his front door, he was surprised not to hear the children's voices and even more surprised that they didn't come running when he shouted "Daddy's home." The only person to appear was Angela and she didn't look very happy at all. "Hello, darling, is something the matter?" he enquired solicitously, whilst thinking that he wasn't in the mood for sulking. "Where are the children?"

"I've asked Julia Bayliss if she would look after them for a couple of hours for me, as we need to talk." she replied.

Jonathan raised his eyebrows. "Don't I get a kiss first?" he asked, leaning towards her.

"No, you don't, Jonathan," she snapped. "You have a hell of a lot of explaining to do, and it had better be good."

Alarm bells started to go off in Jonathan's mind. "At least let me have a drink while we chat. I've been travelling most of the day, you know."

"Have you really?" said his wife. "I wonder?" Jonathan poured himself a very large scotch indeed.

"Can I get you anything, Angela, darling?" he asked. His wife declined emphatically and gave him an icy look as she sat down and started talking.

"How could you, Jonathan? How could you? With the secretary at the children's school as well? You've humiliated me and upset the girls. I always knew you were a professional flirt, but shagging Miss Rowlands really takes the biscuit."

He was going to have to think quickly here. "What on earth are you talking about, Angela? Who's Miss Rowlands?"

"Nice try, Jonathan, but this time you've been caught with your pants down, quite literally. One of the twins' classmates has seen you coming and going from the little tart's house on more than one occasion. She also saw you kissing her this morning and saying that you would see her soon. Alice was so distraught by what her little friend had to say that she physically attacked the girl and so it all came tumbling out then, didn't it? They had to go to Miss Jennings and I've had to deal with the humiliation of having that snooty headmistress telling me that my husband's been shagging around behind my back." Jonathan shook his head in horrified disbelief. "Oh yes, she questioned Miss Slutface, and she was more than happy to confirm that it's all true. In fact, she seems to think that the two of you are actually in love. I can hardly bear to show my face at that school now and God alone knows how you're going to brazen it out, but then brazen should be your middle name."

"I think you'll find that this is all a mistake," said Jonathan lamely.

"Mistake my foot," snapped Angela. "Why would the little tramp say she was having sex with you if she wasn't? She'll almost certainly lose her job now, won't she?"

Christ alive, thought Jonathan. This was a tricky one. No wonder Susie had wanted to talk to him urgently. But why, oh why, had she told the headmistress what they had been doing? "Do calm down, darling, " he said, turning to his wife. "I know who you mean now. I think you'll find she's just being vindictive. The girl made a pass at me on one occasion and I rebuffed her. I think she's just being spiteful, that's all."

"Stop insulting me, Jonathan!" shrieked Angela, finally losing her cool completely. "A school girl says that she has seen you to-ing and fro-ing from this trollop's house over a period of months and you still try and deny it. Let's accept that you're a waster and move on. The worst bit is that you were seen there last night and then again this morning. We have two little girls to comfort and try to convince that you weren't at that wretched girl's house overnight last night. As for us and our relationship, that's another matter completely."

Jonathan decided it best to stop protesting his innocence, because as

Angela said, they must think about the girls. He didn't want to lose his children, but he could also see that they could prove extremely helpful to him in his quest to get Angela on his side. Marriage to Angela suited him. She ran the house well and could be relied upon should he need to do any business entertaining. Clearly, Susie would have to go. She was now far too dangerous. He couldn't believe that the silly little cow had confessed all to the Headmistress.

"I'm not trying to insult you, Angela. I care about you far too much to do that. As you say, we must present a united front to the girls, and we need to discuss just how we are going to do that." His wife gave him a withering look.

"We won't discuss my feelings just now, Jonathan, because we need to fetch Alice and Emily soon and we need to have our story straight."

Jonathan got up and poured himself another drink. He was really going to have to be creative this time. Never in his wildest dreams had he imagined being caught out by a schoolgirl.

*****

Back in Enstone, Susie's mind was racing. Angela would have confronted Jonathan by now. Perhaps she would throw him out and he would come to Rose Cottage, begging to be taken in. Perhaps Angela would want a divorce and then surely Jonathan would marry her? Even if Angela got the house and he had to pay maintenance, they would be happy together in her little cottage.

Thinking about Rose Cottage, Susie began to feel anxious. She'd lost her job. How was she going to pay her mortgage? It wasn't going to be easy finding work, as she didn't think that she would be getting any sort of reference from Miss Jennings. Why, oh why, had she been so foolish?

As the hours ticked by, Susie began to realise that Jonathan was not going to turn up on her doorstep. What could she do? She decided that the best and safest course of action was for her to go to bed. Things might be different in the morning.

CHAPTER 27

Shit, shit, shit! What had she done? Susie's waking thoughts were not happy ones. On the positive side, she didn't have to go to work, but on the negative side, she didn't have to go to work because she didn't have a job! Hopefully she would hear from Jonathan this morning. She was still hoping that Angela would throw him out and that he would move in with her.

Determined to be positive, Susie swung her legs out of bed and headed for the bathroom. Once she had showered and got dressed, she went downstairs. George was waiting for his breakfast. She rubbed the big ginger cat's head and told him that things might be different from now on and that perhaps Jonathan would be coming to live with them. George looked totally uninterested.

As soon as it had turned 9 o'clock, Susie texted Jonathan asking him when he could come over so that they could have a chat. By 11 o'clock, he still hadn't replied, so Susie decided that there was nothing to lose by ringing him. His phone went to answer. She daren't drive up to his office to ask to see him but could she lurk outside on the road and try and catch him on the way home, she wondered?

In the meantime, she had to find a job, so she went and bought a local paper from the Village Stores. She was delighted to see that Alf was advertising for a bar person at The Crown. She jumped into her car and headed for the pub. Luck was on her side, as Alf was standing behind the bar. "Hello, Susie love," he said, "fancy seeing you in here on a Wednesday lunchtime. Got another week off work, have you?" Susie shook her head and Alf noticed that she looked a bit down in the mouth.

"Could I have a word with you in private, please Alf?" she asked.

"Course you can," he said, "I'll just fish someone out of the kitchen to watch the bar and then we'll pop upstairs to my office."

Once seated in Alf's office, with a cup of coffee in front of her, Susie told him a sorry tale about losing her job because the headmistress was a control freak and seemed to think she had a right to tell Susie how she should run her life, in and out of school and that she wasn't going to put up with being treated like that, so she'd told her to stick it. Alf raised an eyebrow and nodded. Susie explained that she had seen his advert for a bar person and would be very interested in the job, as it would tide her over nicely while she was looking for a proper job. Alf smiled at that, and told her that she wasn't really selling herself very well. He was looking for loyal staff who would stay with him. "Oh, Alf, I didn't mean to upset you," said

Susie, "but you see I really do need some work as I have a mortgage and other bills to pay and I'm honest and reliable, I promise you."

"Never walked out of a job before, eh?" Alf pointed out. Susie's heart sank. She really wasn't doing this very well at all.

"Have you ever worked in a bar?" asked Alf. She shook her head miserably. This was going from bad to worse. She was unreliable and had no experience. "Here's what we'll do," said Alf. "You show me that you can pull a decent pint and use the till properly and I'll take you on until I find someone who actually wants the job and isn't using it as a stop gap. Then we're both being honest with each other. How does that sound?" It was better than nothing, she thought, and it might even improve her social life. Susie smiled at Alf and thanked him. He suggested that she went behind the bar right away and if she passed muster she could start the following day. Susie apologised profusely but explained that she had to go to court the next day for her speeding offence. "All right," said Alf. "Come in for 10.00 am on Friday. I'll have you as an extra member of staff and you can work alongside the others to see how you get on, but first of all, you'll have to pass my test. Let's go downstairs and see what you're made of."

Before she knew it, it was approaching 3 o'clock. During the time that she had been behind the bar, Susie had been schooled in pulling pints. Guinness was the most difficult, but Alf assured her that she would get the hang of it; all it needed was a bit of patience. As for the rest of it, most of it was basic common sense. People wanted to be greeted with a smile and have their drinks served in clean glasses, quickly and efficiently. They also wanted to be charged the right price and given the correct change. "If you're serving draught lemonade or coca cola, make sure you put plenty of ice in, unless told otherwise," he said. "That way, there's plenty of profit for me." Susie smiled at him. "I'm not a Yorkshire man for nothing, you know," he told her. "But, even though I'm a Yorkshire man, I look after my staff. I don't suppose you've got much in your fridge, have you love?" Susie shook her head. "Right. Let's go in the kitchen and find you some grub."

*****

It had turned 4 o'clock by the time that Susie got home and as she still hadn't heard from her lover she sent him another text asking him if he was avoiding her. When it came to 5.15 pm and she had still received nothing, Susie decided to go and park on the road near the exit to the airfield where the team's headquarters were and wait for Jonathan to come out and see if she could catch him. After about a half hour wait, she saw Jonathan's car come out on to the main road where she was waiting. Susie leaped out of her car and frantically waved to him. She knew that he had seen her, as where she was standing it was impossible not to, but he drove straight past without turning his head. Furious that she had been ignored, Susie jumped into her car and shot after Jonathan, headlights flashing. She WOULD make him speak to her.

As Susie speeded after Jonathan, all sorts of things went through her mind. She had no job, a court case tomorrow, and now it looked like she had no man at all either. What a mess! It also seemed as though she had no friends in the whole world. Thank God James had said he would go to court with her tomorrow. She sincerely hoped that he hadn't forgotten. Why hadn't Jonathan at least got the balls to tell her that it was all over?

*****

For one dreadful moment, Jonathan actually thought that Susie was going to throw herself under his car. For Christ's sake, he thought angrily as he sped past, couldn't she take a hint? Looking in his rear view mirror, he was stunned to see her red Mini Cooper following him with its headlights flashing. What should he do? Should he just drive home? No, that could be dangerous because the silly bitch might follow him and confront him on his doorstep, and Angela had been very clear that he had to have no more contact with Susie Rowlands if he wished to continue living with her and the children. He supposed the only thing he could do would be to stop and talk to her. Eventually finding a lay-by, Jonathan pulled over. The red Mini Cooper skidded to a halt behind him.

As always, when he saw Susie, Jonathan was blown away by her beauty. This evening was no different. She slammed her car door and came charging towards him. "How dare you ignore me? How dare you?" she screamed.

"Calm down and listen to me, Susie," said Jonathan. "You and I have had some fabulous times together, but don't you realise there are bimbos for shagging, like you, and then there are women for marrying, like Angela. My marriage is on the bloody rocks, thanks to you and your big mouth, and I'm not prepared to lose my wife and children for a bit of fluff."

"Bit of fluff!" screeched Susie, "Is that all I ever was to you?"

"Absolutely," said Jonathan coldly. "As I said. I'm not prepared to let you ruin my marriage, so therefore you have to go." He opened his car door and started to get back into the car. "You will not contact me again. Goodbye." With that he pulled the door closed, started the ignition and drove off, leaving a stunned Susie standing alone in the lay-by. She watched Jonathan's car disappear down the road, got back into her own car and burst into tears. She had lost her job for Jonathan and he had dumped her as though she was just a piece of trash. What the hell was she going to do?

Feeling even more alone than ever, Susie drove home to George. She texted James, who confirmed that he would take her to court the next day, as promised. Not feeling like doing anything, Susie had a bath and went to bed, where she tossed and turned, her thoughts spinning out of control.

CHAPTER 28

James was delighted with the effect he'd had on Greg when he had last seen him. Greg said that he looked amazing and that the colours he was wearing really brought out his blue eyes. He had blushed at all the compliments and been even more ecstatic when Greg had said that they must go out to dinner to celebrate James' new image. It had been a fab evening. Everything felt so right and natural when he was with Greg. It hadn't even seemed odd when Greg had kissed him on the cheek.

James parked his car outside Rose Cottage, and walked up the path. Susie had been looking out for him and opened the door straightaway. "Wow, Jamie, I almost didn't recognise you," she said, "your hair is fab and those shoes are to die for. What have you done with yourself?" James decided to come clean and tell Susie about Penny, as he knew that she wouldn't judge him, and Penny had been Mum's idea, after all.

"What fun," said Susie. "Let's have some coffee, and then we should get going."

George joined them, winding his way in and out of James' legs. James bent down to rub his head. The cat was in seventh heaven and purred loudly to show his appreciation. James looked at Susie and could see that under the makeup she was pale, with dark circles under her eyes. "How are you going to plead?" he asked.

"I've no choice but to plead guilty," she said, "although I did say to the policeman at the time that I was trying to catch a plane. He wasn't interested though." James pricked up his ears at this. Where had his sister been going for the weekend on a plane? The best way to find out was to ask, which he did.

Much as she would have liked to confide in her brother, Susie was so terrified that her parents would get to hear of her affair that she trotted out the same lies she'd fed to her mother. Like Annabelle, James wasn't fooled and told her so in no uncertain terms. "Come on, Suse, that doesn't work with me. What were you really up to and where were you really going?"

"I've told you," she said. "I was going to Monaco. Ask Mummy and Daddy. They saw me on the television."

"Well, you never got that cheap on eBay," said James. "You can trust me, you know."

"There's nothing to trust," replied his sister. "Now, if you've finished your coffee, I think we should get going. I don't want to make matters worse by being late."

"Have you got your driving licence?" James enquired. "I'm sure that you're going to need it." Susie nodded sullenly.

*****

Susie's legs were shaking as she walked into the court room. She felt physically sick. Although she knew that James was sitting somewhere in the back of the court, it really didn't make a lot of difference. Her life was awful.

The hearing was soon over. No-one was interested in the fact that she was driving fast because she had a plane to catch. Susie was fined £240 and had six penalty points put on her licence. Susie guessed she had to be grateful that she still had her driving licence, but the amount of the fine shocked her. She wrote out a cheque with a trembling hand and wondered where she was going to find the money. She supposed that she would have to take out cash on her credit card and pay it in to her bank account. She was very quiet on the drive back to Chipping Norton.

James parked the car and told Susie that he would phone her when he had finished with David Timmins. She nodded, smiled feebly and headed for the shops. She put her credit card into the cash dispenser, and gasped in amazement when her card was returned and her request for £300 cash was rejected. This was going from bad to worse. She had written out a cheque to the court and it now looked as though it was going to bounce. Would that be considered to be another crime? Could it be fraud? Writing out a cheque when you knew you didn't have sufficient money in the bank to pay it. What on earth was she going to do now? No lover, no decent job, and now no money!

*****

David greeted James with a smile and ushered him through to his office. He produced a folder showing James a portfolio of suggested investments. James looked at it gobsmacked. He hadn't heard of any of these things! David started to explain, and James tried to pay attention, but he had to stop David as he was finding it all too complicated. "I'm sorry, David," he said, but my financial knowledge is non-existent. All I want to do is invest my money and be able to get at some of it, should I need it. If you don't mind, I think the best thing I can do is take this home and show it to my dad and see what he thinks. He's a bit of a whizz at investing himself." David's heart sank. He hated it when a third party got involved in his recommendations, but there was nothing he could do.

"Of course," he said, smiling, "let me briefly explain the different products to you and then you will have a better idea of things when you are discussing them with your father."

Half an hour later James left David's office and phoned Susie to tell her that he was ready. They met back at the car. "OK," said James. "This is your territory. Where would you like to go to get something to eat? I don't want to go to The Crown in case David comes in, as I'd like to talk to you on my own."

"That sounds interesting," said Susie. "Why don't we go to Whistlers? I've never had a bad meal there and it's an easy walk."

"Fine by me," replied her brother.

They were soon seated in a table by the window, Susie sipping at a glass of white wine and James nursing a pint of shandy. "What is it you want to talk to me about?" asked Susie.

"Well," said James, "this isn't easy, but you know I've never had a serious girlfriend?" Susie nodded. At that moment the waitress arrived with their starters, so conversation ceased.

James waited until they had finished their starters before picking up the conversation again. "Well," he said, "I think I may have met somebody, but I need to ask you something first."

"Curiouser and curiouser," said Susie laughing. "I really am intrigued now." She did, however, have to be intrigued for a while longer, because the waitress had brought their main courses, which they tucked in to with great enthusiasm. "That was delicious," said Susie, wiping her mouth on her napkin. "I just love salmon."

"And I just love steak," replied James. "Do you want a pudding?"

"Of course I do," came the reply. "Shall we leave your confession until we are having our coffee? I can't cope with all this stopping and starting!" James nodded his agreement, thinking to himself that this did feel very much like a confession.

Pudding plates cleared away and coffee now in front of them, Susie turned enquiringly to her brother. "Come on then, Jamie," she said. "Tell me all about this new woman." James took a deep breath and told her that the new woman was in fact a new man and went on to tell her how he had met Greg. He finished up by asking Susie if she thought he was gay. "You could well be," she replied. "All I can say is that this Greg seems to have made an awfully big impression on you. Your hair is fantastic and I've never seen you look so good. Do you know if he's gay?" James went on to tell Susie that Greg had laughed when he had asked about a girlfriend and said that he had kissed him on the cheek on Saturday night and that it had felt right.

"I guess that sounds as though you might be," said Susie. "Why don't you come right out with it and ask Greg if he's gay and say that you're not sure about yourself, but that you do find him extremely attractive and if he tries to kiss you properly, just let him. That should let you know one way or

ANTONIA ABBOTT

the other!"

"So, you're not shocked then?" James asked her.

"Don't be so silly" said Susie. "It's important that you're true to yourself, that's all." If only he knew about the mess her life was in! She wondered whether she could ask James if he would lend her some money, but decided against it. She would have to come clean and explain why she needed it – because she had lost her job, and she wanted to keep that to herself for as long as possible. She needed to do as many shifts at The Crown as Alf would give her. He was paying £6.50 per hour and a shift lasted for seven hours, which was £45.50 before tax and national insurance. Not very much at all!

Susie gathered her thoughts, realising that James had paid the bill and was asking her if she were ready to leave. They got up from the table and walked back to the car.

As she waved James off, Susie noticed Patsy walking up the lane. She quickly scurried into her cottage. That little snitch was someone she definitely didn't want to see.

*****

The post had come while Susie was out. None of the envelopes looked particularly friendly or exciting and she was tempted to put them to one side, but she swallowed hard and began to rip them open. There was a letter from Woodstock Academy, enclosing her P45. They hadn't wasted any time! That paled into insignificance when she opened the second envelope, which contained her Barclaycard statement. Her credit limit was £6,000 and her outstanding balance was £5,938.67. No wonder she had been refused the £300 earlier. The statement was dated a week ago and she had bought petrol and groceries since then and also spent £35 having her nails done. Damn the Singles holiday to Spain and the Metropole Hotel in Birmingham. How the hell was she going to make her minimum payment, as she didn't have any cash? How was she going to pay her mortgage, which was due on the 1st of next month? How was she going to pay her Council Tax? What was she going to do? Did she have anything she could sell? The only thing she could think of was Granny's ring and Daddy would have kittens if she sold that.

She needed to put herself around the recruitment agencies to see what was around. Alf would put up the rota tomorrow, so she would be able to see when she would have time to go into Oxford. In the meantime she needed to put together some sort of CV, and that would be difficult. What could she give as her reason for leaving Woodstock Academy? Come to think of it, that had been her first proper job. She'd not really done anything much before that. Mummy and Daddy had been very generous

126

and not made her rush out to work. Susie felt even more miserable when she thought about her mother. It would be her birthday and wedding anniversary soon, so she had to find money from somewhere to buy gifts. She might need to ask James to lend her money after all.

CHAPTER 29

When James got home he found his parents watching the news. He waited for it to end and then told his father that he had received a proposed investment portfolio from David Timmins but that he couldn't make head nor tail of it. "Never mind that," said his mother "How was Susie?"

"Fine," lied James, "we went out to dinner at Whistlers in Chipping Norton." His parents certainly didn't need to know about Susie's court appearance.

"If you give me the portfolio I'll have a look at it and then perhaps we could discuss it tomorrow?" suggested Peter. James said that would be great and handed over the paperwork.

Allsort was looking hopeful and James asked her if she would like a walk. Her body shook with anticipation so, despite the fact that it was late, he went and got her lead. After all a quiet walk might help him to think. Susie hadn't been shocked by the fact that he thought he might be gay and the more James thought about it the more he thought that he probably was. Like she said, he had changed his appearance to impress a man. He had never thought about doing that for a girl regardless of how much or how little money he had. He would have to pluck up his courage and talk to Greg. Taking the bull by the horns, he sent his friend a text suggesting that they have dinner the following evening – his treat – and Greg could choose the place. Within seconds he received a reply, "Fab. Let's go to either the Indian or Chinese in Cholsey. You choose." James texted back "Chinese."

*****

The next morning, Peter told James that he had read David's suggestions and would be happy to go through them with his son. Armed with mugs of coffee, they disappeared into Peter's study. "On the whole I don't disagree with what your friend is proposing," Peter said, "but I do think it's important that you understand exactly what you are doing. Did you just switch off when he was talking to you or wasn't he explaining properly?" James thought about this for a minute and replied that he hadn't expected to understand, so he'd not really paid close attention. "OK," said Peter, "I shall give you a crash course and point out to you exactly what these investments are and what your chances are of making or losing money. How does that sound?"

James said that it sounded good to him, and spent the rest of the morning in his father's study. At the end he felt he had a far better grasp of things and thought that he would let David invest £80,000. He had already spent the best part of £5,000, but felt that there might be something else that took his fancy.

James had his final exam to sit on Monday and then college would be finished. He was having so much fun in Oxfordshire that he was no longer sure if he wanted to do a management training course. He also knew that Greg could be a major factor in any decision that he made.

Picking up his phone, James called David and told him that he would be going ahead and investing £80,000, not the £85,000 that they had discussed. David offered to come over to Moulsford in order to finalise the business. They made an appointment for the following Thursday.

James spent the afternoon trying to revise for Monday's exam but he was far too concerned about what he was going to say to Greg that evening to concentrate.

When the time came, James chose his clothes with care – cream linen trousers with a denim shirt and blue shoes – then set off for Cholsey feeling somewhat nervous.

When he arrived in West End, Greg greeted him with a kiss on the cheek and told him that he looked fab. "Have you ever considered wearing more jewellery?" Greg asked. "It can really finish an outfit you know." James looked at his friend, who was dripping in gold, and wasn't sure what to say. He had been brought up rather conservatively and had never considered wearing jewellery, other than his watch and the platinum signet ring that his parents had given him for his 18th birthday. However, he always thought that Greg looked absolutely stunning with his diamond earring and gold bangles. The guy had such style!

"It's not something I've ever thought about," he replied.

"Try on some of the things in my shop," suggested Greg. "You don't know what you're missing until you try." He smiled suggestively. James blushed bright pink.

They had a drink and then walked down into the village where Greg had reserved a table at the Chinese restaurant. All the way there James was wondering what he was going to say and getting more and more nervous by the minute. By the time they reached the restaurant he was desperately in need of another drink and knocked back a beer in no time. "Is anything the matter?" asked Greg. "You seem rather on edge." James gulped.

"There's something I need to ask you," he said, "and I'm not quite sure how to go about it without offending you."

"Of course I am," said Greg smiling.

"Of course you are what?" asked James.

"Gay." came the reply. "That's what you wanted to ask that you were finding so difficult, isn't it?" James looked and felt embarrassed.

"Yes." he mumbled.

"There's nothing to feel embarrassed about," laughed Greg, "I've known for a very long time that I'm gay, whereas I think you are just beginning to wonder whether or not you are. Am I right?" James looked at his friend in amazement.

"How did you know?" he gasped.

"Well," said Greg, "I'm usually only physically attracted to men of a similar persuasion to myself and you must know that I'm physically attracted to you, as I believe you are to me?"

"Yes, I think I am," admitted James. "I guess at the end of the day I've been trying to impress you, and as I've never wanted to change myself for a girl, it's made me wonder if I might be gay."

"I think you are," said Greg, leaning across the table to take James' hand, which he stroked gently.

They walked back from the restaurant hand in hand and when they got back inside Greg's house, they kissed in such a way that it made James' head spin. He had never been kissed like that before. "Wow," he said in amazement.

"Wow indeed," replied Greg. "Now, when we've taken Zizi for her last walk of the day, I think you should ring home and say that you've had a bit too much to drink and are going to spend the night here." James nodded as Greg went to fetch Zizi's lead.

*****

James felt very nervous on the way upstairs, wondering what was going to happen. He needn't have worried however, because all Greg wanted to do was kiss and cuddle, which was wonderful. "Don't be anxious, James," he said, "we can take this as slowly as you need to. We have lots of time to get to know each other properly. We're already friends, and that's a great start, don't you think?" James nodded. The huge double bed was wonderfully comfortable and it wasn't long before he drifted off into a very peaceful sleep. His friend lay watching him, all manner of thoughts going through his head, before he too, closed his eyes and slipped into sleep.

*****

James woke up the next morning to a delightful smell of coffee and before he knew it Greg was standing beside the bed with a tray which held not only the coffee but also freshly squeezed juice and warm croissants. "Gosh, what service!" said James. "I could get used to this you know."

"That's the general idea," replied Greg, climbing back into bed beside him. "Are you coming to the arcade today?"

"Not sure." replied James. "I'll find that out when I get home. Even if I'm not, shall we do something later? I don't think I'll be able to stay here again tonight, though. My parents will wonder what's going on."

"You'll have to tell them sooner or later," replied Greg, "and as you don't have a place of your own, this is the only place we can spend the night together."

"Mmm," said James. "As I'm finishing college now, maybe it's time I thought about renting. I'd rather buy, to be honest, as renting just seems like money down the drain, but I can't get a mortgage at the moment."

"There are advantages to renting, though," replied Greg. "Having a mortgage is a huge commitment. If my business doesn't take off big time, I shall have to re-think everything. I might even need to take in a lodger," he said, looking at James meaningfully. James thought that could be an ideal solution, if things continued as they were. His parents wouldn't question it. They already knew that he and Greg were friends and what could be more natural than for him to move out and share a house with a mate?

Breakfast eaten, the couple had another cuddle before getting ready for the day. James drove back to Moulsford and Greg took Zizi for a walk before getting ready for work. Each of them was thinking intently about the other.

CHAPTER 30

Peter was returning from walking Allsort when James got home. Allsort was delighted to see James and dashed over to greet him, tail wagging. "Hello, pretty girl," he said to the dog. "Morning Dad."

"Morning James," replied his father. "Perfect timing. Your mother has just gone to Wallingford as she has some new stock to sort out, which gives us a chance to discuss her birthday. Sensible decision not to come home last night by the way, if you'd had a bit too much to drink. It was kind of your friend to put you up." James blushed, thinking about Greg and the wonderful time that they'd had.

They went into the house together and James put the kettle on while Peter put Allsort's lead away and wiped her muddy paws. When it was ready, James took the coffee through to his father's study and asked what the plan was for Annabelle's birthday. "Well," said Peter, "I thought I'd get the same caterers that we used for your birthday party and have them cook and serve dinner – just for the family – Grandma and Grandpa, me and your mother, you and Susie, and anyone either of you would like to bring." Without thinking, James asked if he could bring Greg.

"Would it be all right if I brought the chap I stayed with last night, Dad? He works in the arcade with Mum, so she knows him, and you've met him too when he came here the other week."

"I don't see why not," said his father, "although I was thinking more of a girl, but if you don't have a girlfriend, I suppose there's no reason why Greg shouldn't come." James thanked his father.

"I'll phone the caterers now, while your mother is out of the way and then I'll phone Grandma and Grandpa, and Susie."

"I need to talk to Susie," said James, "so I can tell her about the dinner if you like."

"Fine," replied Peter, "just let me talk to the caterers first, so that we're definite about what's happening. I'd like to do it on the actual day, which is a Thursday, because we will also have been married for 28 years on the 28th so that's rather special. Grandma and Grandpa will probably stay on over the weekend and Susie could too, if she would like to. We don't really see that much of her since she bought her house in Enstone. Do you know if she has a boyfriend James?" James shook his head and said that he thought not, as she hadn't mentioned anyone to him and she hadn't brought anyone to his birthday party.

"Let's see if I can get hold of the caterers now and then we can invite the others," said Peter, opening his phone. Twenty minutes later everything was confirmed and Peter told James that he could ring his sister with the details.

*****

Susie was tidying the bar ready for opening when James phoned to tell her about the party and also his news about Greg. He went on to say that he had asked if Greg could go to their mother's birthday party and that his father had said that was OK. He asked Susie if she would be bringing anyone and then reminded her that the next day was Fathers' Day and that their mother was doing a special lunch. Susie's heart sank as she listened to James rabbiting on. She had forgotten it was Fathers' Day and would now have to apologise to Alf and say that she couldn't work tomorrow and what was more she didn't have a present for her father. She needed to put petrol in the car and if she didn't get £240 in the bank pretty damn quick to meet the cheque that she had written out for the court, she would probably have a fraud summons to deal with. She listened to James going on and on about Greg and muttered at what she considered to be appropriate moments, all the while thinking she would have to ask him for a loan.

Finally, James stopped to draw breath and Susie jumped in saying that she'd had a lot of expenses recently and didn't realise that she was up to the limit on her credit card and please could he lend her some money, as she was really strapped and had her huge speeding fine to pay.

James was somewhat taken aback by this and pointed out to Susie that she was the one with the proper job. She cringed at that and told James that running a house was expensive, whereas he lived at home with their parents who were very generous. As she listened to herself, Susie realised that once again her mouth was running away with her, and she really wasn't going the right way about getting a loan from her brother. Taking a deep breath, she tried again. "Look, James, I'm really sorry to ask, but I'm desperate. I really would appreciate it if you could just lend me a couple of thousand." James gasped at that. He had been thinking more like five hundred quid and there was his sister asking for a couple of thou. "I know you've got the money," she continued, "and you know I'd do the same for you."

"I'll have to think about it," James replied. "Anyway, I'll tell Dad that of course you're coming to Mum's birthday, on your own, and that you will be staying over on the Thursday night. Do you think you will stay for the weekend too?" Susie said that she didn't know, thinking that she needed to work, but would deal with that one closer to the time. "I'll let you know about the money when I've had a think," said James, ringing off.

What the hell was she going to do? She had to find the money to buy petrol to get to Moulsford and back tomorrow, buy a present and a card for

Daddy, but worse than all that, it was Saturday, and she had written out the cheque for the speeding fine on Thursday. She needed to pay cash into the bank by Monday at the latest, so that her cheque didn't bounce and she had to tell Alf that she wouldn't be able to work tomorrow aware that she'd only started the job yesterday! What a bloody mess!

First things first. She would go and find Alf and explain about tomorrow. Then she had a brainwave – perhaps Alf would let her have a bottle of nice malt whisky for Daddy for Fathers' Day and offset it against her wages, as he wasn't paying her until Friday. By then she would have done lots of shifts so he'd be bound to agree. Feeling more positive, Susie set off to find the landlord.

She went upstairs and tapped on the door to the flat. Joan opened it smiling and Susie asked if she could have a word with Alf. She was shown through to Alf's office. "Hello, Susie love, what can I do you for?" he enquired.

"It's a bit awkward, Alf," she said. "I'd forgotten it was Fathers' Day tomorrow until just now when my brother phoned me and I'm expected at home for lunch, so I won't be able to work. I'm really sorry. What's more, I haven't bought Daddy a present and I haven't got any money, so I was wondering whether you would let me have a nice bottle of malt whisky or brandy and off-set if against my wages?"

"You don't want much, do you love?" said Alf. "You only started here yesterday. Now you want tomorrow off and a sub against your wages."

"I'm so, so sorry." Susie pulled a doe-eyed face. "It's just that I'm in a complete mess and my parents don't know I've lost my job and I don't want to have to tell them. Please could you help me?"

Alf looked at her and thought about his own daughter. He wouldn't have liked to see Charlotte in such a mess, but also Susie had to learn that things didn't just fall into her lap. "Here's what I'll do," he said, "I'll ring round the staff who are due on the late shift and see if one of them will swap with you for the early one. That'll mean I want you here at 5.00 pm on the dot tomorrow. Do you understand?" Susie nodded. "As for a bottle of booze for your dad. Yes, I'll help you with that. Are you expecting to pay me what I paid for it or are you going to pay me optic price?" Susie gasped. She hadn't thought about Alf's profit, which was probably humungous. She had been planning on spending between £20 and £30. "You hadn't thought it through, had you?" enquired Alf. Despondently Susie shook her head. "You need to think a bit harder, you know, love. I'll do you a bottle at cost plus £5. How does that sound?" Susie thanked him profusely. "Have you bought your dad a card?" She shook her head. "Pop up to the shop now and buy one before people start coming in. When you get back I should have an answer about tomorrow for you and hurry up! I don't want you away from the bar for too long." He smiled to himself as Susie scuttled out.

*****

Whilst Susie was sorting out Fathers' Day, Annabelle was unpacking her new stock and chatting to Greg. "It was kind of you to look after James last night," she said with a twinkle in her eye. "It's really not like him to have one too many when he knows he has to drive. Were you celebrating anything?" Greg knew quite well that Annabelle was fishing, but he wasn't going to be reeled in.

"If we were celebrating anything it was James' new image." He neatly side-stepped. "Doesn't he look fab?"

"He certainly does," Annabelle replied. "I wonder what made him smarten himself up? Could you possibly have had any influence there, Greg?" Greg just smiled. He wasn't biting. If Annabelle wanted to know if he and James were lovers, then she would have to wait for James to tell her in his own good time, when he was ready.

"What are you doing for Fathers' Day?" asked Annabelle, backing off and changing the subject. "I'm cooking a celebration lunch for Peter, and Susie will be coming over from Enstone. Have you met her?" Greg said that he hadn't and that he would be going up to London to have lunch with his parents. "Ah well," said Annabelle "when I've finished arranging this lot, let's go to the George and have some lunch. My treat." Greg thanked her, although he had a feeling the fishing expedition would probably be resumed.

*****

When Susie got back to The Crown it was beginning to get busy, as it had taken longer than she had thought to walk down to the shop, choose a card and walk back. Alf was looking a bit irritable, so she went and apologised to him. "Talk about give an inch," he muttered. "You're in luck for tomorrow, though," he continued. "Nigel will swap shifts with you." Susie breathed a sigh of relief. She had got her present and card sorted and hopefully there was enough petrol in the car to get her to Moulsford. If the worst came to the worst she could say that she had forgotten her wallet, and then one of her parents would be bound to help her out with petrol money to get back home. Her next major problem was the £240 for the speeding fine. Hopefully she would be able to resolve it tomorrow with James. Putting a smile on her face, she turned to serve a customer.

"Good morning, and what may I get you?" she asked.

CHAPTER 31

Peter was delighted by Annabelle's gift to him for Father's Day. It was the latest Mont Blanc rollerball pen. He had a definite weakness for Mont Blanc accessories and Annabelle had impeccable taste so, all in all, it was a good combination. James had come up trumps too with a whisky tasting set which included glasses and a copy of Jim Murray's Whisky Bible. Now Annabelle was busy in the kitchen preparing what he knew would be a delicious lunch, as she was an excellent cook, and he was enjoying a Churchill deluxe cigar and the Sunday Telegraph. Susie would be on her way to join them for lunch, so from his perspective all was right with the world.

Coming home from walking Allsort, James saw that his mother was busy in the kitchen so wandered in and asked what was on the menu. "We're starting off with some champagne and canapés," she said, "and then we're having a rib of beef with all the trimmings, followed by a sherry trifle and cheeses after. I've spent so long fiddling with these blasted canapés that I wanted the rest to be simple."

"Sounds delish," said her son. "Would you like me to lay the table for you?"

"That would be wonderful. Thank you, darling," replied his mother. "Go and ask your father what red wine he would like and then I can uncork it." James did as requested.

*****

Whilst soaking in the bath, Susie considered the day ahead and her plan of action. First of all, her parents must not find out that she had lost her job at the school, and then she needed to work hard on James to at least lend her sufficient money to pay her speeding fine. If the worst came to the very worst she would have to ask her mother for a loan, maybe even admit to speeding. After all, Mummy met Daddy through reversing her car into his so she ought to understand a speeding ticket. She also needed to leave Riverside House promptly at quarter to four, in order to go home, get changed and be with Alf for 5 o'clock. That could be tricky as her parents would expect her to spend the evening with them. She was going to need a jolly good excuse to get away and working at The Crown wasn't going to be it!

Susie chose her clothes with care. What would her parents like? Fairly smart she thought as she peered inside her wardrobe. She finally settled on a white linen skirt with a bright turquoise tee shirt and matching shrug. The skirt would be creased by the time she got to Moulsford, but there wasn't much that she could do about that, she thought, adding a wide gold belt. Definitely better wear Granny's ring, Susie thought – particularly if she had to end up selling it. To make sure the ring was noticed, Susie toned down her other jewellery, just wearing earrings, a necklace and a watch. She thrust her feet into gold jewelled sandals, grabbed her bag and her father's gift and headed for the door. Mrs MacDonald was cleaning her windows and called out to her. Susie answered with a smile, knowing full well that the next thing would be that Mrs MacDonald would notice that she wasn't working and also when it was her turn for the late shift at the pub, would notice that she was coming in gone midnight. She'd deal with all that when she had to. She had today to get through first of all!

Arriving at Riverside House, Susie found everyone engrossed in something different. Her mother was in the kitchen, putting the finishing touches to her canapés, James was in the dining room, double checking that he had laid the table correctly and her father was in his study with a newspaper and cigar. She headed there first so that she could give him his present. "Hello Daddy," she said, "Happy Fathers' Day." She held out her gift bag. In the end Susie had chosen a bottle of Janneau Armagnac for her father, which Alf had let her have for £30. When she saw James' gift, Susie was very glad that she hadn't chosen a malt whisky, as she felt it would have looked insignificant. At least this was a different drink and her father seemed pleased by it. He asked her how things were and she assured him that everything was fine.

"It's nice to see you wearing Granny's ring." said her father. "Do you wear it very often?" Susie shook her head and explained that it was too valuable for everyday wear. Her father told her that she shouldn't let that worry her and that jewellery was for wearing.

At that point Annabelle came into the study. Susie thought how lovely she looked. Annabelle was wearing black linen trousers with a fuchsia pink blouse, belted tightly round her tiny waist. On her feet she had high heeled fuchsia pink suede sandals, a sizeable pair of diamond ear studs in her ears, a diamond bracelet around her wrist, a plain gold watch, her wedding and engagement rings and another three stone diamond ring on her right hand. Yes, her mother knew how to wear jewellery all right!

Annabelle suggested that they all go into the conservatory and that if Peter would open the champagne, she would fetch the canapés. James had already laid out plates and glasses, so all was prepared. They went through and drank Peter's health, whilst nibbling on Annabelle's delicious canapés.

Half an hour later they were all seated at the dining table, enjoying a delicious lunch. Conversation was flowing and so far nothing controversial had come up, but Susie hadn't had a chance to speak to her brother. Lunch over, she suggested to him that they both take Allsort for a walk, as she hardly ever saw the dog or had the chance to take her for a walk. James replied that if she were that keen she could take the dog on her own as he did it most days, and had already been out that morning. That was not the reply Susie wanted and wondered how to get James to go with her. Whilst she was thinking what to do, knowing that she would have to take the damn dog out now anyway, Susie looked at her watch and saw to her horror it had just turned 3.00. She would have to go before too long and hadn't yet made any excuses. This was going from bad to worse.

"Come on Allsort," she called, fetching the dog's lead, "nasty James clearly doesn't love you today, but I do, so I'll take you for a walk before I go home."

"There's no rush for you to go," said her mother. "It would be nice to have a family evening." Susie didn't answer her, but went out of the back door with Allsort. Once clear of the house, she phoned her brother and told him that she had asked him to go for a walk with her so that they could discuss her borrowing some money.

"Look, Suse, I told you yesterday that I would have to think about it and that's what I'm doing," James said to her.

"Yes, I understand, but if I don't put £240 in cash in the bank by tomorrow my cheque won't clear for my speeding fine. Couldn't you please just let me have that?"

"I don't have £240 cash on me," came the reply.

"No, but if I gave you my bank details you could go into Wallingford and pay the cash in to my account first thing in the morning, couldn't you?" she begged. "I'm begging you, James. I'm going to be in serious trouble otherwise."

"Oh all right, I suppose so," said her brother in an exasperated tone, "but I've got to go now. Mum and Dad will be wondering who I'm talking to out here in the hall." Susie thanked him profusely and rang off.

Taking Allsort home, Susie's next job was to borrow some money from her parents so that she could get back to Enstone. They were sitting drinking coffee, so Susie went and told them that she would have to be getting back. "It's only twenty to four," said her mother, "do spend some more time with us. We hardly see you. Do you have to get back for anything in particular?"

"Julie's coming round with a DVD for us to watch," was the first thing that came into Susie's head, "and she said she'd be over between 4.30 and 5.00. I don't want to keep her waiting."

"That's poor planning when you knew that it was Fathers' Day," said Annabelle, a trifle crossly. "Can't you see Julie some other time?"

"It's a bit rude to call her now to change things," replied her daughter.

"Tell you what, why don't you, Daddy and James too, if he would like to, come over and have dinner with me one night next week." Peter and Annabelle did a double take. Susie NEVER invited them over.

"That would be lovely," replied Annabelle, "how about Friday, so that you don't have to go to work the next day."

Susie smiled weakly. God only knew where she would get the money to feed them and what she would feed them on, but at least she would get her wages that day. She would then have to rush from the pub at 5.00 pm when she finished and get some food that was easy and quick to cook, but at least she wasn't going to let Alf down. All she had to do now was borrow some money for petrol.

Picking up her handbag, Susie made a big show of looking for her car key. "It must be here somewhere," she said, as she upended her bag on to the floor. "Oh, shit, shit, shit," she exclaimed, retrieving a lipstick from under the coffee table. "My wallet isn't in here and I need some petrol. Where can I have left it?"

"I have absolutely no idea," said her father, smiling at her, "but I can lend you £40 to put some petrol in your car. I just hope that you haven't left your wallet somewhere with loads of cash and credit cards in it." Susie assured him that she never had loads of cash in her wallet, as she put everything that she could on her credit card, but that she would check as soon as she got home and call the credit card company if she couldn't find it.

She then kissed her parents and brother goodbye, thanked them for a lovely lunch and climbed into her car. As she was about to drive away, James came after her and complimented her on her Oscar winning performance of looking for a wallet that she knew wasn't there. However, as he went back inside the house, he thought his sister must indeed have serious financial problems if she couldn't put petrol in her car. He would have to think hard about lending her money over and above the £240.

*****

Susie was delighted with the £40. £20 would be enough petrol to get her home and, as she only had a few pounds left in her purse, the other £20 would come in very handy indeed and, knowing her father, he wouldn't take it back when she offered it. She got home at 10 minutes to 5, quickly fed an indignant George, changed her white skirt for a pair of jeans and dashed off to The Crown. Much to her dismay and Alf's obvious irritation, she was ten minutes late. Apologising profusely, Susie set to work.

CHAPTER 32

All in all, Susie felt that her first week at the pub had gone well. She enjoyed the work, serving drinks and chatting to people and Alf was a fair boss. He gave the day shift lunch every day, which was really helping with her food bills. She knew the same would happen on the late shift – she would get her supper. Alf had just given Susie her first wage slip. She had opened the envelope with great anticipation, as she had worked for seven shifts at £45.50 per shift, making a total of £318.50. She knew that she had to pay Alf £30 for the bottle of Armagnac, but was surprised to see that she had to pay tax and national insurance on the money before she paid him back the £30. It left her with little more than £200. Next week she would have to pay James back the £240 (as he would expect her to get paid at the end of the month), so it was obvious that she wasn't earning enough money. She would be going onto the late shift tomorrow for a week, so on Monday she could go to some of the recruitment agencies and also see if she could sell Granny's ring. Surely she could get one of those cubic zirconia things that would look like it, so that her parents wouldn't know what she had done?

Susie was on her own in the bar when Alf came in to check that there was sufficient change in the tills. Alf smiled and asked her how she was liking working in a pub. Susie told him how much she enjoyed it. "You'll find the late shifts busier and harder work," Alf told her. "I've been breaking you in gently."

"I'm sure it'll be fine," replied Susie smiling. "There's no way it could be as hard work as tonight's going to be. My parents are coming to supper."

"What are you making for them?" enquired Alf, who was a keen cook himself.

"Not sure," was the reply, "because I've been so short of money I haven't been in a position to buy anything in so I've got to dash to the shops when I finish here. I'm not a good cook, which is a pain because Mummy is just brilliant, so I'll probably show myself up." Alf smiled at that.

"Oh Susie love, you do get yourself in a mess, don't you?" he said. "Stay there for a minute, while I see what's happening in the kitchen."

A few minutes later Alf came back smiling. "Right love, this is what we can do. Philip's making salmon Thai curry for one of the specials today. What do you say that I ask him to put some aside for you for tonight? You'd just need to do some jasmine rice to go with it and hey presto, that'd be your main course all sorted out."

"Oh, Alf, you're a star," said Susie, beaming at him. "Thank you so much. What do I owe you for that?"

"It's a little pressie from me, love. Just enjoy it, that's all I ask. Are you going to do a starter?" Susie said that she wasn't sure. "Tell you what," said Alf, "if you get some Naan bread to serve with the curry, I should think that would be enough. After all, your parents know that you aren't a born cook, so Philip's curry will probably leave them speechless anyway. All you need to think about now is some pud, and what's better after a curry than a few strawberries?"

"Oh Alf, you really are a genius," said Susie. "You sorted out Fathers' Day for me and now you've sorted out my dinner party. All I have to do is get a few bits and pieces now and my evening will be a success."

Alf didn't tell Susie how much she reminded him of his own daughter when she had been in her early 20s. She'd had absolutely no idea about money, and no matter how good the job she had - and she always did have a good job - she could spend way beyond her means. Fortunately marriage had settled her down and he no longer had to bail her out, but he did miss seeing her on a daily basis and doing things to help her, and it gave him a lot of pleasure to be able to help Susie. He didn't know why she had lost her job at Woodstock Academy, but he was fairly confident that she had no idea of what it would mean when it came to getting another job. Still, it wasn't his place to worry about her, but he would give her a bit of a hand when he could, so long as she played fair with him. She was a good little barmaid and very pretty with it.

*****

Peter had decided it would be fun to take Annabelle away for the weekend. It would also mean that they could both have a drink and enjoy themselves at Susie's that evening. James had said he didn't particularly want to go, and was happy to look after the shop for his mother instead. It was the perfect opportunity for him to spend time with Greg.

Peter knew that Annabelle would enjoy staying in the Cotswolds, as there were plenty of antique shops and markets and she would be able to have a good old stock hunt. He was torn between The Feathers Hotel and The Bear in Woodstock. After a few minutes going backwards and forwards between the two, Peter decided on The Feathers. Once he had got a reservation, Peter went and told Annabelle what he had done.

They had an early lunch, packed their bags and were soon driving towards Woodstock. By 3.30 pm they had checked into their room and were exploring the delights of the Courtyard Gin Bar, which stocked over 140 different brands, much to Peter's delight. "I think I'll only have one this afternoon and then one early evening and then I shall drive to Susie's and leave the car there overnight and we can get a cab back," he said to his wife,

"I can get a cab to Enstone in the morning or ask Susie to come and pick me up and you can have a look round the Woodstock antique shops whilst I'm gone. I might even be able to persuade Susie to spend some time with us on Saturday." Annabelle thought that would be a very good idea indeed. They didn't see nearly enough of their daughter, and she was pleasantly surprised that they had been asked over to supper.

Drinks finished, they took a brief stroll round the town which was looking dreary as it had rained for the major part of the day. They then went and got ready for the evening.

*****

Meanwhile, Susie had finished at The Crown and whizzed off to Sainsbury's in Chipping Norton, where she bought some rice, which could be microwaved in two minutes, some Naan bread, two punnets of strawberries and a carton of cream. Heading for the cash desk, she decided to throw caution to the wind and added a bottle of champagne, which she planned to serve as an aperitif. She then dashed home to Enstone to get everything ready. As always, George greeted her with great enthusiasm, sniffing frantically when she carried in the curry. "Hello George, I know it smells yummy, but it's not for pussycats I'm afraid. You'll have to make do with prawn Sheba instead." Susie rubbed his large ginger head. As always, George purred his reply.

Once George was fed and watered, Susie turned her attention to the house. She really wanted to do her best as Mummy was so good at entertaining. She knew that you couldn't go wrong with white linen, so she covered her dining table with a white cloth and found the matching napkins. Looking through the window Susie could see that there were a few roses in the garden so she went and cut them for the centre of the table. She set out the cutlery and wine glasses and stood back to admire the result. Yes, she thought to herself, that would do nicely. She looked at her watch. It was 6.30, and her parents were due at 7.30. No chance of them being late, she thought to herself, so just time for a quick shower and a change of clothes. The champagne was in the freezer and would be fine there until she was changed and ready.

As always, Susie studied her clothes carefully before deciding on what to wear. Finally she chose one of the Monsoon dresses that her mother had bought her on their shopping trip to Bicester Village. It was oranges and browns, which went well with Susie's dark hair and slight tan. Must wear the diamond, she thought, pushing it on to her finger. It could be for the last time! Susie fastened a very bold gold-plated necklace around her neck, added hoop ear rings in the same gold plate, strapped on her watch and finally rummaged in the bottom of her wardrobe for her gold sandals.

Pleased with the result, she went downstairs.

As expected, her parents arrived dead on the dot of 7.30. Watching them get out of the car Susie thought what a handsome couple they made and how well dressed they were. Still, she thought ruefully, money talks, and her parents could afford the very best labels. Putting a smile on her face, she opened the door, and pushed any thoughts of money firmly to the back of her mind. She kissed her parents and welcomed them in.

Susie felt pleased as she showed them through into the sitting room. Her candles were filling the room with a very pleasant smell and it all looked lovely. Her parents looked surprised when she offered champagne, but were delighted. Peter told her that they were spending the weekend at The Feathers in Woodstock, and that he was planning to leave his car in Enstone overnight, so that he could enjoy the evening. He asked if Susie could come and collect him to pick up his car the next morning. She nodded her head, relieved that she was working the late shift the following day.

"This curry is delicious," said Annabelle. "You must give me the recipe." She looked hard at her daughter. "I'm very impressed that you've used fresh herbs. I thought you lived on ready meals."

"I do usually, Mummy, but I wanted to do something special for you and Daddy. I'm so pleased you like it," Susie replied, before quickly changing the subject. "Will you be going on an antiques hunt while you're out this way?" Annabelle nodded and said that was one of the reasons why her father had booked them into the Feathers for the weekend.

"Woodstock's a lovely little place," she went on. "Is that one of the reasons why you decided to work there? Speaking of which, do you think that you'll be able to have next Friday off, so that you can enjoy Thursday evening? You could even stay over for the weekend if you would like to. Grandma and Grandpa will be staying. I could speak to the headmistress and explain that it's my birthday and wedding anniversary, if you would like me to?"

"No, no," gulped Susie. "That's fine. It's all arranged. I've asked Miss Jennings and she's said I can have Friday off." Hell, she thought to herself, she was supposed to be on lates this coming week and she wouldn't be able to do that on Thursday. Alf was going to be really pissed off with her. And, she'd HAVE to make sure that she got away from her parents early enough to work on Friday night, without being late this time. Plenty of time to think of an excuse for her parents during the week, but the first thing she must do tomorrow would be to explain to Alf about the dinner and after he'd been so kind and given her this curry too. She felt a real cow – she loved her parents and she wasn't giving them the time that they would like, and dear old Alf had been so kind and she was letting him down as well.

The reference to her mother's birthday and her parents' wedding anniversary made Susie realise that she was going to have to buy presents and petrol and wouldn't be getting another pay cheque until Friday. What was she going to do? Why on earth had she bought the sodding champagne? That was £27 that she hadn't needed to spend. If James didn't help her out she really was in deep shit. Forcing herself to keep smiling, Susie cleared away the main course and brought out the strawberries.

Around 11.00 pm her parents thanked her for a wonderful evening and Peter called a cab. Susie agreed to pick him up at 10 o'clock the next day, and turned her attention to the mound of clearing up.

*****

Whilst his parents had been enjoying Philip's salmon Thai curry, James and Greg had spent the evening getting to know each other a little better. This time Greg had gone over to Moulsford as Allsort had proved happy to welcome Zizi on their previous meeting. Greg had taken her basket and rug so that she had familiar things with her and the two dogs had a long walk before bed. Checking that they looked happy and settled, James and Greg headed for the stairs, carrying a bottle of champagne.

Greg was impressed by Riverside House. He also knew that James had inherited £100,000 the previous month. He already found him very attractive, but the add-ons that came with him were certainly mind-blowing. He would be a fool to let this one slip through his fingers.

CHAPTER 33

Susie, being Susie, didn't get to The Feathers until almost 20 minutes past 10 the following morning, which, as she knew it would, irritated her father. "I'm sorry, Daddy, I don't know why I'm late," she said apologetically, as Peter glowered at her over the Telegraph.

"Don't worry, darling," said her mother, "you know what Daddy's like. Now that you are here join us for a cup of coffee and then you can take Daddy to collect his car while I have a stroll around the antique shops." Annabelle summoned the waiter and asked for a fresh pot of coffee and another cup.

Susie sat down and tried to relax. She suddenly realised that her mother was asking her to join them for dinner at The Feathers that evening. "Oh, I can't, but thank you," she stammered.

"Why on earth not?" demanded her father.

"It's just that I've got a date," said Susie, blushing. It was the first thing that she could think of and felt it would be bound to put her parents off. "It's a first date," she went on to say.

"That being the case it wouldn't be appropriate for us to suggest that you both join us this evening," said her mother. "Never mind, we shall see you on Thursday for our little party. I hope that you'll be staying for the weekend. I know that your grandparents would enjoy that." Susie felt her heart drop to her boots. She was about to disappoint her parents again. It was becoming a regular thing, but she had no choice. She desperately needed to hold on to her job at the pub. She tried to change the subject by asking her parents how they liked The Feathers.

Annabelle offered to show her daughter their room, which was very pretty and had a large corner bath. "Not that you'd want to stay in Woodstock, of course," she said, laughing. "You must see enough of it, coming here every day." Susie smiled weakly. "Don't let your father upset you, either," continued her mother. "You know what a stickler he is for time and your time keeping is pretty dire. Drive him back to Enstone carefully and he'll be fine. Don't rush, I would like time to have a good look around the antique shops. As you can't have dinner with us tonight, I'll ask Daddy what his plans are for tomorrow. It might be that we could all have lunch together." Susie said she would like that.

Going back downstairs, they finished their coffee. Peter and Susie set out for Enstone whilst Annabelle walked towards the centre of Woodstock.

"I haven't been in your car for ages," said Peter to his daughter. "Do you still like it or are you thinking of changing it? It'll be three years' old on your birthday in November." Changing it, Susie thought to herself, she couldn't afford to put petrol in the damn thing at the moment!

"Oh no, Daddy, I shan't be changing it, thank you. I love it to bits," said Susie. Peter smiled and told her that he was glad. Covertly he studied his daughter as she was driving, and thought how beautiful she was and how odd it was that she wasn't in a serious relationship. Still, she had a date tonight, so that was something. He knew that Susie was a bit scatty, and he would love to see her settled.

"Shall we have a drink at that pub in the next village?" Sodding hell, thought Susie to herself, but instead managed to smile at her father and suggested that it was rather early for a drink.

"Why not come in and have another cup of coffee instead?" she asked. Peter declined politely, saying that perhaps he ought to get back to Woodstock. As Susie didn't seem to want to join him, he decided that he would sample the delights of The Crown on his own. After all, it was approaching midday, and the perfect time for a quick pint to fortify himself for the afternoon's shopping. Parking his car outside, Peter thought what an attractive pub it was, and when he got inside and looked at the menu, decided it would be a nice idea to book a table there for lunch the following day. He decided to book for three, unaware that Annabelle had already asked Susie if she were free. He just hoped that she might be able to join them. After all the table could always be cancelled if Annabelle didn't think it was a good idea, or reduced to two if Susie couldn't come.

Having enjoyed his drink, Peter booked a table for the following day, and headed back to Woodstock.

*****

Susie was at work promptly at 4.55 pm, as she didn't want Alf to be cross. It was going to be bad enough asking to swap her shift again on Thursday. Taking a deep breath, she asked him if he had a minute. "This is very awkward, Alf," she began. "You have been so kind to me giving me this job and helping me out with my dinner party last night – my parents loved the curry by the way – but it is my mother's birthday and also my parents' wedding anniversary on Thursday..." Alf held up his hand to stop her.

"And don't tell me, they want you to go to some sort of party on Thursday night when you should be working for me." Susie nodded her head. "You've only worked for me for just over a week, Susie love, and during that time your need to change shifts has been a bleedin' nuisance," said Alf. "I suppose you didn't tell me about these special dates for fear that I wouldn't take you on. Now then, are there any more parties coming up that I should be aware of?" Susie shook her head and said that she hadn't deliberately misled Alf, but she just hadn't thought about the dates. Looking at her, Alf thought that she was most likely telling the truth. "Right," he said "if I sort this one out for you are we going to be all right for the next few weeks?" Susie thanked him and assured him that all would be well and set about getting herself organised behind the bar.

Saturday night was as busy as Alf had predicted and she felt shattered by the time her shift finished. She'd had a break for supper at 6.30, but that had been it. The rest of the time had been quite frantic. Still, it did make the time pass quickly. David Timmins, from next door, had been in for a few pints and had bought her a drink. Susie had to admit to herself that he seemed a pleasant chap. He'd been very surprised to see her working there. After making him promise that he wouldn't tell James, she explained that she'd walked out of her proper job and Alf was very kindly helping her out until she found something permanent again. David had smiled at that, and said that Alf was a lovely man once you got behind his bluff exterior.

It was almost 1 o'clock by the time Susie got to bed, and she was rather glad that she didn't have to get up early the next morning. Mummy had texted to say she hoped her date was going well and that she and Daddy would pick her up for lunch at midday. What luxury, thought Susie, lunch out with Mummy and Daddy and then something delicious cooked by Philip for supper. Surely Sunday night wouldn't be as busy as Saturday? She went to sleep thinking what she was going to say about her date, as her parents would be sure to ask.

*****

The following morning her father's navy blue BMW drew up outside Rose Cottage at one minute to twelve and Susie walked down the path immediately, as for once in her life she was ready on time. She asked her parents if they had enjoyed their stay at The Feathers. Her father appeared to be most taken with the Gin Bar, but then he always had enjoyed a gin and tonic.

Susie asked her parents where they were going for lunch and was told to wait and see, as they thought it would be a nice surprise for her. It was definitely a surprise, but nice was not the word that Susie would have chosen as her father manoeuvred his way into a parking space in The Crown's car park. Jesus Christ, how was she going to get away with this one? Perhaps she could get to a table in the restaurant before anyone noticed her, but then of course the waiter or waitress who served them would know her and be bound to say something. Why, oh why, had Daddy chosen to come here?

Feeling slightly sick, she got out of the car and followed her parents in to the pub. Alf was meeting and greeting, which he did with great enthusiasm. "Hello, Susie love," he said, "when this gentleman booked a table yesterday I wondered if he was your dad. Good morning Mr and Mrs Rowlands." Samantha, behind the bar, also said "Hi, Susie, can't you keep away?" Susie glared at her whilst muttering a hello. It wasn't going to be long before her parents knew that she worked here. She could feel it coming.

Alf showed them to a table in the dining room and said that he would send someone to take their order. When he had gone, Peter commented that Susie seemed to be very well known in the pub and asked if the food was as good as it sounded. Susie promised him that it was. Oh hell. Simon, the most gossipy waiter, was approaching their table for the drinks order. "Hi Susie darling," he said, "No doubt it'll be a glass of dry white wine for you?" Susie cringed.

"Hello, Simon," she replied, "let me introduce you to my parents."

"Ooh, half your luck, still, you deserve it after working so hard yesterday." Came the cheerful reply. When Simon had gone, Annabelle asked whatever did he mean? Susie shrugged her shoulders and said that perhaps he was mixing her up with someone else. "This pub is so busy," she went on. "The staff try to be friendly, but they're bound to get people mixed up sometimes."

The meal itself passed without incident and Susie's parents told her how lucky she was to have such a lovely pub so close to where she lived. They then took her home and came in for coffee. Susie was very relieved, when at 4 o'clock, Peter said he thought it was time that they were leaving. She just had time to wash up the coffee things and get changed ready for her shift at 5 o'clock.

CHAPTER 34

Susie's week wasn't going well. She had got up early on Monday morning, despite the fact that she felt exhausted from working at the pub on both Saturday and Sunday night. She had printed off several copies of what she considered to be a very smart-looking CV and, with those in her case, and Granny's ring on her finger, she had set off to Oxford.

Full of hope, Susie had started with the recruitment agencies. She was surprised to see that she had been rather well paid at Woodstock Academy, and that the average wage seemed to be some £2k per annum less. The stumbling block came when she was asked for references and she explained that she had walked out of her last job in a fit of temper. All the agencies (and she saw five of them) told her that without a reference from her last employer they weren't interested in her. Susie then asked about temporary work and was given the same answer. What on earth was she going to do? The only thing would be to say that she had been helping her father with his business and that the time had come for her to move on. The snag with that would be that she would have to tell her parents what she had done and that would be just awful.

Feeling very despondent, Susie had then set off on her tour of the jewellers. Granny's ring was valued at £6,550 on her insurance policy and that was what Susie was hoping for. These hopes were soon dashed as the most she was offered was £2,300. Susie went on to ask what it would cost to make a ring just like that one, but with a cubic zirconia instead of a diamond. The sales assistant looked worried at that point, and explained to her that she would not be able to mimic the old fashioned setting if she tried to have something made. "How about just swapping the stone then?" Susie asked desperately. The sales assistant told her in no uncertain terms that they did not deal in cubic zirconia. Susie slunk out of the shop, feeling very small indeed.

By that time it was approaching 3 o'clock, so she left Oxford, still wearing the ring, as she had to be behind the bar by 5.00 pm.

When she got home, Susie decided that she would have to call James and ask him again if he was prepared to help her. He told her very firmly that he was busy and would ring her back later. Alf got cross if anyone took phone calls when they were working, but it was a chance she would just have to take.

True to form, James phoned at the worst possible moment and not only had she not been able to speak to him, she had also succeeded in annoying

Alf. He just had to have been passing at that particular moment, didn't he?

*****

It was now Wednesday, the day before her parents' party, and Susie had no presents for them and very little money. She just had to speak to James and convince him to help her. She daren't ask Alf for a sub against her wages. It was only week 2, after all, and she had changed shifts twice already. She made herself a cup of coffee, sat down at the kitchen table and picked up the phone. This time James was at home and slightly more approachable. "You sound as though you're in a right mess, Suse," he said.

"I am," she replied. "I really wouldn't ask unless I were desperate. I can't turn up without presents for Mummy and Daddy and I have other issues, too."

"Why are you so hard up?" enquired her brother. "I thought your job was pretty well-paid."

"Yes, it was." said Susie.

"Is that the past tense?" came the swift reply. Oh shit, thought Susie, I really have done it now.

"I'd prefer to talk face to face," she said to him.

"OK," said James. "Give me your bank account details again as I've lost them, and I'll transfer £100 when I go to Wallingford this morning. That'll buy you petrol to get to Moulsford and pressies for Mum and Dad. I hope your story's a good one!" Susie asked him if he could possibly make it £250, as she could do with paying something off her credit card, but to her disappointment, he refused.

Still, £100 was £100. She would wait until lunch time and then go into Banbury very quickly and buy Mummy some perfume for her birthday, and she would get on the internet immediately and order some anniversary flowers to be delivered the following morning. Her credit card should just about manage that. Susie thought she had about £25 left to spend. It would soon be Friday and pay day.

*****

When she got up on Thursday morning, Susie laid out what she wanted to wear that evening, as she had to be at the pub before 10 and then wouldn't be back until just after 5, so she knew she needed to be as organised as possible. Her parents had asked her to be there for 7 and that was cutting everything very fine indeed. Although she normally walked to The Crown when she was doing a day shift, Susie knew that today she had to take the car. She packed her overnight bag and put it in the boot and then drove via the garage so that she would have enough petrol for her journey.

The day passed very quickly indeed and it didn't seem to be long before Susie was back home. She rushed through the shower and washed her hair as she didn't want to risk smelling "pubby" and clambered into the long turquoise dress with the low back that her mother had bought her from Monsoon. Stilettos were the order of the night and Susie had some gorgeous gold strappy heels, which went well with the bold, imitation gold jewellery that she had worn last time she went to Moulsford. She also had a gold clutch bag, which she stuffed with the essentials, whilst putting her large, every day bag, into the car.

Coming downstairs at speed, Susie stumbled and heard a horrible tearing noise. She had got one of her heels caught in the hem of her dress and ripped it badly, so that she couldn't possibly wear it. At this point she burst into tears. Why, why, why, she asked herself? For once in her life she had just about been on time and now she had ripped her dress and would have to have a complete change of clothes. What was more, she must stop crying, because she was ruining her make-up. The thought that she needed to stop just made Susie cry all the more. It was now ten minutes past six. What the hell was she going to do? What was she going to wear? She had tried so hard to get everything right for this evening and as usual, everything had gone wrong. She'd have to get herself together and ring her parents and explain why she was going to be late.

Susie decided to ring her mother's mobile as she felt she stood more chance of sympathy from her and was horrified when her father answered it. "Don't tell me," he said, "You're going to be late. What's your excuse this time? I hope it's a good one. You finish school at 4 o'clock and it's now quarter past six and you're still in Enstone. Honestly, Susie, you're useless!" Susie started to cry again. "For goodness sake, stop crying," said her father in exasperation. "Don't even bother with the bloody excuse. Just tell me what time you think you'll manage to grace us with your presence. After all, it's only your mother's birthday and our 28th wedding anniversary. Whatever made me think that would gee you up to be on time?" Susie whispered that she would be there as soon as possible and rang off.

Feeling even more depressed, Susie went back upstairs and washed her face. Her eyes were hideously puffy and she couldn't sort them out just yet. She opened her wardrobe door and looked at the contents. In the end she settled on the black dress that she had last worn in Nice with Jonathan. It was short, so at least she wouldn't catch her foot in it going down the stairs. She changed her gold sandals and bag for black ones and her gold jewellery for pearls, as she felt that would make her look more sophisticated. Susie then turned back to the mirror and was relieved to see that her eyes were looking more normal, so she was able to reapply some make-up. With the addition of a bright red lipstick she was ready. What time was it now? Looking at the clock in the kitchen, Susie discovered that it was 10 to 7. It was going to be well after 7.30 when she finally got to Moulsford, and her father was going to be beside himself. Perhaps Grandma and Grandpa being there would help to calm things down and James was taking Greg too, so Daddy couldn't really create too much of a scene, could he? She kissed George goodbye, and walked carefully down the path to her car – not wanting another accident.

*****

Annabelle's parents had arrived at Riverside House shortly after 3.00 pm, both very much looking forward to the evening's entertainment. They were very fond of their only daughter and delighted that she had married so well. It was clear that Peter worshipped Annabelle and equally obvious that money wasn't a problem. Annabelle and Peter's lifestyle seemed to them to be quite fabulous.

Peter watched his in-laws park their car and carried their bags in to the house. Annabelle was out at the beauty salon being pampered and James was in the antique shop. Peter told them that both their daughter and their grandson would be home shortly. He then set about making a pot of tea.

Just as Peter had said, it wasn't long before Annabelle arrived home, closely followed by James and there was lots of hugging and kissing. The family spent a happy hour or so chatting and then went their various ways to get ready for the evening's entertainment.

Peter had been determined that Annabelle should have nothing to do, as she was always the perfect hostess who worked so hard to make sure that everything ran smoothly for everyone else. He and James had laid the table in the dining room and sorted out the wines. James had arranged Susie's flowers beautifully and they were placed in the centre of the dining table. All that was needed now was for the caterers to arrive. They were serving a hot three course meal. When they arrived Peter briefed them as to which wine should be served with what and then took two bottles of pink champagne and seven glasses out into the garden. It was at this point that Susie telephoned. Peter was really angry. Tonight was Annabelle's night, and as usual, his daughter was going to be late and upset the arrangements.

Promptly at 7.02 pm Greg arrived and James took him through into the garden and introduced him to his grandparents. Greg had pulled out all the stops and was looking simply divine in a cream linen suit and an open-necked blue shirt. His diamond earring was sparkling and his gold necklace was shining against his tanned neck. As he was staying the night, he was accompanied by Zizi, and she and Allsort were soon chasing each other around the garden.

Greg was naturally charming and was soon flattering Annabelle's mother Anne, saying he could see where Annabelle got her beauty from. The elderly lady preened and thought what a nice young man James' friend was. "Where's Susie? She's the only one missing," Anne said suddenly. Peter tried to control the fury in his voice as he explained that for reasons unknown to him, his daughter was going to be late.

At around 7.30 one of the catering staff appeared from the kitchen and asked Peter what time he would like the meal to be served. Having ascertained that everything would be fine for another 15 – 20 minutes, Peter asked for the starter to be served at 7.45 pm. He re-joined the group and told them that they would be asked to make their way into the dining room in few minutes. Annabelle asked if they were going to wait for Susie and Peter shrugged his shoulders and said she would either be there or she wouldn't. He wasn't having the food ruined because his daughter couldn't be bothered to be on time. "No, Belle, don't go and phone her," he said, "this is our special night, and in particular yours. I'm not allowing Susie to take centre stage and spoil it for us any more than she has managed to do already." He then kissed his wife on the cheek and told her that she was as beautiful as the day he married her.

Looking at his watch, Peter then asked everyone to follow him to the dining room. Greg jumped to his feet and offered Anne his arm. She was becoming more taken with him by the minute. As they took their places, everyone was aware that Susie's chair was empty.

*****

Susie had the journey from hell from Enstone to Moulsford. For some reason the Oxford Ring Road was jammed and it was 4 minutes to 8 when she finally parked on her parents' drive. Clutching her mother's birthday gift, she rang the bell, as she had forgotten her key. The door was opened by one of the catering staff who told her that the family was eating in the dining room. Susie groaned inwardly and took a deep breath. This was not going to be pleasant! She was bursting to go to the loo, so she dived in there first, checked her make-up and ran her fingers through her hair. All in all, she didn't think she looked too bad. Susie took another deep breath and opened the dining room door.

It was about as tricky as it could be. Everyone was eating their starter and chatting away, and silence fell as she walked in. "Hello everyone, I'm so sorry I'm late. Happy birthday, Mummy," she said, walking towards Annabelle and holding out her little parcel. Annabelle thanked her and suggested that she sat down. Peter glared at her and told her that as they had nearly finished their first course she could make do with the bread that was on the table and join them when the main course was served. He then nodded to a waitress, who poured Susie a glass of wine. Bravely she raised this to toast her parents and wished them a very happy anniversary, and again wished her mother many happy returns of the day. The others joined in the toast and conversation gradually started again. Seven is not the best number to seat at a long dining table and Susie found herself next to Greg, with her father on her other side at the head of the table. Her grandfather was on the other side of Greg, her grandmother and James were on the opposite side of the table and her mother was at the other end of the table, opposite her father.

James introduced Susie to Greg, who immediately told her that she clearly got her looks from her beautiful mother and that she looked stunning in black. Susie thanked him, thinking back to the last time she had worn the dress and what a happy evening that had been. She found Greg totally charming, but equally she could feel her father's coldness. In desperation she turned to him to try and explain why she was so late, but Peter wasn't in the slightest bit interested and told her so. "You are usually late, Susannah, and I'm sick of it, so let's say no more now and make the best of the rest of the evening," he said. Jesus, she was in his bad books. No-one called her Susannah unless they were really angry with her.

Susie was relieved when the evening was over, but as she went to bed, all she could think about was how she was going to get away the following day to be back in Enstone in time for her shift at the pub.

CHAPTER 35

Susie awoke feeling anxious the next morning. She had two things on her mind. To make her escape from Riverside House as soon as possible, and to get James on his own to talk about her financial mess. She didn't think that either of these things was going to be easy. Showered and dressed, she went downstairs to find Greg and James sitting in the kitchen, eating toast and drinking coffee. They smiled at her and wished her good morning. "There's coffee in the pot if you'd like some," said James. Susie thanked him and poured some.

"What are you guys doing today?" she asked. Greg said that he was working, and James said that he would be going to the lunch organised by their grandparents. "What lunch?" asked Susie in horror. "I don't know anything about it."

"That's because you arrived late," her brother replied. "Grandpa's booked a table at The Beetle and Wedge. You're invited, Suse, so there's no need to look so worried." She nodded glumly. It was going to be difficult to get away by 3.30, but that's what she had to do.

Trying to get back in her father's good books, Susie laid places for her parents and grandparents in the dining room, and set about breakfast. First of all she decided that she would take them tea in bed, as it had turned 9 o'clock and she felt sure that they would all be awake now. She went to her grandparents' room first, where she thought she would get the warmer welcome. They were delighted with the tea tray, but declined Susie's offer of a cooked breakfast, saying that cereal and toast would be fine. She then knocked on the door of her parents' room, to be greeted by Peter asking who was there and telling her to leave the tray outside. She blushed at the thought that she might have interrupted something.

Feeling somewhat deflated, Susie went back downstairs and found a selection of cereals to put on the dining table for her grandparents. She added fruit juices, butter, jams and marmalade, and then went and perched on a stool in the kitchen with another cup of coffee. James, Greg and the dogs had disappeared. Bugger, she thought to herself. James is going to do his best to avoid me.

By the time that James and Greg had returned, Susie was sitting at the dining table with her grandparents, eating toast and chatting away. They were telling her that they didn't see much of her and that it would be lovely if she were to come and stay for a weekend. Knowing that to be impossible at the moment, Susie explained that she was rather busy, but would love to come and stay as soon as she was able. At this point her parents came into the room, so she jumped to her feet and asked them if she could cook them breakfast. Knowing that cooking was not one of Susie's skills, they thanked her and said that toast and cereal would be plenty as they were going out for lunch. Susie went into the kitchen to make more toast and coffee.

When Susie was back at the table, Annabelle asked her if she would be staying for the weekend. Susie replied that she couldn't, as she had to be back in school early that evening and for the following day. It was Parents' Evening with the school's annual open day on the Saturday, so she explained that she was very fortunate to have been allowed to have the Friday off, with all that was going on. Her mother nodded her head and said that it was wonderful that Susie had such an understanding boss. Susie smiled tightly, and began to clear the table.

Once she'd finished with the breakfast dishes, she turned her attention to tracking James down. She finally ran him to earth in the garden, and sat down beside him. "Please, Jamie, can you lend me some more money? Just £1,000 would be wonderful."

"Just £1,000," replied her brother sarcastically. "If it really was JUST £1,000, you wouldn't need to borrow it, would you? I think you should tell me the truth as to why you need money so desperately. It's the end of the month, so you should have been paid."

"Oh, I have," said Susie. It wasn't a lie, as Alf had paid her that morning. "The thing is, I've booked a really expensive holiday and paying for it has left me without the money to pay my mortgage or my bills. And the speeding fine didn't help either."

"I'm pretty sure you're up to no good," replied her brother, "and you're a crap liar too. Tell me the truth and I'll think about it."

"I have told you the truth," snapped his sister, and flounced off.

*****

The family had a very pleasant lunch at the Beetle and Wedge. Anne said how much she liked Greg and was he James' friend, rather than Susie's? They said that he was. "Such a charming man," she replied, "you could do with a young man like that, Susie, darling." If only you knew, Susie thought to herself as she smiled at her grandmother.

Lunch over, Susie said her goodbyes and headed off, arriving at The Crown at 10 minutes to 5. She was filling the ice bucket when she heard a familiar voice greeting Alf. No, it couldn't be! As she turned round, Susie saw the glamorous blonde in tow. "Susie, love, this is Jonathan. Look after him would you please? Go and find a table, Jonathan, Susie'll come over to you."

"Thank you, Alf, but I know Jonathan," she replied. "His children go to

Woodstock Academy. How are you Jonathan?" she asked, turning to him. "Aren't you going to introduce me to your companion?" Jonathan ignored her and escorted the blonde to a table as far away from the bar as he could get.

"That was a bit abrupt, Susie love," said Alf. "Jonathan's a paying customer, and a good one at that."

"I'm sorry, Alf. I didn't mean to sound abrupt. Let me go and see what they would like to drink." With that she crossed the bar and stood beside Jonathan's table with an enquiring look on her face. Christ, Jonathan thought to himself, I didn't know that she worked here. I do hope she isn't going to create a scene. She's already made it perfectly clear that she knows me. All thoughts of impressing and seducing the blonde were rapidly disappearing.

"It's nice to see you again," he said, smiling frostily at Susie. "It must be a rush to get from Woodstock and be here by this time on a Friday evening." Susie smiled and took his order.

As she was pouring the drinks, Susie thought how wonderful it would be to trip with the tray and land both glasses in the blonde's lap, but knew that Alf would know she had done it on purpose and she needed the job too much for that, so she contented herself with placing the drinks in front of the two of them and asking how Angela was, adding that she hadn't seen her for quite a long time. She could see that Jonathan was seething. Finally the blonde went to the ladies' room, so Susie took the opportunity to collect some glasses. She stopped by Jonathan's table to remark that no doubt the blonde was her successor and did he realise she'd lost her job because of him and was having to work here to make ends meet? Jonathan shrugged his shoulders and got to his feet as the blonde returned to the table. Susie picked up the empties and moved on. Why did she still find him so attractive, she asked herself?

She then noticed that David Timmins had come in and was propping up the bar, so much to his amazement, she started to flirt outrageously. So much so, that after about twenty minutes he plucked up courage and asked her out to dinner. "Dinner," Susie shrieked. "I could think of nothing nicer. How about next week? I'm on the day shift then." Heads were turning in her direction, including Alf's, and she noticed that Jonathan was coming up to the bar to settle his bill. She took his money and tried to look condescending. "Do please give my love to Angela," she shouted after his departing back.

"I didn't realise you knew the Brownes," said Alf. "I've never met Mrs and that obviously wasn't her."

"Absolutely not," came the reply. "Angela's a dreary little woman."

"What evening would suit you for dinner?" asked David. Oh hell, I shall actually have to go out with him, Susie thought to herself. She had only said what she had to try and spite Jonathan, but who did she think she was kidding? Jonathan wouldn't have cared if she'd said she was getting married. Mind you, she wasn't having any success on the internet and at least she'd get a free meal, which would save a bit on the groceries. She smiled at David and suggested Wednesday. It was half way through the week and she shouldn't be too tired by then.

David couldn't believe his luck. He thought that Susie was absolutely stunning and he'd got a date with her. Ordering another pint for himself, he bought the woman of his dreams a glass of wine. Alf winked at him. "All right there, son?" David raised his glass by way of reply.

CHAPTER 36

Annabelle's weekend had been wonderful. Peter had asked her parents to bring their passports and he had whisked them all off to Guernsey in his plane on Saturday. Once there, they had taken a taxi to St Peter's Port, where they'd had a walk around the shops and lunch at Government House. Peter had stocked up with cigars and following afternoon tea overlooking the harbour they had taken a taxi back to the airport and flown home. Her parents had really enjoyed the experience because they had never been in a light aircraft before. Then on Sunday she had cooked a roast lunch before her parents set off back to Derbyshire. Annabelle reflected that although game for anything, her parents were beginning to show their age and made a mental note to visit more, as she had not seen them since James' birthday the previous month.

Now it was Monday morning and Mrs Baxter was due any minute to do the cleaning. Once she had Mrs Baxter organised, Annabelle decided that she would ring Miss Jennings at Woodstock Academy to thank her for allowing Susie to have Friday off at such a busy time.

Ten minutes later Annabelle sat down in the Conservatory with a cup of coffee and her phone. She was surprised when Susie didn't answer, but she was soon put through to Miss Jennings. She had never met the woman, and thought her tone was unnecessarily frosty. "Good morning, Miss Jennings," she said, "I am Annabelle Rowlands, Susie's mother, and I am just calling to thank you for your kindness in allowing Susie to take Friday off so that she could join in my birthday celebrations. I understand from her that it was a particularly busy time for you with the Parents' Evening and the Open Day on Saturday."

"What on earth are you talking about?" came a very cross voice down the line. "Susie no longer works here, and hasn't done for some weeks now, courtesy of her disgraceful behaviour. You of all people ought to know that. I have nothing more to say so will bid you good morning, Mrs Rowlands." With that the line went dead.

Disgraceful behaviour? thought Annabelle. *Hadn't worked there for some weeks?* What the hell was going on? Susie was certainly lying to her and had been for a while. She hadn't believed all that nonsense regarding Monaco for a start. How long had her daughter not been working at the school she wondered? Was she working at all? The best thing to do was to get herself over to Enstone and confront little miss butter-wouldn't-melt and see what was going on. Annabelle looked at her watch. It was coming up to 10.30

am. If she went over to Enstone now, she would find out whether or not Susie was working. If she weren't at home, Annabelle could amuse herself with a look round the local antique shops.

Finishing her coffee, Annabelle went upstairs and chose a jacket and handbag to complement her outfit. She asked Mrs Baxter to lock the door when she left and went and got her car out of the garage. As it was a beautiful morning, she put the hood down and set off on her journey.

*****

Arriving in Enstone, Annabelle was interested to notice Susie's car was parked outside the cottage. That suggested to her that her daughter was indeed unemployed. She knocked on the cottage door, but there was no answer. Perhaps Susie had walked to the shops. She then heard a voice from next door, "It's Susie's mum, isn't it?" Turning round, Annabelle saw a figure walking down the path of next door's cottage.

"That's right," she said smiling. "I thought I'd pay Susie a surprise visit, but she doesn't seem to be in."

"No," said Mrs MacDonald, "she went out about half past nine this morning and I expect she'll be back between half past five and six." Annabelle thanked her and said that she would come back later. Perhaps Susie was working locally?

Getting back in the car, Annabelle again looked at her watch and saw that it was getting on for lunchtime. She decided to visit The Crown. Susie had seemed to be very well known there and she might find out something. Worst case, she could at least have something to eat, as the Sunday lunch had been excellent.

Going into the bar, she was greeted by Alf. "Good morning, love," he said, "if I'm not very much mistaken, you're Susie's mum, aren't you? You came to lunch the other Sunday." Annabelle replied that she was. "Susie's in the garden, having a bit of a tidy up. We were very busy last night and the customers left a mess. Can I get you a drink love? By the way, in case you don't know, I'm Alf, and this is my pub." He held out his hand. Annabelle took it and introduced herself. She then asked for a glass of Chablis, feeling that she needed something in order to deal with what was going on. It was apparent that Susie was working in the pub, having lost her job at the school, and she wanted to find out as much as she could from Alf before she confronted her daughter.

She smiled and thanked Alf as she accepted the drink. Taking a sip, she then complimented him on the quality of the wine. Alf preened. "Hasn't Susie told you about my extensive wine list?" he asked. Annabelle shook her head and said that Susie hadn't really told her a lot, except that the food was excellent, which she knew herself, having been there for Sunday lunch the other week. Alf told her that he had spent a lot of years in the meat trade and he prided himself on the quality of his meat and other ingredients too. Annabelle agreed wholeheartedly with him, explaining that she enjoyed cooking herself. "Oh yes, love," said Alf, "Susie said that you're a belting cook and she can't live up to your high standards." Annabelle smiled and told Alf that it was something she enjoyed doing. He said that he loved cooking too, but that he employed a chef, as he wanted to spend his time with his customers, not sweating away in the kitchen. He'd done the cooking when he'd first bought the pub, but things had come a long way since those days.

Annabelle decided to take the bull by the horns. "How's Susie getting on?" she enquired casually.

"Very popular with the punters, as she's such a pretty girl, but then looking at her mum I can see where she gets it from," said Alf. "She needs to learn to be a bit more reliable though. I've let her get away with murder, partly because she reminds me of my own daughter when she was Susie's age, and partly because she has natural charm. I'm sure it won't be too long before she has a proper job again."

Proper job again, thought Annabelle. I could do to get out into the garden and catch her now, while she's on her own. "Look, Alf," she said, "would you mind if I went and had a quick chat with Susie now, before it gets busy and you need her in here?"

"Why not?" said Alf. "Take as long as you like. I can send someone to fetch her, if I need her."

Annabelle thanked him, and picking up her glass of wine, headed into the garden. Susie had her back to her, cleaning a large table, so Annabelle had the advantage of surprise. "Hello darling, you look busy," she said. "I've just been having a nice chat with Alf. He's told me that I can come and keep you company and that he'll give a shout if he needs you behind the bar. I'm sure he wouldn't mind if you sat down for a minute so that we can have a little talk."

*****

Shit, shit, shit, thought Susie as she turned round to greet her mother. How the hell do I get out of this? How much has Alf said? Why is Mummy here? "Hello Mummy," she said, going to put her arms round her and kiss her. Annabelle responded a trifle coolly to her daughter's greeting.

"Sit down, Susie," she said. "Before we start, I don't want any of your lies this time. Why did you leave Woodstock Academy under a cloud?"

"I don't know what you mean," stammered Susie. "Who says I left under a cloud? I just got bored with working there."

"Bollocks," said Annabelle crossly. "You can't afford to be bored. You are extravagant and you have a house and a mortgage. Things are beginning to fall into place regarding your recent behaviour. Now please tell me the truth."

"I am telling you the truth, Mummy," lied Susie. "I got sick of the rich little girls and that old trout Miss Jennings and thought I would do something different."

"Well, this is different, I grant you that," said her mother. "But somehow I don't think it will provide enough money to feed your lifestyle. However, I do know now why you have rushed off every time you have come to see us. You've needed to get back here to work. Maybe Miss Jennings also saw you on tv at Monaco and maybe you missed some school to be there, telling her you were off sick, so she sacked you?"

"Nice try, but wrong," said Susie, praying that Alf would get busy and call her in.

"Well, whatever the reason, I still don't know the truth about Monaco," said her mother. "Frankly I'm not inclined to go home until I get to the bottom of all this. So far, your father doesn't know anything."

"Well, it's nothing to do with either of you what I do," said Susie bravely. "I'm 24 in November."

"Start acting like it then," snapped her Mother. "Always late, pathetic excuses. I wasn't born yesterday you know. What time do you finish here?"

"5 o'clock," replied her daughter.

"Right," said Annabelle. "I'm going to have one of Alf's delicious lunches and then I shall see you at your house at 5.30. You can carry on with your cleaning up now."

Leaving a stunned Susie, Annabelle walked back into the pub and asked to see the lunch menu. She ordered another small glass of Chablis and insisted that Alf join her in something. He poured himself a glass of Leffe and then escorted Annabelle to a table in the restaurant overlooking the garden. Being a kind man, he asked Annabelle if she would like him to release Susie to join her, as he always gave his staff a meal when they were on duty. Annabelle assured him that it wouldn't be necessary and turned her attention to trying to find out more about her daughter's employment at The Crown. Unfortunately Alf got called away, so her plan didn't work. However, she did have a very tasty fish pie with some delightful little vegetables. Lunch finished, Annabelle paid her bill and told Susie, who was now behind the bar, that she would see her later. She thanked Alf for his hospitality and left.

CHAPTER 37

All the way through her shift Susie wondered what she was going to say to her mother. Should she confess all? Well, not all, because she didn't need to tell her mother that she'd been having an affair with a married man. That wouldn't win her any brownie points with a woman who had just celebrated 28 years of marriage. Alf had said what a lovely woman her mother was and Susie was dying to know if they had talked about her, but certainly wasn't going to ask.

Wearily, she left the pub just after 5.00 pm to walk home. It took her about half an hour, and sure enough, there was her mother's car parked behind the Mini on the lay-by outside her cottage. As Susie approached, her mother got out of the car.

"Did you have a nice afternoon, Mummy?" asked Susie.

"Yes, thank you," replied her mother, "but we both know this isn't about me. Now get the door open and the kettle on. I'm not in the mood for being messed with. It was something of a shock to me when I phoned Miss Jennings this morning to thank her for her kindness to discover that you no longer worked at the school. I would like to know what happened and why."

"I've already told you, Mummy. I got sick of the rich little girls and that old cow Miss Jennings herself."

"For a start Susie, I very much doubt that those 'rich little girls' as you so disparagingly call them are any more privileged than you are and always have been and the fact that you didn't particularly like Miss Jennings is quiet immaterial. Now make me a decent cup of coffee and tell me the truth. Or do you want me to go up to the school and ask Miss Jennings exactly what happened?" Her mother was fuming, but Susie didn't have the sense to back down.

"You wouldn't dare," came the reply.

"I wouldn't dare, Susannah? You really don't know me very well at all, do you? Dare doesn't come in to it. I want to know what in God's name is going on in your life."

"I fancied doing something different for a change," said Susie handing her mother a cup of coffee and offering the biscuit tin. "Can't you understand that? Oh no, of course not. You've always had Daddy to keep you, haven't you, whilst you play at being an antique dealer with your dear little shop." She jumped in amazement as her mother's hand slapped her across the face.

"I probably should have done that years ago. Maybe you wouldn't be such a spoiled little cow now," said her mother crossly. Tears started to roll down Susie's cheeks. Her mother had never, ever hit her and she had never called her a cow either. This was mega serious.

"You can go on at me for as long as you like," Susie managed to whisper. "But I've nothing more to say to you. I've told you why I left Woodstock Academy and I can't help it if you don't believe me."

Annabelle realised that she wasn't getting anywhere. Susie wasn't going to budge, so she might as well go home and then try and get an appointment to see Miss Jennings in order to get to the bottom of all this. She didn't want to tell Peter until she had the full facts. Then she could decide how much he needed to know. She knew that he would be angry and disappointed. Susie had always been spoiled, particularly by her father and this, it would seem, was the result. She thanked her daughter for the coffee and biscuits and left.

*****

Susie sat in stunned silence after her mother had left. What the hell was she going to do? Apart from her mother, her finances were in a mess. Who could she turn to? Should she tell James the truth? She couldn't possibly ask Alf for a loan and she had ignored most of her friends recently because she had been so involved with Jonathan. She needed a proper job and she needed it now. She couldn't possibly do any more hours at the pub. She was working seven days a week as it was. George put a paw on her leg to indicate that he would like something to eat and she absent-mindedly stroked his head.

A plan – that was what she needed! She needed to know how much she spent per month and how much she was short. How she was going to find the amount that she was short she had no idea, but at least it would be better to know. She could then go to the bank and explain her temporary problem and hopefully borrow some money off them. Unfortunately, she was working days this week, but at least she could ring the bank and make an appointment. Susie went to look for her latest bank statement so that she could start on her plan – feeling very grown up indeed.

She found it, after a bit of searching, and didn't like what she found! She hadn't realised how much she spent and what she spent it on. What Susie considered to be essentials came to well over £1,000 per month and that didn't allow for the huge interest that she was going to be paying her credit card - 18% on all outstanding balances, and she was just about up to her credit limit. If she was lucky she would get about £1,000 from working in the pub, but she already owed James money out of that. There was also the danger that Alf would find someone permanent soon – she had seen various people come for interview – and then she would be really scuppered.

Susie went and looked in her food cupboard and her freezer. She could live more economically – for a start she didn't have to buy wine and she was getting a good meal at the pub, so with toast or cereal for breakfast and a snack for the other meal she would be OK. She would have to give up the luxuries such as biscuits and chocolate. Poking about in the freezer she found that she had quite a few ready meals in there, so they would also help to keep her going for a while. She'd have to find a cheaper hairdresser too. She could no longer afford to pay £60 for a cut and blow dry and as for her nails - it looked as though she couldn't afford to wear her false acrylic ones any more either!

First thing in the morning, on her way to the pub, she would walk via the shop and buy whatever local papers they had, in the hope that there might be some sort of proper job that she could apply for, and she would ring the bank and make an appointment to go and see someone the following week. Feeling much more positive, Susie opened some salmon Sheba for George and her last bottle of wine, as she felt she ought to celebrate the start of her plan.

CHAPTER 38

Annabelle was deep in thought as she drove home. She was now very concerned about Susie and was wondering what was going on in her life. Equally she was determined to find the answer to that. She didn't want to confront Miss Jennings, but if that was what it took, then that was what she would do. First of all, though, she thought she would start with James. The two children had always been close and she was working on the principle that they still were. Peter had been golfing all day and with a bit of luck he would be firmly ensconced in the 19th hole so she would have the opportunity to speak with James on her own and without Peter's interference.

She was pleased to see that Peter's car wasn't at home and that James' car was. "Hello Mum," came his voice as soon as she opened the front door. "Wait until I tell you what sort of a day I've had." Annabelle smiled and forced herself to listen whilst James rattled on about the various items that he had sold at the shop.

"That's marvellous, darling," she replied. "Now let me get us both a drink. What would you like?" James said that he would like a beer and asked what was for supper. Annabelle confessed that she hadn't thought that far ahead, but as his father was obviously still at the golf club, they would quite possibly send out for a takeaway. "No doubt you're starving?" she enquired. James confirmed that he was, so Annabelle put out bowls of nibbles to go with the drinks and as it was a pleasant evening, she carried them through into the garden.

After she had sipped her drink and eaten a few nuts, Annabelle decided that she must take the bull by the horns and see what James knew about his sister. "I'll come straight to the point," she said, "I'm worried about Susie. Something odd is going on there, and knowing how close you two are, I'm wondering whether you can shed any light on it?"

"What do you mean by odd, mum?" he asked. "I don't know anything other than that she's hard up, 'cos she's borrowed some money from me."

"Really?" said his mother. "How much?"

"£350 in all," replied James. "But she's asking me for more. She says that she's booked an expensive holiday and that has made her a bit short. You know how extravagant Susie is though." Annabelle nodded her head.

"I knew there was something wrong," she said to her son. "Now I know what it is I can try and help her." The conversation suggested that James didn't know that his sister was no longer working at the school.

"Does Susie say much about work?" she enquired casually. James shook his head.

"No, it's not something we discuss. To be quite honest, Mum, I've been a bit wrapped up in myself recently."

"And Greg, perhaps?" asked his mother. "Is there anything you would like to tell me?"

James blushed a deep crimson and took a long swig of his beer. "I don't really know where to start," he said, "but, yes, Greg and I are very close. He's a very special person in my life, if you know what I mean?"

"I think I do," replied his mother. She had been wondering about her son's sexuality for some time and it was evident that James was also questioning it. She certainly wouldn't mention it to Peter until things had moved on a bit more. She wanted to be certain of her facts before she stirred up anything there! Peter would be sure to disapprove and take it personally. She had the Susie hurdle to jump first and as it looked as though all James knew was that his sister was hard up. She had no choice but to brace herself and go and see Miss Jennings which she would do tomorrow. The sooner she knew what exactly was going on with her daughter, the better.

At that moment, Peter walked into the garden. "Ah, there you are," he said. "What's for supper, Belle? I can't smell anything cooking."

"Whatever takeaway you and James would like to order," came the reply.

*****

Annabelle was pleased when Peter announced that he was going to London to his office the following morning. That would give her the opportunity to strike whilst the iron was hot and before she lost the courage to go and visit Miss Jennings. She dressed carefully, selecting a plain cream linen dress with a little shrug and her trademark Jimmy Choo heels. She swept her long dark hair up on top of her head, wishing to look professional as she needed to be taken seriously.

She thought that mid-morning would be a good time to arrive, so set off accordingly. Arriving at the school, Annabelle planned to walk straight in through the front door and locate the School Secretary's office. However, she was surprised to see that she couldn't just walk in because of the school security. She pressed a button, and was asked by a disembodied voice who she was and what she wanted. The door was buzzed open, and Annabelle was directed to the School Secretary's office in order to sign in. Once there, she was met by a stony-faced woman. Annabelle asked to see Miss Jennings. She watched the woman's expression change as she told her that Miss Jennings wasn't available. Annabelle asked when would be a good time to call back and the poor woman looked extremely uncomfortable as she explained that Miss Jennings had told her not to put her through again on the telephone, so she knew that a personal visit would be quite out of the question.

Annabelle raised her eyebrows at this and asked the secretary if she knew why. The woman lowered her voice and said, "I think it's because of what your daughter did, Mrs Rowlands."

"What my daughter did?" echoed Annabelle in amazement. "I wasn't aware that she had done anything. Perhaps you can help me there?"

Fortunately the drab little woman seemed keen on gossip and in hushed tones told Annabelle that Susie had carried on an affair with the father of two pupils at the school and when caught out and confronted by Miss Jennings had been extremely rude to her and resigned on the spot. "Had she not resigned," the secretary continued confidentially, "I'm quite sure that she would have been sacked."

Annabelle really didn't need to hear any more. "I mustn't keep you from your duties," she responded crisply. "I'd hate you to get in trouble with Miss Jennings because of me." With that she turned away and left the secretary wondering whether perhaps she had been indiscreet, but after all, Mrs Rowlands was the girl's mother and quite clearly she had the right to know what had been going on.

Annabelle walked slowly back to her car, wondering what she was going to do next. Peter would have to know, because quite obviously Susie wasn't going to get another secretarial job, or any other kind of proper job, without a reference from the school and working in the pub at Church Enstone certainly wasn't going to fund her daughter's lifestyle. There was no point in confronting Susie again today, so she got into her car and turned it towards Oxford.

*****

Susie had set out for work early, via the shop, so that she could buy the weekend papers. She intended to look through these during her lunch break. As usual, Alf was wandering around when she got to the pub. "Morning, Susie love," he said. "That was a nice surprise your mum coming to see you yesterday." Susie nodded her head, but didn't say anything. "I see you've got the papers." Alf went on to say. "Thinking of leaving me already, love?"

Susie explained to him as nicely as possible that much as she loved working at The Crown, she wasn't earning enough money to cover her overheads and that she couldn't possibly work any more hours and anyway, he was looking for someone permanent, so she could be out of the door pretty soon. Alf said he quite understood and hoped that she found something more suited to her ability, then headed into the kitchen to find out what Philip's specials were going to be.

Susie hadn't had time to ring the bank and as she was quite early, she slipped out into the garden to phone for an appointment. She was surprised and upset by the reception she received. She was told in no uncertain terms that her account was overdrawn and that no cheques, direct debits or standing orders would be honoured. Hesitantly, Susie asked if her mortgage had been paid the previous day and was told very firmly that it hadn't and that she needed to make a deposit quickly as an unauthorised overdraft was very costly. She tried to explain that was part of the reason for wanting an appointment, in order to sort things out, but the person on the other end of the phone clearly wasn't listening, as she had hung up on Susie. That left her with only one thing to do – she must go to the bank in Woodstock first thing the following morning and make sure that she was back at The Crown for opening time.

Thinking quickly, Susie decided that it would be better to have her wages in cash, so that she could decide what money was paid, who it was paid to and when it was paid. Oh God, Alf would probably have a hissy fit, but she was going to have to ask him. Bracing herself, she headed for the kitchen and asked Alf if she might have a word.

"What is it this time, Susie love?" he asked. "Do you need to change shifts again. Have you forgotten someone's birthday?" Susie cringed, but then realised that Alf was smiling.

"No, no, Alf, it's nothing like that," she said. "It's just that I'm having a bit of trouble with the bank and would really appreciate it if you could pay me in cash please."

"Bit of trouble," echoed Alf. "I think you mean that you are in more trouble than you want to own up to, and you're going to be right up shit creek as you won't be able to afford to eat, buy petrol or do anything else. Would I be right by any chance?"

Oh God, thought Susie again, Alf's certainly no fool. She nodded dumbly. "Well, you have to live, and I can't see you starve," he said, "but you're a bleedin' nuisance you know. Yes, I'll sort out cash for you, but mum's the word. I'm not doing that for everyone who works here." Susie threw her arms round his neck and kissed the old boy on the cheek.

"You're a star you know, Alf. You really are," she said.

"Go and do some work." was the reply.

Susie went about her tasks cheerfully. At least she wouldn't be bothered by her mother making a surprise appearance today. It would look odd if she came back again and Mummy had far too much style to let that happen. Little did she know where her mother had been and what information she had gathered.

CHAPTER 39

Peter felt very pleased with himself as he studied share prices the next morning to find a deal he had placed had done more than come good, it had come excellent! He would have to keep a close eye on the company and probably sell soon in order to realise an excellent profit.

Annabelle was delighted to see her husband so full of the joys of spring, and wondered whether it would be a good time to tell him about Susie's troubles. He'd have to know at some point and would be even crosser if he discovered that she'd been keeping secrets from him. Armed with a strong cup of coffee, she approached Peter's study.

"Hello darling, are you busy or may I come in?" she asked, opening the door. "Of course you can come in, Belle. Come in and sit down and let me tell you about the cracking deal I've pulled off. If all goes according to plan we shall certainly have something to celebrate next week. Perhaps we'll take the aircraft and go away for a few days. What do you think? Anyway, this is what I've done..."

Annabelle found her mind wandering. She didn't really understand Peter's wheeling and dealing and frankly wasn't very interested in it. She knew that they had a good, solid investment portfolio that brought them in an extremely healthy income on top of Peter's RAF pension and that occasionally he did some other sort of deal which seemed to bring them in a handsome additional sum. Clearly this was what he had done now, or had nearly done now, if they had to wait until the following week for confirmation.

"That's splendid, darling," she said as soon as he had finished speaking. "Now I, or rather we, have a problem that we need to discuss."

"A problem?" repeated Peter. "What sort of a problem would that be? You haven't backed the car into anything have you?"

Annabelle assured him that she hadn't and said it was a larger problem than a piece of bent metal. She went on to tell him that she had been suspicious of Susie's behaviour ever since they had seen her on the television at the Monaco Grand Prix. "Go on," said Peter. "I'm listening." Annabelle swiftly filled him in on all the details, and Peter's face grew increasingly serious.

"Bloody hell." He sighed when Annabelle came to the end of the sorry tale. "Do you think that the affair is true?"

"I think it has to be," replied his wife. "We haven't seen or heard of a boyfriend for a very long time and why on earth would Susie resign from a good job to go and work in a pub? She doesn't yet know that I know all about her resignation. She told me that she was bored and wanted to do something different, but you and I both know (and so will she by now) that she won't be able to pay her bills. She's in an absolute mess and I'm not sure how we tackle it."

Peter looked thoughtful. "I'm not sure that we do tackle it yet, sweetheart," he said. "It won't do her any harm to be in the shit and wonder where the next penny's coming from. Susie has led a privileged existence and a taste of the real world might not do her any harm. I'm very disappointed that she had an affair with a married man. I wouldn't mind betting that he took her to Monaco. You know how much Susie likes the glamorous lifestyle. I just hope to God she isn't pregnant."

"You're being very philosophical, darling. I thought you'd go berserk," said his wife.

"Oh believe me, I'm really angry," said Peter, "but we need to think about this and be clever. Eventually she will have to come to us for money, but in the meantime let the little madam sweat. By the way, have you told James about this?" Annabelle said that she hadn't. "I think it's best it stays that way for the moment," replied her husband. "We need to think about our next move very carefully indeed."

*****

Susie was looking forward to her night out with David and was smiling to herself as she walked home from the pub. It was a pleasantly warm evening, which helped make her feel good after all the crap weather they'd had recently. George was waiting for her on the mat by the front door along with three letters and after she had fed him and made herself a cup of coffee, she opened the post. The first one was from the Halifax, telling her that she had missed her monthly mortgage payment and would she please pay it straight away. The second one wasn't a lot better – it was an electricity bill for £62.17, but at least it wasn't a final demand, and the third one was to tell her that she was due a dental check-up. Whatever was she going to do about the mortgage? She hadn't got the money– simple as that. Sick to her stomach, Susie went upstairs and ran herself a bath.

After she had soaked for half an hour, she felt marginally better, or at least she didn't smell of beer any more! After towelling herself dry, Susie smothered herself in body lotion, before spraying herself liberally with Chanel Chance Tendre – Jonathan's latest offering from one of his trips abroad. At least she could do David the courtesy of looking and smelling good. Opening her wardrobe door, Susie chose a short black and white spotted dress with a flirty skirt, a pair of black patent high heeled sandals and a black patent clutch bag. She accessorised her dress with a large pearl necklace and matching earrings. Finally, she applied a little make-up and was both pleased and amazed to see that she was ready ahead of schedule. She went downstairs to wait for David.

On the dot of 7.30 a red sports car drew up outside her cottage. Susie had no idea what it was - only that it looked impressive. She told David this as soon as she opened the door. He looked delighted and told her that it was a 1993 Alfa Romeo Spider and that it was one of the last ones produced. The colour apparently made it even more rare – Vinaccia Red. Having admired the car, Susie turned her attention to David. He was tall, slim and very dark, and the white shirt he was wearing under his jacket enhanced his colouring. Not a bad looking date, she thought to herself. At the same time, David was studying Susie and had come to the conclusion that she was quite beautiful and he felt very proud to be taking her out to dinner.

They drove over to Woodstock, where David had booked a table at La Galleria, a very pleasant Italian restaurant. As she sat opposite him, Susie felt quite comfortable, but she was still worrying about the day's post and in particular about her mortgage payment. She hadn't liked the part that had said something about your property being at risk if you didn't keep up the payments on your mortgage.

It wasn't long before the waitress came to take their order. Susie really liked Dover sole, but couldn't bear the thought of having to take the bones out of it, so asked the waitress if the chef could take it off the bone for her. "Why don't you have the halibut?" was her reply. Susie took a deep breath and decided that she wasn't in the mood for messing about.

"Had I wanted the halibut I would have ordered it," she replied. "Now can the chef take the fish off the bone or can't he?"

"I was only trying to help," said the waitress, giving Susie a very sulky look. "I'll go and ask."

Susie looked across the table and she could see that David was trying not to laugh. "Don't you think that was a bit harsh?" he asked.

"No," said Susie, "I don't. For that matter why don't I have the ravioli?" At that point the waitress returned and said that the chef could take the sole off the bone, so they placed their order.

Whilst they were waiting for their food, Susie asked David about his car, and whether cars were one of his interests? He replied that they were and told her that he often marshalled at Silverstone, as he was a fan of motor racing and in particular Formula 1. She then told him about her trip to Monaco for the Grand Prix, with a friend who was involved with one of the racing teams. David looked impressed and said that was something he would love to do. She replied that it had certainly been an experience!

Their starters arrived at that moment, which saved Susie being asked any embarrassing questions about her trip. David then turned the conversation to Susie and asked what her interests were. She found this a difficult question to answer, as her only recent interest had been Jonathan. Looking very sad she replied that she was a keen shopper and enjoyed going to spas and beauty salons. David noticed the sadness and thought it strange that such a lovely girl seemed to be so despondent. He wondered if something was worrying her. Maybe he should try talking about holidays? She'd been to the Grand Prix in Monte Carlo, so clearly she was used to travelling. Looking even sadder, Susie told him about the singles' holiday that she had booked to Spain in August.

Singles' holiday? David thought to himself. Why, oh why, is such a pretty girl going on a singles' holiday?

David smiled to himself again as he watched Susie devour her Dover sole. "This is really delicious," she said to him, "I'm glad that I stuck to my guns with madam over there. It's ages since I've been to this restaurant and I must say that tonight's meal is the best that I've had here." David was pleased and wondered how he could ask Susie what was bothering her.

Suddenly the penny dropped, or at least David thought it did! Jonathan Browne, who worked for Lotus up on the airfield, had been in the pub the night that Susie had been coming on to him. Hadn't Susie said that his children went to Woodstock Academy – where she no longer worked? Hadn't Susie been to Monaco with a friend who worked for a racing team? Could that friend be Jonathan Browne? Could she have been having an affair with him and could she have been caught out? He knew this was all supposition but it would make perfect sense. Interesting, very interesting. How did he move on from here?

Clearly, Susie was extremely unhappy. Maybe she had money problems? Perhaps he could help her there with some sound common sense, but of course she had to tell him of any difficulties. He could hardly ask. At the end of the evening he would ask her for another date. Yes, that was definitely a plan.

*****

On the drive back to Enstone, Susie, who was a little tiddly, decided that she would invite David in for coffee. After all, he had always been nice to her, and at the moment she needed all the friends she could get.

She was a bit unsteady as she walked up the path and as she went into the kitchen, she knocked her post off the worktop and on to the floor, which David picked up and handed to her. Shit! Had he read it?

Being a financial adviser, David was used to reading through masses of information at speed and had indeed skim read the post and realised that Susie was in trouble. When they were sitting down drinking their coffee, he gently told her that he couldn't help but notice the letter from the Halifax, and wondered if he could help her in any way? Susie's chin trembled as she told him that she didn't think anyone could possibly help her, the mess that she was in. "Nothing is ever as bad as it seems," said David reassuringly, "but now is not the time to talk about it. We've had a lovely evening out, it's late and we both have work to go to in the morning. Why don't you come round and see me after you have finished work tomorrow evening and I'll see what I can come up with to help you?" Susie nodded her head and said that she would do just that.

CHAPTER 40

Susie was thoughtful as she walked to work the following morning. She'd had a pleasant evening out with David and was very hopeful, after what he had said, that he would be able to help her out of her financial mess. She was surprised to find Alf already in the bar and even more surprised when he asked her to join him in his office.

"Oh dear, have I done something wrong that you want to speak to me this early?" she asked, laughing at him.

"No, Susie love, you haven't done anything wrong," he replied "but you remember our agreement when you started work here. You were looking for a better job and this was just to get you by and I was looking for a permanent member of staff?" Susie nodded her head, wondering what was coming next. "Well, love, the thing is, I've found someone and he'll be starting a week on Monday, so I shall have to finish you a week on Sunday night. I'm sorry, but that was always the plan. If you're interested I can always contact you as and when I need some casual help – until you get your proper job, that is."

Susie's heart sank. She hadn't thought things could get much worse and was even feeling better after last night, but suddenly things had got very much worse indeed. David was going to have to work a miracle when she saw him later. She thanked Alf for letting her know the situation and made her way back to the bar, fed up to her back teeth.

The end of the shift couldn't come soon enough for Susie. Feeling very downcast, she walked next door to David's cottage. He had left the office early, to be sure that he was home in plenty of time and had changed out of his business suit and into a pair of jeans and a pale pink polo shirt. Susie was taken aback by the pale pink, as she had looked upon David as a serious person who wouldn't wear such a colour, but thought how well it suited him with his dark hair and skin tone. Smiling at her and once again thinking how beautiful she looked, David invited her in.

He asked her whether she would like tea, coffee or something stronger, and feeling that it could be a tough evening, Susie opted for a glass of wine. Sitting down, David started to ask about her financial commitments. "Don't look so worried," he said to her. "I'm sure things won't be as bad as you imagine them to be."

"You must be joking," said Susie ruefully. "They've just taken a turn for the worse today. Alf has a new person starting, so I will be finishing work a week on Sunday. I've been trying to borrow money off James but he's not being helpful. I really don't know what I'm going to do. I can't even get agency work because they all want a reference from my last employer, and the school won't give me one as we parted on bad terms."

David wondered whether or not he should enquire as to these bad terms, but thought better of it. Instead, he asked Susie if she was sure that the school wouldn't give her a reference. "Definitely not," she said bitterly. "And you really don't need to know why. I'm just worried that on top of all the problems that I already have, that I'm going to lose my house as well. I've even tried selling Granny's ring, which is worth a few thousand, but none of the jewellers I went to would give me anything like the price it's worth. I just have no money David, and no chance of getting any and I don't know what to do or how I'm going to live. It was awful when I had the job at the pub but it's much worse than awful now." With that, and to her horror, Susie burst into tears.

Not really sure what he should do, David went and sat beside Susie on the sofa and put his arm round her. Unable to help herself, Susie leaned against David's chest and cried even harder. David then wrapped his arms round her and patted her back and stroked her silky hair. Eventually Susie sat up and started rummaging in her bag for tissues, which of course she couldn't find! David smiled at her and went and fetched some loo roll. "Sorry," he said "but that's the best I can do for the moment." Susie thanked him and proceeded to blow her nose.

"Have a drink," said David, "and let's see what we can do to help you. Have you brought your paperwork with you?" Susie nodded and fished in her bag again, producing a variety of bills and a bank statement. "Right," said David, "let's start with the money you owe, and we'll take it from there."

Half an hour later, David had composed a letter to the Halifax, explaining that Susie was currently unemployed and asking if she could take a payment holiday and another similar type of letter asking if she could spread out her payments, for her to send to utility companies as and when the bills came in. He then went on to write to the council regarding her Council Tax and MasterCard regarding her credit card bill. Susie dutifully typed the letters on her iPad, so that she could print them out when she got home. He told her that she would have to use the little money that she had wisely and only buy essentials such as food or petrol. He went on to say that he really felt that Susie's best bet was to tell James the truth and see if he would then lend her some money, because clearly she needed money whilst she looked for another job.

"But I'm just not going to get one! Don't you understand?" wailed a distraught Susie. "Bloody Woodstock Academy won't give me a reference because I walked out."

"Have you considered apologising to them and saying that you were

180

very hasty?" suggested David.

"After what I said, it would be impossible to go back," she replied sullenly.

David decided to take the bull by the horns. "Look, Susie," he said. "I'm trying my best to help you, but you're only telling me half a story. Please would you tell me what happened at Woodstock Academy? You can be safe in the knowledge that I won't tell a soul."

Susie thought about it for a moment and then decided to go for a half truth. "I was accused of doing something that I didn't consider to be any business of the school's and I ended up by telling the headmistress exactly what I thought of her and then walking out." Well, that was near enough, wasn't it?

Jonathan Browne, sure as eggs are eggs, David thought to himself. Instead he said, "And had you done what you were accused of?" Susie nodded. "Was it that bad that you had to walk out of your job?" he enquired.

"In their eyes it was," said Susie.

As far as David was concerned, that confirmed that she had been messing about with Jonathan Browne. Susie would have had a very rose tinted view of things and she might even have thought that Jonathan would leave his wife for her. An upmarket school such as Woodstock Academy would have taken a very dim view of a member of staff having an affair with a parent and she had no doubt become very defensive and lost her temper. Yes, it all made sense to him, but he did want to hear it from Susie herself, in case he was barking up completely the wrong tree. In her own way, David felt that Susie was not proud of what she had done, hence her reticence in telling him.

"Come on, Susie, please tell me," he said. "I've told you that I won't tell anyone."

Unsure as to whether or not she could trust David, Susie asked if she could sleep on it and perhaps they could have another chat the following evening.

"Tell you what," said David, "you come round again when you've finished in the pub and I'll cook us a bit of something to eat. It's Saturday and I'll have plenty of time to prepare things. What do you say?" Susie replied that she would like that.

*****

When she got home, Susie thought about what David had said. Could she trust him or not? She would dearly like to fully share her problems with someone, but even if she told him, what could she expect him to do? Should she tell James what had really happened? If she did, would he lend her some money? Would he run to her parents? Equally, David knew James and might tell him and in turn James might tell her parents. Her head was going round and round. One thing Susie did know was that trying to sort this out on her own seemed to be impossible. Would she ever work again? She couldn't imagine even trying to go to Woodstock Academy and telling the awful Miss Jennings that she was sorry and asking for a reference. She wouldn't give the old cow the satisfaction of turning her down.

Tentatively, Susie picked up her phone and dialled James' number. When the phone refused to dial out, she gave it a puzzled look and tried again. Again, it wouldn't connect. This time she decided to ring Vodafone and ask if there were problems with the network. They reassured her that the network was fine, but said her phone had been barred due to non-payment of her last bill. Weakly Susie asked how much it was and was told that it was £68.17. She wondered how the hell she could have spent that much money in a month and said so. Vodafone replied that she hadn't paid for two months and asked her if she would like to do so now with a card. Susie whispered that she couldn't and cancelled the call. For the second time that evening she burst into tears. What, oh, what, was she going to do? She picked up George and carried him upstairs for comfort. After all, she might as well go to bed. She couldn't think any more.

CHAPTER 41

Susie woke the next morning with her mind going round in circles. George was still on the foot of her bed and made demanding noises as soon as she moved. As he seemed to be her only friend in the whole world she attended to his needs before her own. Once he was attacking a dish of Purina with gusto, she went back upstairs, showered, dressed and got herself ready for the day.

As she walked to The Crown, Susie decided that she would ring James and ask him again to lend her some money. She would ask Alf if she could use his phone, explaining that her mobile didn't appear to be working and that she didn't have a land line. She wasn't sure what she was going to do if James wouldn't help her. She might have to tell David the truth after all. He did seem a nice bloke, but then she had thought that Jonathan was wonderful and her judgment there had proved to be way off the mark.

Alf wasn't immediately available when Susie reached the pub, so she set about checking the bar over whilst she waited to speak with him. Eventually his cheerful face appeared. "Morning, Susie love, how are you today?" he enquired. Susie assured him that she was fine and told him about her phone. Alf didn't believe a word of it, thinking it far more likely that she had been cut off, but being kind hearted didn't say so, and said that she could use the phone in his office provided that she didn't spend all day on it. Thanking him, Susie went off to ring James. She couldn't believe it when the damn thing went to voice mail, so left her brother a message asking him to call her.

When she went back to the bar Alf asked if she had got through OK. Susie said that she hadn't and she hoped he didn't mind, but she had left James a message to ring her back. "I hope it's not while we're busy. It is Saturday, you know," came the reply. Susie assured him that it was urgent. Alf raised his eyes to heaven at this comment and decided it was time to test the ale, as he was expecting a busy day.

*****

In Moulsford, James had just started to tell his mother that he was going to move in with Greg when his phone rang. Looking at it, he didn't recognise the number, so decided to ignore it. If it were important, whoever was ringing would leave him a message and then he could call back.

"Aren't you going to answer that, darling?" enquired Annabelle. James told her that he wasn't and explained why. "I've got something very important to tell you, Mum, and I don't want to be interrupted by someone ringing me who I probably don't know." Annabelle laughed at that and asked whether the something were ominous.

James decided that he would have to take the bull by the horns. "It's just that Greg is looking for a lodger and I've decided it's about time I moved out of home and as we get on so well…"

"It's OK, you don't need to justify yourself," said Annabelle. "Greg needs a lodger does he? Is there anything else that you would like to tell me?" James went pink and gawped at his mum.

"I don't know what you mean," he spluttered.

"I've never been to Greg's house and was just wondering what it was like," said Annabelle, smiling sweetly at him.

"Oh, if that's what you want to know it's a two bedroomed Victorian cottage in Cholsey – end of terrace, actually," replied her son. "I'll have to share bills and everything. It's going to be a proper arrangement."

"Proper, is it?" enquired Annabelle, smiling up at him. "I know that you and Greg have been seeing a lot of each other. Are you sure that you don't want to tell me anything else?" James shook his head. "OK then," replied his mum. "When are you thinking of leaving us?"

"We thought the 1st August was a good date, as everything will be shared up on a monthly basis," said James, "so I shall be here for another three weeks or so, but will start moving my things over gradually. I've only got a Mini, so it'll mean quite a few trips."

"Dad and I and Allsort will all miss you," said Annabelle. "Are you going to tell Dad or am I?" James asked her if she would, and said that he'd still see lots of her at the shop. "Never forget that this will always be your home, as it is for Susie," replied his mum. "Speaking of Susie, I hardly hear from her these days. How about you?"

James replied that he didn't hear much from Susie either and felt a little guilty, as he knew that his sister was clearly in some sort of trouble and he hadn't helped her out or called her to see how she was. "Tell you what, Mum," he said, getting out his phone, "why don't we ring her now and see how she is? It's Saturday, so she won't be at work." With that he dialled Susie's number, and was stunned to hear a message to the effect that the Vodafone he was calling had been disconnected. "That's odd," he said to his mother. "Susie's phone has been disconnected. She must have a new one with a different number and forgotten to tell us. Typical!" Or she's been cut off, Annabelle thought to herself. It appeared that things could be getting worse for her daughter. She'd have to have another word with Peter about her.

*****

James couldn't wait to get to the Lamb Arcade and tell Greg the news that he'd told his mother they were moving in together and it was only when he was there that he remembered his missed call. He then also noticed that someone had left him a voice message and was very surprised to discover that it was from Susie, asking for a call back at a number he didn't recognise. He was even more surprised when the number he dialled was answered "Good morning, The Crown. How may I help you?"

"I'm so sorry," said James, "I must have dialled the wrong number." With that he hung up, checked the number and tried again. This time the phone was answered by a man with a Yorkshire accent. James explained to him that his sister had left a message asking to be called back on that number.

"Sorry son," came the reply. "It's Saturday lunchtime and the place is very busy. Could you ring again about half past four please?" James said that he would.

"I'm confused," he said to Greg. "Susie's phone isn't working and she's asked me to ring her on a number which apparently is the pub in her village and I've just been told that I can't speak to her now because the pub is busy." Greg shrugged his shoulders. He wasn't particularly interested in James' sister. "Perhaps she's helping them out," he suggested.

James' mind was now working overtime. Susie had not had the money to pay a speeding fine and had borrowed more money from him since. In fact she was still asking for money. Her phone wasn't working – had she been cut off rather than bought a new one? Why had she been trying to ring him that morning? Was she still trying to borrow money to pay her mortgage? Could she be working at the pub for some extra cash? Hopefully he'd find out when he rang her later. As the arcade was getting busy, he had to put thoughts of Susie out of his mind and concentrate on the customers.

James was surprised when his mother appeared in the shop just before lunch. "Well," she said, "I thought I should take you boys out to lunch to celebrate the fact that you're going to be sharing a house." Oh hell, thought James, she's going to pry but there's nothing I can do about it, watching his mother walk across the corridor to talk to Greg. He saw his friend smile, making it was obvious that he had accepted the lunch offer.

*****

Once they were settled in The George, James decided to employ diversionary tactics by telling his mother that he'd had a message from Susie asking him to ring her back, and that when he had done so, he had discovered that the number was The Crown and he had been told to ring back later because the pub was busy. What did she think could be going on? Annabelle replied that it sounded as though Susie was working there and no doubt he would find out what was going on when he eventually spoke with her. She then turned her attention to Greg.

"So," she said, "my son's coming to live with you. What fun. You two seem to have hit it off from the start."

"Absolutely," replied Greg. "I'm really looking forward to James moving in." James could feel himself beginning to turn red and glared at Greg. However, there seemed to be no stopping him. "It seems pointless James staying at home with you, when really all we want is to be together, doesn't it James?" he went on. James muttered something unintelligible.

"Sorry darling, I didn't catch what you said," said Annabelle, who was rather enjoying herself. "What was it you said about moving in with Greg? I thought you were sharing a house, but it sounds a bit more like you are sharing each other's lives?"

"It's really not what you think, Mum," muttered James.

"Isn't it?" said Annabelle, "and what do I think? Do tell me." James was going redder by the minute, so Greg took over.

"Stop being naughty, Annabelle," he said. "I think you have a perfectly good idea of what's going on – James and I are very fond of each other and because of that we've decided to live together. You know that I'm gay, so I'll leave you to draw your own conclusions." Annabelle smiled at him and thanked him for his honesty.

"Oh do stop squirming James," she said. "I've thought for a long time that you were probably gay and have been waiting for you to tell me. Now Greg has saved you the difficulty and embarrassment."

"I don't know what to say," replied her son. "I thought you'd be shocked."

"I'm not," said Annabelle, "but I don't really think that this is either the time or place for this conversation, so let's enjoy our lunch and we can talk more this evening."

"Just one more thing," said James. "What about Dad?" What indeed, thought his mother.

CHAPTER 42

Susie was really fed up that James hadn't rung her back when it was time for her to leave The Crown. She didn't think she could ask Alf to use the phone again. Then, just as she was about to go, Alf caught her at the door to tell her that there was a phone call for her. She dashed into his office, and found to her relief that it was James on the phone.

"What on earth are you doing at the pub on a Saturday and what's up with your phone?" was his opening sentence.

"I'm doing some bar work to earn some extra money – if it's any of your business. I've already told you that I've bought an expensive holiday and had a bloody speeding fine. I'm utterly skint," she replied.

"What about the phone?" persisted James.

"What about it?" replied Susie.

"Look, Suse, I'm worried that you're in some sort of trouble. What's going on?" asked James.

"Yes, so worried that you won't help me by lending me a measly £1,000," she snapped back.

"Really, Susie, that's not the way to talk to someone who you're trying to borrow a measly £1,000 from," said James. "Tell me the truth about what you want it for and I'll think about it."

"I have told you the truth," she shrieked at him. "I can't pay my mortgage or my other bills. Do you want to see me out on the street?"

"Oh don't be so dramatic," said James. "Mum and Dad would never let that happen. I think Mum's worried about you too, by the way. She asked me this morning if I'd heard from you, which is why I tried to call you and discovered that your phone had been cut off. Would that be one of the bills that you can't pay?"

"Look Jamie," said Susie, trying to sound calm. "Will you help me or won't you?"

"This is going to go on for ever," said James, "and I'm bored with it now. Ring me when you're prepared to come clean, and then I'll think about it."

With that Susie slammed the phone down. As she came out of the office, she bumped into Alf, who asked her if everything was all right. "Not really," she said, "but no doubt I'll survive. I'm going next door to see David now. He's cooking me a meal." Alf smiled to himself as he had a fairly good inkling that his neighbour was smitten with Susie and really, he thought to himself, she could do a lot worse. He wished her a nice evening and walked off towards the kitchen to see how Philip was getting on with preparations for the evening.

Susie got herself together and went next door, where she was greeted by a smiling David. Looking at her face, he felt that things had not gone well for her since the previous evening. "Glass of white wine?" he enquired. Gratefully, Susie accepted.

"How are you today?" David asked as soon as they were sitting down.

"Really pissed off," said Susie. "My phone's been disconnected because I haven't paid the bill for two months."

David groaned inwardly. This girl was proving very difficult to help. "And have you talked to James?" he asked.

"I've tried to," she replied, "but he kept banging on about why I need the money and it's nothing to do with him. I put the phone down on him in the end."

"You really aren't helping yourself, are you?" said David. "You want people's help, but you won't even meet them half way. It's perfectly reasonable for your brother to want to know why you need the money. Now use my phone, say you're sorry you hung up on him and for God's sake tell him what's going on."

Susie said it wasn't as simple as that. David told her very firmly that it was and handed her the phone. Susie was stunned by David's assertiveness and sat looking at the phone. "Go on," he said.

"I don't think I can," she replied. "It really is too awful."

"Right," said David. "Tell me then, and we can decide together."

Taking a gulp of her wine, Susie told him all about Jonathan.

It was pretty much as David had expected so he wasn't particularly shocked, just sad that Susie had been so stupid and thrown away her job for a man, particularly one who clearly was a Grade A bastard.

"I can see why you don't want to go and ask for a reference," he said, "but would it be so bad if your parents were to find out what had happened?"

"Mummy would be bound to disapprove," said Susie. "She and Daddy have been married for 28 years so she wouldn't understand."

"Maybe you don't give her, or indeed both of them, enough credit?" suggested David. "Anyway, you do need to talk to James and see if he will lend you some money. You've just had your phone cut off and your job finishes at the end of next week."

"Thanks for reminding me," said Susie. "Although I don't know how you think I could forget," and she started to cry again.

David was cross both with himself and with Susie. He hadn't meant to upset her, but was trying to get her to see sense. "Loo roll again, I think," he said, going to fetch it.

"Look Susie, I'm sorry that you're upset," he said, "but life is tough and you're in a mess and I'm trying to help you out of it. You need some cash, and the only place I can see it coming from is your brother or your parents. I'm doing my best to buy you time, but that's all I can do, put off the day of reckoning. Now pull yourself together and get on the phone to your brother. Apologise to him and ask him for a loan. You should also tell your parents what's happening, but James will do for tonight. I'd like you to ring him and then you can relax over supper."

Susie realised that she had no choice, so after giving her nose a good blow, picked up David's phone and rang James.

*****

James was at Greg's when his phone rang – again a number he didn't recognise. However, raising his eyebrows at Greg and saying he had no idea who it was, James answered it and was surprised when it was his sister on the other end.

"Hello Jamie," she said tentatively. "I'm sorry I put the phone down on you. Can you talk now? Or rather, can you listen?" James groaned to himself. It was Saturday night and he was looking forward to going out with Greg, and now Susie wanted to talk. He mouthed, "This could take some time," at his boyfriend, and went out to the kitchen.

"Fire away, Suse," was all he said.

Hesitatingly and with her voice breaking at times, Susie told her brother the story of Jonathan Browne. For once, she was remarkably honest and didn't hide anything. James did feel sorry for her but still wasn't sure what to do. He knew that he wanted to discuss the situation with Greg, but of course he wasn't going to tell Susie that. Instead he told her that he needed to think about it overnight and would call her back the next day. "Please help me, Jamie," was all she said as she hung up.

"Sorry Greg," said James, returning to the living room. "That was my sister on the phone. She's in queer street and wants to borrow some money."

"Bad choice of words, don't you think?" enquired the love of his life. "But do please tell me more."

James hesitated, but then told Greg what Susie had just told him. "What are you going to do?" he asked.

"I really don't know, and would like to talk to you about it," said James.

"Right." said Greg. "I think we probably need to do this over a drink. Let's take Zizi for a walk to the Red Lion. I'm sure we can get something to eat in the garden to go with the drink." With that he got the dog's lead and the two of them set off for the pub.

*****

When David came out of the kitchen, carrying cutlery, and saying that supper would be about 10 minutes, Susie told him with great pride that she had told James the whole saga and that he would let her know about the cash the next day. As he laid the table, David smiled at her, but thought that it was unlikely that her brother would help her. If he'd been going to, wouldn't he have said so there and then?

Putting his thoughts to the back of his mind, David went into the kitchen to finish off his cooking. It wasn't long before he was back, carrying two different curries – a chicken and a beef. Going back, he emerged with a steaming bowl of pilau rice and a pile of naan bead. "How yummy," said Susie appreciatively.

As she sat there eating the food, Susie realised that she did in fact feel better for having confessed all to David and James. She began to relax, and with that, began to enjoy David's company. He was mesmerised by Susie's beauty but was also very aware, following her revelations about Jonathan, that he would have to tread very carefully if he was going to develop any sort of relationship with her.

Once the meal was over, they moved back to the sitting area of David's one downstairs room and chatted quietly. Susie was very pleased that they had stopped talking about money and was feeling much better, as she felt that now she had told James the truth, he would be sure to help her.

Susie was so wrapped up with herself, that she hadn't given a thought to her brother's circumstances and the fact that he had told her that he thought he was gay and what that might mean to him, his relationship with Greg and everything else he was dealing with.

As it got towards 10.00 pm, Susie thought that she ought to leave, as she had to be back in the pub by 10.00 am the next day. She said this to David and he told her that she wasn't walking alone at that time of night. It was a lovely evening and he would walk with her. Susie realised there was no point in arguing, so the two of them set off together. Parts of the way weren't lit, so David took a torch with him and as Susie seemed a little wobbly (too much wine again) he felt able to take her by the hand without anything being too obvious.

When they reached Rose Cottage, Susie asked him if he would like to come in for coffee but David refused, saying that she had needed to come home so that she would be ready for work the following morning. "Come round after, and tell me what James had to say, won't you?" he said, kissing her on the cheek. Susie promised that she would.

*****

As Susie went into her cottage, James, Greg and Zizi were walking home from the Red Lion. They had had a few drinks and something to eat in the

Red Lion's garden and a good chat about all sorts of things, one of them of course being Susie. Greg said that he felt that James really needed to decide what his life plans were, before he could contemplate lending any money to Susie. He would know what his degree would be the next week and that could also affect what he did.

James told Greg that now they were together he didn't really want to leave the area, but didn't think he could survive on what his mother was paying him for working in the shop. Greg smiled ruefully at this and said that his business was struggling and he didn't know if he could make a career out of the shop either, although in his heart he wanted to work in fine arts and antiques as that was what he had studied for. He went on to ask James if he could commit to lending his sister money when he was basically struggling day to day himself and that he thought James should go to his parents and tell them about Susie. "Or take some money from your investments if you feel that strongly about helping her," he said.

"I can't do that!" said James in a horrified voice. "I've only just taken them out and would lose money."

"There's your answer then," said his lover.

"Well, I've got to say something to Susie tomorrow, because I promised," came the reply. "I'll sleep on it and maybe go and see Mum and Dad first thing tomorrow morning."

CHAPTER 43

Annabelle did not sleep well and slid out of bed early on the Sunday morning so as not to disturb Peter. A multitude of thoughts were whirling through her mind regarding the children and she felt she really needed to have a proper talk with Peter now. She thought that a run would help her to think straight, so pulled on her running gear and went to fetch Allsort, as she knew that the dog would enjoy going with her.

As she ran round the recreation field, Annabelle breathed the fresh morning air and felt much more alive. She called Allsort who was resting under a tree, unable to keep pace with her mistress, and jogged gently home, Allsort panting beside her.

Peter had just come downstairs when she got in, so she kissed him and told him that she would have a quick shower and change and then join him for breakfast.

Half an hour later Annabelle was back, looking as glamorous as ever. After her shower she had blasted her long dark hair with the hairdryer before sweeping it back into a ponytail, and slipped into a pair of jeans and a crisp white shirt. With the addition of her diamond collette, matching ear studs and a touch of make-up Annabelle looked absolutely stunning and her husband delighted in telling her so.

"Thank you, darling," she said, gratefully accepting the mug of coffee that Peter was holding out to her. "As it's Sunday, I'll make us a proper breakfast and then we can have a natter and catch up. I feel that I haven't seen much of you this week." Peter replied that he would enjoy that and went off with the Sunday Telegraph tucked under his arm.

An hour later, after a delicious breakfast, they wandered into the garden to lap up the sunshine for a stroll and a chat.

"You go first, darling," said Annabelle, thinking it would give her longer to decide exactly what she was going to say. She listened dutifully whilst Peter told her what he'd been doing in London and where he felt the Stock Market was and the effect that it was having on their investments. He then went on to tell her that his golf handicap had come down to a single figure. "Oh well done, darling," she said, trying to sound enthusiastic.

"Now then, Belle. How about you? What's been happening in your world? You were out unusually early this morning. Is anything the matter?"

"Oh, you know me so well, Peter," she said, smiling at him.

"I should do after the best part of 30 years," came the reply.

"I went for a run to help clear my head. A lot is going on in our children's lives, some of which you may not be aware of, so I thought this would be a good opportunity to talk to you about everything."

Peter lit a cigar and looked puzzled. He couldn't understand why Annabelle was concerned and said so.

"I think I'll start with James," she said, "I think he's far less complicated than Susie. As you know, he's been friendly with Greg Somerville ever since he started helping me out in the shop and now they're going to move in together. James has realised that he is gay, which I have suspected for a long time, but feel that perhaps you hadn't, darling?"

Peter nearly choked on his cigar. "Gay? James?" he stuttered. Annabelle nodded her head. "Jesus Christ, surely not. Why in God's name does a son of mine find it necessary to bat for the other side? Whatever will people think? Annabelle, wherever have we gone wrong? Our daughter's been screwing a married man, and now you tell me that our son is as bent as a nine bob note. What are we going to do?"

"About James, we are going to do nothing," Annabelle replied. "You are going to calm down and be adult about the whole thing. You've met Greg and said yourself what a nice young man you thought he was. No, Peter, don't try and interrupt me. Let me finish please, and then you can have your say. James will be moving in with Greg at the beginning of next month and you are going to wish him well and if you feel the need to refer to his sexuality, it will be in a positive way, however hard that may be for you."

Peter stared at his wife aghast. "Do you think he might grow out of it?" he muttered. Annabelle glared at him and said she didn't think it was something that you grew out of. "If you think about it," she said, "James has never been one for the girls."

Peter nodded glumly. "OK, Belle," he said. "I hear what you're saying. Thank God he didn't join the RAF, that's all I can say. His life would have been sheer hell."

"Well, he didn't, so that's that," said Annabelle crisply. "What you must remember is that he's our son and he is the same person today that he has been all his life. You just now know that he wants a man for his life partner and not a woman. Shape up. Now then, let's move on to Susie. I know that her phone's been disconnected, which suggests to me that she's in serious trouble and that it might be time for us to move in to help her."

Before Peter could say anything, James appeared through the French doors, shouting, "Hello you two, so there you are."

"Get a mug," called back Annabelle, "there's lots of coffee in the pot." As her son was walking back into the house, she turned to her husband and said, "Now Peter, remember what I've said to you."

When James returned, complete with coffee mug, and after they had exchanged pleasantries, Peter turned to his son and said, "Your mother tells me that you're moving out soon to go and live with Greg. I hope it all goes well for you." James blushed and thanked him. "We were just talking about Susie and the fact that her mobile phone has been disconnected," Peter went on. "Do you know anything about what's going on there?"

"That's why I came round this morning," replied James. "She phoned me last night and we had a long chat. I'm really worried about her." He went on to tell his parents what Susie had said.

"We did know most of that," said his father. "I thought I would let her worry for a bit before I stepped in to help her, but it looks as though I now need to do something. Do me a favour James, ring her this morning and tell her that you won't lend her the money. Could you do it now please?"

James dialled The Crown.

*****

This time it was Susie who answered and when she heard James' voice she held her breath, hoping that he had rung to lend her money. When he said that he had thought about it carefully and couldn't afford to lend her anything she just replaced the receiver without saying a word. She had taken the call in the bar and quickly walked out into the garden to try and get herself together. It had just turned half past eleven and she knew that the lunchtime trade would be brisk, so she needed to be on top form.

She was staring into space with a tear running down her cheek, when she became aware that someone had come up behind her. Turning round, she saw that it was Alf, and tried to smile at him. "Oh dear Susie love, you look as though you've got all the cares of the world on your shoulders," he said. She tried to smile and muttered that she was having a bad time just at the moment. "I know you are love," he replied. "Me giving you your cards at the end of the week doesn't help either, but it's one of those things, I'm afraid, and part of our agreement." Susie nodded and said it wasn't his fault that she was upset and that they could blame her brother.

"Families, eh?" said Alf smiling at her. "Wipe your eyes and put that smile back on your face. We've got a busy pub to run." With that he walked back inside.

*****

Peter and Annabelle had listened whilst James phoned his sister and were surprised how quickly the call had ended. "She just hung up without saying a word." James shrugged. "What are we going to do next?"

"You're going to go and do some work at the shop, whilst Mum and I decide what to do." said Peter. "And by the way, if you need any help moving things to Greg's, let me know and I'll see what I can do."

James got to his feet, said cheerio to his parents and headed off in the direction of his car. When he was safely out of earshot Annabelle thanked Peter for being so tactful, saying that she knew how hard he had found the conversation. "Well, I'm going to have to get used to the situation, aren't I?" he answered. "If it isn't Greg, who does seem to be a nice chap, it's going to be another one. I think, for today, that Susie is our priority and what we need to do now is think about how we are going to handle the situation."

*****

Susie was busy in the bar when her parents walked into the pub and she didn't see them immediately. When she did she wasn't best pleased. "What are you doing here?" she asked. Her father looked hard at her and said, "I could ask you the same question. Kindly get your mother a large glass of Chablis and I'll have a gin and tonic."

When he had paid for the drinks Peter asked his daughter what time she would be finishing work and said that they would see her back at Rose Cottage then. Like hell you will, she thought, as she had agreed to pop round and see David when she had finished. She was already in a state as James had refused to lend her money and the last thing she needed was a session with her parents reading the riot act to her. She would take refuge with David until they gave up and went away.

Drinking up, Peter and Annabelle left the pub, after exchanging a quick word with Alf on the way out. As they had a few hours to kill before Susie would be home, they decided to go to Blenheim Palace, where they could have a walk in the grounds and some afternoon tea as they had missed lunch in their eagerness to get to Enstone.

CHAPTER 44

Having enjoyed a stroll in the summer sunshine and some afternoon tea at the Palace, Peter and Annabelle pulled up outside Rose Cottage at 20 to 6. Susie's car was parked in the lay-by, but there was no sign of her. Thinking that she had probably been held up at the pub, they decided to wait for a while.

When it turned 6 o'clock, Peter looked at his wife and said that he thought Susie was avoiding them and wasn't going to come home any time soon. "What next, then?" said Annabelle.

"Well," said Peter, "we need to eat, so why don't we go to The Crown and have a meal? The food there is excellent and you said that Alf was friendly, so maybe we can get him into conversation and find out something about Susie." Annabelle thought that that was an excellent idea.

They were delighted to find the pub relatively quiet when they arrived, and even more pleased to see Alf behind the bar. Annabelle introduced Peter to him and Peter asked if he would join them for a drink and if they could have a table in perhaps an hour's time? Alf popped a "Reserved" sign on to a table overlooking the garden, accepted a glass of Leffe and suggested that as it was a lovely evening, they might like to sit outside. The three of them went into the garden.

Having found a quiet table, Alf said that he was surprised and pleased, to see them twice in the same day. "Susie's finished for the day, you know," he said. They said that they did know that and part of their reason for being there was in fact their daughter. Alf smiled at them and told them how much Susie reminded him of his own daughter. "She was always useless with money, and the Bank of Alfred was forever having to bail her out," he said. "She's grown up at last though and has a good head on her shoulders. She's a clever girl and I'm proud of her, as I'm sure you are of your Susie." Peter said that they were proud of Susie, but were also worried about her at the moment.

"You've been around a bit, I'm sure, Alf," he said. "I don't like asking people to tell tales, but I do believe Susie has some fairly serious financial problems. She won't talk to us, in fact I think she's avoiding us right now, as we were expecting to see her at home and she isn't there so I'm wondering if you can shed any light on anything?"

"For a start I think you might find her next door," he replied. "She seems to have become friendly with David, my next door neighbour. He's a nice lad, works as a Financial Adviser with his dad in Chipping Norton."

197

"Oh yes, we know him," said Annabelle. "As you say, he seems a nice chap."

"Maybe he's trying to help Susie," said Alf, "As I'm sure you know, she left her job in Woodstock, under a bit of a cloud, and came and asked me for work. Cheeky madam made it clear that it was only a stop-gap until she could find something better and I made it equally clear that I was advertising for a permanent person and would take her on until I found that person. I've now found him, so have given Susie her cards. She finishes a week tonight. On top of that, she's asked me to pay her in cash this last week or so. Sorry to give you such crap news, but if it were my Charlotte I'd want to know."

The Rowlands thanked Alf and said that it was all pretty much what they suspected, apart from the fact that she was about to lose her job at The Crown.

"Kids, eh?" said Alf. "No matter how old they are, they're always your kids and you want to do your best for them, although at times you could cheerfully crown them. I'm sorry that I couldn't give you better news, but that's the way of the world. I've nowt else to tell you so I'll go and get you some menus now."

When Alf had gone back inside, Annabelle asked Peter if she thought they should go next door to look for Susie. "No." he said. "I think I shall come back on my own tomorrow and see Susie. I'll just check with Alf what hours she's working, as I intend to take her by surprise. It's time for you to leave this to me now, Belle."

*****

As soon as her shift was over, Susie had fled next door to see David, having no intention of being grilled by her parents. She explained that she needed to hide out at his place for a while.

David groaned. He didn't want to get off on the wrong foot with this beautiful girl, but tonight wasn't convenient. He was off out for a meal with some mates and then they were going to have a few beers. "Sorry, Susie, but I'm going out," he said.

"Going out," she almost shrieked, "what do you mean you're going out? You asked me to come round after work and now you tell me you're going out!" "Steady on," David replied, feeling somewhat aggrieved that Susie seemed to be taking him for granted. "I asked you to let me know how you got on with James. I didn't invite you to spend the evening with me."

"Bollocks to you as well!" screamed Susie and flounced out of the door. To her absolute horror she saw her father's car drawing up outside the pub. She shrank back into David's porch and waited for them to go in. Somehow she had to get past the pub window without being seen. David could see her lurking there and thought it wouldn't do her any harm to get on with it. She did seem to be very spoilt and to think the whole world revolved around her. He did fancy her, but there was a limit. A night out with the boys would be good.

When he came out of the house half an hour later he was surprised to find Susie still cowering in his porch. "What on earth are you doing?" he asked. "My parents are in the pub and I don't know how to get past without being seen," was the sulky reply.

David burst out laughing. "You are in a mess, aren't you?" he said.

"I don't know what's so bloody funny," she retorted. "I thought you were my friend but now it seems that you don't want to help me either."

"Look, I haven't time for this just now," said David. "If you want to lie down in the back of my car, which will be difficult and uncomfortable, I'll drive you home. How about it?"

"I suppose so," was the churlish reply, "but what will I do if they come back?"

"Either let them in or leave them outside," said David, who was beginning to get very fed up indeed with the way Susie was behaving.

He had actually bought her a pay as you go mobile phone, but because she had been such a pain when she arrived at his house, hadn't bothered to give it to her. Let her sweat a bit longer, was all he thought. He felt that her parents were intending to sort her out, and that was a good thing. Kind as he was, David Timmins was no fool.

He deposited Susie at Rose Cottage and drove off to enjoy the company of his friends and to put women out of his mind for the evening.

*****

Following a very enjoyable meal at The Crown, Annabelle asked Peter if they should go home via Rose Cottage and see if Susie were there. Peter emphatically said that they should not, as the gloves were now off and he would be dealing with his daughter in the morning. Annabelle winced, knowing that he would not pull any punches with Susie, then settled back to enjoy the drive home.

CHAPTER 45

Susie had felt very put out indeed when David dropped her off at home. She'd grown to quite like him and now the bastard had snubbed her. She'd show him. Slightly anxious that her parents might show up again, Susie fed George and went upstairs where she couldn't be seen should anyone look through the window. She then set about the dating site with a vengeance, determined that she wouldn't log off until she had a lunch date for the following day. She wasn't working until tea time and there must be someone she could meet in his lunch hour.

Finally, just gone midnight, success! She was going to meet John, who was an accountant aged 33, at the Pinto Lounge in Banbury. Result! He was nice looking and with a bit of luck would buy her lunch as he would have to eat, wouldn't he?

Exhausted, but pleased with herself, Susie went to bed with George happily curled up by her feet.

*****

Peter was up early next morning as he had no intention of giving Susie the opportunity of going out before he got to Enstone. It was just before 9.00 am when he parked behind her Mini in the lay-by and saw that all Rose Cottage's curtains were closed. Bugger that he thought, the lazy little madam can get out of bed and talk to me, so he went and banged on the front door.

The banging woke Susie up with a start. Pulling on her dressing gown, she dashed downstairs and threw open the front door. "What the..." she said, and then saw her father. "Daddy, what on earth are you here at this time for? Has something happened?"

"Indeed it has," replied Peter. "You were discourteous enough not to be here at tea time yesterday when your mother and I made it clear that we were coming to see you."

"Oh that," said Susie disdainfully. "I'm fed up of being told what to do and how to do it."

"I don't care how fed up you are, young lady. You're going to listen to me – that is after you have gone upstairs and made yourself presentable. I shall make myself some coffee in your absence. Hello George, old chap. Are you looking for something to eat? Where do you keep the cat food Susie?"

Wanting the upper hand, Susie kept her father waiting for as long as she dared. When she came back down, he was sitting calmly on the sofa, drinking a cup of coffee.

"Right, he said. Let's not beat about the bush. You're in serious financial difficulties and don't know which way to turn. Let's have the facts and figures. I can't help you without those."

Susie breathed a sigh of relief. There was a God! Here was Daddy come to sort her out. She had been panicking over nothing. She'd better be a bit nicer to him. "I'll just go and get them," she said, and was quickly back with the spread sheet that David had helped her to compile.

"Mmn," said Peter. "About £8,000 would see you clear. Of course, there's the other problem that you are now unemployable, other than as a barmaid, which won't bring in enough money for your extremely extravagant lifestyle. I understand that your job at The Crown finishes at the end of this week. What are your suggestions for sorting out this mess, Susie?"

"Well, if you could lend me the £8,000, please Daddy, that would be fabulous. I'm sure that eventually I'll get a proper job again and then I'll be able to pay you back. I suppose it was James who ratted on me and told you what a mess I'm in?"

"James fleshed out the bones for us, but your mother discovered quite a lot by visiting Woodstock Academy. I just hope the bloody man was worth all the heart ache you've given yourself and us. You've been a silly little fool, Susie."

Susie pulled a face at him. She didn't need a lecture. "And you can take that look off your face as well, madam. Your brother was concerned about your constant request to borrow money and felt that you needed help. I am now here to offer that help."

"Thank you Daddy," she said enthusiastically. "Does that mean you'll lend me £8,000?" Peter nodded.

"Oh that's wonderful," she said, crossing the room to throw her arms round her father.

"I want all your outstanding bills please Susie, so that I know they have been settled," he said. "Do you have them here now?" She rushed to fetch them, as again, with David's help, they were all neatly put in a file.

"Thank you, I'll take this with me," said Peter. "Now all we have to decide is whether you are going to try and rent out this house, or whether you are going to sell it? If it's the latter, we can arrange to put any furniture that we can't accommodate at Riverside House into storage."

"I don't know what you mean, Daddy," she gasped. "I shall be living here. I don't want to sell the property."

"You certainly won't be living here," came the reply. "You'll be coming to live with me and Mummy. I'm not funding this house for you to play around in after I've settled your debts. What kind of a fool do you take me for? If you can manage to rent it out, it will be here for you to come back to once you have a job again and can pay your bills."

"But this is my home," shouted Susie in a rage. "I don't want to live with you and Mummy. How dare you try and blackmail me?"

"That's fine," said Peter calmly. "You'd better have your file back then." With those words he got up and left, without so much as a backward glance.

*****

Susie was stunned that Daddy could treat her like that. Offer her money with conditions. Perhaps she should talk to Mummy? Shit, she couldn't. Her phone had been cut off and she wasn't going to go and stand in a smelly phone box. Right, she was meeting John in Banbury at 1 o'clock and she had cash, as Alf had paid her on Friday. She would have to go into Vodafone and spend some of her precious cash on paying the phone bill. The only snag was that Daddy would have got to Mummy before she had a chance to speak to her. It wasn't quite 10 o'clock. Dare she go and ask Alf if she could use his phone? She couldn't possibly ask Mrs MacDonald next door, because the old bat was sure to listen to what was being said. Come to think of it, Alf might, too. Hell, hell, hell. What was she going to do?

She was going to Banbury anyway, so she might as well get herself ready for her date. Perhaps she should look a little more conservative to meet an accountant? That decided, Susie chose a pair of jeans and a white v necked tee shirt. She added Granny's ring, because if he noticed it he would be sure to be impressed and what she considered to be plain ear rings and a necklace. Picking up her handbag, she left the house. Immediately she was waylaid by Mrs MacDonald, who couldn't help but notice that her father had visited very early and hoped that nothing was wrong. "Nothing at all, thank you. He was just passing," replied Susie, and rushed towards her car, muttering "bloody woman" under her breath.

Vodafone was less than helpful. They couldn't reconnect a phone – it all had to be done by head office and would take 48 hours. That being so, Susie decided not to pay them and told them airily that if that were the case she would pay head office directly. Mummy probably wouldn't have helped anyway. She now had to kill time before meeting John, so she went to a coffee shop and spent over £5 on a latte and a pastry. Well, after that confrontation with Daddy, she deserved it, didn't she?

Feeling fortified after her little break, Susie wandered around the shops and found herself walking into Monsoon, one of her favourites. They had a sale on, so it wouldn't hurt to just look, would it? Unfortunately, just looking was not something that Susie had ever been good at, and she came

203

out of the shop having bought a top and a pair of ear rings, and having spent £39. Well, they were very good bargains, after all.

Clutching her purchases, Susie arrived at the Pinto Lounge, but couldn't see any sign of John, so asked if she could open a tab, as he would be bound to settle it and ordered a large glass of Pinot Grigio. As she was going to eat, there couldn't be any harm in having one glass of wine. After all, it would be a long day, as she would be working until midnight. She was suddenly aware of a voice saying, "Hello, are you Susie?" and looked up to see John standing over her. She said that she was and that there was a tab open at the bar. Yes, he looked very pleasant indeed. With a bit of luck, she was in for a good lunchtime.

*****

As Peter had expected, Annabelle was waiting for him when he got home. "Well?" was all she said. "Well, what?" he asked, smiling at her. "Don't be perverse, Peter, you know perfectly well what," was her reply.

"Make me some coffee please, and then I'll tell you all about it," he said.

His wife was soon back with the coffee and Peter told her how Susie had been in bed when he got there and how surly she had been until he had agreed to loan her £8,000 whereupon her attitude had changed like magic. Annabelle's eyebrows went up at this. "You don't think that was rather rash, do you darling?" was all she said. Her expression changed when Peter told her of his condition for the loan and Susie's reply to it.

"So," she said, "Susie is in as bad a mess now as before you went to see her."

"That about sums it up," replied her husband.

"Oh Peter, we can't leave her like that," said Annabelle.

"As I said to Susie, Annabelle, I am not paying off her debts, because that is what it will amount to – we both know she'll never repay me – and allowing her to swan around in her house, racking up another set, which will again need sorting out. I'm not made of money. It's perfectly reasonable to me that she should live here whilst I'm keeping her."

Annabelle nodded her head. "I see your point, darling," she said, "It's just that I'm so worried about Susie. Suppose she does lose the house?"

"Oh it won't come to that," replied Peter. "She'll come back here agreeing to anything before that happens. She'll be 24 in November and needs to face up to her responsibilities. We're going to have to continue to play a waiting game. She finishes work this weekend, so time will hang heavy for her then. She'll be back with her tail between her legs, just you wait and see."

*****

Little did Peter realise it, but his daughter was having a very enjoyable lunch in the Pinto Lounge with John. However, this ended abruptly when he got to his feet, kissed her on the cheek, thanked her very much for lunch and said that he must get back to his office. Susie was stunned. She had opened a tab expecting John to pick it up, and now the bastard had swanned off without paying for anything. Feeling very used, she went up to the bar and quietly asked for the bill. She was shocked to find that it was £48.36. John hadn't even said that he would like to see her again and, come to think of it, he hadn't asked for her phone number. He had just got up and left rather suddenly without paying even his share. Perhaps that was how he operated? Met people and didn't pay anything. Feeling like a silly fool, and struggling hard not to cry, Susie walked back to the car park.

CHAPTER 46

David had enjoyed his night out with the boys, but was sad that he and Susie had not parted on the best of terms. On the Monday evening he felt that a visit to the pub would be a good idea. When he walked in, he was greeted by Alf. "Evening, son, how are you?" he said, and then winked, "Not come to see a certain barmaid by any chance?"

David grinned back. "Behave yourself, you nosey old sod, and pull me a pint please."

"I'm just surveying my empire," came back the reply, "but I shall summon someone to serve you immediately." Walking into the other bar, David heard him call, "Susie love, gentleman wants serving in the front bar please."

Susie came through and smiled when she saw David. "Hello, how are you?" she asked. "Did you have a good night out with your friends?" David was relieved that she seemed in a better mood.

"I did, thank you," he replied, "but more to the point, how are you? Have you recovered from yesterday?"

At this Susie shook her head. "No, I've had a visit from Daddy this morning. He tried to blackmail me." David laughed out loud at this. "It's not funny, you pig," she hissed. "You've no idea what my life is like."

"Susie, I've tried my best to help you, but you aren't an easy person to help, you know," David said. "We can't discuss things now, and I know that you're working till midnight every night this week, but let me have a look in my diary and see if I can have a chat with you at some point tomorrow." With that he took out his phone and started scrolling.

"I've got a gap for an hour at 11.30 am. Would you like to come to Chippy for coffee?" he asked. Susie said that she would and that she'd better not stand chatting to him all night, as she had other customers to look after as well. David wondered if she realised how self-centred she could seem at times. Perhaps she wasn't the confident person she appeared on the surface? However, he still thought there was something very lovely about her and knew that she must be very concerned about things.

*****

11.30 the next morning found the two of them having coffee in David's office. Susie looked around with interest. It was a plain room and David didn't have any photos on his desk. Coffee was brought to them by a friendly looking woman whom David introduced as Amanda. She did all the secretarial and administrative work for the firm and David declared how invaluable she was. Susie wished Miss Jennings had felt the same about her and felt a twinge of envy.

"OK," said David, when Amanda had gone out and closed the door behind her. "Tell me about your father and his attempt to blackmail you. Oh, actually, before you do, I've got something for you." With that he reached into his desk and brought out a gift wrapped box.

"For me?" squeaked Susie with excitement. "A present for me? Oh thank you David," and she ran round his desk and kissed him on the cheek. Sitting down again, she ripped the paper off the box and was surprised to see a mobile phone. "It's a basic phone and it's pay as you go, but at least it'll tide you over for the moment," he said.

"Thank you," said Susie. "That's so kind of you."

"Now," said David, "revenons à nos moutons."

"Pardon?" said Susie.

"Let's get back to the point," he said smiling. "Tell me all about your father."

Susie told him about the early morning visit and how she thought her father was going to lend her £8,000, which really would have done the trick and then he had said that she either had to sell her house or let it out and go and live in Moulsford with them, as he wasn't funding her extravagant lifestyle. "Extravagant!" shrieked Susie. "He can't know what the word means. I'm living like a pauper."

"The point is though, that you haven't been," said David. "I've seen your bank and credit card statements and so has your father. There seemed to be a lot of trips to the nail bar and clothes shops."

"Huh, you're as bad as Daddy," said Susie pulling a face. "You keep banging on about wanting to help me and now all you're doing is criticising me. It's not fair."

"I am being fair, Susie. Please listen," was the swift reply. "I understand that you don't want to go and live with your parents, (and neither do I want you to, under his breath) but equally I understand where your father's coming from. Haven't you got two bedrooms in your cottage?" Susie nodded. "Well then," said David, "for a start you could rent one out. You can earn £4,800 a year without having to pay tax on it."

"How much is that a month?" Susie enquired. "Not that I like the idea of a stranger sharing my lovely little house. Particularly as I've got a holiday booked in August. She'd be there on her own and might go through my things."

"A holiday next month?" gasped David. "How on earth are you going to afford that?"

"I've paid for it already," Susie replied. "All I need is to buy my lunch each day and my drinks and have some spending money."

"Listen to yourself," David said, somewhat crossly. "You need £8,000 to clear your debts and you talk about going on holiday next month. You need to get real, Susie."

"How dare you speak to me like that?" screamed Susie, starting to get to her feet.

"Sit down and stop behaving like the spoilt child that you clearly were," snapped David.

Susie was so used to men falling over themselves for the pleasure of her company that she sat down in amazement. "I've never been spoilt," she whimpered. "You know nothing about me David."

"I know what I see," he replied. "You are a stunningly beautiful girl. You are headstrong and used to people doing what you tell them to. I think you're very attractive and would love to take you out. I would also like to help you, but you just don't listen to reason." There! He'd said it. He'd told her that he fancied her, and now he would have to wait for her reaction.

"I think you're nice too David, and I'd like to go out with you," she replied. "I'd also like you to help me, so I'll try and be quiet and listen to what you have to say, but my holiday cost me a lot of money and I would like to go."

"I understand that," he replied, "but there are times when you have to cut your losses. It will cost you even more money to go. Lunches and drinks alone will probably be expensive and knowing you you'll find lots of interesting things to buy as well. Why don't we put the holiday on eBay and see what you can get back? Someone is bound to pay something for it and you can always put a reserve on it. Look out the holiday details, in particular what it cost you and we'll draft something out. Whilst we're thinking about drafting things out, let's try and sort out an advert to put in the local paper to let your second bedroom. Oh, and I never answered your question. £4,800 a year is £400 a month."

"I guess that would be a start," said Susie.

"Look, I've got a client coming in a minute," David said. "Why don't you go home and see what you can find out about your holiday and have a go at writing an advert and I'll give you a ring later and see how you've got on?" Susie said that she would. David walked round his desk, gave her a hug and a kiss on the cheek and then she was gone.

*****

Back in Rose Cottage Susie searched high and low for the details of her holiday, but couldn't find them anywhere. Never mind, she thought, I'll concentrate on the advert for the bedroom instead. After much thought she wrote, "Lady required to share house in Enstone. £400 per month plus share of bills." She would see what David thought of that when he rang. Her mind then turned to David and what he had said to her – that he found her attractive and would like to take her out. She thought he was nice and she was enjoying his company more than she expected and it would be good to have someone to go around with.

Sitting gazing out of the window, Susie was both amazed and pleased to see David's Alfa Romeo pull up outside. How lovely, she thought, he's come to see me because he likes me, so that we can discuss things face to face, rather than ring me up. Smiling, she went to the front door and was horrified to see the expression on David's face. He was ashen white and looked as though he might have been crying. "Whatever's the matter?" she gasped, as he flung himself into her arms.

"Something really terrible has happened," gulped David. "It's too awful to believe."

CHAPTER 47

As he came out of the bathroom, Greg could hear James shouting. "Oh my God, I can't believe it! Oh my God, this can't be happening! Oh my God, I really, really, can't believe it!" His blood turned cold, and he rushed to his boyfriend's side.

"What can't you believe? What can't be happening?" he asked.

"I've only bloody well gone and got five and a star," came the reply.

"What in God's name are you talking about?" asked Greg.

"Euromillions, my darling, Euromillions!" said James.

"Are you telling me that you've won a big prize on the lottery?" enquired Greg, excitement creeping into his voice.

"You bet I have!" James replied, pressing buttons on his phone. £137,973.40 to be precise. There were nine people who had five numbers and a star."

"Fucking hell!" said Greg. "Are you quite sure?"

"Absolutely positive!" said James, "Look, there's the results," passing his phone to Greg, "and here's my ticket, dated for last night." The couple just looked at each other and then they both started to laugh.

"Wowee!" Greg's voice was filled with amazement.

"I know!" said James, "I just can't believe it. I need to look up what I have to do next to get the money. What a great start to the morning!"

Greg started making breakfast whilst James kept fiddling with his phone. "Ah," he said eventually. "I have to ring the National Lottery help line, as it's over £50,000. I think I'll ring Dad first and ask him what I should do, because they might want me to have publicity and I don't want any of that."

"Certainly not," agreed Greg. "I really can't believe this is happening."

The two of them ate breakfast without saying much to each other, as they were both deep in thought. Greg couldn't help but think how lucky he was to have taken up with James. As much as he liked him he had to admit that he also enjoyed the lifestyle that money could buy and which he couldn't afford to fund. James was stunned that he had been so lucky to win such a lot of money.

*****

Peter was reading the newspaper when the phone went. "Morning James, how are you?" he enquired.

"Absolutely fine, thanks, Dad. You'll never guess what's happened, I've just won £137,973.40 on the Euromillions."

"Good grief," said his father. "Are you quite sure?"

"Positive," replied James. "I have to ring the National Lottery help line to find out what happens next, and I think perhaps I need your advice as to what to say."

Peter was delighted that his son was being so sensible. "Might not be a bad idea," he said. "Why don't you come over and make the phone call from here?" James said that he would be over in about half an hour. Peter got on to his computer straight away and did a bit of research into the National Lottery and discovered that they would want to send a financial adviser to see James. Well, he wouldn't need any of that as he used that chap in Chipping Norton and from what Peter had seen, he knew what he was talking about.

Having satisfied himself that he knew as much about claiming as he could at this stage, Peter went off in search of Annabelle. He found her in the kitchen making preparations for a curry. "Guess what?" he said to her. "James has just been on the phone."

"That's nice, but not particularly earth shattering, darling," she replied. "What did he have to say?"

"Only that he's won £137,000 on the lottery."

"What?" said Annabelle. "How marvellous!"

"He's on his way here now," replied her husband. "He's asked me for some advice on what he should say when he rings up to make his claim and I suggested that he came over and we could make the phone call together."

"Very wise," said Annabelle, nodding her head. "I'm pleased that he has so much common sense. Gosh, isn't this exciting? Do you think it's too early for champagne?" Peter agreed that it was indeed exciting, and that it was never too early for champagne, before returning to his study to read some more of the Telegraph.

As they always had champagne in the fridge, all Annabelle had to do was put three glasses on a tray.

*****

It wasn't long before they heard the scrunch of James' tyres on the gravel and saw a very excited James walking towards the front door. Annabelle quickly got the champagne and glasses and carried them through the conservatory and out to the garden. It was a beautiful day, made all the more so by James' news.

Lots of hugging and kissing took place before they sat down to enjoy a glass of champagne, whilst Peter and James discussed the plan of action. James then made his phone call and arranged for someone to come and see him at Riverside House on the Monday to verify his ticket. They agreed that

Peter would be there, so that James couldn't get inveigled into anything that he might later regret.

"What are you going to do with the money, darling?" enquired Annabelle.

"I haven't really thought about that yet," replied her son. "You buy these tickets and kind of hope you'll win, but never really expect to. I think I should like to take the family out for a nice dinner and perhaps invite Greg's parents as well, although I haven't met them yet. Maybe go on holiday, but other than that I'm not really sure. Poor old Susie's in trouble, so maybe I'll give her a couple of thousand. Not sure really."

"There's no rush to decide," said Peter. "Surely you'll invest some though? That fellow in Chipping Norton seemed to me to be very much on the ball."

"Yes, I will have a chat with him," said James. "Maybe I can buy into Greg's property. I know he's struggling a bit, and I can't get a mortgage because I haven't been working long enough, but I could actually put cash into Greg's house, which would help Greg."

"Don't you think it's a bit early to be getting involved with him financially?" asked Peter. "After all, you haven't known him very long and you haven't even started living together yet. Just be careful, that's all I ask. You currently have in excess of £200,000, which is fantastic for a young man of your age. I wouldn't like to see you lose it."

James told his father that he didn't know Greg and that Greg wasn't like that at all. Annabelle glared at her husband and he managed to keep his mouth shut. James went on to say that he couldn't do anything other than think until he had the money anyway, and that couldn't be before next week at the earliest. Peter quietly breathed a sigh of relief.

*****

Over in Enstone, Susie woke up still feeling shocked by what David had told her, and immediately called him to check he was OK. David was very touched by her thoughtfulness and decided that there was a gentle side to Susie and that he was determined to cultivate it, no matter how hard he had to work. He told her that as yet he had no more news and that he was looking forward to the next week when she wouldn't be working, so that they could see more of each other.

Susie winced at that. Yes, after Sunday she wouldn't be working. What was she going to do? There wasn't another pub in the village. Should she look in Chipping Norton for bar work? Maybe if she did it for six months or so, she could convince prospective employers that she had considered training for pub management and decided that getting behind the bar was the best place to start, but not found it to her liking and now she wished to return to secretarial work. Would they still want a reference from Miss Jennings?

Thinking about Miss Jennings made her think about Jonathan and she wondered what he was doing now. She knew that she must put him out of her mind, as David was going to be taking her out and the more she got to know him, she did have to admit, the more she found herself liking him. This was a surprise to Susie, as she had always liked the mad or the bad, or better still both at once and David was neither. However, despite his stuffy job, he did drive a very lovely car. He was also quite funny.

Getting out of bed, Susie noticed that one of her bedside drawers wasn't closed properly, and when she tried to shut it, found that it was stuck. Pushing her hand up the back to try and find out what the problem was, she came across some bits of paper. Reading them, she could see they were notes about men that she had been looking at on the dating site but, joy of joys, what was this? Sunday 19 August – one week half board in Benalmadena, flying from Gatwick - £1,129 and an e-mail address. She could now find out all the details and put the holiday on to eBay. After all, she couldn't go on a Singles' holiday if she was going out with David now, could she? Really pleased with herself, Susie phoned David again to tell him the good news.

David was on his way to see a client when Susie called him. He was delighted that she had found details of her holiday and seemed to be seeing sense about not going. If they were going out together, he certainly wouldn't want her going on a holiday on her own anyway. If things went well between them over the next few weeks and if he could get away from work, he thought he might take Susie to his parents' house in France. He was sure that they wouldn't mind. Besides, he and Dad couldn't possibly take time off together, particularly after what had happened yesterday. Thinking of that, David put in a call to the hospital and following what he was told, then phoned his father. He was so upset that he had to pull off the road and sit quietly in a lay-by to compose himself before driving on to his appointment.

CHAPTER 48

All too soon it was Sunday and Susie's ears rang with the sound of Alf calling time, not just for the punters, but for her days as a barmaid, too. "Time at the bar! If you'd wanted to drink more you should have come in earlier. I've had your money so you can piss off home now." He shouted this out every evening, or a variation of it, depending on who was in the pub and it never failed to raise a laugh. Suddenly Susie realised how much she had enjoyed working there and how good the old boy had been to her. She was very surprised when he appeared from the kitchen carrying a box, which he duly presented to her.

"Here you are Susie love. It's a goody box. I've had Philip put some meals into foil containers for you. All you need to do is put them in your freezer and help yourself when you want one. I know you're hard up and this might help you out a bit. Although you've been a pain in the arse at times, I will miss your smiling face. The customers liked you too." Susie was overwhelmed by the old man's generosity.

"Oh Alf, you really are a star," she said. "I'll miss working here, but I'll come and see you from the other side of the bar." With that she threw her arms round his neck and kissed him on the cheek. She said her farewells to the rest of the staff and walked out to her Mini Cooper.

When she got home, Susie opened her goody box and was delighted to find that she had ten dinners all neatly packaged up. Alf was right, that would help her out.

As she didn't feel tired, Susie sat down with George and a mug of hot chocolate and started to think about David and the fact that they would now be able to see each other properly. She knew that he was still shocked by what had happened earlier in the week. Amanda had been cycling home for lunch when she had been hit by a car and she was in Critical Care in the John Radcliffe hospital. She had worked for the Timminses for almost seven years and both David and his father were very upset. David particularly so. Susie had discovered that Amanda lived alone, and to the best of David's knowledge had no immediate relatives, which was why the hospital was communicating with him and his father. It struck Susie how suddenly life could change – either for the better or for the worse. She did hope that Amanda would soon be on the road to recovery. Finishing her chocolate, she decided it was time for bed. George thought it a good idea to go with her.

*****

The lottery man visited Riverside House on the Monday morning and confirmed that James' ticket was in order and that the winnings would be in his bank account by the end of the week. He was clearly disappointed that he couldn't interest James in any of the other services that the National Lottery provided, but both James and his father were adamant on that score. When he had gone, James grinned at his dad and said how wonderful it was to have won so much money and that now he would have to think seriously about what he was going to do with it all. Peter told him that he had a week to do that in, so not to rush things. James nodded and said that he thought he would have a word with David Timmins to see if he had any bright ideas.

When he phoned David, James was surprised that the man didn't seem his usual cheerful self. Although he made an appointment to see James, when he came off the phone, James did wonder if David had taken in anything that had been said to him, and remarked as much to his father. He also thought it odd that David had answered the phone himself, as it was usually answered by a woman. Peter remarked that perhaps the secretary was on holiday and David was a bit stressed as he would have more to do.

Half an hour before James phoned, David had received a call from the John Radcliffe Hospital to tell him that Amanda had died. He was devastated, and as his father was out visiting clients, he had to shoulder the burden alone. His mind was reeling. David would certainly be relieved when his dad got back to the office. He already had one important suggestion to make.

*****

Susie woke up on the Monday morning to bright blue sky and the thought that she had the whole day and evening to herself. After all, she had been working a seven day week, so she deserved a bit of a break. She was looking forward to meeting up with David that evening for what would be their first proper date and texted him to tell him so. She was slightly put out when he didn't reply immediately, but thought that he was probably extra busy without Amanda's help.

As the weather was so lovely, Susie decided she would spend the morning in her garden as it had certainly been neglected of late. It was only small so it didn't take her long to mow the back lawn and pull a few weeds out of the flowerbeds. Ruefully, she looked at her hands. Her nails desperately needed re-applying but she couldn't afford that, so thought that she would have to try and lever the damn things off herself. Perhaps she could check with the nail bar and see how much it would cost to have them removed. Feeling a bit low, because she did try to look nice, Susie pushed her lawn mower round to the front of the house.

Typical, she thought to herself, there was Mrs MacDonald! Well, she wasn't in a rush, so she could have a conversation with her. Putting a smile on her face, Susie said how nice it was to see her and wondered whether Mrs MacDonald might have time for a cup of coffee?

Mrs MacDonald's face lit up at the suggestion and immediately she was walking up Susie's path. Susie suggested that she go round to the back garden as it was such a lovely morning and that she would bring the coffee out. The old lady was delighted when George appeared from under a bush and came and rubbed round her legs, purring loudly. "You know that I come and feed you, don't you pet?" she said to him.

Susie was soon out with a tray of coffee and a plate of biscuits. She and Mrs MacDonald spent a pleasant hour or so sitting in the sun. The old lady chattered away, asking Susie as many questions as she thought polite. She commented on the fact that Susie's tall boyfriend didn't seem to visit any more. Susie told her that he wouldn't be visiting again as their relationship was over. Mrs MacDonald said that that was a shame, but there were plenty more fish in the sea. Susie smiled wistfully and turned the subject to the vegetables that her neighbour grew at the bottom of her garden and asked how they were doing.

Suddenly, Susie was aware that her doorbell was ringing. Excusing herself, she walked round the side of the house, to find a distraught David.

*****

Susie briefly explained that she was having coffee with her neighbour, before ushering David into the garden. She introduced them and left them to talk whilst she went and made some more coffee. It was very apparent to her that something was seriously wrong, and she guessed it concerned Amanda. Hopefully Mrs MacD would leave soon, wouldn't she? She would surely see that David had come to see her and that it was important.

How wrong she was! Susie realised that hinting was no good; the old lady was determined to stay for as long as possible. When she found out what David's profession was, Mrs MacDonald started to tell him all about her savings! Finally, David had to excuse himself and said he needed to get back to the office and that he would see Susie that evening. "How nice," said Mrs MacDonald, "where will the two of you be going? Will you be going out for a meal?" They said that they hadn't decided yet, and Susie walked around to the front of the house again with David.

"Is it Amanda?" she asked him quietly. David said that it was, and that she had died a few hours ago. Susie hugged him very close.

Returning to the back garden, Susie found Mrs MacDonald eager to find out what she could about David. "He's young to be a financial adviser, isn't he?" she asked.

"I've no idea," Susie replied. "His sister went to college with my brother. That's how I know him." This seemed to satisfy Mrs MacDonald for the meantime, so thanking Susie for the coffee and biscuits, she went home.

Susie cleared the table and then turned her attention to her front garden. As it was minute, she had it in order within the hour and then went inside, thinking about David and poor Amanda. She felt that David probably wouldn't feel like going out that evening in view of what had happened, so decided that she would make supper for the pair of them. Looking in her fridge and cupboards, Susie realised that she would have to go shopping. What could she make that was cheap and easy, she wondered, and decided on spaghetti bolognaise. Everyone liked that, and she could buy a jar of sauce and tart it up with some other bits and pieces as well as the mince. She could also buy salad and garlic bread, which would save on effort. David liked beer, so she would have to see what was on offer at the supermarket, as she wanted maximum results from the minimum spend.

Having written a short list, Susie brushed her hair, got in her car, put the hood down, and set off for Chipping Norton. She wondered if she should call in to the office and see David whilst she was there, but felt that that was perhaps inappropriate, so instead sent him a text to tell him that she was making supper for them that evening and would expect him about 7.00 pm. She smiled at her little phone as she sent the text. It wasn't the same as her iPhone, but it had been very sweet of David to buy it for her.

Swinging the Mini into the car park, Susie wondered about visiting the nail bar to see how much it would cost to have her nails removed, as her hands really did look a mess. She did her shopping, so that it was out of the way, and put it in her boot. She then walked across the road to the nail bar.

"You're in luck," said the nail technician. "I can do them for you now. It'll be £7.50 to have them removed, but better still, as you're a regular customer, we have a special offer on, and I'll do you a new set for £27.50." What could a girl do? Susie said the special offer would be lovely, and settled herself down for a gossip with Kylie. A cup of coffee materialised as if from nowhere and was placed at her elbow. After all, she had been gardening all morning, and was cooking tonight, so she deserved a little treat, didn't she? She could hardly expect David to like her with manky nails, now, could she?

CHAPTER 49

Jonathan Browne returned from work on Monday feeling happy and relaxed. Parking his car, he was slightly surprised to see all the bedroom windows closed. Angela normally had them open, particularly when it was such nice weather. He was more surprised still when he opened the front door and the house was quiet. She must have taken the twins out somewhere, he thought to himself. Shrugging his shoulders, Jonathan went upstairs to take a shower and change his clothes.

"I don't bloody well believe it," he said a few moments later. "The utter cow. How could she do this to me? The scheming, conniving bitch. Well, she won't get away with it, that's for sure." He showered and changed into a pair of shorts and a polo shirt. Pouring himself a large scotch and taking the bottle with him, Jonathan went out in to the garden, where he sat for a while, contemplating what he was going to do next.

He found his mind turning to Susie. After all, she had been a bloody good lay and was clearly infatuated by him. He'd ring her up, that's what he'd do. Jonathan was very surprised to discover that Susie's mobile number had been disconnected. She didn't have a land line, so that was the end of that. He poured himself another drink. Perhaps Susie would be working at The Crown tonight? He'd have something to eat, to absorb the alcohol, and then he'd go over there to see her. Going back inside, Jonathan made himself a cheese and pickle sandwich and drank a pint of milk. That should help to counteract the scotch, he thought to himself.

He quickly changed his shorts for a pair of jeans and was soon in the car heading for Church Enstone. It was a bit annoying, as he'd only left the airfield two or three hours ago, but needs must. Arriving at The Crown, he parked his car and went in.

"Evening Jonathan," said Alf. "We don't normally have the pleasure of your company this late in the day. What can I get you?" Jonathan said that he'd have a small scotch. He and Alf exchanged pleasantries for a while and then Jonathan got to the purpose of his visit.

"I don't see Susie tonight," he remarked conversationally to Alf. "No," replied the landlord, "she doesn't work here anymore." Jonathan chatted for a few more minutes and then left the pub.

*****

David arrived at Susie's at the allotted hour, carrying a bunch of flowers, some beer and a bottle of wine. The flowers had been a bit awkward, as he had walked, but he was touched by Susie's offer to cook and wanted to take her a gift.

She greeted him with a kiss on the cheek, thanked him for his gifts and ushered him through to the sitting room. David looked around him and thought how pretty it was. The table was laid at the far end of the room, and there were candles burning in the hearth. Susie came and sat beside him and said in a sympathetic voice that he must have had an awful day. David nodded his head. They could have supper whenever he wanted, she told him. It would only take her 20 minutes to cook.

David suggested that she started preparing the food after they'd had a chat, as he had something important to ask her. He explained that apart from all the horror that went with Amanda's death, it also left the company without an administrator. He had spoken with his father and had told him about Susie, down to the fact that she had left Woodstock Academy under a cloud and couldn't provide a reference and that she didn't have any experience working in the world of finance, but that nonetheless, he thought she could be a great asset to the company, if his dad was prepared to give her a chance. His dad had said that he would like to meet Susie and they could take it from there. What did she think about that?

Susie looked at David in amazement. "You did that for me?" she asked. "Wow. That's so kind and thoughtful of you. I'd love to meet your dad. When can I do that, please?"

"As you probably know, we really are a family firm," David replied, but didn't tell Susie that he had also told his father that he was dating her, "so Dad has suggested that we go over to supper tomorrow night. You can meet both my parents and have a chat about the job. It will be easier than if you come to the office, as without Amanda, we really are pushed."

Susie said that she understood, and that that would be fine with her. She went on to ask David about his family. David was pleased by the apparent interest that she was taking. He told her that his parents lived in Great Rollright, on the other side of Chipping Norton. His mother was a Marketing Consultant who worked from home and helped out doing some marketing and PR for the family business. The only other family member was his sister Jenny, who Susie had met at James' party, and she was still living at home, waiting for her results. They also had two golden Labradors – Honey and Mustard. Susie laughed at that and said that the dogs sounded like a salad dressing. David retorted that as her parents' dog was called Allsort, he didn't think she was in a position to be critical! Susie laughed some more and thought that David really was beginning to grow on her. He had tried to help her with her finances, had bought her a mobile phone and now wine and flowers and on top of all that was trying to get her a job. He was also easy company and quite entertaining. Not bad looking either – tall and slim. Oh yes, he could also cook, she thought, her mind going back to the curries that David had made on the night when she had dinner with him at Nag's Head Cottage.

David thought it odd that Susie had not mentioned James' lottery win and wondered if perhaps her brother hadn't told her, so didn't refer to his forthcoming appointment to see him, whilst thinking to himself that it was a shame that it hadn't been Susie who had won. That would certainly have sorted out her financial difficulties!

He looked at her as she walked through to the kitchen to get him another beer and once again thought what a pretty girl she was. "Shall I start the supper now?" she called through from the kitchen. David said he thought that a good idea.

Half an hour later Susie was carrying steaming dishes of pasta and sauce through to her dining table. She lit some candles and invited David to join her. He did so eagerly.

The couple were about half way through their meal when the front doorbell rang, followed by loud banging with the door knocker. "Who on earth can that be?" Susie asked. Putting her napkin down, she excused herself and went to answer the door. She was shocked to see that her caller was none other than Jonathan Browne. Her jaw dropped and she was speechless.

"You look as sexy as ever, you gorgeous thing," he said, running his hands down Susie. He stepped past her and waltzed into the living room. "Who the hell are you?" he demanded angrily of David.

"I might ask the same thing," came the calm reply. David had recognised Jonathan immediately from the press and TV, but there was no way that he was admitting to it, as he wondered what the bastard could now want with Susie.

CHAPTER 50

Jonathan had been knocked sideways by the letter he had found on Angela's dressing table when he returned home on Monday evening. It seemed as though he was reading about someone else's life, he recognised so little of his wife in the words.

Dear Jonathan

By the time you read this, the twins and I will have left. We are going to live with someone else. You don't need to know who. I have known this gentleman, in the biblical sense of the word, since Alice and Emily started at Woodstock Academy. However, unlike you, I don't need to flaunt myself publicly. I wouldn't have left you had it not been for that little tramp. You see, I have the ability to conduct an affair with discretion. A word you clearly don't understand.

The girls have met the gentleman we are going to live with over the last month, since your indiscretion became public, and like him very much. The school term will finish on Thursday, so I'm not in the least bit concerned about having taken them out a few days early. They won't be returning there in September.

We will sort out the mechanics of a divorce, as I shall expect you to support your children. There will be a lot we need to sort out over the coming months. When I have chosen a solicitor I will let you have details.

Angela

*****

Angela had left her husband for a widower, some twenty years older than herself. Alex Drummond was an ex-RAF officer, who had served at one point in his career with Peter Rowlands. She had met him one morning in a café in Woodstock. He had asked if he might join her as the café was busy and there was a shortage of tables. She had immediately been struck by his charming manners and when he had told her that he was looking for a house in the area she had suggested a couple of estate agents. Alex had been living near Newbury but was very fond of Oxford and wished to move to the area.

Angela had actually looked at properties with him, as he said he would appreciate a woman's input. Little did she realise that she was selecting her future home. Clearly a man of means, Alex had chosen a well-proportioned detached house on the Woodstock Road in Oxford itself.

They had seen each other very discreetly and were lovers within a month of meeting. However, Alex had never visited the Brownes' home in Kirtlington. Angela always went to him. As soon as her husband left the house in the morning, Angela would do her chores and would then be free to spend the rest of the time with Alex, until she had to collect the twins from school. The duplicity of it all had quite amused Angela – she being viewed as the little mouse, grateful to be married to the handsome Jonathan Browne. Of course she knew of his affairs, but was prepared to tolerate them, until Susie Rowlands became public knowledge in Woodstock.

She had been telling Alex how upsetting she found it all, when he suggested that they move in together. Always putting her children first, Angela said that it would depend on whether or not the girls and he got on well together. They had met for a picnic when Jonathan was away for the European Grand Prix, and although he was older, the twins had taken to Alex immediately. So much so, that Angela had cried off from going to the British Grand Prix a fortnight later and they had gone away together to the New Forest for the Saturday night. As that had been so successful she had no qualms in accepting Alex's offer. He had more than sufficient means to care for them all, as he had inherited a small fortune when his wife had died some ten years previously.

Now here she was, sorting out who was going to sleep where in Alex's house in Oxford. The beginning of a new chapter of her life. Angela dreaded telling her parents about what she had done, but that could wait for another day. She had switched her phone off for the evening, as she didn't wish to have Jonathan haranguing her, as he was bound to be screaming down the line as soon as he had read her note. That could wait for tomorrow! In fact, she would probably buy another phone and reserve the old one just for him, so that it didn't need to be switched on very often.

As the twins were happily choosing their new bedrooms, Alex called up to tell them that supper was ready. Such luxury, she thought to herself as she and the girls all went downstairs together.

*****

Jonathan hadn't thought about ringing Angela. He was too preoccupied with replacing her and was positive that Susie would jump at the chance to share his life. Confidently, he had parked his car behind the Mini in the lay-by outside her house, as it didn't matter a bit who saw him now.

With a beaming smile on his face, Jonathan rang the bell and then banged on Susie's door but got the shock of his life when he saw that she was sharing a meal with another man.

Susie was thrown into turmoil by Jonathan's arrival. "Why on earth have you come here?" she asked him.

"That's not a very friendly greeting, Susie, sweetheart," he said, trying to kiss her. Susie turned her face away, feeling very embarrassed. If this meeting did have to take place, she would have much preferred it not to have been in front of David. She couldn't help but find Jonathan devastatingly handsome and, despite herself, her stomach was doing cartwheels, but sitting at her dining table was the man who was trying to help her and who she was beginning to find rather attractive.

"Oh go away, Jonathan," she said crossly.

"Go away," he drawled. "Don't be silly. I've come here to ask you to come and live with me. I've no intention of going away." Susie felt like crying. If he had said that a month ago she would have jumped at the chance. "Aren't you going to offer me a glass of wine?" he continued, eyeing up the bottle on the table.

"I think you've had enough already," Susie ventured.

"Who do you think you are to tell me how much I can drink?" Jonathan replied angrily.

David decided it was time to step in. "You heard Susie ask you to leave, now I'm asking you as well," he said, walking towards the door.

"And who the fuck do you think you are to ask me to leave?" roared an incensed Jonathan.

"I'm a friend of Susie's," replied David, "and she has made it clear that she doesn't want you here."

"Doesn't want me here," sneered Jonathan. "Let me tell you something mate. She used to welcome me with open arms and legs." Susie gasped and turned bright red.

"Please just go, Jonathan," she whispered. How could he say that about her? She was seeing a side of Jonathan that she didn't realise existed.

With that Jonathan stormed out of the house, slamming the front door behind him, and shouting, "You'll regret this. You've had your chance!"

*****

Wow," said David after Jonathan had left. "That was some entertainment." Susie was still looking embarrassed and upset by the scene that David had just witnessed. "Never mind," said David, taking her hand and leading her over to the sofa. "We have tomorrow at my parents to look forward to. I'll pick you up about 7." Susie nodded automatically and started thinking about what she should wear to impress a prospective employer. She was particularly concerned as she didn't want to let David down.

They chatted for a while, but Jonathan had spoiled the evening. They kissed briefly, which Susie rather enjoyed and then David set out to walk home.

As it was only 10.30 when he got to Church Enstone, he decided to have a drink in The Crown. "Just don't ask," he said when he saw Alf approaching. The landlord grinned at him and asked if he should pull him a pint.

CHAPTER 51

Susie had spent a restless night thinking about Jonathan versus David. She liked David much more, but she still found Jonathan amazingly attractive and he could offer her a glamorous lifestyle too. Wasn't it just like life that he should ask her to live with him when she no longer wanted to? He had been drinking though and she was pretty sure that he wouldn't have asked her had he been sober. Round and round the thoughts went in her mind, until it was time to get up.

David would be picking her up that evening to go and meet his parents. She couldn't afford to mess things up there. However, she and David weren't even an item yet, so what would be the harm in perhaps having lunch with Jonathan? Susie lay in the bath and fantasised about living with the man she had thought Jonathan to be – the glamour, the fast cars, the high life, but she knew in her heart that she valued David over Jonathan. Going downstairs, she asked George what he thought, but all he did was chirp and ask for his breakfast. Susie fed him and made herself some coffee and toast. Who could she talk to about this one? Perhaps Grace? She hadn't spoken to Grace in ages – just used her as a foil for her mother when she was gadding about in Monaco with Jonathan.

Nothing to lose, decided Susie, and dialled Grace's mobile. Because she had changed her number, courtesy of David, Grace didn't realise who was calling and was surprised to hear Susie's voice.

"This is a surprise, Suse," she said. "I haven't heard from you in ages." Susie apologised and proceeded to tell Grace about her affair with Jonathan and that he had now asked her to live with him, but that there was also David. "You really pick your moments, don't you?" said Grace irritably. "I've just got to the office and I have a busy day ahead of me. If you want my honest opinion, have nothing to do with the married man. What he did to his wife he will do to you in due course. Leopards tend not to change their spots. Now you'll have to forgive me, but I must get on. Why don't you call me one evening?" With that, Grace replaced the receiver. Susie felt slightly miffed. Grace didn't seem to be that interested in what she had to say. It hadn't occurred to her to ask Grace how she was and what was going on in her life!

The words "what he did to his wife he will do to you in due course" stuck in Susie's mind as she went through the day.

She tried to focus her thoughts on the evening ahead and wondered what gift she should take for the Timminses. She felt that wine wasn't appropriate. Maybe she could get chocolates at the village shop, which would save her the trouble and expense of taking the car to Chipping Norton.

As she closed her front door on the way out, who should be calling "good morning" to her but Mrs MacDonald. Susie smiled. "I see that the young man you said you were no longer seeing came to see you last night," ventured the old lady. Jesus Christ, thought Susie, trust that old bat to have seen Jonathan.

"Yes, he did pop in," she replied guardedly.

"He didn't stay long," said Mrs MacDonald, hopeful of a titbit of gossip.

"No," said Susie and set off towards the village shop. Mrs MacDonald stood looking after her, not sure what to make of it all. Curiouser and curiouser, as Alice would have said.

*****

Over a couple of pints at The Crown, David had also been thinking about Jonathan. He fancied Susie very much and felt that he would have to move things forward, as he didn't want her rushing back into Jonathan's arms. Bugger it! Just when things had been going along fairly smoothly. He hoped that Susie would hit it off with his parents and that his father would offer her a job. That would surely help his cause. Alf commented that David looked very thoughtful and David just nodded his head absentmindedly. When Alf called time, he walked next door, still deep in thought.

*****

James had also been thinking about Susie and whether or not he should help her financially. He didn't feel that he wanted to discuss this with anyone. His parents might or might not approve and he wasn't sure that he needed Greg's input, as this was very personal. The only possible person was David Timmins and he had seemed a bit vague when they last spoke. They had a meeting set up for next week but if he was going to do something he ought to do it now. The question was, how much should he give her? It would have to be a gift, as Susie stood very little chance of ever repaying him and as he'd won so much money, surely he could afford to be generous? At the moment everything was going his way and Susie seemed to have the chips stacked against her.

The other thing that James wanted to organise was a special family dinner to celebrate his winnings and he was wondering about whether or not to invite Greg's parents. Perhaps he would ask his dad about that one. He wouldn't ask him about Susie though. He would sort that out for himself.

All of a sudden and out of the blue, James made a decision. He would go over and see Susie the next day and take her a cheque.

*****

Susie had just got in from the village when James pulled up outside. "Jamie! This is a surprise!" She said. "Come on in." James followed her into the sitting room and asked how things were going.

"Oh, you know," she said, "life has a mysterious way of working," and she told him all about David and Amanda being killed and that she was going to see David's parents that night. She had just been up the village to try and buy some chocolates but the shop only had Milk Tray, so she would have to go into Woodstock or Chipping Norton now.

"Tell you what," said James. "Why don't I take you and we can have a bite to eat as well. I've lots to tell you. Can we go to Woodstock, as I haven't been there for ages?" The next minute they were heading for James' car, watched by an increasingly incredulous Mrs MacDonald.

Once seated in Hampers and with their food in front of them, James told Susie all about his plans to move in with Greg. "Daddy and Mummy know?" Susie asked.

"Yes, and Dad has taken it surprisingly well," James told her. "However, I have some even more exciting news."

When Susie heard about his lottery win, her jaw dropped. Why couldn't it have been her? Why was it always James? He was the one with the brains. All she had to rely on was her looks. She couldn't match up to the rest of the family. Daddy had flown the Queen about, Mummy was the most perfect domestic goddess imaginable and not only had Jamie got the brains, he'd got the luck as well, with love and money. Susie felt like a complete failure.

She suddenly realised that James was offering her a present. "This is for you, Suse," he said. "I want to share my happiness with you." Susie pulled off the ribbon, eager with anticipation. The box was as light as a feather. What could it possibly be? Inside the wrapping was another box. When she opened it, it revealed a cheque for £5,000. James was sitting there looking very pleased with himself, and whilst she was pleased to receive it, sadly Susie couldn't stop herself from thinking that with all he had just won, James could have given her more. That wasn't going to buy her any happiness. All it would do would be to pay off some debts.

She smiled and tried to sound enthusiastic as she thanked him, but was sure that her words sounded hollow.

James was now burbling on about a dinner he was organising to celebrate his win and saying that it would probably be in a couple of weeks' time. Getting fed up with golden balls and his wonderful life, Susie interrupted him to tell him that she was dating David, as well as being considered for a job with his firm. "That's wonderful," replied her brother. "He can come to the dinner with you."

Lunch eaten, Susie said she would quickly look for some nice chocolates for Mrs Timmins and would also pay her cheque into the bank. That would shut the bank manager up and get him off her back.

As she couldn't find any quality chocolates, Susie changed her mind and bought David's mother a bouquet of flowers. She couldn't wait to tell David about the cheque from James. She felt she ought to ask him who it was most important to pay. At least she could now use her debit card again. Perhaps she could buy David a present? Obviously not this afternoon, as she had James in tow, but she could go to Banbury or Oxford tomorrow, as she could now afford to buy petrol. Life was on the up after all.

*****

Susie chose her clothes with care that evening, settling on an elegantly cut pale grey maxi dress. It showed off her figure to advantage and looked sober and sensible at the same time. She felt that Granny's ring would also be appropriate. Financial people would be sure to appreciate these things. She had given herself a good talking-to in the bath, about being ungrateful. After all, James hadn't had to give her anything and £5,000 certainly got her off shit street. She was ashamed of herself for being jealous of his good fortune, but ever since they were children she had been resentful of her younger, more talented brother. Little did she realise that he was envious of her bubbly, spontaneous way of dancing through life.

David arrived promptly for her at 7.00 pm. He hugged her close and kissed her cheek, saying that he didn't want to smudge her lipstick and that she would have to wait for a proper kiss until later. He then stood back and told her that she looked absolutely beautiful. She told David that he didn't look too shabby himself and the pair of them walked down the path to his Alfa, where Susie carefully put the flowers on the back seat. She turned a blind eye to Mrs MacDonald who was frantically waving from an upstairs window.

It didn't take long to get to Great Rollright and soon David was pulling up outside his parents' house. They were greeted by both his parents as well as Honey and Mustard. Mrs Timmins looked delighted with Susie's bouquet. Like her son, Julia Timmins was tall, dark and slim. His father, George, was also dark, but stocky. They made Susie feel very welcome as they walked through to the sitting room. Julia handed round glasses of Pimms and then George started to tell Susie about the business and asked her a few questions too. "Don't be too formal, George. Susie hasn't come here to be interrogated," Julia warned him. George smiled and apologised.

Dinner was delicious. Julia had made a pâté, which she followed with lamb cutlets and young vegetables and to finish off they had a rhubarb crumble and clotted cream. Susie complimented her hostess on the yummy food. Over coffee they talked a little more about the business. The conversation ended with George asking if she would like to work for them for a few weeks on a trial basis. He said that he and David would formalise things the next day and that David would advise her of the details. Susie thanked him very much and said she would look forward to receiving the offer.

All too soon the pleasant evening ended and David drove her home. Susie asked him if he would like to come in for more coffee and he said that he certainly would. She was feeling pleasantly light-headed from the Pimms and Prosecco and really enjoyed the long, lingering kiss that David gave her as he left. Perhaps Jonathan wasn't so special, after all?

CHAPTER 52

The next day Susie hit the shops in Oxford, looking for a present for David. She had no idea what to buy him, as she didn't know him very well. She was also vaguely conscious that she shouldn't spend too much money yet. David was coming round that evening to talk to her in more detail about the job and to help her sort out which bills to pay. However, for the moment she didn't have to worry about that boring stuff. She was out in the sunshine and her debit card was burning a hole in her pocket.

She had parked in the Westgate car park and had already popped into Monsoon and East and thought that she would go back later to buy, as there was no point in carrying unnecessary bags around with her when those shops were on her way back to the car. But what to buy for David? Aftershave? A bottle of something? Well, she needn't have come to Oxford for that! A shirt? What size? Cufflinks? A bit too personal perhaps. She didn't know him that well yet. Maybe a cup of coffee and a pastry would help her think.

Suitably fortified, Susie continued on her walk, but the only things that caught her eye were ones she would like herself. In the end she settled for a bottle of Eau Sauvage for David, as she was fairly confident that he wore it and she liked it anyway! That sorted, Susie continued to look round the shops and with the security of James' gift and the promise of a job, she felt she deserved something for herself. She had no trouble in finding something - a top from East, a dress from Monsoon and some Mac make-up. Having spent over £200, mostly on herself, Susie set off back to Enstone.

Whilst in Oxford, she had also popped into Marks and bought a bottle of champagne and various goodies for dinner, as she had told David that she would do dinner that night, as it would be easier to discuss things at home.

*****

When David arrived Susie was wearing her new Monsoon dress with a pair of strappy sandals and he thought she looked gorgeous. He kissed her and told her so. He was slightly surprised when she opened a bottle of champagne, saying that he mustn't drink too much as he had driven up. "We need to celebrate," she replied, " so let's take this in to the garden as it's such a lovely evening." When they were outside she asked him if he could tell her about the job first, as she thought they might need to look at some paperwork to sort out how she was going to allocate her money.

The patio table was looking very pretty, covered with a white cloth, and with a candle burning in the middle. There was also a bowl of crisps and another of cashew nuts. David was impressed that Susie had gone out of her way to make things special. Before he could start telling her about the job, she dived under the table and came up with a beautifully wrapped package. "This is for you, David, to thank you for all you've done for me," she said. He opened it at once and smiled when he saw the contents.

"My favourite," he said. "How did you know?"

"I thought I had smelled it on you," replied Susie, "and I like it too, so it seemed just right." David told her that it was very just right.

He went on to tell her that he and his father had discussed her and the job and what they suggested was that Susie should join them for a month on a trial basis and they could all see how they got on and whether or not they worked well together. If they did, she would then move on to a proper probationary period of three months. Her salary for the four months would be £20,000 pro rata. Susie looked blank at this, so David explained that that equated to £1,666.67 per month! If all was well after the four months, she would then go on to a permanent contract, at a higher wage to be negotiated, and she would also have an opportunity to join the pension scheme. How did that sound to her?

Woodstock Academy had paid Susie £22,000 a year, plus something into her pension which she didn't understand, so she felt that £20,000 on a trial basis was quite acceptable. I'll make myself indispensable she thought and then they'll want to pay me loads to keep me. She smiled at David and said that it sounded very good to her. "OK then," he said. "I'll get all that written up and bring it over. Could you start on Monday please?" Susie agreed enthusiastically.

As they drank their champagne, enjoying the sun's last rays, they touched on the subject of Susie's debts. She explained that she had paid James' cheque into the bank, so that her account was now working again and that she had a bit of cash left, courtesy of Alf. David said that her first priority was to get her mortgage back on track and then make sure that her council tax and utility bills were up to date. He then suggested that she pay as much as she could off her credit card and cut it up. "Cut it up?" squealed Susie. "What would I want to do that for?"

"To teach you to control your spending habits and not get into a mess again," he replied smiling. Susie looked horrified. "Tell you what, then," said David, "you can give it to me to keep for you and I'll give it back if you still want it when you've cleared the balance."

"That could take a long time," said Susie ruefully.

"Not if you do as I suggest," was the swift reply.

With that they went inside for supper. Over the meal David asked Susie if she had advertised her spare room in the local paper and put her holiday on eBay. She said that she had done neither, but agreed with David that the holiday was a priority and needed to go on there straight away. Between them they concocted the listing, giving the holiday a minimum price of £100 and setting the auction to end in ten days' time. Susie said that she would like to hold fire about letting the room, as things were no longer so tight for her. David reminded her that she would only receive a week's wages for July and she would then have to support herself through August before she got any more money, so she still needed to be careful.

Susie sighed and said that it was all so dreary! They had finished the champagne by now, so Susie went to the kitchen and came back with a beer for David and a glass of wine for herself. As she was handing the beer to him, Susie thought that he was becoming something of a fixture in her life and that it was rather nice. David was thinking much the same thing about Susie and praying that she would be good at her job and become a part of the family business. He rather fancied her as a permanent person in his life, but realised that was rather a lot to ask for just yet.

David was hoping that he could take Susie to his parents' holiday home in France, but he would have to talk to his dad about that, as he mightn't appreciate him whisking Susie away during her probationary period.

They had been curled up together on the sofa for quite a while, listening to music, when David realised that he was on his fourth beer. Add that to half a bottle of champagne and he knew that he shouldn't be driving. Oh well, what the hell? There were taxis and he also had a pair of feet. He'd just have to get up a bit earlier to collect his car the next morning. He was certainly in no rush to leave. He suddenly realised that Susie was offering him coffee and wondered whether it was a cue to leave after he had drunk it.

After they had finished their coffee, David glanced at his watch, and saw that midnight was fast approaching. He gave Susie a long, slow kiss and ran his fingers through her hair. "I'd better be going, otherwise I'm not going to be much use at work tomorrow."

"I thought you might like to stay," Susie replied tentatively. David held her even closer and said that he could think of nothing nicer.

CHAPTER 53

James was delighted when he checked his bank account on the Friday morning to find that the lottery money had indeed been paid in. Over breakfast he told his parents that he was now officially rich and that he was planning to organise a celebration dinner and wondered whether or not they had any suggestions? He felt that everyone invited should be offered accommodation, as they wouldn't want to be travelling after they had been drinking, which made having the meal in a hotel seem like a good idea.

They chatted around various locations and couldn't come to any decision, so Annabelle suggested having the meal at home as there wasn't going to be that many of them. Greg's parents couldn't come as they were away on a three week cruise and James wanted to have the dinner sooner rather than later. That only left Annabelle and Peter, Greg and James and Susie and possibly David. Peter and James both said immediately that that wasn't fair on Annabelle as she would have to do a lot of work. "Oh for heaven's sake," she said. "You know I love cooking. James can tell me what he wants to eat and choose the drinks and we can take it from there. Someone else can faff around and lay the table and be my general lackey. James?"

"Are you sure, Mum?" enquired her son. "And of course I'll help you."

"Positive," she replied. "Now just pick your date and menu."

Annabelle also pointed out to James that although he had won all this money, he didn't need to throw it around unnecessarily. "I'm sure you and Greg will be planning a luxury holiday somewhere," she said. James said that he hadn't got that far yet, but it was certainly a good idea. He told her that he had an appointment with David Timmins on Monday as he wanted to do some more investing.

"Very wise indeed," Peter nodded. He then picked up his newspaper and wandered off.

Once they were alone together, James broached the subject of bedroom arrangements with his mother. "How will dad react if Greg and I sleep together?" he asked.

"He won't react at all," replied Annabelle. "That's what you do and that's what you'll do when you stay here." James thanked her for being so understanding.

"Now, as for the party menu," said Annabelle. "What do you fancy?" James said he didn't really know and asked if he could leave it to her as she was so good at those sorts of things. "Shall I ask your father to select the wines, then?" asked Annabelle. James said that would be wonderful, and that he would sort out a date with her when he had spoken to both Greg and Susie.

He then went and rang his sister. James was pleased that Susie sounded much more relaxed and she thanked him again for the cheque and told him that she was now straight with the building society and all her other bills were up to date. "Wait until you hear my other good news, Jamie," she said excitedly and then went on to tell him that she was now properly going out with David and that she was starting work with him next week, on a trial basis. James laughed at that and said that he would be seeing her on Monday, then. He also said that if she and David were now properly dating, would she like to properly confirm that she would be bringing him to the dinner party. Susie replied that she would love to. James decided that he would let his mum deal with the rooms. Enough was enough!

James was aware that Annabelle was calling him, "Post, James darling." He went and took the envelope from her and opened it. "Today is just the best day," he said, "first my winnings hit my account and then I get my results. I've got a 2:1, Mum."

"That's wonderful, darling," Annabelle said, kissing him. "Let's go and tell Dad."

"Let's go and tell Dad what?" enquired a voice, as Peter came down the hallway. "I'm in search of more coffee. The Telegraph's making me thirsty this morning."

"I've got my results Dad and I've got a 2:1," James almost shrieked with excitement.

"Marvellous, son, marvellous," said Peter, shaking James' hand and hugging him close. "We've got even more to celebrate now. Mum will have to do something extra special."

James was soon on the phone again. This time to Greg, to tell him both about his degree and the fact that he now had his money. "Book a table for us for tonight anywhere you like," said James, "and Mum's going to cook for my celebration dinner and we're going to have it here at Riverside House, and I've spoken to Susie and it's going to be next Saturday – that's a week tomorrow." He could feel Greg smiling down the phone as he congratulated him on his fantastic news.

"You're a very lucky young man, you know," said Peter emerging from the kitchen minutes later. "I'll bet there aren't many chaps your age in such a fortunate position. You'll have to start thinking about what you're going to do for a living now that you know what your degree is. I presume that you'll be applying to the big boys for a management training course?"

"I don't know, Dad," came the reply. "To be quite honest, my life has been so exciting just recently that I haven't given it much thought."

Peter looked hard at his son. "I realise that everything seems to be rosy in your garden at the moment," he said, "but this is the real world. You haven't sufficient money to create an investment portfolio that will keep you in the manner to which you are accustomed, although you could take some sort of income from it. Therefore you need to carve out a career. You just need to sort your head out and find out which direction you're going in. You know that I'm always here to help you if I can."

James nodded in agreement, whilst thinking that he didn't particularly want a business career. He was enjoying the antiques world and spending time with Greg. He would have to discuss all this with Greg later and see what he thought. Maybe they could open a shop together somewhere different? Get better premises and have a shop of their own, rather than be in an arcade? Perhaps Mum would also be interested in that? He would have to sound them both out. After all, he would be able to do something substantial. That could be another thing to discuss with David. Fancy Susie going out with the guy as well! Such a small world. So much had happened in the last few weeks. It was quite amazing.

With that James took out his phone and dialled Jenny's number. She was over the moon, as she had also got a 2:1. They congratulated each other, chatted for a short while and then finished the conversation.

*****

When she had finished talking to James, Susie got straight on the phone to David and told him all the exciting news – about James' degree and the dinner at Riverside House. She then remembered to ask about Jenny and her degree. David said he hadn't heard, so he would have to ring his sister and let Susie know later.

After he had put the phone down and before he rang Jenny, David thought to himself that things were progressing very nicely indeed with Susie. Life was indeed good.

CHAPTER 54

Susie was confident that life was really on the up. She had a new boyfriend, the promise of a job and she was out of debt, relatively speaking. She felt that she should tell her parents that all was well and that she should do this before James' dinner party the following Saturday. With this in mind, she set off for Moulsford first thing on the Saturday morning, hoping that they would both be at home.

"This is a surprise darling," said Annabelle, wondering what had now gone wrong in her daughter's life. "Go through and find Daddy and I'll bring us all some coffee."

Susie found her father in his study, reading his beloved Telegraph. He looked up in surprise when he saw her. "To what do we owe the honour?" he enquired.

"I've lots of news to share with you both," was Susie's reply. "I'll wait for Mummy before I start."

It wasn't long before Annabelle appeared with the coffee and a plate of biscuits.

"Now that you're both here I can tell you my good news," said Susie. Her parents fixed their eyes on her. "I'm going out with David who does James' financial advice. I've also met his parents, who are really nice and his dad has offered me the admin job in his office. James has given me some money from his lottery winnings and I'm now straight with the mortgage and my bills. I'm starting work for George and David on Monday," she gabbled.

Peter and Annabelle looked at her. "That all sounds marvellous, darling," ventured Annabelle. "Things certainly happen at a pace in your life."

Peter spoke then. "I know that David's given James some sound advice, so hopefully he can get your feet back on the ground. You've been very foolish lately, Susie and you're very fortunate to get a job in an industry that you know nothing about. Don't cock this one up."

"I won't, Daddy, I won't," said Susie. "I'm on trial for a month to start with, but I know I can make it work. George has taken me on without references you know."

"From where I'm sitting George didn't have much choice," remarked Peter drily. "You were hardly likely to get a reference from Woodstock Academy, and let's face it you haven't had a proper job anywhere else."

Susie made a face at him. Trust Daddy to have something horrid to say.

"Don't pull a face at me, Susannah, you know I'm speaking the truth and you don't like it," Peter retorted sharply.

Quickly Annabelle intervened. "Regardless of everything, Susie's life has definitely taken a turn for the better, and we're very pleased for you darling, aren't we Peter?" she said, glaring at her husband.

"Yes of course we are," he replied. "We're also very pleased that you took the trouble to come over and tell us your good news. I shall take you and Mummy out to lunch to celebrate." Susie thanked him.

*****

Whilst Susie was making her peace with her parents, James and Greg were discussing possible plans. They'd had a great evening out the night before. They had been to the Crazy Bear in Stadhampton, where they had consumed a magnum of pink champagne alongside their Thai dinner, before being shown to their luxurious suite. When they had checked out of the hotel that morning, after a night of extreme passion, the bill had been enormous, but what the hell, they had a lot to celebrate. Now they were back to reality, in the Lamb Arcade.

"How about a holiday, James darling?" Greg suggested.

"Oh absolutely," enthused James. "Do you want to go and get some brochures whilst I look after things here?" James asked. Greg said that he would, delighted that he had been asked, as he could make sure that he got brochures that he found appealing. James was young and impressionable and Greg felt that he could lead his new lover. It wasn't really that Greg was avaricious, but he did have a taste for the high life and he hadn't had the wherewithal to fund it – until now. He had a mortgage and a struggling business, but he now had James and hopefully some of James' money could be used to Greg's advantage. Ignoring his fuzzy head from the night before, Greg hit the travel agents.

Whilst he was gone, James sat wondering whether he should re-arrange his celebration dinner for the Crazy Bear. He had never been there before, and the place really was something else. He smiled, thinking about his father's face when he saw the bedrooms. He and Greg had been given a suite with a bath built into the bottom of the bed. They had seen a selection of the other rooms too and they were all equally bizarre. If they went there, it would save poor mum from doing all the work. She was a star and an excellent cook, but for heaven's sake, she deserved to enjoy the party as well. There would only be six of them, so it would only be three rooms. They could start off with a jeroboam of champagne and take it from there. He'd only learned last night what a jeroboam was and he could see no reason why they shouldn't have one. He could afford it! They could all meet up at Riverside House and have a stretch limo to take them to the Crazy

Bear late afternoon, then check into the hotel, sort themselves out and have dinner in the evening. He could order the limo again for the following day to take them back to Moulsford. Sorted! He dialled the hotel and started making enquiries. Yes, they could certainly provide accommodation and a table in the evening for six people. He was straight on the phone to Moulsford to tell his parents what he had done.

"Hello Mum," he said. "You're off the hook for doing the cooking on Saturday night. Greg and I went somewhere last night that was ab fab, so I have booked rooms and accommodation for us all on Saturday. That will save you tearing your hair out in the kitchen. I'm going to organise a stretch limo to take us and bring us back."

"I really don't mind cooking, darling," said his mother, "but that is extremely thoughtful of you. Where are we going? Can't we drive? A stretch limo is rather tacky, don't you think?"

"I won't tell you where we're going, because I want it to be a surprise," replied her son. "We could all meet there, but I thought it would be nicer to go a bit earlier, then we could check in to our rooms and get ready at the place itself. It would make it more of an occasion, and it really is very special." Annabelle smiled at her son's enthusiasm. After all, it was his night and his money.

"Very well, James, that would be lovely," she said. "I'll tell your father, and Susie's here at the moment, so I can tell her too. You were very kind to give her some money, James. As I'm sure you know, her life now seems to have taken a turn for the better." James agreed and said that he would see his mum later.

His next job was to find a stretch limo, which he did without too much difficulty. Feeling very pleased with himself, James settled down to wait for Greg to return with the brochures.

He didn't have long to wait. Roughly half an hour later Greg was back enthusing about various exotic locations and saying that he reckoned they could have a great holiday for about £8,000, and that they had lots to discuss.

James started to tell Greg about his change of plan for Saturday, saying that he had booked the rooms and a table at the Crazy Bear. Greg was delighted by that. He had introduced James to the hotel and James was definitely picking up on style. This was something that he needed to be taught. He had come a long way since they first met, but he now needed to learn about the right places to go to. And boy, oh boy, could Greg show him!

CHAPTER 55

Susie awoke full of excitement on Monday. It was her first day in her new job and she was desperate to make a good impression. She had chosen her clothes the night before, as the last thing she wanted to do was to be late. She got up early and was on her way to Chipping Norton before 8.30, and in her new office promptly by 9 o'clock.

David and his father were already there. They smiled when they saw her. Susie smiled back and told them how much she was looking forward to the day. "That's good," said George, "For this morning, at least, we'll be gentle with you."

David took Susie to a large desk in the front office. He showed her the computer. "It's an ordinary pc with Windows. You'll be familiar with that, won't you?" Susie nodded her head. "The filing cabinets are all along that wall," he went on, pointing at them. "Clients are filed alphabetically, so that's all straightforward, but to start with this morning, just concentrate on answering the phone and putting the calls through to us and opening and sorting the post. You also have a copy of our diaries there, from which you will see that your brother is coming to see me this morning. You must chase us to keep that up to date. We're supposed to tell you when we make appointments and where we're going, but we don't always remember. Amanda was always nagging us." At the mention of Amanda's name, David's face clouded over and Susie could see how upset he still was.

Pulling himself together, David went on, "The kitchen's through that door there and the loo's opposite. Coffee and tea are your responsibility, and you take the money out of the petty cash tin, which is kept in the top left hand drawer of your desk. It's normal to offer a drink to visitors." Susie nodded again. "As we're a very small office we have a cleaner who comes in once a week, but the rest of the time it's down to us to keep everything clean and tidy, so washing up needs to be done as we go along. That really means you most of the time."

The front door opened and the postman arrived. As it was a Monday he had a huge pile of mail. "I'll leave you to get on with sorting that out," David said, grinning at her. "The phone will no doubt start ringing soon too. Are you familiar with the system?"

"Yes, I am, thank goodness," said Susie.

She sat at her desk and enthusiastically set about her task of opening and sorting the mail. It wasn't long before she heard the outside door open and James walked in. "Hello, Suse," he said. "How are you settling in?" "Just fine, thank you," she replied. "I'll see if David's ready for you and then I can make you both a drink. What would you like?" James told her that he would like coffee. Susie checked with David and then showed her brother into his office and closed the door.

*****

"Well, aren't you the lucky one?" said David by way of greeting. "First your inheritance and now this lottery win. Well done you. Remind me again how much it is that you've won." James smiled and told David that it was just under £138,000 and that he had all sorts of ideas about what to do with it, going on to explain about Greg and perhaps putting some money into his house or his business. David took a deep breath and said that he wouldn't necessarily rush to do that as James and Greg hadn't known each other for very long. "Also if you pay into the house, you aren't actually seeing a return. You're just helping your friend to reduce his mortgage. Which, although kind, doesn't benefit you financially." James said that he understood.

David went on to tell him that his role as a financial adviser was to look after his clients and until Greg became a client, his sole concern was for James' finances. James said that for the time being he would like to have this new money available, in case he and Greg came up with a business plan. David asked for a couple of days to come up with some suggestions.

The conversation then turned to the dinner party on the Saturday. David said how much he was looking forward to it and James said he was sure that it would be a good night and reminded him to be at Riverside House for 4.00 pm. Saying goodbye to his sister, James drove home to Moulsford.

*****

Susie really enjoyed her first day and worked very hard indeed. She found it a total contrast to the work she had done at Woodstock Academy, as the school systems hadn't been automated. She had looked at the client data base, but not actually used it yet. She was to have instruction on that later in the week. She hoped that David and his father would like her, as she was sure that she would enjoy working there.

That evening, Julia Timmins asked her husband how Susie had got on. "She's a very personable young lady," was the reply, "and it's quite clear to me that David's besotted with her. From that point alone, I hope she works out. It's far too early to say yet, but at least she's very willing."

"That's good," replied his wife. "I must say that I liked her the evening she came here and it would do David good to have a lady in his life again

246

and a very attractive one at that."

Julia smiled. "Dinner won't be too long. Let's go and sit outside and have a nice cold drink whilst we're waiting. I'll go and grab a bottle of wine."

*****

Peter was keen to know how James had got on with David when James got back to Riverside House. James told his father about his suggestions for buying into Greg's house or perhaps them setting up in business together, and went on to say how David had advised caution. Thinking "thank goodness for that," Peter merely said that David seemed to have his head screwed on in the right direction, as James didn't want to rush making important decisions. James laughed and said he'd never realised that having money was such a big responsibility.

"That looks an important envelope, Dad," he continued, eyeing up his father's desk. "Is it something exciting?"

"Never you mind," replied Peter. "You'll find out as and when."

"Top secret, eh?" replied his son. Peter just smiled. The contents of the envelope had come as a huge surprise and he couldn't wait to discuss them with Annabelle. He knew that she would be delighted.

CHAPTER 56

Susie enjoyed her first week at George Timmins and Son and both David and his father were pleased with her progress. She had a naturally sunny personality and got on well with people. She also dressed nicely and added some very welcome colour to the office. When they all finished on Friday evening George told Susie that it was customary practice to have a management meeting in a local pub and that he very much hoped that she would join them. Susie said that she would love to and the three of them adjourned to the Blue Boar. George ordered the drinks and they went and sat at a small window table.

"Well Susie," George smiled, "What do you think of us so far?"

"I'm really enjoying myself, George," was her reply. "The work is very interesting. I know that I have a lot to learn, but I'm sure that I can do it."

"I'm pleased that we haven't frightened you off," he said. They all smiled and the conversation turned to James' dinner the following evening.

"Do you know where you're going yet?" asked George.

"No, it's all a big surprise," said his son. "We could be going anywhere." Susie chipped in.

"I'm wondering if it might be London, but I think that not knowing is all part of the fun. I'm really looking forward to it." David said that he was too.

They finished their drinks and went their separate ways. Susie and David arranged to meet up later.

*****

For their magical mystery tour on Saturday, Susie decided on a short black dress with high-heeled strappy sandals and some very bold costume jewellery. She had a pretty little beaded evening bag, which added the finishing touch to her outfit. She was travelling to Moulsford in shorts and a baggy top, as it was a beautiful day. In case they were staying in a 5 star London hotel she was taking a pair of white linen trousers and a selection of other tops with her.

David was astounded when he saw the size of Susie's case. "I thought we were going for one night, not one week!" he exclaimed.

"You never know what you might need," came the reply. Silently, he put her case in his car.

They said goodbye to Mrs MacDonald on the way out. The old girl was in her element as she was in charge of George and she was very pleased to see that Susie was going away with that nice young man. She much preferred him to that other one who used to slope around all the time; he'd never even given her the time of day.

David had the hood down on the Alfa, and the two of them were somewhat windblown by the time they reached Moulsford. Greg was already there, so James introduced him to David.

"Where are we going then?" asked Susie. No sooner had she got the words out of her mouth than a huge white stretch limo pulled up outside the front door.

"Well, that chap must be in the wrong place," said Peter, rising to his feet. "I'll go and sort him out and find out who he's looking for."

"Sit down, Dad," said James. "That's the car that I've hired to take us to where we're going." Peter cringed and prayed that they wouldn't see anyone he knew. Sensing his discomfort, Annabelle suppressed the desire to laugh. The chauffeur rang the bell and loaded all the bags into the car.

"Isn't this fun?" said Susie as they all climbed in. Her mother agreed with her. Her father looked uncomfortable. Susie giggled to herself as she saw his face. "Don't be such a boring old fart, Daddy," she whispered in his ear.

The chauffeur handed them each a glass of pink champagne, causing Peter to cringe again, before pulling smoothly out of the drive and turning the car towards Wallingford. At that, with the exception of Greg and James, they played guessing games as to where they were going. Susie chose London, David said Henley, Annabelle thought it might be Le Manoir in Great Milton and Peter opted for Malmaison in Oxford. James was delighted that they were all wrong. He settled further back into his seat. He really was enjoying himself and looking forward to seeing their faces when they arrived.

Some twenty minutes later they were pulling up outside the Crazy Bear, and shortly after that they were shown to their rooms.

"Bloody hell," Peter said to Annabelle. "It's like being in a Chinese brothel. Just look at it. Have you ever seen anything like it?" Annabelle said that she hadn't, but that she had also never seen a Chinese brothel.

"It's certainly opulent. Now you remember this is James' night and he's paying for it, so don't rock the boat. I'm going to try out this enormous bath and get dressed for the evening. It's just turned 5.30 and we're meeting in the bar again at 7.00."

*****

Susie and David were thrilled with their suite and in no time at all were trying out the huge bed and finding that it was very much to their mutual satisfaction. They then shared a bath and were only just ready on time, so rushed down to the bar to find the others already gathered there. "Last as usual, Susie," said Peter smiling at his daughter.

"Someone has to be," she retorted.

"Hmm," replied her father. "Be warned David. If you're used to being on time, my daughter will soon knock that out of you." David smiled, but didn't answer.

James had organised cocktails for them all. Peter groaned inwardly. He would far rather have had a decent gin and tonic. He was a real man for Christ's sake and he didn't drink bloody girlie drinks. He was equally sure that David would have liked something different too. He knew that he mustn't slip away, as Annabelle would kill him, so bracing himself, he sipped the offending mixture. He noticed that Susie was in her element, and to his disgust James was gazing adoringly at Greg.

He was relieved when a waitress appeared and showed them to their table. That was peculiar too, in Peter's opinion. It was more like a coffee table than a dining table, but he supposed this was all part of the Thai experience. He raised his eyebrows when he saw the jeroboam of Veuve Cliquot champagne that was on ice.

David did more than raise his eyebrows. He had seen from the menu that the Veuve was £495. He would have to talk to James fairly seriously. Yes, the chap had money, but he wouldn't have it for long if he spent it like this. David mentally totted up the cost of the evening and inwardly shuddered. He also noted that Greg seemed very comfortable and at home with all that was going on. Clearly he was a great influence in James' life.

Annabelle was thinking much the same thing. She was looking back at the James of a few months ago, who used to dress in jeans and awful white trainers. Now he was wearing an Armani suit and a very expensive pair of shoes. He was also gazing at Greg admiringly. Like David, she felt that Greg had quite a hold over her son.

She then turned her attention to Susie and David. Susie was looking stunning and the couple seemed very much wrapped up in each other. She hoped that was a good thing. Would she always worry about her children, she wondered.

*****

Despite Peter's misgivings and to James' great delight, the evening was an obvious success. The Thai food was absolutely delicious and the champagne was perfect with it. David thought what a handsome family the Rowlands were and could see where Susie got her looks from. He hoped to himself that their relationship would long continue. He also hoped that James would be OK with Greg. Something there was making him slightly uneasy and he wasn't sure what. Putting his thoughts to the back of his mind, David turned his attention to Peter, who was asking him whether or not he played golf.

All too soon it was time for the party to break up and wend their way, somewhat unsteadily in some cases, to their respective rooms, having arranged to meet for breakfast the following morning. Each couple was pleased to return to their room after a very indulgent evening, where they continued to indulge themselves in their different ways.

CHAPTER 57

There were one or two sore heads at breakfast the next morning; Susie's in particular. She had enjoyed the cocktails and champagne rather too much! The drinks had been followed by a night of passion and very little sleep, and she was feeling extremely delicate indeed. As she nibbled a piece of toast, Susie thought about the night and just how loving David was. She had always thought that Jonathan was the bee's knees in bed, but David was proving that to be wrong. She smiled across the table at him.

"You're looking peaky Susie," her father observed. "Too much booze last night?" Susie glared at him.

"I haven't had your years of practice, Daddy," she replied.

Once breakfast was finished everyone went and got ready to meet the limo. The chauffeur again greeted them all with glasses of pink champagne. This time it was Susie who cringed.

Once safely back in Moulsford and drinking some restorative coffee, everyone began to wonder how they would spend the rest of the day. Sleeping came fairly near the top of Susie's priorities! "Someone should stick their head in at the arcade to see if anything exciting's happening there," suggested Annabelle.

"As you're saying someone, I take it you don't want to do that, Mum," said James. "Don't worry. We can do that, can't we Greg?"

"I shall take my beautiful wife out for lunch," said Peter, "and if any of you young things would like to join us you would be most welcome." The others declined, so after finishing their coffee and thanking James for his extreme generosity, David and Susie left for Enstone, while Greg and James made their way to Wallingford.

"Wasn't that fab?" Susie enthused once she and David were alone together. "Such a fun place and such an amazing bedroom."

"Very expensive though," said David. "James' bill must have been well in excess of £2,000. It really was most generous of him."

"Well, he's got the money," Susie replied, "and you can't take it with you, after all." David winced. He thought he had begun to educate his new girlfriend on spending and extravagance, but now he was not so sure.

"Talking of money," he said, "how's your holiday getting along on eBay? Doesn't it end soon?"

"Yes," Susie replied. "It ends tonight. Last time I looked it was at £300, which is nothing really." David sighed inwardly. This girl was going to take some taming! However, she had started out well in the practice, which was definitely a step in the right direction. It was obvious too that she came from a privileged background, where Mummy and Daddy had provided rather a lot and she hadn't had to worry too much about money. "Anyway, I'm going to sleep now," Susie continued. "Wake me up when we get home."

*****

James and Greg called in at Cholsey on their way to the arcade to collect Zizi from Greg's neighbour. Greg also picked up the holiday brochures, as they hadn't yet had an opportunity to discuss a holiday. He intended to strike while the iron was hot.

The Lamb Arcade was relatively quiet for a Sunday lunchtime, so they were able to have a good look at the brochures. Greg suggested that they wait until the schools were back and that it would then be a good time of year to visit Mauritius. James asked him if he had been there before and Greg said that he hadn't, but knew lots of people that had. "Le Saint Geran's coming in at around £8,500 for a fortnight without flights and meals," he said casually.

"Around £8,500 without flights and meals," gasped James. "You can probably add at least another 4 to that with flights, drinks and food. "Maybe," said Greg casually, "but aren't we worth it after all that you've won?" James looked at his friend with surprise, realising that he was expected to pay for all of the holiday. He would also be paying Greg rent and sharing the bills in the house. Was this the time to re-negotiate? He was saved from answering the question by someone needing help with a piece of porcelain.

James tried to focus on answering the man's questions about the jug, but he couldn't help feeling a bit hurt. He had taken Greg out to the Crazy Bear as soon as his money had come through and paid for everyone to go there last night, which as David has correctly guessed, had cost him in excess of £2,000 and now Greg was looking at a £12,000 holiday and expecting him to pay for the whole thing. Panic hit James. Was Greg using him? No, he couldn't be, surely? He knew that Greg was struggling with the business, but thinking about it logically, they had become lovers before he had had his lottery win. Suddenly things didn't look quite so rosy. He would definitely take David's advice and tread carefully. His dad had said that too.

Having sold the little jug, James returned to Greg and the holiday question. "I do think that £12,000 is rather a lot of money to spend on our first holiday together," he said. "I know that I have just won money, but I do need that to last. There may be other things that we would like to do. Don't forget that I don't have a proper income yet. I'm only helping Mum out."

Greg pulled a face. "Perhaps you'd prefer Benidorm?" he asked sarcastically. "We could always do self-catering as well."

"Don't be like that, Greg," James replied. "Just let me think about things for a while. It's only the end of July. We've plenty of time for September. It's also not worth falling out over it."

"Who's talking about falling out?" enquired Greg quickly. He slipped his arm round James' shoulders. "I wouldn't fall out with you in a million years, you know that. Especially when you're just about to move in with me. No more time split between two places. I'm really looking forward to it, aren't you?" James replied that of course he was, although he and Allsort would undoubtedly miss each other, but he and Greg would be visiting Riverside House and he could see her then.

*****

Peter and Annabelle were having a quiet pre-lunch drink at the Beetle and Wedge and discussing the contents of the envelope that had so fascinated James. As Peter had supposed, Annabelle was both thrilled and delighted. "I'm so proud of you, darling," she said as she raised a glass of Pimms to her husband. Peter shrugged his shoulders nonchalantly.

"I guess I'd better accept then," he said smiling.

"You wouldn't dare refuse," said Annabelle, laughing up at him. "But neither would you want to." Peter nodded his head. "Can I tell the children?" she continued.

"Absolutely not," came the immediate reply. "You know what they're like. They can't possibly know until after Christmas."

"What did you think of last night then?" she asked, still laughing.

"I'm glad I wasn't seen by anyone who knew me," replied her husband. "First that ghastly car and then that poofters' paradise with those poncey cocktails. I've never felt so uncomfortable in my life."

"James did his best to take us somewhere special and unusual," said Annabelle.

"Hmmn, he certainly succeeded with the latter," came the reply. "Casting aside his sexuality, do you think James is OK with Greg? You don't think he's a user, do you?"

"I've not given it a thought, to be quite honest," replied Annabelle. "What makes you feel concerned?"

"There's something that I just can't put my finger on," replied her husband. "I may be being unnecessarily nervous in view of the amount of money that James has at such a young age. I think once James has graduated, we really should talk to him about a career. At the moment, because he has money, he probably thinks that he doesn't need one, but that really isn't the case."

Before Annabelle could reply, the waiter came to tell them that their table was ready.

*****

Susie and David spent a quiet afternoon sitting in Susie's garden and waiting for her eBay auction to end. David was logged in and watching it keenly. "It's up to £407 with ten minutes to go," he told Susie excitedly.

"That's better," she replied. "I wonder if I can make £500. That would be a reasonable amount. Perhaps we could go away for a weekend with that. I really would like to get away at some point." David nodded his head and suggested that they waited for a while before making any decisions, as she was on probation and it wasn't really appropriate for her to take holiday. Raising her eyebrows, Susie said she supposed she understood.

Ten minutes later there was great excitement. The holiday had finally sold for the princely sum of £607. "What a result," a delighted Susie said. She whooped so loudly that Mrs MacDonald, who was never very far away if she thought anything interesting was going on, wondered what on earth had happened.

CHAPTER 58

August passed quickly. Susie worked hard and was delighted when George Timmins told her that he was pleased with the progress she was making and said that he was now ready for her to begin her proper probationary period and that he and David would make a decision regarding permanent employment at the end of the year.

She asked David if this meant she could now take a holiday and he replied that she could. Of course he wanted to go with her, so he asked his father whether his mother would be prepared to step in and help for a week or two. George said that he would discuss it with Julia that evening and asked David what his plans were. David explained that he would really like to take Susie to France and show her their house. George smiled and said he didn't think that would be unreasonable, provided that Julia could help out.

David told Susie that he had spoken with his father and that they were trying to work out some dates, so that the two of them could go off together. Susie thought that would be wonderful. She was beginning to realise that everything David did for her was for the best. She was trying hard to pay off her credit card and the balance was gradually reducing. She had been very good and used all her eBay money to help pay off her card. She was still using the phone that David had given her, although she was thinking that soon she might go back to her iPhone.

David had fallen in love with Susie. He felt he knew her really well and was delighted that she seemed to have changed from the very angry person he had first met into a loving and happy girl. They had talked a lot, and he understood her demons. David also knew that his parents liked Susie very much. His father was impressed by the way she was working in the office and his mother thought her to be charming and fun. She had actually told David that Susie was good for him, as he was inclined to be too serious, and Susie helped to bring out his fun side.

James and Jenny had graduated, but Susie and David had been unable to get tickets to attend the ceremony. Both sets of parents had gone though, and had met each other for the first time. Each couple had approved of the other. Annabelle and Julia had both looked stunning, so there was common ground there immediately. Peter told George how impressed he had been by the way in which David had helped James with his finances. Naturally, this pleased George no end.

David had emphasised to James not to get financially involved with

Greg this early in their relationship and after the holiday discussion James had been more than happy to take David's advice. He and Greg had been living together for a month now and everything was fine as far as James was concerned. He was happy. The next hurdle would be explaining the situation to his grandparents.

James and Greg had compromised on a holiday. They were going to spend a fortnight in Kenya. This had come in at less than half the price of Greg's suggestion, so James was feeling a lot more comfortable, although Greg was still a little miffed.

*****

Peter and Annabelle were also planning on going away. It seemed that all the Rowlands wanted to holiday in September. They were celebrating Peter's exciting news, which they didn't yet feel they should share with their children. "Where would you like to go Belle?" Peter asked his wife. "Shall we take the plane and go somewhere?" Annabelle said she would like that and she also felt it to be rather appropriate. After some discussion they settled on Le Touquet, as they had been planning to go there for several months. Annabelle left Peter in charge of the arrangements.

She had been spending more time in the Lamb Arcade, as she had promised Peter that she would keep a closer eye on James and Greg. She felt that she hadn't got very far. She knew there had been a bit of a disagreement over the holiday and felt that James was quite correct not to spend £12,000.

She did report this back to Peter, who was horrified that such young people should even consider spending such a sum of money on a holiday. "What's Greg's background, Belle? Has he perhaps been used to his parents spending lavishly?" Peter asked. Annabelle said that she didn't know, and that her next task would be to find out about Greg's parents. "Tell you what, though," said Peter. "I'm bloody proud of James that he didn't just capitulate. After all, it's a new relationship, and we all know what that's like."

Annabelle thought back to when she first met Peter. She had reversed her car into his when she was trying to park and had nearly died when she saw a tall, handsome RAF Officer bearing down on her. There had been little damage and as they'd had to exchange names and addresses, Peter had phoned her and asked her out to dinner. She had been 19 at the time and was very impressed by a man who was some nine years older. Soon after, he had been posted to Cyprus for twelve months, but it seemed an eternity to Annabelle. However, they kept in touch and on his return Peter had asked her to marry him.

Peter's voice broke in on her thoughts. "Penny for them, Belle."

"Sorry, darling," she said, I was just thinking back to how we first met, and you going to Cyprus…"

"Mmm, I thought then how beautiful you were and you haven't changed a bit. You're as beautiful now as the day I met you, all those years ago. I have a wonderful marriage and two fantastic children, well, most of the time, they're fantastic and I have you to thank for all that."

"Darling, that's lovely," said Annabelle, leaning across to kiss him. "All we can ask for our children is that they are as fortunate as we are."

"That's precisely why we need to watch out for them," came the reply.

CHAPTER 59

Julia was delighted when George told her that David wanted to take Susie to La Petite Maison. "It will mean I'm going to have to ask you to help me, though," her husband said.

"That's fine," replied Julia, "let me have a look at my schedule. The kids will have to fit round us. I'm so pleased, George, that David is going out with Susie. I think she's really bringing him out of himself." George agreed with her. David did have a tendency to be serious, and having observed him with Susie, he could see that she really did have a good effect on him.

"Do you think this could be a permanent relationship, Julia?" he asked.

"I don't know," came the reply, "but I for one would be very happy if it were. I fancy a new hat." George looked at her and laughed.

"Look at that schedule of yours and see when you can grace me with your presence."

Julia went away to her office and came back with a large diary. "Friday 14th is the earliest I can do," she said, "but I really must be in London on Tuesday 25th. How does that sound to you?" George said it sounded good.

"I'll ring David now and tell him," he said. "Have you fed these dogs, by the way? They seem to me to be looking extremely hopeful."

"Oh George, of course I have. They're dogs. It's part of their job to look hopeful."

George was already dialling David to tell him the good news. "That's great Dad, thank you so much," his son said. "I'm with Susie now, so we can start making our plans."

"Making our plans for what?" enquired Susie, who was in the kitchen, preparing their supper. David went through and told her about the conversation he had just had with his father and about the family's holiday home on the outskirts of Montmorillon, saying how much he would like to show it to her. "We can take the Alfa and drive down, spending a night or two on the way," he enthused. "I just love France. How about you?" Susie had to admit that she didn't know it very well, but that she thought the holiday sounded great fun. "Would you like to leave all the planning to me and I'll surprise you?" he asked. Susie said that she loved surprises and to be taken away on holiday when all she had to do was to pack her case would be just wonderful. Remembering how much stuff she had taken to the Crazy Bear, David wondered what might be necessary for a week in France! He pointed out to her that it would be a very relaxed, casual holiday, so she didn't need to take loads of things. "There's a swimming pool in the garden and we have a barbecue, so you'll be partaking of my culinary talents," he told her.

"They're going to be better than mine," said Susie laughing. "Besides, you've cooked for me before, and you're jolly good. Look, I haven't started supper yet, I'm just fiddling about. Why don't we see if Alf's got a table and we could go there and celebrate, then I could stay over at yours tonight." David smiled at her and said that he would ring Alf.

Half an hour later they were heading for The Crown. Alf was pleased to see them and told them so. "You're both looking very happy," he said.

"We're off on holiday soon, Alf, that's why," Susie told him. "David's taking me to his holiday home in France."

"Aren't you a lucky girl, Susie love?" Alf replied. He looked hard at David and winked. When Susie wasn't looking, David winked back.

*****

While David and Susie were organising their trip to Montmorillon, Peter and Annabelle were planning theirs to Le Touquet. They decided they would go the following weekend, provided the Hotel Westminster could accommodate them. Peter got on the phone and confirmed that the hotel could offer them a suite for five days, starting on the Friday. "How lovely, darling," said Annabelle. "I do so enjoy Le Touquet. I wonder if James could look after Allsort for us. When is it they're going to Kenya?" Peter got on the phone again.

"They're not leaving until the 17th, so he says they'd love to have Allsort," he told Annabelle, once he'd finished his call to James.

"Have you found out anything interesting about that Greg?" Peter asked Annabelle.

"Oh don't call him THAT Greg," his wife replied. "He's our son's partner."

"I know," said Peter. "That's what concerns me and not for the reasons you imagine." Annabelle poured him another gin and tonic and told him to relax – the weekend was starting and the weather looked good.

"Shall we take the plane somewhere for a day trip tomorrow?" she suggested.

"That would put pressure on me to file a route," said Peter. "Could we make it Sunday instead?" Annabelle said that they certainly could. They set about discussing where to go. In the end they settled on Guernsey. It was only a short flight and somewhere they visited quite often, but they liked it.

"Let's pick up a car at the airport and spend the day on the beach," said Annabelle. "We could leave early and be on the beach by 10.00, couldn't we?" Peter said he would get the flight plan in and see what he could do.

The phone rang, and they were delighted to hear from a very excited

Susie that she was going to France with David and that they would be staying in the family home near Montmorillon. "It's between Poitiers and Limoges," went on Susie. "We're travelling down in David's Alfa and he's planning the route and all I have to do is pack my case and get in the car."

"That'll suit you then," replied Annabelle. "I'm really happy for you darling. When are you going?" Susie told her mother that they were leaving on the 14th September. "Just as we come back from Le Touquet," said Annabelle.

When she had put the phone down Annabelle turned to Peter and said how nice it was for Susie to be back to her old self again, and that she really thought they had David to thank for that.

"I think we've got quite a lot to thank him for, actually," said Peter. "He's certainly keeping James on the straight and narrow financially. He's stopped him pumping money into that Greg." Annabelle glared at him. "Sorry," he said, "but you know what I mean."

"As for Susie," Peter went on, "I'm delighted that she's landed herself a decent job and a decent boyfriend. Provided she doesn't manage to cock up her trial period, it might be that she could make a career for herself in financial services."

"It might be that she could make a career for herself with David," came the swift reply.

"That might not be such a bad thing either," said Peter. "George and Julia seem like a nice couple. Maybe we should suggest a meal sometime?"

"I think it might be best for Susie and David to have their holiday first," replied Annabelle. "There's plenty of scope for something to go wrong. I hope it doesn't, but you never know. If it did, it could be somewhat embarrassing if we had a meal booked with his parents." Her husband nodded his head.

*****

In Cholsey, Greg and James were discussing their forthcoming holiday to Kenya and wondering what they should do about Zizi. "I guess I could always ask Mum and Dad if they would look after her," said Greg, "but she wouldn't have much fun in London. Perhaps one or both of them could come and stay here."

"I would ask my parents," James replied," but Mum'll have her work cut out with the arcade with both of us away and Dad flits backwards and forwards to London. That said, though, someone will have to walk Allsort, so they could also walk Zizi. The dogs do get on well together. Shall I ask them? It would save troubling your folks." Greg said he thought it would be a good idea.

James rang Riverside House and spoke to his father. "Didn't think of it when you were making plans for Allsort Dad, but we're wondering if you could take Zizi for a couple of weeks while Greg and I are in Kenya?"

"Bloody hell, that's a long time, isn't it?" replied his father.

"Well," said James, "isn't it just as easy to walk two dogs as one? They are great friends, after all." Peter laughed.

"OK, son, you've sold it to me," he said. "She can come here."

James and Greg returned to their holiday discussion. Greg was pushing for a limo to take them to and from the airport. "We'll have to take my car otherwise," he said, "and I don't know if I'll be able to relax properly if we have to leave it at the airport for all that time, and long term parking is so expensive, I don't imagine there would be much in it, cost wise. We don't have to have a stretch limo. Just an ordinary one will do. It'll also mean that we get dropped at the door and then all we have to do is to check in and on the way home the car will be waiting for us." James saw that it made sense and agreed.

Feeling pleased with the result, Greg turned his attention to private transfers in Kenya. "Do you really want to be squashed up on a bus with loads of other people?" he asked. "I know I don't."

"The hotel is an hour and a half from the airport, so that will be expensive," replied James. Greg pulled a face.

"Don't be so penny pinching," he muttered. This annoyed James, who retorted, "I haven't seen you put your hand in your pocket for much since I had my win," he said. "I'm paying for this flaming holiday and all you want is more and more. You're beginning to get greedy, Greg, and I don't like it."

Greg was horrified. He hadn't thought that James would query him. "Oh sorry, darling," he said. "Tell you what, I'll pay for private transfers. I wouldn't like you to think that I'm mean. Surely you know me better than that? We're going to have a wonderful holiday and I just want everything to be completely perfect for us, that's all." With that, he reached over and kissed James on the cheek. He was going to have to watch his step, that was for sure.

CHAPTER 60

Susie and David spent a very happy weekend together, thinking about their upcoming holiday. David booked the ferries and reserved a room in Le Cheval Rouge hotel in Versailles for the first Friday and Saturday nights, as he planned to show Susie the Palace. He thought that Le Cheval Rouge would be fun, because although it was only a two star hotel, the building used to be the stables for Louis XIV. The ambience would get them in the mood for the Palace! That would mean they would reach Montmorillon on the Sunday and probably start working their way back towards Calais on the following Friday. David also had a special surprise for Susie. He had discussed it in detail with his mother, who had been a great help and come up with some useful suggestions.

All too soon it was Monday morning and back to work, but it was less than a fortnight until their holiday. The two of them worked very hard indeed and the time flashed by. Julia came into the office the day before they left, so that Susie could update her with the files that she was working on. "I hope this will be a very special holiday for you, Susie," she said, as the couple were leaving.

"Thank you. I'm really looking forward to it," Susie replied.

The couple had agreed that they would go to Susie's first of all, where she would pack and give the spare keys to Mrs MacDonald. They would then have supper at The Crown, and spend the night at David's, before an early start on Friday morning to catch the 7.30 am ferry.

Susie had already semi-packed, so she didn't take too long getting the last bits and bobs together. She had listened to what David had said about not needing much and only had a suitcase and an overnight bag. He was both impressed and relieved.

By 7.45 pm they were seated in The Crown and tucking into Alf's excellent steaks. David assured her that it wouldn't take him long at all to pack and then they would go straight to bed. "I like that bit," said Susie, looking at him lovingly.

"To sleep tonight," he replied. "We've got a long day tomorrow. I shall be setting the alarm for 3.00 am." Susie groaned. She was not fond of getting out of bed early in the morning.

Just after 8.30 the pair wished Alf goodnight and walked next door. An hour later they were in bed. Susie went straight to sleep, but David lay awake for a while wondering whether this holiday would be all he hoped for.

*****

The crossing from Dover was smooth, and with the hour's time difference it was just after 9.30 when they docked at Calais, and the port was bustling. "If we push on we could reach our first hotel by lunchtime," David said to Susie. "What do you think?"

"As I have no idea where we're going, that sounds absolutely fine," she replied. David manoeuvred the Alfa off the ship and set his satnav. He couldn't ask for Susie's help as he wanted everything to be a surprise. "No peeping," he said to her as they drove away.

Susie was more than happy to gaze out of the window. She wondered, from the road signs, if they might be going to Paris, but soon discovered that the destination was Versailles. She was a little surprised when she saw the hotel, as she had been expecting something grander, but was fascinated when David told her about its history. They went to reception to see if it might be possible to check in and were directed to an upstairs room across the courtyard. Although somewhat basic, it was large and clean and had a balcony which overlooked the car park and the small seating area.

The sun was beating down, so David suggested that they leave their luggage and set off in search of something to eat. They wandered off, hand in hand, and soon came to Les Halles, with its fascinating choice of eateries.

After lunch they strolled round the gardens of Versailles, deciding to leave the interior of the palace until the following day. It was blisteringly hot and they had to make frequent stops for ice creams and cold drinks. Despite that, they had a lovely afternoon, even if they did end up with rather sore feet!

After a long soak in the bath, Susie was keen to hit the town and suggested that they drive to Paris for the evening. David was very emphatic when he said no, explaining to her that he wasn't going to risk taking his car into Paris. Besides which, he wanted to join her in a few drinks. "How about the train then?" Susie asked. David felt that would be a lot of trouble and said so. After a slightly heated discussion, David got his way, and they set off, again on foot, into the town.

They didn't think that Versailles had a great deal to offer in the way of restaurants and what was on offer was expensive for what it was. Having accepted that, they had a reasonable meal with a carafe of wine for 84 euros.

The hotel didn't have air conditioning, so the couple spent a very hot and disturbed night. David suggested to Susie that he would see if they could cancel their booking for the coming night and move off. He appreciated that would mean not seeing inside the Palace, but felt they could do that on another occasion. He sincerely hoped that he and Susie would frequently be passing through Versailles en route to La Petite Maison. Susie said that would be fine with her, so David went and tackled the chap on reception. As luck would have it, the guy had just promised someone first refusal on a double room should he receive any cancellations, so was kind enough not to charge David anything.

"Madame Moreau won't be expecting us until Sunday, so I thought we'd stay in Lussac at Les Orangeries for tonight," David said to Susie. "Who's Madame Moreau?" she enquired. David explained that Madame Moreau was the local lady who looked after La Petite Maison. She was on a retainer from his parents and they told her when they would be visiting, so that she had everything as it should be for their arrival. "She's quite elderly and I don't want to get her flustered," he explained, "and anyway Les Orangeries has the most superb restaurant. That will help to make up for last night, and at least you'll have had one decent meal before I start with the old barbecue." Susie laughed at that. She was so enjoying David's company. Already he seemed very relaxed and so different from his formal office self. She was slightly scared that she might be falling in love with him.

"I've booked a table for dinner outside," David went on to say. "It really is scorching again today and it can be very warm inside Les Orangeries."

"That's fine," Susie said. "I'm so glad that we can put the hood down on the car. It would be unbearable otherwise."

They glanced round the room to ensure that nothing had been forgotten, and while David was paying the bill, Susie made herself comfortable in the passenger seat. She was glad that she didn't have to drive, as she'd never driven on the wrong side of the road! Feeling tired from yesterday, she pulled her baseball cap down over her eyes and prepared to sleep.

David spent the drive to Lussac-les-Chateaux in a very thoughtful mood indeed. Should he or shouldn't he? Was tonight the night? They were going to be somewhere rather lovely. Certainly more glamorous than a barbecue at La Petite Maison.

*****

Susie awoke as they were approaching Lussac. "I'm sorry, David, but I'm absolutely knackered," she said. "Yesterday was a long day and then that hot room last night just about finished me off and it's hot and sticky today too. Not that I'm complaining, I love the heat."

"Les Orangeries has a lovely pool," he replied, "so I suggest that once we're sorted out we have some lunch in the garden and a swim in the pool."

That was Susie's idea of heaven. Once they had been shown to their room, she hunted through her case until she found a very skimpy navy and white spotted bikini which she put on under a low-cut white sundress. "Jesus, you are so beautiful," said David, when she emerged from the bathroom. "I could make love to you right here and now."

"No you couldn't," she replied laughing. "We're going for lunch and a swim. Your desires will have to wait until later."

"Depends on how busy the pool is," came the swift reply. Susie gasped and blushed bright red.

They had a very happy afternoon, swimming and lazing around. The garden offered plenty of shade as well as the sunshine, so all in all, everything was perfect. Maybe this should be the moment? David wondered to himself. He excused himself and went back to the room, where he took something from his case and put it in his shorts' pocket.

Returning to the garden, David changed his mind, thinking how lovely it all would look after dark. It would wait. He smiled across at Susie, who was stretched out like a cat, lapping up the sun. "I think I could stay here for ever," was all that she said. David said he was glad that she was happy, and she would be pleased that there was also a pool at La Petite Maison. She nodded her head and told him how much she enjoyed being in the water. With that David swept her up in his arms and dropped her into the swimming pool. He was careful not to make too big a wave, so that he didn't upset the other guests, who fortunately seemed to think it was funny, judging by their shouts of "Bravo!"

Still in their swimming gear, Susie and David enjoyed a glass of champagne before going up to their room to get ready for dinner. David had bought a bottle and asked the waiter to keep it on ice for them as they would enjoy some more when they came back down.

Once in the bedroom, David had no hesitation in ripping off Susie's bikini and making passionate love to her there and then. "What a lovely start to the evening," she said, smiling up at him.

"Wear your most glamorous outfit tonight, Susie darling," David said. "I feel that this will be a special meal."

Always eager to please him, Susie delved around and finally settled on a long midnight blue dress with a very low cut back. She slipped her feet into silver mules and added some delicate jewellery. "Will I do?" she enquired.

"Do?" said David. "As always you surprise and delight me, Susie Rowlands. Let me escort you to dinner before I ravish you again."

Susie's eyebrows shot up. This was a new David, but one she rather liked! She noticed that he had been fussing with his appearance and seemed to be patting his trouser pockets somewhat anxiously. "It's so hot that I'm not going to wear a jacket," he said to Susie.

"I don't blame you," was the reply.

Once downstairs and outside, Susie and David were shown to a table on the edge of the patio overlooking the beautiful garden and swimming pool. David was glad that the days were getting shorter, because he was looking forward to nightfall. They sipped their champagne and studied the menus. The champagne disappeared as if by magic, so David ordered a second bottle. "Wow, and you call me extravagant!" said his companion. David smiled.

"Tonight is as special as you are," he replied.

Dinner over, they continued to sit and drink their champagne, enjoying the beautifully lit garden. Eventually Susie got up and excused herself to go to the ladies' room. Once she had gone, David felt in his pocket and opened the little box. He looked at the ruby and diamond ring that lay there, twinkling up at him. He had been guided in his choice by his mother, who had told him that Susie would look wonderful in rubies, and both of them had noticed that she already had a very large and beautiful solitaire diamond.

David looked up and saw that Susie was coming back. Without a moment's hesitation, he dropped the ring into her glass of champagne. As she sat down again, much to her surprise, David held out the glass to her, at the same time as getting down on one knee. At this point, Susie saw the ring swirling about in the bubbles and gasped. "Susannah Rowlands, would you do me the very great honour of becoming my wife?" he asked.

Now read what happens next to the Rowlands family in this sample chapter from the second volume in Antonia Abbott's *Emotions trilogy*:

HEIGHTENED EMOTIONS

AN OXFORDSHIRE WEDDING

CHAPTER 1

The Rowlands family made a very handsome group standing outside Buckingham Palace in the wintry sunshine. There was Peter, looking distinguished in a morning suit with an MBE pinned to his chest, and beside him was his pretty wife Annabelle, stunning in a full-length silver fox coat and matching hat. They were accompanied by their two children, Susie and James, both of whom were feeling very proud indeed of their father. They had posed for a variety of photographs and were just about to leave when a small child rushed up to Susie, saying, "Miss Rowlands, Miss Rowlands, we haven't seen you for ages, and then we see you here! Has your daddy got an honour too?"

Susie looked at the child in amazement. It was Emily Browne, one of Jonathan's children. Jonathan, her ex-lover - what the hell was he doing here? He'd cost her her job at Woodstock Academy and then he'd shoved his way into her house one night when he was drunk, asking her to go and live with him. Fortunately David had been there and had got rid of Jonathan, as Susie still didn't know how she would have dealt with him had she been on her own. Were he and Angela back together, she wondered?

"Mummy and Uncle Alex and Alice are over there," continued the excited child, "why don't you come and say hello to them?"

"Who's Uncle Alex?" enquired Susie, trying her best to smile at Emily, and wishing the ground would just swallow her up. As Susie was asking who he was, Uncle Alex, followed by Angela and Alice, walked over to them. Uncle Alex was heading straight for her father, hand outstretched, saying, "Rowlands, what a surprise. I was standing there wondering if it might be you, and now Emily has proved that it is, as she recognised your daughter."

"Well I'm buggered," replied her father, taking the proffered hand. "If it isn't Alex Drummond. There's no need to ask what you're doing here, but what a surprise that we should both be here at the same time. How many years will it be?"

Susie looked on in astonishment - Daddy actually knew Uncle Alex. How? And what on earth was she going to do about facing Angela? Daddy was introducing them all to Alex Drummond, who in turn was introducing Angela to them and the twins to the other members of her family. Alice was busy explaining to Mummy that they used to go to Woodstock Academy, which was how they knew Miss Rowlands. Alice went on to tell Mummy that, since her Mummy and Daddy had split up and they had gone to live with Uncle Alex, they had been going to the Dragon School.

Annabelle smiled at the child, all the while gripped in the chill realisation that it must have been Angela's husband with whom her daughter had had the affair. This was not very comfortable. Horror of horrors, she then heard Peter agreeing to Alex's suggestion that they should all go for a drink and that the Ritz seemed to be as good a place as any. They left the Palace and each family got into a separate cab.

Once safely inside the taxi Annabelle turned to Susie and asked her if it were Angela's husband who was her ex-lover. Susie nodded glumly.

"This is wonderful, Peter," Annabelle said. "We are going for drinks with the woman whose husband Susie was playing around with."

"Sorry, Belle, but how the hell was I supposed to know that?" enquired Peter. "Drummond and I were at Cranfield together all those years ago and I thought it would be fun for us all to have a drink. I wasn't to know that Susie had been shagging his partner's husband, was I?"

James listened to all this with great interest.

"I'm sure no-one will refer to the affair. After all, young children are present," continued Peter. "This is a very special day. Let's enjoy the rest of it."

*****

In the other cab, a similar conversation was taking place, albeit somewhat guardedly as the twins were present. "I can't believe that I'm going to have a drink with Susie Rowlands after all that has gone on," Angela said. Alex apologised and said that he couldn't have been thinking straight when he made the suggestion, but he had been stunned to see Peter Rowlands after such a long time. They had trained together at Cranfield and then been sent on their first posting together. They had got on well, but inevitably lost touch over the years, and he had been pleased to see his old friend again. Angela sighed and said that they would have to make the best of things.

It didn't seem long at all before their cab was pulling up outside the Ritz. The twins were very impressed that a man wearing a top hat came and opened the car door for them. They were having such an exciting day! Uncle Alex had received an MBE for his charity work and Mummy had bought them new outfits for their trip up to London. It was a shame that they hadn't been able to see the Queen for themselves, but Uncle Alex had told them what she had been wearing and what she had said to him, so that was next best thing.

They were followed into the hotel by the Rowlands, as the cabs had virtually been behind each other. A waiter showed them to a table that was large enough to accommodate them all, and once they were seated, asked them what they would like to drink. Peter felt that champagne was the most appropriate drink for the occasion and had no hesitation in saying so! Annabelle thought that Angela and Alex looked a little surprised by this, but, gamely, they agreed, and a magnum of Bollinger 97 was ordered.

"What would your little girls like?" Peter asked, turning to Angela.

"They're old enough to answer for themselves," came the somewhat tart reply.

Peter raised his eyebrows in frustration and then turned to the children. Emily said that she would like a Coke and Alice opted for lemonade. Mummy didn't approve of fizzy drinks, so they were seizing the opportunity, as they knew that they wouldn't be corrected in front of other people. That was one of the best things about seeing Daddy, he let them have anything that they wanted.

Thinking about her father, Alice turned to Susie and asked her if she still saw him. Susie had the grace to blush as she shook her head. Hell, she thought to herself, I must get away from these children, as surely everyone will be talking about something different by the time I come back. With that in mind, Susie excused herself and headed for the Ladies' Powder Room.

Oh no, she thought, it's going from bad to worse, for as she came out of the cubicle, who should she see touching up her lipstick but Angela. Susie smiled at her weakly.

"I've always been fascinated to know more about the woman who caused me such heartache," said Angela conversationally. "Do please tell me why you thought it such a good idea to have a tawdry little affair with my husband and ruin my marriage?"

"I'm sorry," stammered Susie. "I just found Jonathan so attractive and he asked me to meet him after you had viewed Woodstock Academy and things kind of developed from there."

"I'll say they developed," snapped Angela. "I'm just rather surprised that the two of you didn't get together after I threw him out."

At this point the Powder Room door swung open to admit Annabelle.

"You've been rather a long time, Susie darling, and I was beginning to wonder if you were all right," she said.

Susie assured her mother that she was fine, smiled at the two women and scuttled back to the bar and a restorative glass of champagne.

What was said between Angela and Annabelle will never be known, but the conversation that took place in the bar after they both returned was very civil indeed.

*****

"The engagement is announced between Susannah Elizabeth, the only daughter of Wing Commander and Mrs P J Rowlands of Riverside House, Moulsford, and David Anthony Timmins, only son of Mr and Mrs D K Timmins of Great Rollright". Kevin was so pleased that he had read that announcement in The Telegraph a few months previously, and was still scheming on how best he could use this knowledge to his advantage...

Kevin needed to find out more about Mr and Mrs Timmins of Great Rollright, that was for sure. They might well be interested in what he had. That would be one in the eye for that snotty bastard Rowlands. He hadn't missed his name in the New Year's Honours list. But now that his little girl was about to be wed, things might be different. He might be happy to pay for Kevin's silence. After all, the daughter would hardly want her future in-laws to know that her mother had been photographed nude, would she? Did the girl even know herself? Where did Susannah Elizabeth live? The Timmins wouldn't be hard to find. He'd looked up Great Rollright and could see that it was only a small village. Directory Enquiries or 118 118 as they called themselves these days, should probably do the trick. Kevin scratched his groin with enthusiasm. There just had to be money to be made here, and he was going to make sure he got his hands on it.

He didn't know what had made him look through the New Year's Honours list, but when he saw that Wing Commander Rowlands had received an MBE, it had brought that little cow Annabelle to the forefront of his mind. He would make her sweat!

His first job was to find his old drinking pal, Malcolm, Annabelle's half-brother. He had discovered that relationship some while ago. He would never forgive the snotty bitch who had kicked up about taking her clothes off for him, and, to boot, had got him fired from his job at *The Buxton Echo* when she had gone to the editor and told him about the photo contracts Kevin was signing up on the side. The disgrace had stuck with him, and he hadn't had a decent job since.

Kevin knew that Malcolm was resentful of Annabelle. He considered her to be a spoiled little rich girl, married to that pillock of an RAF Officer and living in luxury in that posh house on the Thames. What also stuck in his throat was that she had refused to help him out any more. It wasn't Malcolm's fault that he'd been born a bastard and given away, whilst she seemed to have been born into privilege, and married into even more of it.

He'd always liked Malcolm, ever since his schooldays, and when Malcolm had learned what that cow Annabelle had done to him, he had helped devise the blackmailing scheme, as the perfect way that the two could make some money. He might know where Susannah lived. That would be a very good starting point indeed. Kevin folded his newspaper, scratched his groin one more time and set off for the local Weatherspoons.

Heightened Emotions: An Oxfordshire Wedding will be published in early 2015.

CONTACT DETAILS

Visit the author's website:
www.antoniaabbottauthor.co.uk

Follow on Twitter:
twitter.com/Antonia_Author

Like on Facebook:
facebook.com/AntoniaAbbottAuthor

Cover Design by: www.StunningBookCovers.com
Cover photography © oxfordshirevillages.co.uk

Published by: Raven Crest Books
ravencrestbooks.com

Contact us on Facebook:
facebook.com/RavenCrestBooksClub

31554269R00161

Made in the USA
Charleston, SC
22 July 2014